ANGEL FALLS

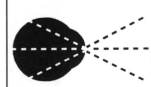 This Large Print Book carries the Seal of Approval of N.A.V.H.

A JOSEY ANGEL NOVEL, BOOK 1

ANGEL FALLS

A FRONTIER EPIC OF LOVE AND WAR

DEREK CATRON

WHEELER PUBLISHING
A part of Gale, a Cengage Company

Farmington Hills, Mich • San Francisco • New York • Waterville, Maine
Meriden, Conn • Mason, Ohio • Chicago

LIBRARY OF CONGRESS CIP DATA ON FILE.
CATALOGUING IN PUBLICATION FOR THIS BOOK
IS AVAILABLE FROM THE LIBRARY OF CONGRESS

ISBN-13: 978-1-4104-9695-9 (softcover)

Published in 2018 by arrangement with Derek Catron

Printed in Mexico
1 2 3 4 5 6 7 22 21 20 19 18

As the Colonel says, "A man's character is shaped by the women in his life." I'm a fortunate product of this truth. Wife, daughter, mother, sisters, grandmother, aunts, friends; I wish they were all still here to see what they made of me.

CHAPTER ONE

Annabelle Rutledge heard the big miner plod into the store before she saw him.

His boots fell heavy against the pine board floors. Without looking she knew she would have to sweep again. The miners tracked in so much mud from Virginia City's gold-laced streams it was a wonder the town's surrounding hills hadn't been worn to rocky nubs.

Her eyes flickered past the errand boy from Kessler's brewery who stood at the counter, and she took in Clawson's burly figure. He stood before a row of shelves filled with canned goods. His head bobbed like a grazing buffalo, but his dull eyes never left her.

Annabelle took her pencil to Kessler's shopping list. The boy was illiterate, so she showed him her mark next to each item on the list and where she had packed it in the boxes on the counter. The boy nodded as if he could read the words. He smiled at her diligence, grateful, she suspected, for being saved a cuffing if he failed to return with everything.

Clawson cleared his throat with an animal grunt until she met his gaze.

"I'll be with you in a moment." She forced a smile she hoped struck as cold as the winds off Montana's snow-capped peaks.

She returned her attention to the boy and calculated the bill. Gold was the region's currency since its discovery in Alder Gulch in 1863. A dollar's pinch of dust could buy a man a dance and a drink at one of the hurdy-gurdy houses. Annabelle wondered what two dollars might procure, but she never asked. The trip west after the war had shed many of her conceptions about what constituted good manners, but vestiges of her Charleston decorum endured.

While she completed the tally, the boy fingered a set of tools her father had purchased that morning from a miner headed back east. Years of hard labor in the gulch had left the man richer in experience than in the pocket.

Optimism gleamed like gold in the boy's eyes, and she recalled the words an old man once spoke to her. *"A young man's hope will outlive any run of disappointments."*

She smiled, recalling the Union cavalry officer who'd led her family's wagon train most of the way from Omaha. The Colonel — no one dared call him by his given name — was laid up at Fort Phil Kearny near the Bighorn Mountains, wounded in a battle with Indians. She missed his avuncular wisdom, but he had never been a miner, and life in the goldfields might have tested his aphorism.

The boy hefted a pick in his soft hands while she completed the invoice. "You have a mind for staking a claim, do you?"

"Yes ma'am."

Annabelle intended her query as a jape, for the boy was too slight by half to work as a placer miner. Seeing his earnestness, she knew he meant what he said. Thousands of miners had rushed to the area, pulling millions of dollars from the creeks and hillsides in the past three years. With the war's end, even more settlers came. By the time Annabelle and her extended family arrived two months earlier, intent on rebuilding their fortunes as shopkeepers in a boomtown, Virginia City stood as capital of the country's newest territory.

"I'm saving my money to buy a stake," the boy said. Pride showed in the set of his jaw.

"It's hard work."

Early arrivals told of scooping a pan into the stream, swirling the water over the edge to carry away the sand and walking away with enough gold in the bottom of their pan to buy dinner. It was no longer so easy. Deposits lay as many as twelve to twenty feet below the creek's surface, making for backbreaking work even for men as big as Clawson.

He moved to hover over Annabelle and the boy, his frame casting a shadow across them and the shelves behind. Standing so close, Annabelle choked on the stench of dried sweat and dead animal. She had been ill that morning, and her stomach roiled at his odor. She stepped behind the counter to give herself space as he loomed over the boy.

"If you're not going to buy those tools, why don't you skedaddle?"

His face split into a grimace Annabelle figured was supposed to be a smile. Clawson was a powerful man, the muscles in his shoulders and back bulging beneath his cotton shirt. Such a man would have unnerved Annabelle once, but she had endured too much in her twenty-five years to quake before anyone in the store that bore her family's name.

After her husband's disappearance during

the war, she oversaw a plantation. She mourned the deaths of two brothers and made the decision on her own to sell out and finance her family's trek west with enough goods to start a business. Not everyone had survived the journey through disputed Indian lands, but those who did were made stronger by the experience.

"Wait your turn or go," she snapped.

Clawson scowled at the boy and cleared his throat with a menacing rumble.

The boy took the hint.

"I need to get," he told Annabelle, his eyes turned up toward Clawson. "Mr. Kessler will tan my hide if I'm gone too long."

He swept the packed boxes from the counter, staggered a moment beneath their weight, and shuffled toward the French doors, leaving Annabelle alone with Clawson.

The look Clawson gave her brought to mind a man who sits down to a steak dinner after a week of hardtack. The man often visited the store but rarely purchased anything. He came instead to look over the wares, including Annabelle — appraising her dark hair and lithe figure as if she were for sale like one of the girls in the town's many sporting houses.

Annabelle sighed. She was accustomed to unwanted attention from men, but there was a lot more of it since Josey had left.

Josef Anglewicz, known even in these parts as Josey Angel, had been the wagon train's scout but became much more to Annabelle. She had mocked him the first time she saw him. Wearing four pistols and a rifle slung over his shoulder, he looked to her like a boy playing bandit. That was before she had seen him use those guns.

She didn't doubt Josey loved her. For the six weeks he stayed with her while they recuperated from the trail, she knew the kind of love she'd convinced herself existed only in fairy tales and poetry. Then Josey left, gone to retrieve the Colonel, he said. Annabelle wondered if he would return. They'd exchanged harsh words before their parting. Well, she had spoken harshly. Annabelle had never known Josey to speak that way. A man who worked a Henry rifle the way he did had little use for sharp words.

No, Josey just brooded. And left. Which was worse. Because when Josey Angel came into the store, even men like Clawson stood back. Now there was nothing to forestall Clawson's attention. His eyes took her in head to foot and lingered at what lay between.

"Do you want anything?"

Another grimace-smile split Clawson's wide face, his lips thick and wet behind a beard so coarse it brought to mind a buffalo snout. The gears in what passed for the machinery of his animal mind were grinding their way toward a clever retort, and Annabelle regretted her choice of words.

"Be careful what you say next if you ever want to shop here again."

He nodded, but his expression hadn't changed. He pointed to the shelf over her shoulder. "Are those peaches?"

Annabelle didn't have to look to know the cans were marked. "That's what it says."

"I like peaches." He smacked his lips for emphasis. "I'll take those."

Annabelle knew his mind — it wasn't hard to figure. The peaches he pointed to were on the top shelf. She would need the ladder her father kept behind the counter to reach them, providing her uncouth customer a generous view of her bustle as she did so.

She would have laughed at the pathetic ploy if she hadn't thought Clawson would be charmed by her reaction. Not for the first time she saw the parallel between the attentions of men and those of a dog begging at the dinner table. His mouth was open as she reached for the ladder — and stopped.

13

"Let me see your money first."

His snout glistening in the light from the windows, Clawson drew a gold nugget from the pocket of his vest. Nuggets were rare for placer miners. A gold nugget the size of a silver dollar carried a value of two hundred-fifty dollars. This one, the size of Annabelle's smallest fingernail, was worth about twenty. Finding such a nugget could make a man feel full of sand.

"You can make change, I expect."

"No doubt."

Her fingers twined around the ladder's side rail. She turned her back to him, feeling his eager eyes on her. She placed one foot on the ladder's bottom rung — and stopped. "Oh, look. I have some peaches here." She drew out an identical can from a lower shelf and placed it on the counter. "That will be one dollar."

His eyes hardened, and Annabelle sensed anger that made her cautious. Stupid men were the most dangerous of all.

His voice thundered. "I don't want those peaches." He pointed to the top shelf. "I want those."

Annabelle spoke in the soothing tone she would use on a skittish horse. "All right. Just a moment."

She'd had her fun. Now he would have

14

his. No harm would come from looking. He could brag about it later to the boys at the faro table before he lost the rest of his money. She climbed the ladder, mindful of her long skirt and heeled shoes. She extended her arm toward the peaches. Just as her fingers wrapped around the can, something pushed against the fabric of her dress.

"I aim to get my money's worth."

His voice was hoarse and throaty. Annabelle felt cool air against her leg as he hiked up her skirt and petticoats past the knee. Her breath caught as his callused hand, rough as a bristle brush and cold as iron, raked across the bare skin above her stockings.

"It's warm in here," he said.

Annabelle closed her eyes against his touch, her body rigid, feeling his fingers reach higher. She balanced against the ladder with one hand. With the other she reached into the pocket sewn into the right-side seam of her skirt. His thick fingers snagged in her garters as he stretched for more. Annabelle shuddered, her spine arcing so she had to grasp the ladder to maintain her balance. Her free hand took hold of something else, just as Clawson's coarse fingers extended toward their objective.

"Looking for this?"

The derringer had been designed for pockets. While the single-barrel pistol could fire only once and was difficult to reload, Annabelle was confident she wouldn't need a second lead ball at this range.

Clawson fell back against the counter. Annabelle descended from the ladder, keeping the pistol's front sight lined up with his wide chest. With her free hand she re-arranged her skirt and petticoats, never taking her eyes from him.

"It looks like a child's toy," she said, "but this was the very type of gun that killed Abraham Lincoln. Isn't it funny to think what trouble such a small gun can cause?"

The miner didn't laugh as he retreated around the counter. "I meant no harm," he whined, raising his hands in a defensive gesture.

"You should learn to keep those to yourself." The memory of his hands against her skin brought the taste of bile to her throat. *I should shoot him just to teach all these miners a lesson.*

She might have pulled the trigger, but she couldn't remember when she had loaded the derringer and worried that moisture in the tube might prevent it from firing. Josey had warned her about keeping guns clean. How many mornings had she watched him

16

clean his rifle and revolvers?

With the counter between them, Clawson found courage in her hesitation.

"Put that away. You wouldn't shoot a man."

"The last man I held a gun on thought the same thing. He was my husband."

Confusion washed over Clawson's snout. "I didn't know you were married."

"I'm not any longer." She lifted the gun with both hands so he could see into the barrel as she pulled back the hammer. "Do you see my point?"

CHAPTER TWO

Josey rode hard the first day out from Virginia City. He stopped to sleep for a few hours when the moonless sky grew so dark he feared his gray Indian pony might stumble and break a leg. He rose before dawn, maintaining a measured pace to spare the horse but determined to spend another full day in the saddle. The farther he got from her, he figured, the clearer he would think.

The Yellowstone River was low and flowed so slow cottonwoods growing along its banks reflected against the water like a shimmering canvas. Branches showed through in places. Soon the trees would be bare.

It had snowed once already, and the weather could turn again at any time in the mountains. He told himself that was the reason for his haste. He had to get to the Colonel while there was still time to get back before winter set in. If he rode far enough, he might believe it.

The day turned warm when he kept out from the shade. At times the trail left the river and wound up into the hills. The grass was brown and dry. Mottled with dark sage and other brush, fields and hills rolled all the way to the mountains. Josey enjoyed riding through an emptiness where his thoughts could roam, and the only sounds were the plodding footfalls of his horse and the flap of the wind as it whipped across the plains. Yet even here his thoughts felt crowded. He rode on.

By dusk he was falling asleep in the saddle. If he'd been more alert, he would have seen the fire's orange glow against the boulder in the cleft between two bluffs. He'd hoped to avoid other travelers as well as Indians. Before he could turn clear, a voice called out.

"Hey stranger. Why don't you come sit by our fire before you fall off of that horse?"

Josey eased his mount toward the sound of the voice. A man, bowed under the weight of years and the bucket he carried from the river, watched him from the shadows among the rocks. A set of white whiskers ringed the old-timer's round face like a halo encircling the moon.

"That's kind of you, but . . ."

19

The man spit, a messy, wet sound. "Rather have you 'round our fire t'where we can see a friendly face than wonder where you are in the dark."

Josey didn't need to see to know the man was heeled. Probably had his hand on the grip of a revolver, just in case the strange rider proved a threat. Josey dismounted and approached. "That's an invitation a man can't refuse."

The old-timer's face stretched into almost a perfect circle when he smiled. He spit while he waited for Josey, tobacco juice leaving a stain against the gleaming whiteness of his beard, like piss in the snow. He introduced himself. Josey forgot the name the moment he heard it.

"Josef Anglewicz," he replied with a nod and a touch to his broad-rimmed hat.

The old-timer's rheumy eyes rolled past Josey and the twin gun belts he wore at his waist and settled on the rifle butt extending from the saddle scabbard at his horse's side. "That be Josey Angel to friends?"

"That's how most men say it."

The man hooted like he'd won at faro. He treated Josey to another full-moon smile and spit again, more stains on the snow. "We ain't got much, just some beans and bacon I'm stirring up, but you're welcome to join us. I'd sleep easier with that rifle of yours in our camp."

Josey forced a smile. "I'd be obliged."

The others returned to camp after seeing to their horses and pack mules. There were four of them, younger men, closer to Josey's age. Two looked like brothers. They appraised Josey while the old-timer made introductions.

"I thought you'd be bigger," said the older brother, standing to his full height so he could look down on Josey.

"I thought he'd be older," the other said, hanging back a bit and not meeting Josey's gaze.

The old man ignored them. "They say he shot fifty Indians at Crazy Woman Creek this summer. Held off the entire Sioux nation and saved an army patrol."

Josey shook his head. "Wasn't like that."

Humility fueled their curiosity. "What was it like?" one of the brothers asked.

"Yeah. If it weren't fifty, how many did you kill?"

Josey looked away. Someone always had to ask, like it was a card game and there was a way of keeping score. In a fight, Josey didn't think so much as react. He aimed. He fired. He levered in another round and aimed again. There wasn't time to see what happened after the first shot. Any corpses left afterwards weren't his to claim. They belonged to God. Josey had learned His appetite for slaughter was insatiable.

"Enough," he said.

They liked that answer, and Josey regretted saying anything. A vague response permitted their imagination to fill in the account. The next time he heard the story it might be three score or more dead Indians.

People were always eager to build up a man — until they were ready to take him down. Those like the old-timer praised a man so they could feel bigger for knowing him. He'd be swapping stories of Josey Angel for the rest of his life. There was no harm in it, least not for him. He might even get a few free drinks if he told the stories well enough.

The harm came when the stories grew too big for some men. Men who felt small in the hearing of them. Men who could see no way to feel better about themselves than by killing the man from the stories. It was one of the reasons Josey first came west. Stories from the war had spread so far he couldn't go into a town without drawing a challenge from someone looking to make his own reputation. Josey hadn't been able to outrun the old stories, and when some of those were forgotten, new ones replaced them. Josey worried about the next time someone heard one of the stories and decided to test their truth. There would always be a next time.

Leaving the fire to tend to his horse, Josey unsaddled the gray gelding and picketed it on a loose tether so it could graze. The night breeze carried some of the old man's words. He was telling the others about Griswoldville. Yankees loved that story. The numbers were big, and a partisan storyteller left out the parts of how the Georgia militia by then was mostly boys and their grandpas. Josey brushed the horse down, losing himself in the task.

At supper, he learned his hosts were miners who'd seen the elephant. They'd been working the stream near Nevada City, finding just enough dust to nurture a flicker of hope before time and backbreaking labor snuffed even that. The brothers were first to pull up stakes.

"Got a letter from our ma," the younger brother said. He had the lean face of a boy who's known too much hard work on an empty stomach. "Our pa's sick."

"We're needed on the farm," the other said, his hard look a challenge to anyone who thought to contradict the account.

They weren't quitting. Their ma needed them.

Josey knew enough of mining not to begrudge the "gobacks" who abandoned the mining camps. For every man who hit a strike, hundreds like these poured their sweat into an unyielding earth.

"Where are you headed?" the younger brother asked.

"Phil Kearny," Josey answered. He explained that his friend remained behind at the fort.

"Is he a invalid?"

Josey choked. The Colonel was an old man, but he would have shot anyone who suggested he was a cripple in his presence. "No. He was wounded in the Indian attack and had to lay up at the fort while we continued."

The old-timer nodded, like he knew that part of the story. "Why didn't he just come along with another wagon train? Why do you have to go back for him?"

Josey chewed on his beans. He'd heard the question before. "Because I promised him I would."

After eating, Josey returned to his horse. "You'll be warmer by the fire," the old-timer called.

"I'll sleep better knowing the horse is fine."

"Suit yourself. Hope we don't find you scalped in the morning."

Josey waved an appropriate salute. The stars were out, and in the absence of the moon they sparkled like icy snow in the sunlight. Had it been any brighter, Josey would have helped himself to some coffee and pressed on.

By rising early, he figured he could be on his way before the others woke. It was at least a six-day ride to the fort, and the miners would slow him down. Worse, they would ask more questions, want to talk about things he'd crossed the country to forget.

The Colonel called him a misanthrope, partly because he liked to think Josey didn't know the word's meaning. Josey understood it well enough not to dispute the label. A few years spent watching those around him die and hiding from strangers who would shoot him on sight had eroded Josey's regard for his fellow man.

Maybe war was God's way of culling the herd, something every generation had to endure until the horror and waste sated its bloodlust. God demanded a sacrifice, and Josey did his part to see it done. More than his part. The Colonel said he possessed a rare clarity of thought when everything around him was going to hell. Plenty of soldiers shot targets as well as Josey, but it was different when bullets flew back. Instead of panicking, Josey found a focus in those moments — along with feelings he didn't like to admit, even to himself.

The Colonel called it a gift. The gift, to Josey's mind, was the sixteen-shot Henry his father gave him when Josey left for war. The repeating rifle meant Josey could keep firing while everyone around him stopped to reload. *That* was his gift, he told the Colonel.

Gift or blessing, Josey's skill came at a price. He had no hope for quelling the nightmares. Not until he met Annabelle. In surviving their journey west together, Josey discovered more to live for than he'd ever expected to have again. Yet still there were days, even when he was with her, that his mind cast about for something lost and forgotten.

She was angry with him for leaving to fetch the Colonel. He didn't have the words to make her understand why it was important that he go back. Even if he could explain himself to her, he wasn't sure that he should.

Josey led his horse a short distance uphill from the camp. He hoped he would be warm enough with his thick buffalo-skin blanket. As he settled in he recalled another starry night on the trail when Annabelle came to him wearing nothing but a thin cotton gown. He recalled the feel of her warm body pressed against his. The way her dark eyes lit up whenever she saw him. No one else in the world looked like that on seeing him. He tried shutting his mind to the memories. He'd find no sleep chasing such a line of thought. Then, worse, he pictured her dressed for one of those fancy balls people liked in Virginia City, dancing with the newspaperman she'd met. Josey didn't dance. He'd been glad there'd been someone to take his place when the dancing started. He wasn't so glad now that he was gone and the newspaperman was still there.

It was a fitful sleep with such thoughts in his head, yet Josey drifted off, his mind freed from Griswoldville and Crazy Woman Creek and the effort to separate fact from the stories that were told. He pondered new philosophies. If none of the stories we tell ourselves are true, then anything we choose to believe should seem real enough. He wished the Colonel was around to chew on that with him.

■ ■ ■ ■

The raised voice of one of the miners woke Josey later than he'd intended.

"They've got our mules!"

Josey rolled to his rifle and was up in an instant. He liked to clean and reload his guns first thing in the morning, but it was habit more than necessity. He levered in a cartridge and went to his horse, the sound of pounding hooves coming from near the campsite.

Clambering to higher ground, Josey saw two Indians atop the next bluff, surrounded by four mules. One of the horsemen dismounted and inspected the forelock of his pony. Josey couldn't see the miners, but he heard them giving chase.

"His horse is hurt. We can catch them!"

Bad idea.

Two riders — they looked like the brothers — scrambled up the ridge toward the Indians. Their big horses struggled for footing in a scree. Loose stones tumbled down the slope. The Indians watched, even the one who was supposed to be worried about his pony. Before the miners drew within range for their revolvers, the Indians remounted and disappeared over the far side.

Don't chase after them.

The riders crested the hill. They spun their horses around at the top, maybe looking for signs of where the Indians had gone, maybe gathering courage. Josey hoped it was time enough for their wits to catch up with them. The other two young miners were mounted and climbing the ridge after them.

Josey looked east. The sun wasn't up, but he saw mountains silhouetted against a gray sky. There wasn't enough light to tell if the gray rose from clouds or morning haze. Even if he could maintain his pace, he was still days out from the fort. He saddled his horse and wished he were on his way.

"I see 'em!"

One of the riders — it looked like the older brother — pointed and urged his horse in the direction the Indians had gone. For a moment Josey thought the younger brother might hold his position, that he might return to the relative safety of the camp, but the hesitation was just the time it took him to bring his horse under control. He followed after his brother.

Josey slipped his rifle into the scabbard. He tied both gun belts around his waist. They were heavy and made walking awkward, but a man need only try loading a black powder revolver once under fire to determine he couldn't have too many guns. Josey led his horse to the campsite.

The old-timer was there, as agitated as a squirrel in a wolf den. "I told them the mules weren't worth it. They said they were all they had left, and they wouldn't go home empty-handed."

Josey walked to the edge of the camp. It was far enough removed from the bluff to provide good sightlines. Boulders on the backside provided a natural screen. He tethered his horse there and drew out his rifle. An old log the brothers had used for a bench the night before lay by the firepit. Josey dragged it to the edge of the clearing and sat down.

The old man wore a gun belt and paced the campsite. He stopped at each of the places where the men had slept to sort through clothes and bedding. "I can't find my powder flask. It was here last night."

Josey watched how the man's hands shook. "Won't be time to reload, anyway," he said. He turned away so he wouldn't have to see the old man quake.

They didn't have to wait long. An explosion of gunshots echoed over the hill. Too many to count, then silence. Another shot. A few more seconds of quiet. Another shot. Then nothing.

Josey looked back to the old man. At least he was still. He nodded toward the man's holstered gun. "I hope you know how to use that thing."

Josey slid down from the log and lay behind it. He inhaled, a tang of pine on the still air. He tested the sightlines again with his rifle. Its wooden stock felt warm in his hands, like a living thing. A meadowlark fluted, invisible in the field. Pounding hoofbeats, like the roll of thunder, drowned out the bird's call. Their rhythmic beat drew nearer. Josey waited, his mind as clear and cool as the snow-fed streams from the mountains.

CHAPTER THREE

Annabelle picked her way across Wallace Street, breathing through her mouth and avoiding the horse droppings and the worst of the sludge that transformed Virginia City's main thoroughfare into a quagmire whenever it rained.

The street brimmed with activity. She paused to watch a Wells, Fargo and Co. stage pass by. Mud reached up to the horses' fetlocks, and dollops of the stuff caked their tails. The stage carried more dreamy fortune hunters from Fort Benton. They just kept coming, though the scarred and dirty coaches no longer left empty. The town's population had been dwindling since miners found gold near Helena the previous year, and Annabelle wondered how long Virginia City's cosmopolitan ambitions could last.

There was no sign of declining fortunes today. Most miners took Sundays off, so commerce ruled the day. With eight billiard halls, five gambling parlors, and numerous bawdy houses and saloons, even the faithful could be distracted from the Sabbath.

Annabelle found more solid footing on the boardwalk. Her long wool skirt, held low in the wind by the lead shot she sewed into the hem, swished above the loose planks. A pale autumn sun offered some heat, like a hand caressing her face. The season's first snow had melted away, but there was no way of knowing how many sunny days remained before winter settled in.

Crowds kept to the sunny side of the boardwalk, as people fled the long shadows cast by the false-front second stories on the street's southern half. Annabelle never understood why the false fronts were so popular in the West. They were meant to lend the town a resemblance to bustling cities back in the states, but to Annabelle they emphasized what was absent, like a man who hides a balding head under an ill-fitting wig.

She pulled tight her shawl about her shoulders and increased her pace past the brick façade of the Pfouts store. Her father's late return to the store had left her running behind for a dinner appointment.

Langdon Rutledge remained a vital man, though war had aged him even as it ruined his import business in Charleston. He'd lost most of his hair, and his beard seemed to turn white overnight. The journey west had rejuvenated him, as did starting a business and laying roots in a new town. He stood more erect these days, and Annabelle told him he looked good in the wide-brimmed hats the men wore here.

On returning from his midday meal, her father asked if there had been any sales.

"The boy from the brewery was here. I left the invoice so you can settle later with Mr. Kessler." Annabelle paused as her father looked over the paperwork, amused to wonder if he was still listening. "Oh, and I sold some peaches for twenty dollars."

She set Clawson's gold nugget on the counter beside the invoice.

That got his attention. "You sold twenty cans of peaches?"

"One can." She masked the grin that came at the memory of Clawson's abrupt flight from the store. "It's like you've always taught me, Father: It's not just the goods; it's the service."

Annabelle stopped beneath the arched battlements that adorned the roofline at the

Montana Post building just long enough to peer through the cleanest windowpane and confirm the newspaper office was closed. She hurried to the café across Jackson Street.

Mr. Blake waited inside. Of course, he did. Her friend would have arrived first even if Annabelle had been on time. He sat alone in the corner at an intimate table for two, set with a spotless white tablecloth and real china that distinguished the café from the rough-hewn dining houses farther down Jackson Street.

Henry Nichols Blake was the editor of the town newspaper and a new friend, despite Annabelle's misgivings about his Yankee provenance. Though not yet thirty, Mr. Blake affected the appearance of an older man. His thick, wiry beard and the round, wire-rim spectacles completed a studious countenance he'd earned studying law at Harvard.

She had met Mr. Blake a month earlier at a formal ball given in honor of Annabelle's family soon after their arrival. Virginia City could be a rough place, yet the town also attracted men of means with cultural standards cultivated in cities like Charleston or, in Mr. Blake's case, Boston. These men held aspirations for Virginia City evident in the new schoolhouse under construction, the active literary society, and frequent performances of the Montana Theatre.

Annabelle had attended the cotillion with some trepidation. Josey was no help. He despised crowds and took the occasion to scout the land between Virginia City and Bozeman. The prospect of seeing Annabelle in a formal gown — a sight he confessed stirred his blood — wasn't enough to overcome his disdain for dancing.

Josey needn't have feared. Gossip of Annabelle's attachment to Josey — and his dangerous reputation — left Annabelle standing alone as the musicians played. Only Mr. Blake proved bold enough to approach.

"There will be no wallflowers tonight," he said, his eyebrows arching in what she came to recognize as a cue to his smile. He proved his manners were the equal of even a Southerner that night, holding a handkerchief over his hand so that he would not directly touch her back as they danced.

Mr. Blake now stood as she came to the restaurant table, offering a gallant bow before taking her hand and tickling her fingers with his dark beard in the slightest of kisses. Annabelle hesitated as the tang wafting from the kitchen of oyster stew, normally a favorite, turned her stomach and left her feeling flushed.

Concern creased Mr. Blake's wide forehead as he guided her to a chair. To her relief, he said nothing and sat down, his eyes alight as he asked of any news.

She resisted telling of her morning's most interesting customer. Some things she wouldn't share even with Mr. Blake, who had proven himself discreet, despite being a newspaperman with an unfathomable network of gossips.

The waiter brought tea and took their orders. Annabelle asked for toasted bread.

"Such plain fare?" Mr. Blake's eyebrow cocked with curiosity. He wore his thick beard like a mask, leaving his dark brows as the most expressive part of his face.

"I had a large breakfast and don't want to spoil my supper."

Mr. Blake allowed the lie to pass, his brows betraying his complicity. He turned instead to the story of a new arrival who had taken a steamer up the Missouri River to Fort Benton, the same route he had taken.

"You recall the savages I told you about?"

"They can hardly be called savages."

"It's true, the Indians along the river are tame in comparison to those you encountered," Mr. Blake said. "Real first-class beggars, more eager for handouts of tobacco than a white man's scalp."

"They cannot be confused with the Sioux."

Mr. Blake shifted in his chair and cleared his throat. "No, of course not."

Though he served with distinction in the war — having been wounded at Spottsylvania — Mr. Blake spoke modestly of his record. He never appeared comfortable around Josey, whose exploits were well known, and Annabelle noticed their paths crossed far more often when Josey was away.

"I've told you how you should have traveled by steamer. It would have been far safer and more comfortable."

"Yes, but they would not have permitted us to transport five wagons full of goods. Plus, there were other benefits to overland travel." A memory of raking her fingers through Josey's thick brown hair brought a smile to her lips.

Mr. Blake cleared his throat. "Well, the Indians along the river, many of them carried certificates that testified to their character, written by officers or members of steamboat crews. These certificates usually said something like, 'The bearer is an honest Indian. Treat him well.' "

An arched eyebrow signaled a turn lay ahead in Mr. Blake's account. Annabelle prompted, "Did your new friend meet an Indian like this?"

"Better. His Indian, of course, couldn't read, so he didn't know what his certificate said: 'The bearer is a damned thief. Shoot him on sight.'"

Annabelle covered her mouth to stifle a laugh and hide her reaction to the vulgarity. Mr. Blake looked so pleased with himself — even a smile broke through that wiry beard — that she failed to contain her mirth.

He shared more gossip over the meal as Annabelle picked at her toast. She thought she must eat something, but her stomach turned even at bland food.

"Perhaps you should see a doctor." Mr. Blake avoided her gaze.

Annabelle had received the same advice while passing through Fort Phil Kearny from the commander's wife, Margaret Carrington. She eyed Mr. Blake, not trusting the coincidence. "I wasn't aware of discussing my health with you."

The newspaperman contemplated his soup. "People tell me things."

A flash of anger settled Annabelle's stomach. "I can assure you that this is none of your business."

Mr. Blake retreated from the topic, his brows flattening with concern. "Have I told you what it was that drove me to Montana?"

Grateful for the change of subject, Annabelle encouraged him to continue.

"I was in Boston after the war and sought a policy of insurance. The physician, on learning that two uncles and aunts on my father's side were victims of consumption, focused the entirety of his examination on that scourge. He listened to my breathing for minutes on end. His stethoscope was new, and I think he was disappointed not to hear evidence of my imminent demise."

"I'm sorry. I had no idea —"

"Pray, save your pity for someone in need of it." He patted her hand. "You are confronted not with an invalid, but a fool."

"You are not ill?"

He sat erect, as if at attention. "Hardly a cough since the day he saw me. But the doctor had embedded the notion in my brain to such an extent that I could think of nothing else. Having read descriptions of the climatic conditions of the Rocky Mountains, I decided to come west."

He sat back in his chair, his story concluded, yet Annabelle had yet to determine its point — and her Mr. Blake never told a story without a point.

"I am happy you chose to come west," she began. "The dry mountain air must agree with you."

Mr. Blake appeared impatient. "Yes, yes, but I was never sick. I don't believe I was any more at risk of developing consumption than you. Yet I permitted that quacksalver to put the fear in me without seeking another opinion."

Annabelle's eyes narrowed. The conversation had strayed in a direction where the man should have no knowledge. "Is that your point?" She tried to keep her voice neutral, but Mr. Blake detected its thorny stem.

"Mrs. Holcombe, I have only your well-being in mind."

The use of her married name, which Annabelle had ceased to claim on her arrival in Montana, reminded her that Mr. Blake knew more of her history than she had ever shared with him.

"Again, sir, my well-being is not your business." She no longer attempted to hide the anger in her voice.

"I must contradict you in that. As your friend, your well-being *is* my concern. Seeing another doctor might remove any doubts you harbor."

How did he know so much? Annabelle

41

wouldn't give him the satisfaction of asking, though she could think of a couple of her former traveling companions with whom she would be more circumspect in the future.

Mr. Blake encroached on her most private shame: a miscarriage she suffered early in her marriage, just before the war. A doctor said she could no longer conceive children, and the news devastated her. It was why she had never sought to remarry after her husband was presumed dead during the war. Men pursued her for her beauty and apparent strength, yet she felt unworthy knowing she couldn't give them a child.

It never occurred to her to doubt the doctor's diagnosis, but he had been working for her husband, whom she later discovered was a traitor and murdering thief. Just before his death, Richard implied the doctor's assignment had not been to treat a miscarriage, but to see that one occurred. She wished now she had learned what he had meant. *Perhaps I shouldn't have been so quick to shoot the bastard.*

"I have it by all accounts that Doctor Daems is a good man, a knowledgeable physician, and a discreet professional."

Annabelle scoffed. "No one, it seems, remains discreet around you."

Mr. Blake held wide his hands in a gesture of innocence. "If I am the exception, who better to judge a man's discretion?"

"What you're suggesting just isn't possible."

"Oh? Have you been chaste?"

Annabelle blinked as if slapped and required a moment to absorb his words. She felt heat rising up through her chest and into her face. Blake saw it. Too late he held up a placating hand.

"How dare you —"

"A newspaperman must learn to ask impolite questions to get at the truth."

"That far exceeds even the bounds of 'impolite,' *sir.*" She spat the last word. Her voice had risen, and she felt the stares of others in the dining room.

She pushed back her chair. Her vision blurred as her eyes grew moist, and she didn't wish for Mr. Blake to see the effect of his words. Before she could stand, he took her hand. She couldn't face him, tried blinking away the tears.

"I'm sorry, Annabelle. I mean only the best for you, and you deserve to know."

But she already knew. Besides the morning sickness, there were signs a woman wouldn't confess in the presence of a gentleman, even if she had chosen to dismiss them at the time.

She spoke the next words so softly she doubted even the sharp-eared newspaperman heard them. They were words she never thought to utter, especially now that she had driven away the only man she ever loved.

"I'm with child."

CHAPTER FOUR

Josey found the Colonel waiting in the dining mess at the boardinghouse where he'd taken rooms. An enormous fire burning in a central hearth warmed the long, low-beamed room. Josey's stomach rumbled at the smell of fresh bread and a meaty stew as he navigated between the rough-cut trestle tables. The place was busy with civilian contractors who mowed the hay, felled the trees, and cut the boards that built Fort Phil Kearny. They came here for the food and stayed for lingering looks at Elisabeth Wheatley, the proprietor's little wife, all of nineteen years and as pretty as the first flower of spring.

She favored the Colonel with a wide smile as she set the table next to the big stone fireplace with tin plates and cutlery. She scurried away when Josey approached, her booted feet shuffling through the fresh straw her husband spread to keep the mud from puddling.

"Seems reputation of your charm precedes you." The Colonel's thick, gray mustache flattened into a wry smile. He no longer wore the buckskins he'd favored on the trail. He now sported flannel with a dark vest that looked like it had been part of a store-bought suit. His thick, denim coat had a blanket liner sewn in for warmth. He kept the coat on despite the fire, though he left it unbuttoned.

He'd removed his hat for the lady, and his bare head shone in the light from the kerosene lamp on the table. "You could have at least waited until we got some food before frightening the little bird away."

Josey removed his hat and ruffled his hair. Crowds and loud places unnerved him. "I suppose we can thank *him.*"

He nodded to the next table, where the old-timer held court, a mug of beer cradled in one hand while the other hovered over a shot of whiskey. With his back to their table, the white-bearded miner hadn't seen Josey come in. His voice carried above the din of the crowd.

"The Indians came in waves, but Josey Angel held still, moving only enough to lever in another shot. He put that Henry rifle to use like a farmer with a scythe, cutting down any brave foolish enough to rear his savage head."

The Colonel's thin eyebrows popped. "The scythe is a new touch."

Josey replaced his hat and sank low on the bench. He'd never appreciated the bastardization of his surname or the references to "angel of death" he'd heard during the war. He picked at a splinter in the tabletop with a fingernail still rimmed with dirt even after a bath. "It was just a small raiding party. They wanted no part of a rifle from a well-defended position."

"They made short work of the other miners. Four of them, wasn't it?"

Josey rubbed smooth the table with his nail. "They were fools. If they hadn't chased after those mules, they'd be here now."

After Josey drove away the Indians, the miner had wanted to find and bury the bodies of his comrades. He called it the Christian thing to do. His convictions faded once he understood Josey wouldn't wait. They packed and fled before the Indians could return in greater numbers. The journey had taken a full week. The old-timer yammered the whole way. *What were you thinking when you saw them coming? Which one did you shoot first? How many did you kill?*

47

On arriving at the fort earlier that afternoon, Josey found the Colonel outside the post headquarters. Their reunion made the trek worthwhile. The old man gripped him hard and pulled him close, like they were family, which, in a way, Josey felt they were. They had just never spoken of it.

With his head caught in the crook of the old man's arm, Josey heard the Colonel's voice break as he spoke in a rough whisper. "I thought I'd never see you again, my boy." Josey felt too strange in the moment to ask what he meant. There was too much news to tell, anyway.

While the Colonel walked him to the boardinghouse just outside the fort's gates, Josey filled him in on all that had happened. They had been apart less than three months, but it seemed longer in the telling. Josey talked about the road agents who'd stalked their wagon train through Montana. He explained that the settlers had unwittingly been carrying a cache of stolen Confederate gold, and how it had nearly cost Josey and Annabelle their lives. When the leader of the bandits turned out to be Annabelle's supposedly dead husband, Josey had been eager to kill him — but Annabelle got to him first.

Josey had never been one to stretch a yarn

the way the Colonel could, so the old man peppered him with questions, pressing for details. The gold, divided among the settlers, had eased their transition to frontier life. Josey had saved a share for the Colonel, who seemed unaffected by the news. By the time he was done, Josey couldn't remember when he'd talked so much. His face was sore, and he rubbed his cheeks.

The Colonel put a hand on Josey's arm. Josey hadn't talked about what passed between him and Annabelle after they arrived in Virginia City, but the Colonel seemed to glean enough from what he had said.

"I don't think I've ever seen you smile so much. You've done hurt your jaw."

Josey enjoyed the Colonel's laughter. The old man's grip was rough against his arm. The spotted skin on the back of his hand looked fine as paper. Josey studied his face. The gray mustache drooped like a frown, just as it always had. But his sunken cheeks and sallow complexion spoke to just how hard the last year had been. The Colonel had been slow to recover from a bout of ague this past winter, and with all the hard riding they'd done since then and the blow to the head he took in the Indian fight, he'd never put back his normal weight.

When he'd wrapped his arms around the old man, Josey felt like he was holding somebody's frail grandfather, the kind of man who needed an extra blanket and a seat by the fire at night. Josey had called him old man since the day the Colonel first saved his ass, but he'd never thought of him as aged.

Talked out and tired, Josey felt the way he did after a fight when his mind emptied. The Colonel's question threw him.

"Why did you come back for me, son?"

Josey looked at him. "Because I told you I would."

"You did?" The Colonel stared off toward the hills that ringed the fort and the valley. "I suppose I wasn't thinking too clearly then. Even if I was, I'm not sure I would have held you to a promise like that."

"You never had to hold me to anything."

The Colonel's eyes moved to the ground, but his attention seemed focused elsewhere. "You should be back with that pretty little filly of yours, building that ranch house you talked about, setting up a good business for you and Byron."

"Who's going to make sure we build it proper?"

"You still mean to put me on the porch in the shade?"

Josey grinned. "We'll build one of them wrap-around verandas so there will be shade no matter the hour."

"Maybe put a glass of lemonade in my hand?"

"Annabelle will make it extra sweet for you."

The Colonel launched forward, swatting Josey with his wide-brimmed hat. "You might as well dig me a grave and carve up a headstone while you're at it. Is that why you came back? 'Cause you think I'm too feeble to make it on my own?"

"No, I —"

He took another swing, not as energetic as the first, and stepped back. The few strands of hair the Colonel had left fell akimbo, exposing the brown spots on his scalp that reminded Josey of the Appaloosa the Colonel rode. They stood in silence a moment while he caught his breath.

"I'm not dying, you know."

"I'm counting on that."

Afterward, the Colonel took him inside the boardinghouse and sent him off for a bath and fresh change of clothes while he made arrangements with the Wheatleys. Now that it was evening, Josey was ravenous and more than ready for Mrs. Wheatley's return, her approach signaled by a wake of silence as heads turned to watch her pass.

"I think you'll like the stew, Colonel. Fresh antelope. James shot it himself."

"That sounds wonderful, Miss Elisabeth."

She set platters heaping with boiled potatoes and cabbage on the table before them. Josey saw a flash of blue eyes as she glanced his way before lowering her head and nodding. She retreated before Josey could stand and remove his hat. The Colonel's eyes trailed after the young woman.

"A man's character is shaped by the women in his life as a mountain is carved by wind and water." The room was filling up, and some of the men who had finished their drinks claimed seats along the benches at their trestle table, practicing their "boardinghouse reach" on the plates of vegetables.

The Colonel always warmed to a crowd. He nodded to a young man who stepped past their table with an armful of logs before returning his attention to Josey. "Show me a noble man, and I'll find you a good woman in his life. Probably more than one: mother, wife, maybe a pretty thing he was too fool to keep."

Josey squirmed on the pinewood bench, wondering if the man had added too much wood. "What about a fellow with no woman in his life? There's plenty of them."

While Josey scooped large spoonfuls of potatoes for them both, the Colonel leaned back as if to study the question. Josey knew he already had an answer. The old man had an answer for everything. He was just waiting for the newcomers at the table to settle down and listen.

After swallowing a bite of potato, the Colonel gave a satisfied smile. "A man without a woman is shaped just as surely by that absence. The absence of a woman can turn a man mean and cruel."

"I don't see a woman with you." Josey meant it as a joke, but something sad passed across the Colonel's eyes. The old man didn't like to speak of his life before the war.

The Colonel cleared his throat. "Mean and cruel aren't the only outcomes of being without a woman. For some men, it brings on a clarity of thought and purpose. A wisdom that isn't possible to a man besotted." He stared a hole through Josey. "Even that doesn't mean the man in question wasn't shaped by a woman, just as some of these ravines were carved by rivers gone long ago."

Josey welcomed the change of conversation when the young man who'd toted the wood returned. The Colonel introduced him as James Wheatley, the proprietor. He carried a big Dutch oven filled with stew. His wife trailed behind with a dish of poverty pudding, layers of bread and apples sweetened with a little sorghum. Wheatley seemed eager to meet Josey.

"I got me a Henry rifle, just like you." Wheatley couldn't have had much more than a score of years, and he tried to mask his youth with a beard so patchy it looked like dark tree moss glued to his chin and cheeks. "I've hunted with it but haven't had a chance to see what it can do in a fight. Not like you. I reckon I'll get my chance sooner or later."

While the men dug into the stew and pudding, Wheatley fetched the rifle for inspection. The walnut stock shone in the lamplight. Josey admired the well-oiled magazine tube and the ease with which it twisted open for loading. He handed it back with a nod.

"Keep it clean, and it will serve you well."

Wheatley grinned like a schoolboy who'd brought home good marks. He scooted onto the bench beside Josey. "Will you stay for the winter? There will be no trouble finding work for a shot like you."

Josey shook his head. "We're headed back to Virginia City before the weather turns."

No one spoke for a moment. A look passed between Wheatley and the Colonel. Josey faced the old man.

"I'm not leaving, Josey," the Colonel said. "The commander hired me to help train up the garrison. Most of them are just raw recruits, and the mounted infantry — many of them city boys have hardly ever ridden a horse."

"I told Annabelle I'd come right back."

"Go back. I'll follow in the spring, when the wagons start coming through again. Carrington plans to go on the offensive once the snows set in and the Indians pull back to their winter camps."

"You should stay, too." Wheatley's voice cracked in his enthusiasm. "It's not safe to travel, what with the Indians so stirred up. Besides, civilian contractors make five dollars a day. That's a lot better than what they pay soldiers. A private makes only fifteen dollars a month. If you stay through spring, you won't have to worry about the Indians, and you'll go home with a full purse."

The Colonel chuckled. "Our young traveler is already a rich man," he told Wheatley. "Rich in coin — and in love."

Josey felt himself redden from the heat of Wheatley's fire. He hadn't avoided talking about Annabelle, but he'd steered clear of specifics about how things stood between them. The Colonel didn't miss much. Josey should have known the old man's silence on the subject didn't equate to ignorance.

"Not the kind of rich to be a big rancher," Josey said.

He never thought much about money, so long as he had what he needed to get by. He should probably start thinking about it more. Annabelle had been a wealthy plantation owner's wife before the war. She came west hoping to help her family rebuild their fortunes, and Josey had never felt on an even footing with her.

The discovery of the stolen gold should have made things easier for everyone. But to Josey the money revealed how much more there was to being a rich man than having some gold. Fancy balls excited Annabelle, but Josey didn't dance. He didn't enjoy making small talk with bankers and lawyers and newspapermen. Annabelle spoke with longing of San Francisco and London and places where they didn't even speak English. He wondered how some dirty ranch in the mountains could ever content her.

Wheatley was right. Waiting for spring and the arrival of the year's first wagon trains would be safer. Annabelle might be disappointed, but he could write to her. The military couriers made regular runs up to Fort Smith on the Bighorn River, and from there it would be easy to get a letter to Virginia City. He would tell her about the money he'd make here. If he could afford to build the biggest ranch house in Montana, maybe Annabelle would stop talking of going someplace else.

"I'll talk to the commander tomorrow," Josey said. Henry Carrington had offered him a job once, and Josey was confident the offer stood.

The Colonel's mustache drooped a little more than usual, the way he looked when he puzzled over something. Wheatley appeared pleased even beyond the prospect of another long-term boarder with the means to pay. His position in the fort community made him a storehouse of gossip and knowledge. He started counting down a litany of "opportunities," as he called them.

Josey cut Wheatley off. "I figure I'll just work with the Colonel. The last time I was here, the infantry didn't even have enough ammunition for target practice. And they're still armed with those worthless Springfields? I expect there's plenty of need for training."

Wheatley swallowed hard. "I'm sure you're

right, but there's a greater need for guns like yours with the wood wagons. The Indians are harassing them nearly every day they go out to chop wood. Besides, Carrington's got all his officers now." He looked to the Colonel as if unsure how much he should say. "Lieutenant Grummond has been handling more of the training, and Company C from the Second Cavalry just arrived with Captain Fetterman and a couple more officers."

Josey perked up at the mention of Grummond.

"Do you know him?" Wheatley asked.

"We've met, but I don't know him well." What he knew wasn't good. Josey looked to the Colonel for confirmation. He'd finished his stew and pulled his pipe from the pocket of his vest, but he hesitated before packing it with tobacco.

"I knew *of* him," the Colonel said. "Like Josey here, George Washington Grummond was a man who inspired more than his share of campfire stories."

Wheatley let the comment pass. Like the best camp gossips, he knew when to press and when to file away something for later. "Well, it's Fetterman who bears watching. His first night here he told anyone who would listen that with eighty men he could

58

ride through the entire Sioux nation."

Josey scoffed. "Eighty men?"

Wheatley nodded. "He was a hero at Jonesborough, they say. I'll tell you this: the men feel a lot better about having an officer around who knows how to lead men into battle."

"Sounds to me like a man who's never fought Indians," the Colonel said. He was rubbing the back of his head where he'd been struck by a war club. "An officer like that could get a lot of men killed."

CHAPTER FIVE

Annabelle saw the doctor the next day. She'd had time to absorb the news and figure out what she must do, so that when Doctor Daems confirmed her condition, she matched his enthusiasm at the good tidings.

A baby. *Josey's baby.*

Believing herself barren had devastated Annabelle, left her feeling like a lesser woman. She'd been so ashamed she hadn't even told her parents. This changed everything. And yet nothing was different. She was in Virginia City and Josey was . . . where was he now? *Was he safe?* He had said he would return as soon as he could, but in their parting she had given him little reason to hurry. Now she was with child. Unmarried and alone. The prospect of a town scandal didn't bother her. Not much, anyway. Her thoughts were for Josey. Something in the idea of Josey becoming a father made him more vulnerable in her mind. Worry muted her joy, like daybreak delayed in a mountain's shadow.

The doctor could only guess at the date the baby would arrive. With an awkwardness she found charming, he asked about the possible conception time. Recalling a perfect summer day on a riverbank near Fort Laramie, Annabelle conceded it could have been as early as July, but the doctor dismissed that as too soon.

A different day came to mind — at the start of September, soon after they arrived in Virginia City. Annabelle celebrated her twenty-fifth birthday with her family and Josey. He gave her a rifle like his, a gesture recognized as romantic only by someone who knew Josey Angel. The next day they rode to the Madison River valley, about halfway between Virginia City and Bozeman. They rode all day. Josey taught her how to shoot and care for the Henry, which she liked better than a revolver.

They slept under the stars high on a slope where Josey told her warm air from the valley would flow as the sun set. They made love by firelight, lulled by the sound of water gurgling over the rocks in a nearby creek. In the morning he promised to show her where the water cascaded down the cliff face. He told her of his plans to build a ranch house overlooking the river with a veranda that wrapped around the house so there would be shade at any time of day.

"We should call the ranch 'Angel Falls,' " she said.

He frowned. "Like a fallen angel?"

"No, silly. The waterfall." She could tell his mind had drifted elsewhere. He had never much cared for the nickname. A few subtle movements of her hand brought him back to the moment. "Tell me about the ranch," she cooed.

He relaxed and told her every detail. Not just a house to live in, but also a thick-walled icehouse where blocks of ice cut from the frozen stream could be preserved through most of the summer, and a smoke-house with three fireplaces where meat and fish could be cured. She ran a finger along the pale ribbon of skin that wrapped across his forehead where his hat shielded him from the sun and watched his soft brown eyes narrow and expand as if he saw everything he described. She laughed to hear him so content.

Josey was not a big man. When she wore her heeled boots and he stood in his socks, her eyes cast downward to meet his. He didn't seem to mind, but she never spoke of it, believing most men to be sensitive about such things. She rarely noticed his height or slender frame. She noticed other things. In warm weather with the sleeves of his shirt rolled up to his elbows, the muscles in his forearms rippled beneath the skin like tight cords of rope. When he went without his vest while working around the house, the fabric of his shirt pulled tight against the muscles of his chest and back.

She told him once he seemed larger with his clothes off, but he took the comment to mean something else. They laughed so hard that day she forgot he was Josey Angel. For that afternoon, he was just her Josey, a sweet man with a shy grin and a funny crease of pale skin across his forehead.

In the moments after their lovemaking, Josey was the most open with her. Some people made the mistake of thinking him ignorant because he spoke so few words, but he hadn't always been like that. Something in the war had changed him. In these unguarded moments, Annabelle glimpsed the studious child he had been, like an image in a daguerreotype. She saw the boy who read aloud to his father the poetry he loved. She pictured him lying by the family's fireplace while his mother played a Beethoven sonata. Josey would never be a loquacious man, but Annabelle encouraged him to share more of his past and his thoughts. It delighted her to hear where his mind went.

Josey didn't mention marriage, and she didn't construe his ranch fantasy as a proposal. Yet their intimate time together was more than the mere "horizontal refreshment" miners enjoyed in the bawdy houses. Annabelle understood without Josey saying that his vision included her. That was enough.

The day had been warm, but the cloudless night turned cold. Annabelle shivered as she slipped away to answer the call of nature. Josey's eyes followed her, gleaming in the firelight like stars impatient for dark.

She hurried back, and he pulled aside the buffalo-skin blanket. She nestled beside him, his skin so warm she didn't need a cover. No matter how many times he washed, his hands smelled of the oil he used to keep his guns clean, his fingers slick with it as they glided across her body. Her nose once wrinkled at the scent, but now she accepted it as a part of him. He traced a line along her bare hip that curled into a circle. Her skin beneath his fingers puckered with goosebumps.

"What if the Garden of Eden wasn't really a place?"

The incongruity of his words startled her into a laugh. "What do you mean?"

"I mean what if it's just a symbol, like in a poem when the words mean more than one thing."

"A metaphor?"

He nodded. "Eden's not just where life began but a paradise. A place of earthly delights." The increasing circumference of the circles he drew on her body brought his fingers into the spongy softness of the hair beneath her waist.

"I don't know what you could mean." She sought his gaze, trying to appear stern, but the effect of his straying fingers distracted her. A few moments later she had forgotten his point.

"Then there's this serpent," he continued. He leaned over her, draping a leg across hers.

She laughed again. The man was drunk on lovemaking. "You don't have to go to such trouble to seduce me."

"I'm serious."

"Are you?"

He failed to conceal the tug at the side of his mouth that she recognized as a smile. He slid on top of her and held her eyes with his.

"Tell me about the serpent."

65

He adjusted his position, and she opened to him. "He imparts knowledge onto Eve."

"Onto?"

"Something like that." He lifted his weight from her so she could move against him.

"And this is supposed to be something wicked?"

"Just you wait."

Afterwards, their bodies slick with sweat, Josey pulled the buffalo-skin blanket over them. When he turned to sleep, she poked at him until he looked at her.

"What was that silliness about the Garden of Eden?"

"I had a point. I just got distracted."

He turned away. She poked him again. "Well, what was the point?"

She leaned across him, expecting to laugh at whatever he said, but his eyes dulled and he looked away. "It was nothing. Silly, like you said."

"No. Tell me."

"I don't have the words to say it right."

She pressed her hand against his chest until he looked at her. "You don't need the right words, not with me. Just tell me what's on your mind."

His eyes turned toward the sky as if the words he wanted could be found among the stars. "It's what's on your mind."

She waited while he sought the rest of the words.

He said, "You worry I will be unhappy without a child."

Despite her promise to be understanding, Annabelle felt her stomach turn. Her jaw clenched as she bit back a response. She had convinced herself no man worth having would want a barren woman. Josey had told her he didn't care, yet when they were separated on the trail to Montana she had feared he meant not to return. That fear had never gone away.

He reached to her, his hand cupping her cheek. She turned to feel his rough hands against her, hoping he didn't see the tears.

"Don't be sad. What I wanted to explain is why I don't want children."

She looked at him. Her doubt must have been apparent.

"Really," he said. "Who would want them? You suffer for nine months, and it ends in a moment that could kill you. Then you're a slave to this helpless, mewling monster who's of no practical value for years."

Her throat tightened, and her voice croaked. "What does any of that have to do with the Garden of Eden?"

He sat up, throwing the blanket aside in his enthusiasm. The words that had been hidden among the stars fell like summer rain. "I started thinking of the first people. Who would choose to have a baby? But it wasn't a choice, you see. It was this" — he ran a hand over her body — "this garden of earthly delights. There's never been a man, certainly not many, who could resist its lure."

"Women, too," she said, smiling at his ardor even if his words bewildered her.

"Exactly. And it's only later, with the arrival of the baby and all the risks that presents, that these first parents came to recognize the ruse, a knowledge that altered how they viewed the garden."

He sat silent, looking pleased with himself. She couldn't resist piercing his pride. "I hope you don't repeat any of that to a mother."

Instead of wounding him, the tug at the side of his mouth revealed the true intent of everything he had said. That Josey would defend her from bandits and Indians Annabelle never doubted. Now he sought to protect her even from fears of her own making. It was as if he could see into the darkest places of her heart and shine light there. A million oaths of love couldn't prove his feelings for her more.

She returned his smile and reached for

him. "My dear, sweet Josef," she said, her fingers walking across his thigh. "You may be an impudent philosopher, but fortunately for me you have other skills."

The memory of Josey warmed Annabelle as she headed down the shaded side of Wallace Street to the livery stable.

She never thought Josey meant what he said about not wanting children. The words were intended to comfort her. But her news brought on new fears, and she wouldn't be at peace until she dealt with those.

She carried an apple in her pocket for her horse, an Appaloosa Josey had traded for at a Crow village. Josey refused to buy one of the big American horses. Indian ponies were more surefooted in the mountains, and they managed on whatever forage they found along the trail. Staying with their tradition of simple names for horses, she called hers Apple, and Annabelle enjoyed spoiling her horse with treats. She wished there was something she could bring to Lord Byron that would assure an agreeable reaction from the former slave who had been riding at Josey's side for two years.

In Josey's ranch fantasy, Byron homesteaded the land alongside his, and they worked cattle together. She wasn't sure if

Josey had ever spoken of this with Byron, given their natural reticence, but he probably didn't have to. The men had spent so much time together one could finish the other's thoughts without a word passing between them.

That brotherly bond meant Lord Byron was the one person in town who might be angrier with Josey than she. Byron and Josey had agreed to fetch the Colonel together after Byron returned from Salt Lake City. He'd gone there on a freight run with Annabelle's uncle and Willis Daggett, a hired hand who'd come with them from Omaha. They had hoped to make a final run before the snows made travel between the towns difficult. The supplies they purchased would give them enough provisions to make for a profitable winter at the store.

Josey, still recuperating from his wounds in the fight with the road agents, stayed behind. Lord Byron had been happy to take on the chore to allow his friend time with Annabelle. That Josey left early was a betrayal to Byron, who didn't understand why Josey was gone but didn't press Annabelle when she proved reluctant to speak about it.

Annabelle found him brushing an Indian pony that looked too small to carry such a large man. He spoke to it, as a mother to a babe, patting with one hand while he brushed with the other. Despite the reassurances, the horse would not remain still and turned its head to watch him. Lord Byron was careful to stay out of nipping range.

"I would think after riding with you to Salt Lake City and back this pony would know to love you," she said. She found a knife in her saddlebag and quartered the apple.

"Horses don't take to me," he said, frustration in his deep voice.

"He knows you're nervous." Annabelle brought a piece of apple to the horse, careful to hold her hand flat as she offered the gift. She wasn't sure how much she trusted a horse that couldn't sense the goodness in Byron.

Before he had been freed, the big man known as Old Hoss spent his life working in the fields. He'd never ridden a horse when he met Josey and the Colonel while trailing Sherman's army through Georgia. He'd learned to ride because it was a condition of remaining with the Union officers after the war. He'd crossed the country three times now, yet horses still made him uneasy.

Not unlike the way I feel around him.

71

Annabelle felt guilty for the thought. This man had been nothing but kind to her and her family during the long trek from Omaha. When she'd been separated from Josey on the trail, Byron's presence reassured her.

Her thoughts now weren't hard to read.

"He's coming back," Byron said. "As soon as he gets the Colonel, they'll be back before you know it."

"If the Colonel's well enough to travel. If the weather doesn't stop them." *If I haven't driven him away for good.*

Byron continued brushing, and she appreciated that he didn't try to placate her with empty reassurances. The mustang calmed as she stroked its forelock, allowing Byron to clean its hooves.

"You're better to this horse than it deserves, given how it treats you."

"Oh, he don't treat me bad." Byron had a missing tooth, and when he grinned its absence made his smile shine brighter. "Ain't bit me yet."

"Yet," she said and laughed.

He moved on to brushing out the horse's tail, even though it looked like the job had already been done. "I figure so long as I's good to him, he'll be good to me."

"I don't have to tell you the world doesn't always work that way."

"No, but it'd sure be a better place if it did."

He looked at her. The smile disappeared, and his face slackened, wide shoulders slumping as if weighed down. "I can't help the world, only my place in it." With a deep breath, he turned back to the horse. A hint of mirth laced his voice. "So that means my horse won't have no nettles in her tail."

Annabelle watched him finish, already feeling guilty for what she intended to ask. She had no right. She fed a second piece of apple to his horse, saving the rest for her own.

"I'm going after Josey."

She had decided this as she sat in Doctor Daems's office behind the drugstore he ran with his wife. The plan came to her even as the doctor lectured about the care she required in the coming months. That morning she had sold supplies to five miners who'd quit their stakes and were returning home before winter arrived. She could accompany them as far as Fort Phil Kearny, but she shied at the idea of traveling with five strangers. She would be safer with Byron, and she knew he, too, would be eager to see Josey and the Colonel again.

"He's coming back," Byron said.

She believed that, even if it weren't for

73

her but to gather Byron and ride off with the Colonel on some new adventure. It might be next month. It might be next spring.

"I can't wait that long."

"It's not safe."

"I'll be going with a group of miners. We leave in two days." She met his eyes. "I hope you'll be with us."

"Indians are stirred up now."

"That's the Sioux. We'll be traveling through Crow lands most of the way. They hate the Sioux more than we do."

"Josey'd shoot me if I let you do this. And that's if nothing bad happens."

Annabelle understood the dangers. After three months on the trail from Omaha, the idea of more hard riding and sleeping outdoors as winter approached held little appeal. Yet she couldn't sleep, haunted by the memory of Josey riding straight into a pack of road agents. Josey told her he never expected to outlive the war, and he behaved at times like he still didn't feel comfortable in the world.

On the trail, Josey saved her from her husband's gang in part because he had been prepared to die. Surviving the war imbued him with a belief that a disregard for life had been the thing that saved him. While

74

that might explain his survival to this point, it was a dangerous philosophy going forward. Every day he was gone from her was another day Annabelle feared Josey might take another heedless risk.

"He needs to know how much he has to live for."

Byron turned his head, surprised at her words. "Oh, he knows, Miss Annabelle."

"He doesn't know that I'm with child."

The worry in the big man's face dropped heavy as a horseshoe, replaced with the biggest gap-tooth grin Virginia City had ever seen. He took a step toward her as if to sweep her off her feet into his bear-like arms. He stopped himself, crossed his arms as if embracing himself.

"Whoo-eee, Josey's going to be a daddy!"

Annabelle felt a twinge of disappointment that Byron didn't embrace her, though he might have broken her in his enthusiasm. She smiled to see such unrestrained joy, trusting she would witness its match at Fort Phil Kearny when she delivered the news to Josey.

CHAPTER SIX

From the ridge overlooking the river, Light Hair looked down on the white soldiers and wished he could kill every one. His grip tightened on the war club as he imagined his arm's arc delivering the strength of the swing to the club's stone head just as it made impact, hearing the sound as it crushed the hairy face of a soldier like a melon dropped from a cliff.

Today is not the day for that. He relaxed his grip and lifted the farseeing glass he had taken off a dead officer months earlier. He crouched for a better look from behind the thick trunk of a fallen tree, moist with rot. A storm must have blown over the tree, its height and girth leaving it vulnerable because its roots did not reach deep enough in the shallow soil atop the ridge. The strength of a tree, the old ones say, comes not from growing thicker in good years when there is water but from surviving in the bad, dry times.

Light Hair hoped they were right. The *wasicu,* or white men, were like a big tree on a hill. They appeared strong in their forts, but they were not rooted to the land. His people were fewer, and they had grown weaker since the *wasicu* poisoned the land, their diseases killing the people, their stink driving away the buffalo.

Yet for all their suffering, Light Hair's people were rooted to the land, like a spindly pine that grows on a mountainside, its trunk and branches twisting toward the light while its roots stretched far for purchase in the craggy places where no other life could last. *We will outlast these white devils and burn their forts to the ground.*

Through the glass, he studied the structure, the smallest and northernmost of three forts the soldiers had built that summer on the trail they followed along the shadow of the Shining Mountains, what the *wasicu* called the Bighorn Mountains. Burning it to the ground would make Light Hair smile, but he would not be content until the bigger fort, the one the soldiers called Phil Kearny, a few days to the south, was nothing but ash.

This little fort was an open square with pine log walls driven into the ground, strengthened with long, narrow buildings where the soldiers lived and worked. A pole stood near the middle from which their flag flapped in the winds that swept along the valley cut by the nearby river. The fort's corners were built higher and held the great rolling guns that shot twice — once when the soldiers fired it and again when their giant bullets exploded a great distance away, scattering burning metal that could shred a dozen warriors at a time.

Light Hair closed his eyes and pictured what his warriors could do if they managed to get past the guns-that-shoot-twice. High Backbone fell in beside him, reaching for the glass without asking. His old friend knew Light Hair's mind.

"We can never take the fort."

"Not unless we can get inside."

High Backbone scoffed. "Are they going to invite us? With our bows and guns?"

Light Hair shook his head. Taking the fort had been a daydream. "We will think of a way."

"The men who made things like this" — High Backbone gestured with the farseeing glass — "are not dullards."

As a boy, Light Hair had followed High Backbone on his first great raid. Now High Backbone followed Light Hair since the Big

Bellies, the men the *wasicu* called chiefs, named him a Shirt Wearer, one of four young warriors held within the tribe as examples of courage and character. Light Hair accepted the honor, but he questioned his worthiness, knowing the sins of his heart. He thought of Black Buffalo Woman. The flash of her black eyes when she spied him in the village. The way the hides she wore pulled tight against her body when she turned away, knowing he would follow.

Light Hair closed his mind to the image before the shame could show on his face. He felt the same sense of unworthiness concerning his name. For his bravery in battle, Light Hair had been awarded a great name, the name of his father, who took a new name to honor his son. But in his mind, he remained Light Hair, an outcast taunted by other children because his light skin and wavy, brown hair resembled a half-breed child. For that, he had hated the *wasicu* before he had ever seen one. Seeing what they did to his people made him hate them more.

"No, they are not fools. But they think we are as simpleminded as children. We will teach them their error."

Just not today. Even with High Backbone, his friends He Dog and Lone Bear and his

79

brother Little Hawk, all fierce warriors, they were too few to challenge the *wasicu*. Light Hair had eight in his raiding party, including a couple of untested boys and a Cheyenne warrior still burning too hot after the massacre of his village two years earlier.

Once the autumn buffalo hunts were over, if Red Cloud and the other Big Bellies could draw together the people into a single camp, they might have enough warriors to confront the white soldiers. The tribes were not accustomed to fighting together the way white soldiers do. The *wasicu* had more guns, more powder and lead, but Light Hair was determined to find a way his people could win.

Until then, raiding parties such as his would continue picking off those stupid enough to wander away by themselves or in small groups. They would weaken the rest by driving off horses and the spotted buffalo the white men herded in pens.

"They have built a new pen for the horses." High Backbone returned the farseeing glass.

Light Hair had already seen. "It will be a simple thing to loose them."

He focused the glass on the fort's interior and watched the soldiers moving about. He was too far away to see, but he pictured their hairy faces and bald heads. He knew they did not all look like that, but it is how he imagined them. Ugly and dirty.

They thought the same of his people, which amused him. His people had the sense not to stay in the same place so long the smell of their shit hung in the air like marsh gas. The *wasicu* stink made Light Hair grateful to be upwind of the fort. Even the spotted buffalo they herded were dirty, living among their own filth. They stank like rotting flesh even before they were slaughtered. Consuming such food had to make a man weak. There was no strength gained from the hunt. No thrill from the kill. And the dirty meat could not be good for the body. Maybe that was why the *wasicu* were pale and so many were bald. Buzzards ate rotting flesh, and they were bald, too.

Yet High Backbone was right that the *wasicu* were clever in the things they made, like the farseeing glass, the pistol Light Hair wore under his belt, and the rifle strapped to his pony. Some of the people thought these things made the *wasicu* too great to fight. They lived near the forts waiting for handouts of flour, beef, and coffee. They grew weak and went hungry when the *wasicu* chose to withhold or delay the handouts they had promised when they seized the

81

land. The people lost their way. Only old women could still sew with bone awls. Young men forgot how to chisel arrowheads from flint, needing iron from the white man's barrel hoop instead. Instead of spending days scraping and softening an elk hide, a maiden in a few minutes could trade her body for a wool blanket.

Light Hair carried the glass, revolver and rifle, and a pouch for powder and lead, but he wore no white man's clothes, not even the blue coats many warriors adorned to commemorate a kill. He would use their magic to kill the *wasicu,* but he would not live like them.

Yet the magic was tricky. The people could take their guns, but that was not enough. They needed powder and lead or the cartridges that were used in the new fires-many-times guns. The people could not make their own, so the full strength of the white magic eluded them.

Light Hair had tried to steal some of this magic for himself by counting coup against a white warrior, a man who rode an Indian pony instead of a big American horse and shot as well from horseback as most men did standing. In the Moon When the Chokecherries Are Ripe, Light Hair saw this man almost singlehandedly hold off the biggest raiding party the people had gathered that summer. Once Light Hair saw him fight, he wanted some of his magic.

He should have killed the man. He had been helpless before Light Hair. Instead, Light Hair merely touched him, claiming some of the man's magic for his own. Later, he followed the soldiers' trail to the fort and learned the man was a scout. He had a large family, including a white-black man brother and a dark-haired wife who rode better than most white men. The white warrior led his people away from the fort, north and then west into Crow lands. Light Hair was glad. Let the Crow face the white warrior's magic.

The magic Light Hair stole failed him. Without more cartridges, Light Hair could not learn to shoot from horseback as well as he wanted. He would not waste the cartridges practicing, not when every one he owned could mean the death of another white man.

Light Hair looked back to the horses outside the fort, more than a score of big, heavy American horses. They had arrived a day earlier, probably all the way from Fort Laramie. Little Hawk, brave but impatient, had wanted to steal the horses the night they arrived. Light Hair demanded they wait.

"They are tired. Tomorrow they will be rested and will have eaten their fill. Then, when we take them, we can run them hard."

Now the horses were ready. Light Hair turned the glass to the fort. The soldiers were moving in the direction of one building near the wall. Smoke rose from the big black pipe that extended from the dirt roof. Light Hair closed his eyes and pictured what must be done, seeing it in his mind like the moves of the scalp dance — a strange way for him to think, for Light Hair never danced.

"They will be eating soon," he told High Backbone. "That is when we will move."

He crawled back from the edge of the ridge and went to the others. His instructions were simple and clear. No one interrupted. They followed him, he knew, because he did not risk lives in raids until he held a vision of success in his mind.

High Backbone spoke to embolden the younger members of the raiding party.

"Remember, it is better to die young on the prairie than be wrapped up on a scaffold as an old man."

The others smiled to hear him repeat this bromide of the Big Bellies. He Dog contributed another, his voice quivering like an old man's: "We must pray that courage is always

84

the last arrow in the warrior's quiver."

They laughed and went to their horses. The youngest boy would remain with the travel horses that were trained for endurance. The rest took to their warhorses, which were fearless and faster over short bursts. Light Hair traveled on a yellow paint, a gelding that never seemed to tire. For battle, he rode a sorrel with four white socks. He dusted his horse with dirt from a prairie dog mound. The prairie dog held the power to deceive, and he would invoke its magic to protect his horse from bullets.

Before mounting, he hefted his war club. It felt good in his hand.

High Backbone grinned at him. "Maybe you will get to use that today."

"I hope not."

If Light Hair's plan worked, they would be gone with the horses before the soldiers knew they were there.

High Backbone nodded in approval. "Patience serves you well." In a sign of respect, he called his old friend by his warrior's name.

"Soon even the soldiers will learn the name of Crazy Horse."

They drew close to the fort by riding out of sight in the gully along the river. High

Backbone and the second boy had ridden ahead, to wait north of the fort. Little Hawk and He Dog dismounted and crawled forward to open the gate on the corral. Light Hair and the other riders were at full gallop by the time they were in the open. They waved blankets and fired pistols to panic the American horses, which bolted through the open gate and past the fort.

Light Hair and Lone Bear brought horses to Little Hawk and He Dog, and they rode off together in pursuit of the fleeing horses. Soldiers emerged from the fort wide-eyed and open-mouthed and too late to do anything. Guards in the tower fired off a few shots, and Light Hair circled back on a dare ride, hoping to draw their fire toward him while the rest escaped.

Once the fleeing horses cleared the fort, they found High Backbone and the boy waiting for them. The two of them waved blankets and fired their pistols, turning the herd toward a ravine that led out of the valley. Light Hair grinned. Everything was going as he had seen it.

As he followed after the others, a shot from the fort whined over his head and struck Lone Bear's horse. His friend hurtled to the ground over his collapsed horse. He lay still a moment, and Light Hair feared the worst. Then Lone Bear rose, shaky on his legs. He kept his wits, pausing long enough to take the bridle from the horse to show he was not afraid. He turned to face the fort, shaking a fist and blowing on his eagle bone whistle in defiance.

The soldiers had rallied, taking to the horses they kept saddled within the fort and giving chase. There was not much time. Light Hair urged his sorrel forward, his quirt popping, the pony digging hard into the soft soil along the river. The big American horses the soldiers rode were fast over short distances, and their hooves set a frantic drumbeat that seemed to grow louder with every stride. More bullets whined past him, and he threw himself from side to side on his pony to avoid the shots of his enemies, hoping he had done nothing to defy the spirits and nullify the prairie dog magic.

Lone Bear was known for bad luck in battle. He had more wounds and injuries than the rest of them combined, and Light Hair was determined his childhood friend would live long enough that they could tease him about this day as well.

He stood ramrod straight beside his fallen horse, still blowing his whistle as if to challenge the soldiers in the fort and their long guns. Light Hair watched puffs of dirt explode in the ground near his friend as the soldiers sought their mark, each shot growing closer. Light Hair was not sure how long it would take the soldiers to train one of the guns-that-shoot-twice at them. One well-aimed shot would kill them both.

Before that could happen, he swept alongside Lone Bear, extending an arm to his friend, who reached up and leaped, timing his movement to slide into place behind Light Hair. This was a game they played as boys. A thousand times Light Hair had "rescued" Lone Bear. A thousand times his dark-skinned friend, so much the opposite, so much the same, had saved him. With Lone Bear behind him, Light Hair veered off to avoid the aim of his pursuers, heading toward the ravine, where he trusted he would have help in turning back the white soldiers.

He need not have worried. The few soldiers giving chase could not draw closer than a couple of hundred yards before rifle shots from the ravine turned them back to await reinforcements. By then, the raiding party would be long gone with their stolen horses.

They rode hard to their meeting spot and found the boy with their travel horses. Light

Hair's sorrel was spent from carrying two warriors. On his return, Little Hawk panto-mimed an elaborate fall from his horse to mock Lone Bear, drawing laughter from the others now that they had returned with nothing worse than Lone Bear's bruises.

He Dog, High Backbone, and the boys began removing the noisy iron shoes from the captured horses. They were not much as prizes. Light Hair intended to give the American horses to widows and the old to be used as packhorses or to pull drag poles. If the winter proved as bad as he feared, they might wind up in stew pots. The horses were not good for much else because they moved with such difficulty over rough country and fared poorly without the hay and oats they had been reared on.

But the white soldiers would feel their absence, and that was enough reason for taking them. In the coming war, Light Hair knew the people would need every advantage they could get. If all went as he hoped, they would soon be strong enough to attack the soldiers in the big fort.

CHAPTER SEVEN

Fort Phil Kearny sat along the road to Virginia City near the confluence of Big Piney and Little Piney Creeks, nestled against the foothills that sloped down from the snow-peaked Bighorn Mountains.

The views were striking, and the supply of water and wood plentiful, but Josey sensed he was being watched as he covered the short distance between the boardinghouse and the high walls of the fort. The braided path of Big Piney Creek flowed through a valley between a low rise called Sullivant Hill just north of the fort and Lodge Trail Ridge to its east. Soldiers spoke of seeing Indians watching from the heights, creating an impression that the fort wasn't an outpost in Indian country so much as a pen for beasts destined for slaughter.

Josey's eyes swept Pilot Hill, about a mile south of the fort, seeking the silhouette of the pickets stationed there. They waved flags to signal attacks on the woodcutters' wagons, a near-daily occurrence as the wagons made the five-mile trek between the fort and the pinery. The knot in Josey's stomach loosened a bit to see nothing stirring now, but his neck and shoulders were tight with the tension of constant vigilance.

The Sioux had fought the Crow for generations to claim this land. They looked on the white soldiers and passing emigrants as a blister that needed to be pricked. The sharper the knife, the better so far as the Indians were concerned.

But they had no answer for the eight-foot stockade that encircled the fort. It was constructed of heavy logs buried three feet into the ground. Firing notches were cut into every fifth log for soldiers who manned the platform inside. Gun bastions stood at opposite corners, providing a wide field of fire in either direction. The soldiers had planted stakes to mark their effective firing range from the fort. The Indians knew better than to cross that line.

There were two gates on the fort's east side. The southernmost led inside to the quartermaster corral and the warehouses and teamsters' equipment and civilian workshops. Josey walked through the main gate into the military camp. It had been less

91

than three months since he'd been here, yet he almost didn't recognize the place. Tents had been replaced with small wooden structures encircling a large, square parade ground, the grass gone brown.

A flagpole towered more than a hundred feet at the center of the parade ground. The Stars and Stripes, big enough to cover the roof of one of the buildings, billowed and snapped in the wind. The whine of sawmills carried from just outside the fort. The air smelled of livestock and latrines.

Uniformed soldiers and civilian contractors moved about the interior with a sense of purpose. An officer led an infantry company through drills on the parade grounds. A couple of privates pushed carts stacked high with fresh-cut wood. Enlisted men wearing kerchiefs over their faces shoveled lime over the sink behind the barracks.

Josey stopped a private to ask directions to the commander's headquarters. Only a wisp of brown fuzz on his upper lip separated the soldier from childhood. From his accent, Josey figured he must be a galvanized Yankee, a Confederate who'd enlisted after the war.

The soldier pointed to a row of low buildings along the eastern wall of the stockade. "It's over there, sir, between the guardhouse and the sutler's store." All the buildings looked much the same to Josey. The soldier added, "Here comes the K.O.W. She'll be headed there. Just follow her."

The boy was off before Josey could make sense of his instructions. Turning around, Josey saw two women approach. They wore plain dark dresses without coats on the unseasonably warm day. He recognized Margaret Carrington, who carried a small straw basket on her arm. She stopped and tilted her head, as if seeing him from an angle might jostle her memory.

Josey greeted her, removing his hat and offering a bow that he hoped would conceal his discomfort. The commander's wife was a thin, attractive woman in her mid-thirties whose regal mien held a civilizing influence over the military outpost. She had formed a quick friendship with Annabelle during their brief stay at the fort, and Josey dreaded the questions she was sure to ask. He was not confident his evasions would hold up to her clear-eyed scrutiny.

Her tiny face lit on recognizing him. "Mr. Anglewicz. What a pleasant surprise."

She glanced about him. "Does your presence signify an unexpected visit from Annabelle? She is such a dear."

"Sadly, no. She remains in Virginia City,

but she is well. I came to fetch the Colonel."

A quizzical look knitted Mrs. Carrington's brow. Josey hastened to interpose before she could ask anything else. "I was looking for your husband's headquarters. The private told me to see the K.O.W. . . ."

Her thin lips twisted into a sardonic smile. "He meant me: Commanding Officer's Wife."

"He said 'K'?"

"The literal abbreviation would not do."

With a self-deprecating laugh, Mrs. Carrington introduced her companion, a young woman with a shy smile and deep-set eyes. Frances Courtney Grummond reminded Josey of Annabelle, though he wasn't sure why.

"You must be the lieutenant's wife," he said. "We both marched with Sherman in Georgia."

Mrs. Grummond brightened. "George will be pleased to discover a friend at the post."

"We weren't friends. I mean, we were in different regiments. He fought with the infantry, I believe. I rode with the cavalry."

"No matter. We shall have you to dinner some night. I know how soldiers love to tell stories."

Josey said, "Mrs. Carrington can tell you I'm poor at making supper conversation."

"Josey is reticent on the subject of his war service," Margaret Carrington said.

"Margaret can tell you, I'm poor at making supper," Frances Grummond said with a musical laugh. "I nearly set fire to the officers' quarters row with one of my first attempts."

Her laughter again reminded Josey of Annabelle. There was little physical resemblance between the two. Annabelle was taller and leaner and a few years older, but the younger woman's manner of speaking could have made them sisters.

They crossed the parade ground to the headquarters, Josey now carrying Mrs. Carrington's basket. The women remarked on the pleasant temperatures. Frances Grummond told of how a terrible snowstorm greeted her arrival at the fort a month earlier.

"Our quarters weren't completed then, and we slept in a tent," she said. "We failed to draw tight the tent that night, and the wind was so penetrating I awoke with my face covered with snow, the melt trickling down my face like tears."

Josey laughed along with the women, and as he listened to Mrs. Grummond, he realized why she reminded him of Annabelle.

"Your accent," he said. "I thought you

95

were from Michigan."

"My husband is from Michigan," she said with a look of surprise. "I am from Tennessee."

"But I thought —"

Josey stopped himself. Something in her words surprised him, but he couldn't say what. Since the war, he suffered frequent lapses of memory. He could recite lengthy poems or excerpts from books he had favored as a child, and the faces of every man he had killed were seared in his mind. But he couldn't read a book now and remember much of what he'd just read. He embarrassed himself at cards and other games that required any level of attention.

Josey tried to remember what he could of Grummond, but it wasn't much. George Washington Grummond was not a name a man forgot, and there were myriad camp stories about how the young officer had risen to the breveted rank of lieutenant colonel. Grummond had faced a court martial for his treatment of the men who served under him, Josey recalled, but this was no topic to consider in front of the man's wife. He put the matter from his mind. As they reached the plank-board post headquarters, out walked the lieutenant himself.

"Fannie —" Grummond's startled attention turned to his wife's companions, and his face darkened. "Josey Angel?"

"Lieutenant," Josey said with a nod.

The two men appraised each other for a moment. Grummond, a tall and handsome man, carried himself with the erect bearing of someone born to command. Josey wondered what a blow to Grummond's pride it must have been to lose his higher rank upon reenlisting after the war.

Always alert to awkward lulls, Margaret Carrington said, "Mr. Anglewicz was kind enough to accompany us here. I've brought Henry's lunch."

Grummond recovered. "The commander is inside with Captain Fetterman and your colonel," he said, his hooded eyes focused on Josey. He turned to his wife. "I'll escort you home, Fannie." He led her away without another word.

Margaret Carrington's thin eyebrows arched in curiosity. "Is there a history between you two?"

"None that I can remember."

With a discreet cough into the handkerchief she kept in the pocket of her dress, Margaret Carrington let the comment pass. Josey turned to the stairs so that he might open the door for her, but she stayed him with a delicate hand on his arm.

"Annabelle is all right, then?"

The question sounded innocent, but Josey squirmed beneath the gaze of her sharp blue eyes. "She is well."

"See me before you leave. I am overdue in writing to her, and I'm certain my letter will arrive faster with you."

Josey picked at a hangnail on his thumb. "I think we've decided to stay until spring. It will be safer to travel then."

With a night to think about it, he'd grown comfortable with the decision to delay his return. The fight on the trail and the old-timer's stories in the boardinghouse dining room reinforced the wisdom of waiting. It wasn't only his and the Colonel's safety that concerned him.

What Annabelle refused to see was that *she* was safer when he was away. Josey drew danger the way a river draws predators searching for easy game. Bad men would keep coming, seeking Josey out to slake their thirst for the notoriety that would come from killing the man in the stories they'd heard.

Josey felt no fear for himself — he'd come to terms with the likelihood of a violent death long ago — but he had no defense in his feelings for Annabelle. After surviving his first battle, he'd never known terror in a fight — until he'd faced the prospect of losing her. The experience exposed him as a coward.

So he would give her time to come to her senses. If by the time he returned to Virginia City she had decided to move on to San Francisco or take up with that newspaperman, they might all be better off. Annabelle would be safer and happier without him, and Josey could live with that. It was better to be without her than live in constant fear of losing her. At least a part of him wanted to believe that.

Margaret Carrington was watching him, but if she read in his face any of what passed through Josey's mind, she possessed the manners not to judge him as they made their way into her husband's headquarters.

Chapter Eight

Leaving Virginia City, Annabelle and Lord Byron circled behind the Tobacco Root Mountains and rode east, through the pass at Bozeman. New buildings, their fresh-cut planks gleaming in the sunlight, marked the passage of time since they last came that way. On the third day they picked up the course of the Yellowstone, which tripped musically over round river stones, not as deep or as wide as when they'd passed going west. Cottonwoods adorned the river's banks, their diamond-shaped leaves turned to rust by the changing season.

Lord Byron pointed out landmarks from their journey two months earlier, but to Annabelle one copse of pines or a bend in the river looked much like any other. The mountains that girded their route now held more snow on their peaks, and she wondered if the weather would hold long enough to see them through to Fort Phil Kearny.

The journey west had taken four weeks, but they hoped to halve that by traveling without wagons. Annabelle and Byron rode sure-footed Crow ponies. Byron led a pack mule. Their traveling companions, a motley mix of five goback miners, were similarly equipped.

Grumbling about traveling with a woman and "a Sambo with a gun" came to an end the first night at camp when Byron and Annabelle outclassed the others in a shooting competition. Seeing how the pair handled their Henry rifles, the miners welcomed their company, especially after the winners agreed the wagers could be repaid in overnight guard duty instead of gold. A white-haired miner the others called Old Ben proclaimed seven to be a lucky number. Considering his failure in the gulch, Annabelle wasn't sure Old Ben was a good judge of serendipity.

They passed few travelers, given the lateness of the season. The weather held for the first week, and the river valley's wide plains gave way to rolling prairie. Annabelle grew quiet when recognizing the crossing where she had been taken by her husband's band of road agents. Her mood darkened further on seeing clouds thick with rain gathered over the mountains, like a herd of Holsteins in a corral. *That fence won't hold.*

Despite the threat of inclement weather, traveling suited Annabelle better than she ever would have thought before coming west. She enjoyed riding. She appreciated the sweet smell of pine forests and campfires. Bacon and coffee never tasted better than when cooked over an open flame. Best of all, Annabelle hadn't been sick a single morning since leaving town.

That's because this is Josey's baby.

She liked that her baby would be born in this country. Leaving Charleston had been a necessity, a new start for her family before the loss of their way of life destroyed them. That world before the war seemed a different lifetime now, small and constraining, like a corset drawn too tight. Living beneath a sky that stretched farther than her imagination made anything seem possible. Her free hand moved to her belly. It felt no different to her yet, but she smiled as she stroked the soft skin beneath her shirt. Her child would know these limitless possibilities.

Her child would know his father, too. *Or her father.*

She hadn't told the doctor about her plans to ride after Josey. To her parents, she left a note. They would have tried to stop her.

102

How can I find peace until I see Josey? The more she thought about it, the more she believed the fort was the best place to have the baby. She respected the fort's doctors, and having Margaret Carrington at her side would be a comfort when the time came.

Annabelle wished Margaret were with her now. Without conversation, a two-week ride through the wilderness leaves too much time for reflection. Annabelle's mind whirled between thoughts of the baby and what she would be like as a mother to what she would say to Josey when she found him. *Would he welcome the baby? Would he welcome her?* She knew Josey loved her, but some men weren't meant to be corralled. She feared she had driven him away by pushing too hard for things he wasn't ready to give.

Annabelle recalled Margaret's parting advice when she had been uncertain of Josey's love: "Let nature be your ally." They had proven wise words, and she trusted in them again as she anticipated a reunion with Josey. Nature would bring him back to her arms. *Would the baby be enough to hold him?*

In the time they shared, Annabelle had uncovered all of Josey's sore spots. He rarely spoke of the war. He didn't speak of his parents, whose memory stirred shame in him because of the things he had done. Crowds and loud noises agitated him. He grew sullen whenever she brought up traveling to San Francisco or almost anyplace else, as if the man who had done nothing but crisscross the country since the war now felt rooted.

Knowing all the places where Josey was sensitive didn't mean she avoided them. It wasn't Annabelle's nature to let a thing lie, and she wanted him to understand her the way she hoped to understand him.

But she didn't understand, not yet at least. She saw that when Josey left. In Charleston she knew men who returned from the war with empty sleeves that flapped against their bodies, pants legs that ended in stumps. Just because Annabelle couldn't see Josey's wounds didn't mean he didn't carry them. She thought if she loved him enough he would trust her enough to talk about what happened, like lancing a blister to save the new skin underneath. She now understood she had been naïve to think that. She may as well have hoped to cure an amputee with needle and thread. Josey might yet heal from his unseen wounds, but it would be on his time, not hers, and if it took a lifetime of love to cure him, he deserved that.

And so does our baby.

She tried to discuss these matters with Byron, but he proved an even worse conversationalist in the saddle than Josey. Byron behaved as if talking about his friend represented a form of betrayal, so Annabelle did most of the talking. She rehearsed some of the things she intended to say to Josey, thinking if Byron found sense in the words, then Josey would as well.

She should have known better.

As they rode, Byron's eyes swept the tree line along the trail so Annabelle couldn't be certain he was listening. When she asked how he put behind him the terrible memories of his life before the war, he seemed to brood for a minute or more.

"Talking about what happened before never helped me none now," he said. "It's living now that helps me forget what happened then."

The weather turned cooler, the wind picking up as the skies darkened with the clouds Annabelle had seen earlier. She dropped a pile of kindling beside the fire and pulled Josey's buffalo-skin blanket around her shoulders. She wore her riding clothes — pants and shirt cut for a boy almost grown. No one could tell yet from looking at her that she was with child, though she wanted to believe her pants were growing tighter. With a wide-brimmed hat to complete the ensemble, she must look like a man from a distance — not a bad thing in the open country.

They camped along the banks of the river, among rolling hills that stretched to the horizon like patches of a quilt sewn together. Old Ben sat beside the fire with his rifle from the war. The single-shot Sharps had a grinder built into the wood stock that saw more use than the firing end.

"I know how you Charleston girls love your grits," he said, grinning through his thick white beard.

The other miners were down at the river, testing their luck with the trout. She found Byron staking out his tent at the edge of the camp, a discreet distance from hers but near enough to give her comfort.

His sense of loyalty to Josey and, by extension, to her, was a palpable thing. Annabelle valued it as a treasure beyond gold, but felt she had done nothing to earn it. There had always been an awkwardness between them. Though Byron never said a cross word to her, history strained their relationship in a way that left Annabelle with a sense of debt she felt she could never repay. She sat beside his tent, wrapped in her blanket. The smell of rain hung heavy on the wind.

"Byron, tell me how you chose your name."

He answered without looking up. He smelled the rain, too, and it pushed him to complete his task. "You heard that story. The Colonel likes to tell it so much everyone from here to Omaha must know it."

"I've never heard it from you."

He paused to look at her a moment. He shook his head and smiled, the gap in his teeth providing an extra warmth to the expression. "I took the name from a book Josey used to carry."

"A book of poetry," she said. "Did you like the poems?"

"The words, they's pretty, but they don't mean much to me. I guess I just liked the name. The Colonel, he tells me now that I'm free, I should have me a free name. I ain't never heard a name that sound more free than Lord Byron."

"I like your name very much."

Byron stood and tested the tent's lines to be sure they would hold in a strong wind. The motion pulled at the sleeves of his blue cotton shirt, exposing the jagged white scars that laced his wrists. Byron was sensitive about his scars and wore long sleeves to cover them. The one time she saw the angry red ribbons that crisscrossed his back like Roman numerals, she became ill. Josey had told her what he knew of Byron's life on the Georgia cotton farm. He had been taken from his children and their mother and never saw them again, learning after the war they had died of fever.

Annabelle kicked at a river stone, flipping it over with her booted foot as she weighed her next words. "I want you to know that at my plantation we never separated families."

His brow creased with curiosity. "I figured that."

"We never whipped slaves. Those who worked in our house, they were treated better than hired servants."

" 'Cept they couldn't leave."

Annabelle winced as if struck, but if she stopped now she would never say what she wanted. "We cared for them. Housed them, fed them, clothed them. When they grew old, we didn't turn them out onto the streets."

Byron was tightening some of the tent's lines. He gave no indication that he was listening, so she tried a different tack. She told him of Mr. Pock, the Chinese servant her mother hired for their house in Virginia City. Mr. Pock cooked, washed, and kept house in return for a salary generous enough that he wouldn't leave for another household. It was still less than it would have cost to keep a slave.

And at the end of every day, Mr. Pock left their home for a drafty tent that he shared with three other men near the Chinese temple at the end of town. Annabelle had been there once. The place smelled of pigs and the laundries that boiled all hours of the day. Back the next morning, often before dawn, Mr. Pock warmed himself before the wood stove in their kitchen because he couldn't afford fuel for his tent.

"Before the war, the Negroes who worked in our house lived better than poor Mr. Pock." As she spoke, Annabelle watched Byron's reaction to ensure she didn't offend. "I won't defend owners who abused their slaves. What they did was wrong, and there is no excuse for it. But it's important to me that you know we weren't like that."

Byron had finished with the tent and looked at her. "You've been kind to me."

"But I want to be your friend, like Josey is your friend, and I don't think that can happen if we don't understand each other."

Byron chuckled, the sound a deep rumble in his chest.

Annabelle said, "You must think I'm a fool."

Shaking his head, Byron's gap-toothed grin spread across his face. "I just never knew a white woman to care so much about what a black man thinks."

She laughed at the truth of that. She overturned another rock with her boot, exposing the moisture on the underside. "Things are different now."

"Yes, they are."

"Do we understand each other?"

The grin fell from Byron's face, and his dark eyes turned sad. He crouched before her, unable to meet her eye. He picked up the stones she'd kicked over, feeling the heft of them in his large hands.

"You think Mr. Pock is bad off, worse than the slaves you had back home," he said, looking at the stones as he spoke.

She nodded, a little wistful that he couldn't meet her eyes.

"Mr. Pock doesn't work for you so he can live well." Byron set the stones down, turning them back the way they had been. "He does it for his children, so they will have a better life. A free life."

Annabelle covered her mouth as the impact of Byron's words fell upon her. He stood and turned away, looking east toward a past so horrible Annabelle wouldn't try to imagine.

"You never had that," she said.

He fell silent for a long moment. "No, ma'am."

Annabelle closed her eyes, wishing, not for the first time, that she could be as comfortable in silence as Josey and Byron. "I *am* a fool."

If Byron heard her, he chose not to respond. He stepped away from her toward the ridge overlooking the river. Annabelle figured she deserved to be shunned. She stood, brushing the seat of her pants. "I guess we better go see about supper before it starts to rain."

Byron continued to ignore her. Annabelle tried not to let it bother her. It wasn't the first time a man had tuned out her conversation, and the rebuke shouldn't sting any more coming from a Negro. She waited for him to notice she had stopped talking while he squinted toward the horizon.

"My eyes ain't so good as Josey's, but I don't think I like what I see."

Atop the ridge Annabelle spotted a lone rider on a yellow paint pony. An Indian. She described for Byron what she saw.

"Where there's one, there's sure to be more." He stooped to pick up his Henry and cartridge box. "If not right away, then soon."

CHAPTER NINE

The post headquarters was a long, narrow structure built of one-inch plank board. Beside it stood a forty-foot tower from which flag signalmen could send and receive messages to the pickets on Pilot Hill.

Josey held the door for Margaret Carrington and followed her inside. They entered a spare room that smelled of coffee and cut pine. A large table stood in the center. The chairs had been pulled back against the walls so that men could move around the table, which was covered with papers and maps. A doorway led to a second room, which Josey took to be Carrington's office. The commander excused himself for a moment with his wife, leaving Josey with the Colonel and Captain Fetterman.

After hearing of Fetterman's boasts that he could ride through the Sioux nation with just eighty men, Josey steeled himself to meet a rough braggart or at least a fool. The captain proved nothing of the sort. He was about thirty, with thick, dark muttonchops that helped mask his relative youth. He spoke with the refined manners that promised the kind of bright future Josey never imagined for himself in the army. *They love their West Point gentlemen.*

Fetterman flattered Josey, filling him in on the fort's situation as if he were still a fellow officer. The garrison's strength was under two hundred effective troops, with almost an equal number of armed civilian workers. Recent supply trains from Fort Reno left them with sufficient ammunition, along with corn and grain for the horses and mules that remained.

The fort had suffered fifty-one attacks, most of them directed at the herds or the wood trains that made near-daily trips to the pine forests five miles away. The post had lost more than six hundred mounts and head of livestock, with six dozen men killed, most of them civilian workers. The soldiers claimed to have killed four times as many Indians, but Fetterman's tone implied that he found the figure as dubious as Josey did. Fetterman made the case for taking the fight to the Indians, and Josey realized the captain was sharpening his arguments, hoping his audience could help sway a reluctant Carrington.

"With fifty mounted men and another fifty well-armed civilians we could strike at the Indian villages on the Tongue River and make them think twice about continuing their raids on the fort. It would be like halting a bully by bloodying his nose."

The intensity of Fetterman's speech suggested smoldering ambition but didn't come across as boastful. Before he could solicit their opinion, the Carringtons returned. Margaret Carrington made her farewells as the commander greeted Josey.

"Has the captain been pitching you on his plan to attack?"

Carrington's jocularity befitted the man in charge, but a tightness in the skin around his eyes and mouth conveyed an insecurity that didn't match his tone. With a stooped carriage and small frame, Carrington resembled the lawyer and man of letters he'd been before the war. His dark-ringed eyes looked sad even when he smiled, as if he overheard the whispers of the soldiers who resented serving under a man with more political connections than experience in battle.

Josey deemed it a harsh judgment. Carrington had spent his war years recruiting volunteers in Ohio and Indiana, and his skills at organization had served him well in his new post. Fort Phil Kearny — named for a heroic Union general — had been built with remarkable speed under difficult circumstances. The soldiers forgot how vulnerable they'd been until the stockade was completed.

Fetterman stood by his proposal. "It would be good for the men's morale, sir, to teach the Indians a lesson."

The Colonel interrupted. Though no longer commissioned in the army, he'd led more men into battle than all of the fort's officers combined.

"It's not much of a lesson if the Indians win."

Fetterman's coal eyes lit up. "You don't question the valor of the men —"

Carrington raised a thin-boned hand to quell Fetterman's distress. "I'm sure the Colonel means no disrespect. His is an honest assessment of our circumstances."

The commander sighed and ran a hand through dark hair that hung down to his uniform collar. He was in his mid-forties, Josey figured, but the months of command had weighed on him. His beard was streaked with more white than three months earlier.

"Our men are equipped with obsolete, muzzle-loading rifles. I have requested more carbines and repeating rifles, but General

Cooke fears we will waste ammunition with such weapons."

As he spoke, Carrington circled the big table so that he faced the other three men.

"Most of the enlisted men are so raw they've never seen battle, and their officers have never fought Indians." He looked at Fetterman as he spoke the last. The captain looked down at the table.

The Colonel, who'd been helping to drill the soldiers, interjected. "Most of your mounted infantry had never even ridden a horse before the army assigned them to one. The Sioux would ride circles around them."

Carrington nodded as he approached Fetterman. "Until your arrival with the cavalry, Captain, I barely had enough officers to keep the men in line and handle administrative duties."

He placed a hand on Fetterman's shoulder. "I welcome your enthusiasm and concern for the fort's morale, and I assure you I want the same thing. By winter, we will have trained these men to be a disciplined fighting force."

"The Indians will be vulnerable come winter," the Colonel added. "Their horses will be weak with so little grass to forage. They'll have to break into smaller camps. We can take them one at a time instead of facing all of the Sioux at once — and maybe the Cheyenne as well, if Bridger's to be believed."

"What does Bridger say?" Josey asked.

Jim Bridger had to be three score years, stooped with rheumatism and an arthritic spine from where he'd once had an Indian arrowhead removed, yet the army had no better scout.

"His friends among the Crow say Red Cloud is drawing the Sioux together in camps along the Tongue River," the Colonel said. "Cheyenne war parties have added to their numbers. They said the village was so big a man could ride through it from sunrise until the sun was above his head."

Carrington cleared his throat, a skeptical sound. "We'd best be careful where we repeat that information. We don't want to frighten the women. You know how Mr. Bridger likes to stretch his stories."

The old mountain man enjoyed a tall tale. He once told Annabelle he'd been scouting the area for so long Chimney Rock was just a hole in the ground when he first saw it. Yet Josey didn't think Bridger would exaggerate something so important as the size of the enemy force.

Fetterman stared down at the maps spread across the table, his clean-shaven chin puckered in a frown. His fingers circled the hills, etched with tiny marks to suggest their height, and traced along the thick, dark lines that denoted the creeks that cut between them. Whether he was seeking a way to outmaneuver the Indians or his reluctant commander, Josey couldn't tell.

"I see that you will not be moved on this matter," Fetterman said.

"I'd prefer you see that I am right," Carrington replied.

Fetterman continued to study the maps.

"Time is our ally, Captain," Carrington said. "Use it to train the men so they will be ready to fight when the time better suits our circumstances."

Outside the headquarters, Josey squinted against the harsh light of a low-hanging autumn sun while he waited for the Colonel. The office faced the parade grounds, and the giant flag cast a shadow that stretched toward the main gate. After setting aside attack plans, Carrington had promised to arrange work for Josey protecting the wood wagons. Wheatley had been right; there was a lot more money to make from the army as a civilian worker than Josey had ever earned as a soldier.

The Colonel stepped beside him, tamping tobacco in the bowl of his pipe as he puffed.

"Do you think Bridger could be right?"

Josey recalled the wagon train of soldiers he guided that summer who'd been ambushed and surrounded by a couple of hundred Sioux. Bridger had been the man who led reinforcements to them, driving off the attackers. If his assessment about the size of the Indian camp was right, they might be facing not just a couple of hundred mounted warriors, but ten times as many.

Josey said, "I ran across only a raiding party."

The Colonel relit his pipe and looked to the horizon. Carrington had wanted to be close to water and timber, but the site he selected left the fort in view of the surrounding hills. Even on days the Indians didn't attack, soldiers saw flashes of Indian signal mirrors.

"They watch us because they can't figure out a way to take this fort," the Colonel said. "With the howitzers and the stockade, fifty men could hold this place against any number of Indians, even if Bridger is right."

Josey considered his new job guiding wagons. "Yes, but they've got enough warriors to overrun the woodcutters any time they'd like."

The Colonel patted Josey's shoulder. "Not once they get a taste of your rifle. You know

Indians don't have the stomach for the casualties a direct assault against a defended position would demand. An attack like that could decimate a whole generation of warriors. Chiefs value the lives of their braves too much to risk that."

"More than our generals ever did."

The Colonel drew on the stem of his pipe and exhaled smoke in tiny puffs, like a signal fire. "Their best option is to keep stealing horses and cattle, keep trying to pick us off a few at a time until they bleed us dry."

Josey thought he saw a flash from atop Lodge Trail Ridge, like a twinkling of a star. He wondered if the signals meant anything. The Indians had no written language, and Josey couldn't imagine they could convey anything but the simplest of messages with a stolen mirror glinting in the sunlight. He supposed they didn't need to say much. Perhaps it was enough to remind the soldiers they were being watched.

We are here. We are always here.

CHAPTER TEN

Gray skies and cooler temperatures drove the raiding party to take shelter in a hollowed-out space among the boulders that were scattered in the hills like playthings of the thunder beings.

Light Hair sensed a tense frisson among the others. They talked more, moved about more than usual. They had not spoken of their plans for the next day, but in their mood they made clear what they wanted to do: kill *wasicu.*

Little Hawk, riding ahead as their wolf, or scout, had spotted the whites first — a small party on horses and mules heading east along the river trail to the forts. They were not soldiers. Though they were headed in the wrong direction, Little Hawk said they dressed like the men crazy for the soft yellow iron.

It did not matter who they were. Warriors killed soldiers because they fought without honor, and their presence meant more *wa-sicu* would come. Other whites were a threat, too. When the people had allowed them along the river the whites called the Platte, their passage brought disease to villages and drove buffalo from the hunting grounds. The people could not allow the *wasicu* to destroy these lands as well.

He Dog built a fire in a dry spot against the rock, and they gathered near it beneath a shelter Climbing Bear rigged with a lodge cover and poles. The musty smell of eight men pressed together made it difficult to breathe at first. The wood was moist, but no one complained about the smoky fire when the night turned cold.

After returning to the village and giving away most of the horses stolen in the raid at Fort Smith, Light Hair had been eager for another venture before the autumn buffalo hunts. Lone Bear, still sore from his fall in the last raid, and High Backbone remained behind. Climbing Bear enlisted two fellow Cheyenne to take their place. They were brothers, both tall and broad-shouldered. They looked so much alike Light Hair had trouble telling one from the other. Like Climbing Bear, they were eager to kill *wa-sicu.*

They had ranged beyond Fort Smith into

Crow lands, following the trail of a small band Light Hair suspected might be spies. The traveling miners presented a new opportunity.

The warriors sat cross-legged near the fire eating pemmican and dried meat. They warmed themselves with stories of summer days and successful raids. Most were warriors' tales of courage and daring, smooth as river stones in the telling from having been shared so many times.

After everyone but Light Hair had spoken, Climbing Bear addressed him by his warrior name. "Why do you not tell us a story, Crazy Horse? Even far to the south we have heard of your raids."

Light Hair remained silent. He had been half-listening as he pondered what they must do the next day. The stories that first came to Light Hair's mind rubbed against him like pebbles in his moccasin, preventing his comfort so long as the *wasicu* held sway over the people's land.

He Dog said, "Crazy Horse never speaks of his deeds."

"My brother is always first into battle, and the last to take something for himself from the spoils, including the stories of his successes," Little Hawk added. "These were commands to him from a vision."

The others nodded as if they had heard of this but had not known whether to believe it. Light Hair's humility set him apart from most warriors. He had always stood out because of his light skin and wavy brown hair usually seen only among Indian girls. As a child, older boys pulled at his breechclout and told him he should wear dresses. Others mocked him with chants. *"Light Hair is a white man. Light Hair is a white man."*

Light Hair had never been large for his age. Even now he stood a hand's span smaller than most of the warriors who followed him. But the childhood taunts had driven him to work twice as hard at the tasks that distinguished men. Where other boys grew frustrated with the game of shooting arrows at grasshoppers, Light Hair grew more determined. Light Hair rode twice as far as anyone else before stopping for water. Young Light Hair never returned empty-handed from a hunt even if it meant days of hunger in the wild. The old ones said Light Hair could never keep a great horse because he rode them so hard.

On becoming men, boys sought out visions that guided their behavior for the rest of their lives. In Light Hair's vision, a plainly dressed horseman floating above the ground told him not to adorn himself for battle as other warriors did. Instead of wearing an eagle feather bonnet to denote the enemies he slew, he wore a single feather and a small stone behind his ear. The horseman told Light Hair to never keep anything for himself besides what he needed, instructions Light Hair forgot on his first raid. He took two scalps that day and was struck by an arrow in the leg as he took the second.

He never forgot the commandments of his vision after that day, but following them isolated him from other people. His quiet ways and habit of going off alone for days at a time earned him a nickname that was not spoken to his face: "Our Strange Man."

The holy vision infused Light Hair with courage that made him a leader after twenty-six winters, yet the vision's demands also meant he could not live as other men did. He had loved one woman in his life, Black Buffalo Woman, and her father had chosen another for her. Among a people where wealth was measured in horses, a warrior who gave away most of what he took was not a good prospect for a husband. Light Hair held that story so close it chafed at his heart.

Without intending to, Light Hair's reflections spread a somber mood over the group. The excitement at the prospect of battle had run its course, leaving the men spent and vulnerable to dark thoughts. The hour was late, but no one was ready to sleep.

Climbing Bear kicked at a charred log, stirring new life into the fire. "We should go kill the *wasicu* now, while they sleep."

The Cheyenne brothers barked war yips in assent. They rose as if to prepare for battle, stopping only when they saw no one else moved from the fire.

Light Hair sensed the eyes of the others on him as he studied the flames. Night raids were fine for stealing horses and mules, but they were dangerous when gunfire was involved. It was too easy to shoot the wrong person in the dark.

"I will ride with Little Hawk tomorrow to watch these white men." He nodded to Climbing Bear and the Cheyenne brothers. "You will ride ahead as wolves. Scout to make sure no other whites are coming from the opposite direction. When I have a vision of victory, we will attack and kill the *wasicu.*"

Climbing Bear snorted in disgust. "Dog Soldiers do not need a plan. We ride down the *wasicu* and kill them where we find them."

He Dog, who knew Light Hair's mind better than anyone, spoke out. "And how many

Dog Soldiers die in your raids? We follow Crazy Horse so that no one will die but the *wasicu*."

"You speak of war like old men who dream of dying wrapped in a thick buffalo robe." Climbing Bear raised an ax as he turned to the brothers. "It is better to die in battle. Am I right?"

Anger spread across Little Hawk's face, and he moved toward Climbing Bear as if to knock away the ax. Light Hair stilled him with a hand on his elbow. Seven winters younger than Light Hair, Little Hawk's blood ran hot like the Cheyenne, and Light Hair knew he held back out of respect for his brother. The boys who rode with them also looked keen to follow Climbing Bear, their eyes large, nervous grins spread across their faces.

Light Hair understood their eagerness. He had felt the same way when seeking his first scalp. Light Hair sensed he was losing the group. *Would that be so bad?* If they used knives and axes, they might sneak into the *wasicu* camp and kill everyone without danger to themselves.

Light Hair yearned for more. The raids that killed a few *wasicu* at a time were not enough to drive the white men from their lands. Stealing their horses and spotted buffalo was not enough. By learning more of the white man's ways, he hoped to discover a vision for how to defeat them.

He stared into the fire as he spoke. "Killing these miners will satisfy your blood lust for a day, but it will soon leave you hungry again. We must kill all of the soldiers to sate your appetite."

Looking around at the faces glowing in the soft firelight, Light Hair felt he had most of them again. He Dog was with him no matter what. Little Hawk's regard for him outweighed his impatience. As eager as the boys were for scalps, they were nervous, too, and would not fight without Light Hair's assent. The Cheyenne remained unconvinced.

"You do not understand." Climbing Bear had made the same assessment on the group's leanings and directed his words to the others. "If you had been at Sand Creek, you would not wait to kill any *wasicu* you found."

His words fell upon them like a dark shroud. Even the light of the fire seemed to dim as Climbing Bear continued with the story that had been too painful to share earlier. They all knew the bare outline of it. Two years earlier, while the Cheyenne Dog Soldiers raided farms and wagon trains in the lands south of the Platte, the old chief Black Kettle made peace with the white soldiers.

Climbing Bear had resisted the call to fight and settled with his wife and family in Black Kettle's camp at Sand Creek. In the Moon of the Rutting Deer, he rode off with most of the warriors on an autumn buffalo hunt to gather meat for winter. They did not fear for their families because Black Kettle flew an American flag over his lodge so soldiers would know they were protected.

That did not matter to the white chief known as Chivington. His men surrounded the camp and attacked, firing guns-that-shoot-twice before charging on horseback to kill everyone, mostly women, children, and men too old to have gone hunting. Word of the massacre had spread among all the tribes. Climbing Bear, his face set like granite, shared details only someone who had been there could know.

"They could not even fight back," he said. "We had given over our guns earlier to the army to make peace."

A few were quick enough to escape, some digging holes in the banks of the creek where they could hide while the soldiers rode down and killed the rest. Climbing Bear lost his wife, two children, and his mother that day.

"They did not just kill the people," Climbing Bear said. "They cut the bodies into pieces. They scalped even children, sliced off fingers and other parts, then adorned weapons with their trophies. They cut the baby from a mother's stomach while she lived so that she could watch them smash her child's skull before they killed her."

After the massacre, Climbing Bear and the other warriors joined the Dog Soldiers. Their sole ambition: kill *wasicu* before they were killed themselves.

"They think us lower than dogs," Climbing Bear concluded. "They will not stop until they have killed all of us."

Climbing Bear's story was turning the minds of everyone to charging after the *wasicu*. Even Light Hair felt his blood grow hot for the killing. They sought more than revenge. The *wasicu* left the men feeling helpless in a world that grew smaller and harsher every year. They felt as much power to stop the *wasicu* as they did to halt the wind and the rain from wearing down the mountains. They looked in the faces of children in the village and saw a future of living on handouts from the forts, wearing white man's clothes, going to white man's schools, digging in the dirt with white man's tools, and never knowing the thrill of a buffalo hunt.

They never spoke of this, yet fear ate at every one of them like a wasting disease. It was worse than any single massacre on a village for it infected all the people — and it would not stop with the slaughter of one camp of miners.

"We are not here to kill a few fools who hunt rocks in the dirt," Light Hair said. "That will not bring your people back."

Climbing Bear scowled as if he did not believe what he heard. "You do not understand our need for revenge. If you had been there —"

"I was there." The effect of Light Hair's whispered words could not have been greater than if he had shouted them from a mountain.

"You were not —"

Crossing his arm with a closed fist over his chest, Light Hair said, "In my heart, I was there."

"My brother knew a woman from your village," Little Hawk told Climbing Bear and the other Cheyenne. "Her name was Yellow Woman."

Climbing Bear's curiosity quelled his anger for the moment. "She was my wife's friend. She was a good woman." He looked to Light Hair. "How did you know her?"

Listening to Climbing Bear's story, Light Hair's mind had turned to another peaceful village, on Blue Water Creek where he had lived when he had fifteen winters. As Climbing Bear described what he had seen in the ruins of his village, Light Hair closed his eyes and saw everything just as he remembered it eleven winters earlier.

Left behind when the warriors went to raid horses from a neighboring tribe, Light Hair went off alone for days on a hunt that saved his life. He returned to a burned-out village, riding past the corpses of the old, the young, and the women. They, too, had been mutilated, much as Climbing Bear had described. Light Hair found a lone survivor, a Cheyenne woman who had been visiting relatives with her husband. Mad with grief, she still held the lifeless body of her baby, her husband's slain body nearby.

Finding another horse, Light Hair managed to take the woman back to her people. They traveled three days together and not once did she speak. She recovered her voice after he returned her to her family. In the subsequent years she demonstrated her gratitude by treating Light Hair as a beloved brother.

Light Hair saw his pain reflected in Little

Hawk's eyes, and he heard it in his brother's voice as he told the tale. Light Hair did not stop him.

"It was Yellow Woman you saved?" Climbing Bear asked.

Light Hair's silence proved answer enough. He thought of the last time he had heard from Yellow Woman. She had sent to him a pair of moccasins she had beaded herself. They were winter moccasins, the buffalo skin turned in so that the fur would keep his feet warm. She also sent a message: "She who made these smiles at the sound of your name." Now she was dead.

No one spoke. Glowing embers were all that remained of the fire, and in the gathering darkness Light Hair felt the eyes of the others upon him.

"We will attack and kill the *wasicu*," he said, hearing the grunts of approval from the Cheyenne and waiting for silence before he continued. "But this will be done only once I have a vision that will help us take vengeance on the soldiers as well."

The next day Light Hair rode with Little Hawk to trail the miners. Climbing Bear and the Cheyenne rode ahead to scout the trail. He Dog and the boys followed with the warhorses. Light Hair would not attack

133

until he could see victory in his mind. The *wasicu* were as numerous as locusts. His people were not. Every death was a tragedy, mourned by wailing women who cut their hair and arms in their grief.

They followed the miners at a discreet distance. Light Hair counted seven men. They brought no wagons, only horses and mules. Two of the miners rode Indian ponies. So much the better. The people could make use of the ponies and mules.

As he studied the white people, Light Hair tried to think of a way he could use their capture to lure soldiers into a trap, but they were too far removed from the fort. Perhaps Climbing Bear was right, and the best they could hope to accomplish was to slaughter these men where they slept. Light Hair held back from calling for an attack because something struck him as odd about the group. He drew closer as the day wore on.

A storm stalked their path through the afternoon. Light Hair smelled rain on the wind that stirred the branches in the trees. Thunder echoed through the hills.

The rain did not bother Light Hair, but only fools did not seek shelter from lightning. Light Hair recalled the stories his father, a holy man and healer, told him as a boy, how spirit riders cast lightning to the earth, punishing any who ignored the commandments of a vision. The hooves of their giant sky horses pounding among the clouds created the sound of thunder.

As he grew older, Light Hair dismissed the stories as fables parents told their children. Then one summer he rode with his uncle and father far into the badlands and saw for himself the huge bones of the sky horses, gleaming white in the sand and cliff faces where they were buried in their fall to earth. Their bones made even buffalo look tiny. Proof of these things gave Light Hair a new respect for the power of visions.

The miners sensed the storm's approach as well. From a hill overlooking the trail, Light Hair watched them settle into a campsite near the river where the next hill climbed steeply.

"We will come at night, after the storm passes," he told Little Hawk. The sounds of water dripping from the trees would mask their movements. "We will steal their mules and horses. Then we will kill the white men."

Little Hawk nodded and turned his horse. Light Hair began to follow on his yellow paint, but a thought stopped him. He took out his farseeing glass and turned back to the miners. Something troubled him about the group, and he used the glass to study the two miners who rode Indian ponies.

"What is it, brother?"

Light Hair turned the glass to sharpen the image. He studied the face of every white man in the camp, looking for one he had hoped to never see in these lands again. He did not see the face he sought. He searched the faces again, counting to be sure he did not miss one. There was no mistake. The white warrior whose magic he had tried to steal was not among these miners.

Yet Light Hair did not doubt the identity of two who were: one, a white-black man, was the warrior's brother. Light Hair had followed their wagons long enough that summer to be certain he was not mistaken. The other, though she dressed like a man, was the dark-haired woman who rode better than most white men, the warrior's woman.

In his surprise, Light Hair lingered longer than was safe, but as he studied the woman, a new plan came to his mind. His vision of victory extended beyond the taking of this camp. That would be simple. In Light Hair's mind, he began to see a way that the people might capture the big fort.

When Light Hair closed the farseeing glass and turned away, Little Hawk narrowed his eyes, a question on his lips that he did not speak. It took a moment for Light Hair to realize the cause of his brother's confusion before it occurred to him.

Light Hair was smiling.

CHAPTER ELEVEN

The woodchoppers' road looped from Fort Phil Kearny for five miles behind Sullivant Hill to Big Piney Creek. The road ended near the creek's widest point, at a wooded island of thick pines that grew straight as an arrow and ninety feet to the first limb. The woodchoppers had built a blockhouse there with loopholes for firing out whenever the Indians attacked. While they worked, Josey rode among the big trees, alert for snipers.

Since an attack in early October before Josey's arrival, the Indians no longer harassed the workers near the blockhouse. They preferred attacking the wood wagons when they were most vulnerable, during the drive from the fort to the blockhouse or on the return. The picket on Pilot Hill monitored the wagons' progress. Pulled by six mules each, the wagons moved in trains of a score or two. If Josey or one of the guards riding the flanks called out an alarm, the front wagons turned in to meet, the others falling in to form a large corral with the rear wagons closing the circle. The drivers turned the mules to the inside of the corral so the wagons could bunch close, forming a barricade.

Everyone in the train was armed. Most were better equipped than the soldiers, with breech-loading rifles or repeaters like Josey's Henry. The Indians managed little more than to harass the train until the signalman on Pilot Hill alerted the fort and the soldiers rode to the column's relief, driving off the Indians.

No one had been killed in the first week Josey rode with the wood wagons. He heard a few stray shots from the woods along the road and a few arrows landed nearby, but the Indians rode off before he could get close enough to engage the attackers. Twice the Indians came in numbers, but the firing from within the corral drove them off before the soldiers arrived from the fort. Josey doubted the Indians suffered any losses either. They rarely rode close enough for a clean shot, and as much as he valued his Henry, it didn't pack the punch needed to be deadly at long range.

The work reminded Josey of the patrols he rode during the war. Long periods of inactivity lulled a man's senses until a sudden threat put him at risk. Dullards didn't last long on patrol. Josey felt sharper; the air smelled fresher; the sun shone brighter. The whoosh of wind through the boughs soothed him like a musical interlude, leaving him alert to any discordant notes. Dry pine needles rustled amid the brush off the road. Crows cawed when disturbed from their perch among the trees. Mules panted and snorted. Leather traces creaked against their pull. All might represent routine movements of the day. Any could be portents of danger.

By the day's end when a bugle call heralded their safe return to the fort, Josey was exhausted. Even when little happened, the hours of jangled nerves took a toll. He could feel it among the soldiers and civilians alike. No one had died this week, but they'd seen the little fort cemetery grow by ones and twos most weeks. Rumors that the Indian village was swelling left the fort's inhabitants feeling they were hemmed in and forgotten. And yet the work was a welcome distraction to Josey, an excuse to disengage his mind from the questions that nagged him since leaving Virginia City. Within the fort, he found no such protection.

One Sunday Margaret Carrington approached him. The officers' wives and children had been playing croquet on the parade grounds. She broke away for a rest and joined Josey when she saw him pass. The exercise outdoors brought a bloom of color to her pale cheeks. After exchanging a few pleasantries about the warm autumn day, she got right to the point.

"I was expecting a letter from Annabelle announcing wedding plans, yet I sense in your manner that my wait may be prolonged."

Josey might have been put off by such directness from another woman, but he had taken Margaret Carrington's measure on their first meeting. He knew she had Annabelle's best interests — and even his own — at heart.

"The subject has not come up."

"I suppose there wasn't time, not with you scurrying back here —"

"I had promised I would return for the Colonel."

"Oh, yes. I had forgotten." Margaret Carrington's voice had risen to a level that a pair of enlisted men leading a water wagon turned to look. "You must excuse me, for the Colonel doesn't seem the type of man to require such coddling. I suppose looks can be deceiving."

The path turned muddy as they reached the well-trod area in front of the barracks. Margaret Carrington stepped into the thick, brown grass near where the powder magazine was buried. She waited for Josey to offer his arm, and they continued across the uneven ground. After a deep breath, her voice returned to its normal level.

"You know, Josey, it is natural for a man to have doubts. Women have them, too."

Josey said nothing. *Annabelle should have doubts.*

Margaret Carrington knew him well enough not to wait for a reply. She patted his arm. "I don't know what passed between you two in Virginia City, and I don't suppose you'll tell me."

Josey felt her eyes on him but continued to stare straight ahead.

"I do know what love looks like when I see it. When a man loves a woman the way you love Annabelle, she will forgive anything if he will just ask."

Josey stopped and faced her. Annabelle's mother had once told him almost the same thing, and he wondered where this women's wisdom was written that so many should know it.

"If she really knew me . . . if she knew what I'd done . . ."

142

Margaret Carrington poked his chest with a finger. "She knows you. She knows what's in here. The rest is a page in a book that's been read countless times. Turn the page, Josey. I know how this story goes, and it's a happy ending."

In Virginia City, Josey had rented a cabin on a bare hill overlooking town. The cabin was made of logs with a dirt roof. Josey threw out the broken furniture, moldering animal skins, and rotted foodstuffs abandoned by the previous occupant. He aired it out for a week before he allowed Annabelle in. By then it was clean, though spartan, smelling of lavender, pine, and wood fire. A south-facing window permitted plenty of light during the day. At night he used candles.

The structure was well chinked against cold winds, and the single room stayed warm even when the fire burned low in the fireplace. The bed was the only proper furniture. Annabelle teased Josey about his priorities, but she didn't seem to mind.

Despite the uphill ride, she came often to see him. She brought food, as if Josey couldn't be expected to feed himself in her absence. Sometimes they ate sitting on the bed. Sometimes they ate in rickety chairs set outside on a porch that overlooked the town. Between the foothills that enclosed it, Virginia City was platted with vertical and horizontal streets that reminded Annabelle of Charleston and other cities she'd known back east.

While they ate, Annabelle would tell Josey about Charleston and muse about places she'd never been. Josey liked to hear her talk, even when his wandering mind missed the words. Her voice soothed like a lullaby. He always slept better when she stayed with him, even when they didn't make love. He liked it better when she talked, but when she ran out of things to say she grew annoyed with him for not speaking more. She confused the peace he felt with her for an absence of interest, and it nettled at her.

"Aren't you happy to be with me?" she asked him once.

"I am happy."

"Can't you show it?"

She didn't expect an answer, and he didn't offer one. Most times she understood him without being told things. On occasion, she ran out of patience or up against subjects he could never tell her about, not if he wanted her to ride up the hill to see him again.

It was like that when she asked about his

parents. Josey hadn't seen them since he left for the war. He'd stopped sending letters before the war's end, and that bothered Annabelle as if she were the one aggrieved.

"At least write to them. Let them know you're alive." Years of believing her husband dead without knowing had left Annabelle sensitive to the topic. "Thinking somebody dead without knowing is a torture worse than grief."

"I'll think about it."

"What is there to think about?"

"I have to think what to say. It's been a long time."

What Annabelle didn't understand was that it wouldn't end with a letter. His mother would want him to return home — or she would rouse his father to come looking for Josey. Writing a letter would never be enough; he would have to see her.

And then what? She wouldn't recognize her boy in the man Josey had become. One look in his eyes and she would know how many mothers had lost their sons to her boy's actions. Better she think him dead than know him as a killer.

That night after Annabelle left, Josey sat in his chair and watched the sun set over the gulch. He wore his buffalo blanket against the wind that whipped down from the Tobacco Root Mountains. The rolling brown hills around the town were freckled with sagebrush. He tried to imagine the view before the hills were shorn of trees for building and firewood and the ground was dug up and scarred in the search for gold. From this height, it looked like a giant boar had been rooting in a yard.

The lowering sun drew his eye to a hill just north of town. Five evenly spaced white boards cast shadows across the dirt. Boot Hill. The painted boards marked the resting spot for road agents hanged more than two years ago by the Vigilance Committee, respected men of the community who saw themselves as upholding order in the absence of law.

Josey had ridden with them for a time when he came to Virginia City a year earlier, had helped them on occasion carry out their rough form of justice. He was certain the men buried on Boot Hill had deserved their fate. But he would never think to dig the graves for those he killed in a place where he would have to look at their markers.

Hills rolled to the horizon in every direction. When Josey closed his eyes he imagined every one of them a Boot Hill, covered with blank markers for the nameless men he had killed. Some he still saw in his dreams, recognizing their faces in the moment when the light left their eyes, like snuffing a candle flame between his fingers. The sun slipped beneath the western hills just as fast, leaving Josey in darkness. He rose and turned to go inside, knowing he could never remain at peace in this place.

The next day he set off to get the Colonel.

CHAPTER TWELVE

Annabelle woke with a start, her heart racing as if she had been running up a hill. She tried to still her breath and listen. *There.* A shuffling outside her tent. The noise must have woken her. It was Byron. The big man's low rumble wasn't meant for whispering.

"Something's bothered the horses," he said.

"I'll be right there." She reached for the Henry rifle. She had loaded it before she tried to sleep, but she checked it again just as Josey would.

She had thought she would never sleep. Byron's sighting of the Indian put them all on alert. They tethered the horses and mules closer to the camp among the miners' tents and set an extra watch for the night. The storm already had everyone on edge. They hurried to prepare dinner to the drumbeat of approaching thunder. Two of the miners had brought back a string of trout. Annabelle ate as much as any man these days and still walked away from meals hungry.

A pelting rain started while they cleaned up. They redoubled their efforts, and Annabelle was in her tent before the worst of it came, carried by powerful gusts of wind that shook her canvas confines. The downpour's furious pounding drowned out all other sounds. A tribe of Sioux could have ridden through their camp and no one would have heard them. The rain and intermittent lightning made sleep impossible. She kept feeling around the tent, worried water would seep in or that a flash flood would sweep away everything. She bundled her things in hopes of keeping them dry. The last thing she remembered was placing her rifle scabbard on top of the rest so that it wouldn't get wet.

The day's first hazy gray light unfurled from the eastern horizon as Annabelle stepped outside. Byron was down among the miners and the horses. She counted five miners and two horses as she made her way toward them.

"I never even got a shot off." Old Ben's plaintive protests sounded like an apology for falling asleep. "They came in so quiet I didn't know they were here until the horses were running off."

"The mules, too?" Annabelle asked.

Old Ben wouldn't meet her eyes. Annabelle shook her head. She couldn't blame the old man for falling asleep after the day they'd had.

"We're going after them." The biggest miner, a man named Jeremiah, held a rifle in one hand and the bridle of his horse in the other.

Annabelle glanced toward Byron, who shook his head.

"Bad idea," she said. "You'll never catch Indians in this country, especially with those big mares."

"We've got to try." Jeremiah had left a wife and two young children in Arkansas, promising he would return a rich man. "If we have to walk out with just two horses we'll be going home with nothing."

Annabelle looked around at the tents and gear, mostly provisions to see them through the journey. "There's nothing here worth risking a life over."

"We've got to try."

"They were just boys," Old Ben added. "One of them looked like the horse he was riding was lame. He stopped on that ridge right there, checking its fetlock like something was wrong. If you hurry, you might catch them."

Jeremiah looked at Annabelle, daring her to try to stop him.

She turned to Byron. "If we're going to be walking, we better start sorting through our things. See what we can afford to leave behind."

Jeremiah mounted his horse. Avery, a boy too young to have fought in the war, took to the other horse. Old Ben handed him a revolver. "Good luck."

The two riders ascended the slope on a switchback. At the top they emerged from the morning shadow and paused in the bright sunlight. Avery waved down to them before turning his mare to follow Jeremiah down the other side.

Annabelle cleared the things out of her tent, discarding what she couldn't carry. She had purchased gifts for the commander's wife before leaving Virginia City, things that wouldn't be included in the wagons that resupplied the fort.

"I suppose Mrs. Carrington won't be getting her new hat or parasol."

Byron had borrowed an ax from the miners and nodded toward the pines that grew from the side of the slope like whiskers on a man's chin. "If we can make us some poles, we can fix 'em to the horses like the Indians do."

She nodded. "I don't want to leave any of the food or ammunition behind."

A sharp clap echoed over the ridge. The night before she might have convinced herself it was thunder, but this morning she knew better. Three more claps, in quick succession, then a whole fusillade.

Ambush. The fool Jeremiah had ridden right into them. She turned to Byron. He already held his rifle, his forehead furrowed with worry. She tossed him a box of cartridges and picked up her rifle, breathing deeply to still the fluttering that felt like ospreys taking flight in her stomach.

She looked down the slope to the other three miners. They had heard it, too. Old Ben had his rifle ready, a powder flask in his shaking hands. Byron had her elbow. When she turned to look up at him, he nodded toward the slope's summit.

"We'll be safer there."

Higher ground. Of course. She stooped to pick up a canteen and Josey's buffalo blanket and followed. They picked their way amid the rocky outcropping that overlooked the river. There were boulders near the top, large enough to provide cover. Even before they crested the top they heard the Indians.

Maniacal war whoops and barks, like Satan's dogs loosed from hell. The sound turned her mouth dry as cotton.

Byron urged her on, but Annabelle looked back. Old Ben got off a shot. His hands shook powder all around him in a vain effort to reload before the Indians rode him down, a tomahawk crushing half his skull. The other two miners didn't get off a shot. They broke into a run for the water. They weren't even out from under the trees before their bodies were pierced with so many arrows they looked like pincushions.

Everything happened so fast, Annabelle didn't have time to scream. She stumbled ahead to the shelter of the boulders, bracing herself against a rock as she caught her breath, transfixed by the horror below. She forced herself to look away when the savages brought out their big knives and began to saw at the scalps, their arms straining to cut away hair and skin. She hoped the miners were dead — but they were not. Inhuman cries, sounds she didn't know men could make, carried up the slope. Annabelle ducked behind the boulder, closed her eyes, and covered her ears. Still, the noise assailed her, like a physical pummeling. To block the screams, she recited a lullaby her mother used to sing.

Slumber on, baby dear, do not hear thy mother's sigh. Breathed for him far away, while she sings thy lullaby.

Three times she repeated the song before the screams stopped. The miners' death cries rent the melody unrecognizable, but the silence that followed was even more awful. Annabelle's heart thrummed like a violin string from beating so fast. Her curiosity got the better of her, and she had to look. The scalps hadn't been enough. The savages stripped the clothes off the corpses and cut away parts from the bodies.

"Trophies," Byron said.

The Indians were a small band, maybe eight, the exact number difficult to figure because they never stopped moving. Despite the cool morning, most were dressed in breechcloths, with buffalo robes draped over their shoulders. Their bodies, even their ponies, were painted, some with streaks of color, others with spots like jungle cats.

Once done with the bodies, they tore through the campsite like children at Christmas. They ripped off covers and broke open trunks and boxes, splitting with axes any that were locked. Their glee at discovering the most mundane things might have been comical if not for the mutilated corpses that littered the scene. Annabelle couldn't watch any more, the nausea she hadn't felt since leaving Virginia City making her whole body tremble.

The rising sun promised the kind of bright, warm day Annabelle might have rejoiced in at any other time. She closed her eyes and wished for the savages to hurry, take what they wanted, and leave them be. Maybe they would be content with the scalps they had.

As much as Annabelle wished them away, she couldn't ignore the Indians for long. They were aware of her and Byron but in no apparent hurry to approach. A couple of shots from Byron's rifle discouraged any attempt to ascend the slope, but the range proved too great for him to cause any damage. At least the same was also true for the Indians, who valued their powder and shot too much to waste it. They were more concerned with sorting their booty.

One Indian stood out. His skin was a paler shade than the others, his long, braided hair such a light brown Annabelle wondered if he might be a half-breed. Instead of a headdress or fearsome jewelry, he wore a lone feather. Though he was not the largest, he moved among the others as an officer might, each brave giving him their full attention before he moved on to the next. She

155

shivered with a sudden chill when he looked their way.

Her hopes for an easy escape evaporated with the morning dew when the Indians settled in and built a fire. What plunder they could not carry off on horses, the Indians piled together and lighted. She judged by the sun it was mid-morning, but the day grew warm among the rocks where there was no shade. The bright light splintered her head, which had been pounding since her failure to drown out the miners' screams. Annabelle took a sip from the canteen and offered it to Byron.

"You think they mean to wait us out?"

"No telling."

Looking at the mutilated bodies, Annabelle knew the Indians were in for a long wait. *I'll starve before I let them do that to me.*

Once the fire was going, she counted seven Indians seated around it. She used Byron's spyglass to watch them. They were a joyful party. From their gestures and the sounds that carried up the slope they seemed to be reliving the glory of the miners' slaughter. They went on like they were describing Bull Run or Fredericksburg.

Byron had been exploring the opposite side of the ridge. While the ground sloped

156

from their camp, the ridge ended in a long drop to the river.

"What do you see?" she asked.

"Not much. I thought we might find a way down while they's distracted, but the other side's too steep."

Annabelle studied the Indians around the fire. The light-skinned one was alone in not participating in the boasting. He sat silently, his attention never straying for long from the crest of the slope.

"I don't think they're as distracted as we need them to be," she said. "It's almost as if they're waiting for something."

"Reinforcements?"

She didn't see how more numbers would help. Only a few men at a time could make the ascent up the slope no matter how many they had in reserve.

"I don't know."

The Indians were in no hurry. One of them drew out a pipe and lit it with a twig from the fire. Before drawing on it, he raised the pipe in each direction of the compass then held it overhead like an offering to the heavens. He drew in the smoke, passing the pipe to his left as he exhaled.

"Maybe they'll leave once they've had their smoke. Maybe it's a tradition."

Byron didn't match her optimism. "They

157

look awful comfortable."

So they settled in. They stood the rifles on end and used the buffalo robe to form a screen that shielded them from the sun when it reached its zenith. Despite the heat of the day, Annabelle shivered. The initial rush of fear had worn off, yet she remained terrified now that she had time to consider their position. They had no food, not much water, and no escape route. They had retreated to a place where the Indians could not easily get to them, but with enough time and patience the savages would prevail.

Is this where I die? If only that were the full cost of her error. She'd brought Byron here. His death would be her responsibility. She'd also put her baby in danger. Josey's baby. *What was I thinking?* At this point a quick death might be the best she could hope for.

On the journey west, Annabelle's mother terrorized herself with newspaper stories of massacres and white women taken captive by Indians. She would read parts of them aloud until Annabelle demanded she stop. Her mother even took to sleeping with an ax beside her. That frightened Annabelle's father, who feared she would wake one night with a start and dismember a limb — his or hers — before coming to her senses.

158

Annabelle had accused her mother of creating an irrational fear of Indians with all her reading, but that was before she knew what the Sioux could do.

Recalling some of those stories now, Annabelle doubted any of the authors had witnessed what they described. Their accounts lacked the visceral horror of what she had just seen — and heard. From the stories, Annabelle had imagined taking a scalp to be a simple thing, like a butcher cleaving a steak. The memory of what she had seen brought back her nausea, and this time she couldn't blame the baby.

In many of the tales, a white man gave a pistol to a woman so she might "save" herself if all else failed. On listening to such stories, Annabelle had wondered what she would do in that position. Martyring oneself seemed easy in the abstract. It felt different now. Could she take her own life? How would she even manage with a rifle? Would she have to rely on Byron? A bullet to the head seemed preferable to how she imagined the Indians might use her before torturing her to death. Some of the books told of women burned alive, like witches from a more superstitious time.

Yet there were also stories of women who survived their captivity. Mother had read an account of an Irish woman taken by Indians two years earlier. She had been ransomed to the army and returned to her husband.

That hope glimmered, as delicate as the life inside her. In all the nightmares of Indian savagery her mother's readings had inspired, Annabelle never dreamed there might be another life at stake. Stroking her hand across her belly, Annabelle wished she could feel the baby inside, to be reassured that it still breathed, however it was babies drew air inside their mother. She had to take it on faith that her child lived. Faith was all a person had sometimes.

Annabelle's trust in God had been shaken by her brothers' deaths during the war. She felt like a hypocrite for allowing her thoughts to turn to faith now. *Better to live as a hypocrite than die beneath an Indian knife.* Annabelle would do whatever it took to see that her baby lived. She clasped Byron's hand in hers and closed her eyes.

"Because he loves me, says the Lord, I will rescue him. I will protect him, for he acknowledges my name. . . ."

CHAPTER THIRTEEN

Josey spent the afternoon seeing to his gray pony. Carrington permitted him to keep the gelding in the cavalry stables, but Josey didn't trust the horse's care to anyone else. Before crossing the parade grounds on his way back to the boardinghouse, he checked to make sure Margaret Carrington was gone. He wished to avoid another interrogation about his feelings for Annabelle. Instead, he spied Frances Grummond leaving the temporary hospital, appearing unsteady on her feet. Josey rushed to her side.

"Ma'am, are you all right?"

"I'm fine now," she said with a dramatic wave of hand. Her voice held a singsong quality, and her deep-set eyes appeared unfocused. She clutched a handkerchief stained with a shade of red he knew too well.

"What's happened?"

In her other hand she held a tiny bottle. "Doctor Hines gave me laudanum for the pain. I think he meant for me to wait until I returned home to take some."

Josey put his arm around the woman to steady her. The officers' quarters stood just ahead. "Why did the doctor give you laudanum?"

She removed the handkerchief, exposing a ribbon of stitches across the loose skin between her thumb and the palm.

"I must look like Frankenstein's monster," she said. "George will be furious."

"He will be relieved to know you aren't hurt worse." Josey hoped he was right, but he knew too much of her husband's history to be certain. "What happened?"

She looked up at him, her eyes avoiding his gaze. "You will laugh at me if I tell you."

"Of course I won't."

"I was making biscuits."

Making biscuits? "I don't understand."

"I told you I was a terrible cook." Her voice held a trace of girlish squeal, reminding Josey of just how young she was. She must have been practically a child when she married Grummond, whom Josey judged to be about thirty. "The biscuits came out so hard, I thought I would need a hatchet to separate them into halves."

Josey failed to stifle a laugh. "Tell me you didn't use a hatchet."

"No, but I needed a butcher knife. The blade slipped. You promised you wouldn't laugh at me."

"I'm not laughing at you. I'm laughing at your story. You intended it to be funny."

"I did," she said. "You like my jests. I can never make George laugh."

"That is his loss."

Frances Grummond had a liveliness and sense of humor Josey found hard to reconcile with her gruff husband. *People probably think the same of Annabelle and me.*

At the center of officers' row stood the post commander's quarters, a handsome house with two brick chimneys and a shingled roof. Plain wood structures housing the other officers stretched from either side. They were single-room affairs with dirt floors and stovepipes jutting out from their earthen roofs. Josey's nose wrinkled at the smell of lime. The privies behind the officers' quarters were treated more often than the others.

"I fear I shall never learn to cook," Mrs. Grummond said. "At least not well. My pies are nearly as bad as my biscuits."

"At least your pies aren't responsible for any injuries," Josey said, enjoying the sound of her musical laugh. It struck him as odd that she would be such an inept cook for as long as she'd been married. His interactions with Grummond were limited, but he remembered a night around a campfire when the officers read aloud letters from home. Grummond had a letter from his wife, though Josey couldn't remember anything he'd read.

Mrs. Grummond turned at the sight of her husband. "Oh, there's George."

She called to him, "George, don't be angry with me. I am such a lummox." She went to him, extending her hand for his examination.

"What's this?" He strode past her, coming straight to Josey. Grummond's height seemed even greater from the way he stood ramrod straight.

"Mr. Anglewicz was kind enough to see me home from the hospital," Mrs. Grummond said.

"The doctor gave her laudanum for the pain," Josey said. "I didn't think she should be left alone."

"And you judged your company to be appropriate?" Grummond looked down on Josey through hooded eyes. Something in his manner left Josey to wonder if he didn't have a laudanum supply of his own.

"Fannie, go inside." Grummond turned to Josey. "I can see to my wife's care myself."

■ ■ ■ ■

That night Josey found the Colonel in the boardinghouse dining room with Fetterman and Grummond. The room smelled of stale beer, smoke, and the sweat of a couple of dozen men who bathed infrequently. A fire raged in the hearth, leaving half the room uncomfortably warm while a chill lingered in every corner. Fetterman was buying drinks. Grummond already looked to be in his cups. He slumped over the table, his hooded eyes nearly shut. Josey ignored him and went around the trestle table to sit beside the Colonel. Fetterman offered him a shot of whiskey, but Josey stuck to a mug of warm milk Elisabeth Wheatley favored him with. It was a rare treat given all the cattle the Indians had driven off.

Josey tried to listen while the other men talked about their progress training the new recruits. The noise in the crowded room left him on edge. A clatter of glasses at the bar jolted him. Voices raised in laughter at a table to his left spun him round. On reflex, his hand reached to his waist, but he'd left his guns in his room. His fingers drummed a beat like a racing heart on the tabletop until the Colonel slid a hand over his arm and gave a light squeeze.

The arrival of a couple of privates to the table interrupted the training talk. Enlisted men were rare in the boardinghouse. On their meager pay they could afford to eat only in the fort mess, but the lure of the fresh meat James Wheatley managed to bring back from his frequent hunting excursions was worth an occasional splurge.

The men looked a score of years each. Fetterman knew them by name and introduced them as new recruits to the Second Cavalry. He sat up straighter as he addressed them. "Fitzgerald, Clancy, what can I do for you?"

Clancy responded, a thick brogue revealing his distant origins. "Begging your pardon, Captain, but we want you to know we're with you, at least we hope you'll take us with you."

"Am I going somewhere?"

Fitzgerald, who'd been twisting his cap in his hands as if reluctant to speak, blurted out, "When you convince old Ichabod to let us take the fight to the savages."

The Colonel leaned toward Josey and whispered, "He means Carrington." The commander had been a personal secretary to Washington Irving as a young man. Josey had heard whispers among soldiers who

166

compared their commander to the author's craven Ichabod Crane.

Fetterman said, "Your valor is a credit to the Second, gentlemen." The young soldiers beamed to be addressed as such. "See that you continue your training under Lieutenant Grummond here, and we'll soon give the Indians a fight they won't forget."

He nudged Grummond, who looked ill. His bloodshot eyes failed to focus as he looked across the table and up at the soldiers. He towered over the privates when he stood, even on shaky legs. They edged away from him, now uncomfortable in the officers' presence.

"Thank you, sirs," Clancy said. "We'll be leaving you to yours then. A good night to you."

They were gone before Grummond could make his way around the table, fumbling at the buttons on his trousers. The Colonel followed after him to ensure Grummond got outside before he relieved himself.

"What was that about?" Josey asked, nodding in the direction of the privates.

"They grow bored with the constant drilling," Fetterman said. "I can't blame them. They see the Indians sallying against the wood trains every day. It pricks at a man's pride to cower within these walls."

"Better a wound to the ego than they wind up as headless horsemen." Josey wondered at Fetterman's failure to correct the show of disrespect for the commander. "Didn't they teach patience at West Point?"

Fetterman's face clouded over. "Your jest hews too close to the mark, sir."

Josey blinked in surprise. "What do you mean?"

"My father and my uncle attended West Point. I did not."

"I had no idea."

Fetterman appeared mollified by the compliment the mistake implied. "My father died when I was nine. Had he lived, perhaps the army would have seen fit to accept my petition. I was a bank teller in Rochester. When the war started, I saw my opportunity to show the army its error."

"You seem like a West Point man."

Fetterman's coal eyes smoldered. "I like to think myself better than that. West Point men carry the burden of entitlement. None ever outworked me."

Josey raised his cup in a toast to Fetterman, who allowed himself a smile.

"We are not so different, you see," Fetterman said. "Our blood pulses with the beat of war's drums. West Point can't teach that."

"I am not like that."

"Of course you are. I grew up reading of Caesar, Alexander, the legends of Arthur, the song of Roland. Every time I read it I would pray for Charlemagne's return. I would think, 'Blow your horn, Roland.' Do not try to tell me as a boy you didn't imagine yourself a character in such stories."

Josey recalled a conversation with Annabelle about Achilles and Hector, but he did not share it with Fetterman. "A boy's fantasies. They mean nothing."

Fetterman shook his head, his thick muttonchops turning in the lamplight like the tusks of a boar. "They mean *everything*. There would be no story if Roland called for aid. These stories are about how heroes face mortal danger. They teach us of character and honor, everything that's important about being a man."

Josey's thoughts remained elsewhere.

"What about love?"

"Love?" Fetterman uttered a dismissive sound. "Love is not for heroes. Love is for fools."

"Then I am a fool."

Fetterman held his glass to the light and swirled the liquid. A smile tugged at the corner of his mouth. "A fool who is here, in a fort at war, while his love is . . . where is she, exactly?"

Josey didn't answer. Fetterman finished his drink with one swallow.

"Your silence does not bring to mind a man who is a fool for love. You know I am right. The crucible of combat exposes weakness in some but reveals the mettle in others. War is where we found our true selves, Josey. You can pretend otherwise if it gives you comfort, but I recognize a kindred spirit. I think you do, too."

The Colonel returned, and Josey rose to use the privy. His head felt muddled, and he wondered if it was the din of the room and sitting too near the fire or Fetterman's words. *Maybe I should have had a drink.* He welcomed the bracing effect of the cool night air.

The clear sky illuminated a crescent moon that cast a silvery glow over the path to the privy. A small shed stood just off the path. From behind it, Josey heard retching and a cough that cut through the thin air like a rifle shot. He stepped around the corner.

"Do you need help?"

"Just stay away from me." The shadow crouched behind the shed rose into a towering silhouette Josey recognized. "And stay away from my wife."

Grummond hawked and spat and wiped his mouth. His figure swayed in the moonlight, and for the second time that night Josey reached toward a gun belt that wasn't there.

"I have never sought out your wife," he said. "Your affairs are none of my concern."

"My affairs? You leave that out of this. They have nothing to do with you."

Josey's fingers rubbed together with an agitation he could not quell. Grummond posed him no threat, yet he couldn't control the reaction of body and mind. Something set Josey's mind whirring, but he couldn't figure out what it was, like the spinning spokes of a wheel that fails to find purchase in a sandy path.

He kept his voice even. "I never imagined they did."

Grummond fell silent, perhaps waiting for his legs to steady. "Stay away from Fannie. Don't talk to her again."

Josey had no intention to go looking for Frances Grummond. But her husband, he decided, would bear watching.

Chapter Fourteen

The Indians continued their sojourn, and the day carried on like any other. The sun traced its arc overhead. The river flowed below. A crow cawed from a pine growing sideways from the eastern cliff face. Tall trees that shaded their looted campsite creaked and groaned where their boughs rubbed together in the afternoon breeze. Annabelle might have dozed but for the dread that squeezed at her insides, making it difficult to draw breath. She felt exhausted, and she was ravenous. She wished she had thought to bring the pack with food.

A whistle broke her reverie, like the sound of an eagle cry. She no longer heard the crow, and she wondered if it, too, had fallen victim to a cunning predator. She swept the blanket aside and raised Byron's glass. The Indians were stirring.

"Are they leaving?"

Abandoning their piles of booty near the

fire, the Indians came to the slope, carrying bows or rifles. Their leader, the pale one, held a tomahawk. Annabelle shuddered; he seemed to be looking straight at her.

"I don't think so." She grabbed her rifle and levered in a cartridge.

There was little natural cover along the slope, but the Indians bounded like deer from rock to tree, their leader always dancing ahead as if daring Byron and Annabelle to shoot. The four men who carried bows paused to fire arrows up the slope while the men with rifles waited.

After an arrow clattered against a boulder a few feet in front of them, Byron said, "They mean to draw us out so those with the rifles can get a shot at us."

He kept low and used a rock to steady his aim, but his first two shots sailed high. The afternoon sun was falling behind the Indians and not helping Byron's aim. He adjusted his rifle, and his next shot landed at the feet of the pale Indian, who bounded away like part of an elaborate dance.

The attackers came in turns, one moving up the slope to a place of cover while the others diverted their attention. The Indians slowed their advance after drawing within rifle range. The leader drew closest. He remained in the open as if taunting Byron to shoot.

"They're hoping we run out of ammunition."

Byron patted the brick of cartridges in his vest. "Now they the ones with a long wait."

He turned to fire again, but Annabelle stayed him with a hand on his arm. "Let them think we're worried and draw them closer. We might have a surprise for them."

Byron nodded, grasping the rest of her meaning. "They haven't seen many Henry rifles."

For the first time all day Annabelle smiled.

Like frustrated children, the Indians grew bored once they felt their dance was being ignored. They began to advance on three fronts. To their right, a slender young Indian moved among the rocks, never stopping long enough for Byron to take his measure. To their left, a husky buck picked his way along the edge of the slope, using for cover the trees that grew from its sides.

In the middle, in the open, came the pale Indian, unhurried but always in motion, gliding one way then the other, never a pattern to his movements that Byron could anticipate. The others advanced more slowly, all of them whooping and hollering a terrible noise.

Byron fired twice more in the direction of

the pale Indian. It seemed as if he knew where the bullets were going, and he danced away. After Byron's second shot, Annabelle noticed that the other two Indians in the front broke from their cover to move up the slope to another place of concealment.

"They think we're reloading," she said.

"They are used to fighting soldiers with old muzzle loaders."

Byron fired two more shots to test his theory. Sure enough, the Indians on the flanks burst forward after the second shot, when they assumed their quarry had to reload. That would have been true if Byron and Annabelle carried old Springfields. But the Henry was a repeating rifle. Its barrel could be loaded with sixteen forty-four-caliber cartridges, a new one levered into the chamber after every shot. The Confederates, who had nothing like it, called the Henry "that damn Yankee rifle that can be loaded on Sunday and fired all week."

Annabelle smiled to imagine the surprise coming to the Indians.

"Are they close enough?" Byron asked.

"I think so. The one on my side is a little slow. And he's getting careless with all the attention you're paying to the pale one."

"Then let me pay a little more attention to him."

Byron took aim on the leader. Annabelle hoped he might get lucky, but she wasn't confident. There was something about that Indian. He acted like he thought the bullets *couldn't* hit him.

Annabelle pulled back the hammer and brought the rifle to bear on that big buck. He was too big to conceal himself behind the tree where he'd taken cover. She slid her left hand along the rifle's octagonal barrel, careful of the tab that held the cartridges in place. She leaned forward against the boulder to steady her aim and braced herself so she wouldn't flinch when Byron fired. She breathed naturally, listening for her heartbeat, willing it to slow so she could lie still. Leaving both eyes open, she put the front sight onto the Indian's shoulder, then adjusted, leading the Indian so she would be ready when he broke from cover. She wouldn't waste a bullet on a shoulder wound.

"Ready?"

"Yes." She took a breath and released it the way Josey taught her. Even though she was ready for it, she shook at the sound of Byron's shot so close to her ear.

One. Two.

The big Indian stepped from behind his cover. He had to move along the ledge where the trees grew at odd angles from the cliff face. He stepped over one to get to the next place of concealment. Annabelle lined up her sight in the center of his chest and adjusted to account for the angle of the slope and the wind coming up from the river. A couple of seconds had passed from the last of Byron's shots.

She pulled the trigger.

The rifle's recoil rocked her back, giving her a view of the Indian as he stood erect, staring forward. The Henry wasn't powerful enough to knock such a big man from his feet at that range, but her aim had been true.

The Indian halted. His right hand moved to his chest. When he drew it away, it was dark with blood. She levered in another round, the cartridge kicking out and spinning in an arc over the rifle's barrel. She imagined a look of surprise on his face as he turned to his comrades and called out something. She released another breath and waited for him to look back.

"Got you."

With that shot, the Indian fell, first to his knees, then back, his lifeless head striking the rocks, his body sliding back a foot or two until it caught against a tree.

Stillness fell over the scene. Annabelle heard nothing but the echo of her last shot ringing in her ear. The Indians fell silent, their surprise palpable. Even the pale Indian halted his dancing. Too late Byron thought to get off another shot in his direction. By then the man had broken from his trance, and the ricochet of the bullet off the hard ground behind him reawakened the rest. Their mournful cries filled the air, sounding even more dreadful than their war whoops and shouts.

All of the Indians came running toward them, too fast for Annabelle to get a good aim. She fired twice more, missing the mark as the Indians clambered up the hill.

Two of them paused at the body of their fallen comrade. Reaching under his arms, they dragged the larger man down the hill and out of range of the rifles. Annabelle was more concerned with the others. Byron managed to shoot the slender Indian who had been coming up on their right. He had gotten the closest to them, within twenty paces.

Annabelle handed her rifle to Byron when he fired his last shot. The barrel was hot to the touch, but burned fingers were the least of her concerns. She twisted open the tube to reload. Her fingers fumbled with the cartridges as she slid them in. It was an effort to keep from looking up at the advanc-

178

ing Indians as Byron tried to hold them off with his fire. The spent cartridges from his rifle spun free and plinked against the hard ground.

She held the rifle flat in her lap so the loaded cartridges wouldn't slam against each other. After filling the tube, she twisted the end of the barrel back into place and returned the rifle to Byron just in time to reload the other.

"I think we stopped 'em," he said.

She risked a glance. The Indians had taken cover where they could. Byron's rapid firing had convinced them of the foolishness of a direct charge. Annabelle breathed for what felt like the first time in minutes. She clasped her fingers together in a vain attempt to cease their trembling, but her entire body shook.

"I suppose they can't resist the opportunity to have a black man's scalp." She tried to laugh past the quiver in her voice as she patted Byron's nappy head.

"They ain't gettin' this one."

Annabelle finished reloading her rifle and heard another eagle cry, like a whistling on the wind. A shadow passed over her head, and she looked up. An Indian shouted a fearsome scream and leaped down from a rock.

Annabelle rolled away, raising the rifle just in time to block the downward arc of the man's arm, a large knife clenched in his hand. She lost her grip on the gun as the man's full weight fell across her, knocking the breath from her lungs and filling her head with a dizzying animal stench. The man screamed again, a terrible sound, and raised his knife hand, but Byron was just as quick, swinging around with his rifle and catching the Indian across the side of the head with the wooden stock.

The motion forced the man to shift his weight, and Annabelle, still fighting for breath, managed to squirm out from under him. The Indian turned on Byron, but he had levered in a new shot and fired, the barrel of the rifle nearly touching the Indian's chest. Before the Indian fell back, Byron put a second shot into the warrior's head.

There was no time to relax. The other Indians had begun to move up the slope to take advantage of the distraction. Her breath coming in painful wheezes, Annabelle fired down the slope, not even bothering to aim, praying that the sound alone would freeze the Indians and halt their advance.

A chill gripped the air as the sun fell behind

the foothills. Wrapped in the buffalo robe, Annabelle offered to share it with Byron, but the big man refused. He watched the Indians through the glass. They had returned to their campfire.

"I shot that skinny one," Byron said. "I don't know how much longer he can last before they need to leave."

"How many are left?"

"Six, including the one I wounded."

Annabelle looked to the body beside them. He had grown rigid where he lay, his knee raised at an unnatural angle. "I thought I had counted eight. This one must have been sneaking up the cliff face while the others sat around the fire." *Clever bastards.* "If he could make it up, we can make it down."

"You think?" Byron sounded doubtful. He shuffled past the body and looked down the other side. "It's awful steep."

"But he made it up . . ."

"The light was better then." Byron craned his head around the rocks that obscured his view. "There ain't no natural path."

"It won't be full dark for a while."

A plan formed in her head. She rose to stand beside Byron, taking in the view of the river, the Bighorn Mountains smudged the darkening horizon far to the southeast.

181

Fort Smith stood somewhere at the foot of them. "If we could get down to the river, we could float with the current, come out somewhere on the other side. Even on foot we could be too far away for them to find us by morning." The more she thought about it, the more the idea appealed to her. "It won't be too hard. I'm a good swimmer."

"I ain't."

She put a reassuring hand on Byron's shoulder. "I'll help you. We'll find a branch or something you can hold."

Byron stepped back and turned to look at the Indians' fire. Annabelle could smell the smoke as it floated their way and imagined she smelled something cooking, which reminded her of how hungry she was. It was enough to make up her mind.

"Let's start before it gets any darker."

The climb down was as hard as Byron had predicted. They maneuvered away from the sheer drop at the ledge, but the descent along the rock face was too steep to see a path to the bottom. They wound between boulders to where they could find footing in narrow crevices.

Byron went first. Annabelle held the rifles, a canteen, and the blanket as he wedged himself between the rocks and dropped one body length to another foothold. Then she tossed him the gear and attempted to follow his path. Byron was much larger, with a longer stride and powerful arms to support his full weight when necessary. More than once Annabelle's footing failed, and she slid down the rock face, kicking loose scree so that the small rocks tumbled in a noisy clacking. She cringed, fearing the Indians might hear it.

It was darker on this side of the hill, the long shadows deepening into a dusk that played tricks on their eyes. They were screened from the wind, and their movements kept them warm despite plummeting temperatures.

Once they came upon an impossible drop and had to retreat up the rock face and attempt another approach. Annabelle's arms shook with the effort as she pulled herself up. Her hands were gummy with pine resin, but that didn't seem to improve her grip. Byron found another route closer to the river. Annabelle heard the water sweep past as she waited for him to maneuver to the next rock. *We're close now.*

Darkness came on, and she couldn't see Byron well, just tossed the rifles in the direction of his whispered call and hoped he could see well enough to catch them. She eased her way down, moving by feel, maintaining her footing until with a gentle hop she landed beside him. She smiled as she looked for him, but his attention was already on the next drop, nearly as great as the one that had forced them to turn back.

"I don't know . . ."

Annabelle glanced around. There had to be another way. "How did the Indian get up this way?"

"I don't know . . ."

Annabelle's irritation mounted, but she held her tongue. Hunger, weariness, and fear left her short-tempered. She looked back the way they had come — couldn't imagine herself making the climb, and to what point? There weren't any alternatives. In the growing darkness, it was impossible to judge the drop. Twenty feet? Maybe less?

"We have to jump."

"From here?" Now Byron sounded irritated with her.

"Not here." She pointed to the rounded edge of the boulder where they stood. "We can crawl out along the edge as far as we can go. The drop won't be as far."

Byron looked to be questioning her sanity. "Do we have a choice?"

He handed her the rifles, sat on the rock,

184

and crawled forward, crab-like, to where the boulder folded down onto itself. He peered over the edge. "I don't know . . ."

Annabelle held her breath. Byron crawled forward a few inches, peered down again.

If he says "I don't know" one more time . . .

He shuffled ahead a few more inches. Craned his neck forward as far as it would go. And disappeared.

"Byron!"

He landed hard with a grunt that sounded painful.

"Are you all right?"

"I think so." He was silent a moment. "When you jump, be sure you're out away from the rock."

"Did you hurt yourself?"

"Nah." A tightness in his voice suggested otherwise.

She gave him a moment to collect himself before tossing the gear to him. Her heart raced, and she shivered as she mimicked Byron's crab crawl. Peering over the edge as he had, she couldn't see the ground, only Byron's luminescent smile — or was it a pained grimace? She inched ahead, feeling like invisible ropes pulled at her knees, tugging her forward and down even as she shuffled her feet, hoping to purchase a few more inches before the fall.

Then she was gone. Too soon. In the suddenness of the drop she forgot to launch herself clear of the rock. A painful impact threw off her balance. Her full weight landed on her left foot, which twisted into an unnatural angle. Agony sharp as a rifle crack shot through her leg, and she tumbled forward onto her face.

Annabelle writhed. Byron said something, but she couldn't make out the words through her anguished screams. She bit down on her arm to stifle the sound, hoping the pain from her teeth might relieve the torture radiating from her ankle. Bile rose on cresting waves of agony, followed by dry heaves, for there was nothing in her stomach to come out. She lay spent on the ground. She unclenched her jaw from around her arm, relieved to see she hadn't drawn blood. Somewhere, far away it seemed, she heard Byron's voice.

"— I could carry you —"

She sucked air. Hoped the pain had been a moment's shock. *Wishful thinking.* She rolled to her side, testing her ankle against the ground.

Oh, sweet Lord!

Her mind hadn't exaggerated the pain. From somewhere Byron continued speaking.

"— the Indians —"

His words cut through the fog in her head. She opened her eyes. Full darkness. How long had it taken them to climb down? What if the Indians had checked on them? Tried another attack under the cover of darkness and discovered them gone?

She felt the hoofbeats through the ground before she heard them. Without a word, Byron thrust the rifles upon her and scooped her into his arms. She couldn't see the Indians, but their whoops and hollers made it clear they saw Byron lumbering along with her. She looked ahead in the darkness. The ribbon of water gleamed in the faint light of night's first stars and appeared just as distant. The river had seemed so near when they were far above it on the rocks.

Her ankle throbbed, and her body shook with each of Byron's ambling steps. As strong as he was, her dead weight slowed him too much.

"You have to let me go."

She felt him shake his head, his breath coming in great pants like a winded horse.

"They won't kill a woman." Annabelle said the words with more confidence than she felt.

Byron stumbled but kept his footing.

"They may do *worse.*"

She tried not to think of what that implied.

The river looked closer now, but even if they reached it they couldn't escape Indians on horses. "Leave me a rifle. I can hold them off long enough for you to get away. Just float with the current as far as you can. They won't be able to track you in the dark."

The horses closed in.

"They may hold me for ransom. If they kill you here, Josey will never find me."

She thought he would argue, but he set her down. Kneeling beside her, he fired in the direction of the Indians, halting their advance. Annabelle took the other rifle. Sixteen shots. Could she make them last long enough for Byron to get away? Would she save the final round for herself?

Ignoring the pain in her ankle and hip, she swiveled her body to an upright position. Annabelle raised the rifle. It was too dark to see well, but there were places where the shadows loomed darker against the lighter horizon. She fired once. Levered in another shot.

"Go. Get Josey."

Byron stood. He started to say something, but words failed him.

"Go," Annabelle repeated. "Tell Josey about the baby."

CHAPTER FIFTEEN

The wood train returned late after a wagon busted a wheel, the hour casting the fort in a rose-limned gloam by the time Josey returned with the others. The drivers had been forced to pull into a corral while the woodchoppers made repairs. They unloaded the wagon before they could replace the wheel, and the minutes dragged like hours while they sat immobile, peering into the surrounding trees made menacing by lengthening shadows.

No attack ever came. All should have been well, but as they approached the wide wooden gate at the quartermaster corral Josey sensed something amiss. No bugle call heralded their return, and men and horses gathered in unusual numbers at the main stockade gate. With duties remaining on an already long day, Josey set aside his curiosity. He'd be sure to hear of any news at the boardinghouse.

Josey stabled and unsaddled the horse. After brushing down Gray he heard his name called. One of the privates from the cavalry company ran toward him. He was a shy, gawky fellow. Wild muttonchops framed his face, and he stunk of cigarettes. Unsure of the protocol, he gave an awkward salute while trying to catch his breath.

"Courier's come from Fort Smith. They had a black man with them. Name of Byron? Colonel sent me to fetch you."

Byron's here? Josey handed the private the brush and set off toward the post headquarters, then thought better of it. He loosed Gray from his stall, not even bothering to saddle the gelding, and raced the weary pony across the parade grounds.

Good news would have waited.

The Colonel waited for him outside the commander's office. He helped still Josey's horse while he dismounted. The old man's eyes remained fixed on the gelding.

"What's wrong?"

The Colonel patted Gray and led the horse to the lookout tower, finding a rope to tether it to a post. Josey had no patience for chores.

"Tell me what's happening."

"Byron's here."

191

Josey braced himself for something terrible. Guilt twisted in his belly like a knife. *I'll never forgive myself if Byron followed me because I didn't wait for him.*

"Is he hurt?"

"Nothing that won't heal, but he's been through a lot." The Colonel faced Josey and put his hands on his shoulders, steadying him the way he'd done for the horse. "There was Indian trouble. Took him days without food to make his way on foot to Fort Smith. They thought he was in no condition to ride, but he insisted on coming to see you."

"I don't understand." If Byron was all right, why did the Colonel act like disaster had struck? Josey started to slip past him, but the old man's grip held firm.

"Annabelle was with him."

Was? The words punctured Josey's mind like an Indian lance, scrambling his head so that he doubted what he'd heard. Every form of question came to his tongue, twisting his mouth to the point he couldn't utter anything. Finally, he managed, "Where is she now?"

"The Indians got her, Josey."

Josey's world collapsed in on itself. His legs folded, as if the bones had been removed. He slumped to the ground, breaking the Colonel's grip on his arms. His ears filled with a wailing that seemed to originate from a great distance until Josey drew breath and realized he'd been responsible for the sound.

This is my fault. She came after me.

The Colonel hovered over him, unmoving, his image shimmering as if Josey viewed him from underwater. Self-pity and blame flooded over him. He felt he was drowning. He needed something, anything to cling to, or he feared he would wash away, unmoored from his sanity. He found his lifeline when Byron stepped out of the headquarters. Josey crawled toward him, a motion like swimming with limbs that had no solid form.

Anger like molten iron surged through his limbs, granting him the strength to stand.

"You left her?"

Byron flinched as if struck.

"She told me to leave. I didn't want to go."

Fury stoked the fires raging within Josey.

"I never would have left her."

Even as he said it, guilt doused the inferno. *I did leave her.*

Byron shrank back, and the Colonel wrapped his arms around Josey. The Colonel's voice was a harsh whisper in his ear, urgent and commanding.

"It's because Byron kept his head that we

have a chance to find her, Josey. He can lead us to where she was taken. We can track her to their camp."

Josey trembled with rage and guilt and fear. Another cry of anguish emptied his lungs. He buried his face against the Colonel's chest.

"I never should have left her. This is my fault. I've killed her."

The Colonel shook him.

"Don't talk like that. We don't know she's dead. They don't always kill women, Josey. You know that. Maybe we can ransom her."

The Colonel's words sunk in. The rage that had burned within him hardened into angry resolve, sharp as steel. Byron came to them, looking like a smacked puppy as he waited to absorb whatever punishment Josey needed to mete out. Josey placed a hand on his thick shoulder. Through phlegm and an uncontrolled trembling, Josey choked on the words in his mind.

"I'm sorry," he managed.

I'm just frightened. The look in Byron's eyes confirmed his understanding, and Josey knew his friends would ride with him through the entire Sioux nation if that's what it took to get Annabelle back.

Josey demanded every detail. The Colonel

and Byron had convinced him rushing out after Annabelle would end in his death and hers. Byron had lost track of the time it took him to make his way to Fort Smith, the army's northern outpost. As near as they could figure, nearly a fortnight had passed. Any hope of rescue would require a careful plan, so Josey bit back his impatience and tried to clear his head. He needed to know what happened. Where were they when the Indians attacked? How many were there? What did they look like? What was their manner?

After making Byron repeat his account for more than an hour, the Colonel accused Josey of punishing himself with the story. The old man might have been right. Only after Josey set aside his guilt did he think to ask about Annabelle's motives.

"Tell me," he said to Byron, "why was Annabelle so determined to come to the fort?"

No reason Josey came up with explained her actions. Annabelle was a headstrong woman, but she wasn't reckless. It was even harder for Josey to imagine Byron agreeing to anything that put her in danger.

"She said she needed to see you."

Byron's voice was hoarse from the telling. He looked toward the Colonel as he spoke.

Josey turned to the old man. "Am I missing something?"

The Colonel reached into his vest pocket for his pipe and tobacco.

"Now, Josey, trying to understand a woman's motives —"

"Stop. Both of you." Josey looked from one to the other. The Colonel studied his pipe. Byron's eyes were cast to the ground. "There's something you're not saying."

After a moment, the Colonel spoke.

"Annabelle was going to come, whether Byron helped her or not. What Byron said was true: she had something she needed to tell you."

"What?"

The Colonel and Byron were dancing about the subject like it was a coiled rattlesnake. They were trying to spare his feelings, but Josey's patience had run out.

"We aren't married. If she wanted to leave me, she could have just done it. There was no need to come all this way."

The Colonel looked like he'd swallowed turpentine.

"She didn't come out here to leave you. She came to see you because she's with child. She was afraid if she waited you'd get yourself killed before she could tell you."

For the second time that night, Josey's

world collapsed in on him.

Talked out, Josey raised no objection when the Colonel insisted they take Byron to the boardinghouse for a bath and a long sleep before making any plans. While he saw to Byron's care, Josey sought out Wheatley in the boardinghouse kitchen.

"I need whiskey," he told the caretaker.

"Sure," Wheatley said, failing to conceal his surprise. He'd never served Josey liquor. He grabbed a glass from a table by the door.

"Just give me the bottle."

Wheatley nodded and uncorked a bottle. If he meant to say something or ask a question, he swallowed it after looking in Josey's eyes. Josey left without a word.

He took a deep draw on the bottle, feeling the once-familiar burn down his throat, impatient for the liquor's clouding effects on his mind. If he couldn't have forgiveness, he would settle for forgetfulness. Anything was better than imagining what the Indians were doing to Annabelle.

He headed away from the fort toward Big Piney Creek, drawn by the sound of water spilling over rocks in the streambed. He found a half-rotted log at the water's edge and sat down. He took another swallow. The creek's flow was low this time of year. He

197

breathed in the musty smell of decaying leaves and moist soil along the banks.

The news that Annabelle was with child hit Josey like a lightning strike on a cloudless day. The very idea of fatherhood seemed alien to him, a responsibility for other men — older, full-grown men like his father. Josey was twenty-five years old and still didn't think of himself like that, even though his father had been no older when Josey was born.

Of course, his father hadn't been through a war. There wasn't time to think of the future then, only enduring another day and surviving the next fight. Even after being with Annabelle, Josey didn't give any thought to being a father. She had told him she couldn't have children.

Confronted now with the prospect of fatherhood, he didn't know what to think. The whiskey wasn't helping, but he took another long draw anyway. One moment he grinned, as if he had accomplished something no man before him ever had. The next he buried his face in his hands, overwhelmed by guilt and a mounting sense of responsibility. What did he know of being a father? The thought of holding a baby terrified him. What if he dropped it? What if he squeezed too hard? What was too hard?

Could the whelp's insides burst out like an overcooked sausage?

As his mind whirled, he recalled a conversation with the Colonel soon after the war about riding to Mexico. They'd rejected the plan because neither spoke Mexican. Maybe it wasn't too late to learn.

He took another sip. Josey hadn't eaten after returning from the pinery, and the liquor roiled in his empty stomach. Even through its welcome haze, he never doubted he would go after Annabelle. The more he thought on it, the more sense it made. He had never believed he would outlive the war. Afterwards, he'd felt adrift, struggling to find a purpose that explained his survival. Now he had one: to save Annabelle and her child.

My child.

Whether he lived or died in the effort made no matter. The thought of dying to save his child made sense. This was what he was meant to do. It was a better fate than riding off to Mexico.

Josey rose on unsteady legs. The bottle was empty, though he hadn't remembered finishing it. He stumbled through the brush toward the fort. He needed to find Fetterman.

CHAPTER SIXTEEN

They came for her at the first gray hint of dawn.

Annabelle had exhausted her bullets long before then in purchasing time for Byron to escape. Her pursuers maintained a safe distance until they could see she was resigned to capture. Her last act had been to hurl the spent rifle into the river so the Indians wouldn't get their savage hands on it.

They came on their ponies, forming a half-circle around her ragged form. She was spent. Hungry. Tired. Cold. She had covered herself with the buffalo robe, but the frigid ground she lay upon leached all warmth from her. At least her ankle had grown numb. By morning it felt like it was encased in a block of ice. She wouldn't look at it, afraid to see how much it had swollen overnight.

No one spoke. The pale one nodded to

one of his companions, a big buck who dismounted and picked her up like a sack of flour. He tossed her across the back of a spare horse, securing her with tight binds around her wrists and ankles.

They rode, and all her pains from the previous day redoubled in intensity, along with new ones caused by her position across the horse's back. Her ankle throbbed as if some tormentor took a hammer to it with each of the horse's strides. Her hip burned, and her back felt like it might crack in two after she shifted her weight off her belly, hoping to protect the baby. They didn't ride far, across the river valley and around the hill to the campsite where this nightmare had all begun, but in her tortured state it felt like riding all the way to Omaha.

At the campsite, the big Indian dropped her to the ground. The warriors gathered their plunder and the horses and mules they had captured. The bodies of their fallen comrades hung over the backs of two mules. She sat, still dazed, the Indians' harsh language sounding like the yips and barks of dogs to her ears. Annabelle's captor transferred her to a pony — her own Apple. She wondered how they knew it had been her horse.

Through a mixture of hand signals, grunts,

and other noises, he made her understand she was to lead Byron's pony behind her as she rode. A hard pinch on her arm made clear the consequences for failure. The man's face twisted into a smile, his hard eyes implying he would welcome any cause for further torture.

Painted and dressed for war, he was a fearsome sight. Like the others, he wore a breechcloth with a buffalo robe draped across his shoulders and wrapped around his waist. His long, black hair was pulled back into two braids. Bead necklaces dangled around his neck, clacking together as he moved. Holes pierced his outer ear leading to the lobe, adorned with great brass rings and silver jewels. A crown of eagle feathers encircled his head, extending past his neck to his shoulders. He had painted his horse with vivid stripes like lightning across its sides, its ears also pierced. Bells and a human scalp were woven into its mane.

No one offered her food, and she feared asking. Any hope Annabelle harbored for ransom melted beneath her captor's angry glare. They would not forgive the murder of two of their own. They would bring Annabelle along, either to extend her torture or because they needed her labor to bring the captured horses, and then they would kill her in as diabolical a fashion as their savage imaginations could conjure.

They headed east, into the rising sun. There were six Indians, including the one Byron wounded, who seemed only slightly hurt. He didn't look much older than a boy and treated the scratch upon his upper arm as the grandest of battle souvenirs. The faces of the older warriors were set in grave expressions. Their watchful eyes made clear the impossibility of escape. At least they were heading closer to Josey. She hoped their vigilance would not outlast whatever purpose her survival served.

They soon left the trail, taking paths so steep and covered with broken stone they would be inaccessible to white men, dashing any hope she held that they might come across wagons or a patrol of soldiers. They rode in single file, Annabelle in the middle, leading Byron's pony on a rope. The elaborately adorned Indian she came to think of as Pierce rode behind her, beating her with the end of his lance any time she stumbled or dropped the line. As they rode, the Indians chanted a song that soon grew as monotonous as the throbbing in Annabelle's ankle. Only the pale Indian didn't sing.

They wound up the clefts between hills, on trails invisible to anyone but an Indian. The sound of their progress echoed between the cliffs so that Annabelle always had the sense someone was tracking alongside them. Her heart swelled at the sound, imagining Josey at the lead of a cavalry attack, yet she knew this was a false hope. Assuming he lived, it would take days for Byron to get word to Josey, and no cavalry could manage the trail the Indians took. If Annabelle was going to survive, she had to save herself and find her way back to Josey.

On reaching the far bank of a wide river, the Indians separated into every direction but north. Annabelle continued with the pale Indian and Pierce. Leaving the rivers, they came into dry and barren country, scarred by countless buffalo trails. Trees gave way to sage and chaparral. The trotting horses kicked up puffs of dust with every step, and she choked on the dirt and grime. Despite her best efforts to memorize the compass points of their route, Annabelle's focus wavered. She had been hungry for so long. Weariness dulled her mind, and she thought only of enduring pain and privation.

She found relief in brief moments of unconsciousness, her body holding its place in the saddle through habit alone. The rope leading the second pony slipped from her hand once, inviting blows and stinging whip strokes across her back and neck from an all-too-eager Pierce. He shouted at her with an impressive vocabulary of blasphemous English, apparently the only words he knew of her language. The pale Indian who rode ahead never spoke or even glanced back.

At evening, they came upon a pine grove beside a thin creek. The other Indians were already gathered there. They had built a large fire, and the idea that they might burn her in it came almost as a relief. Only thoughts of the baby kept Annabelle from doing something that might invite a quick release from her suffering.

The Indians spread blankets around the fire, not bothering with tents. Pierce threw her to the ground beside his blanket, binding her hands and securing her legs with a leather strap like a horse hobble. The pale Indian continued on, as if he and his horse had no need of rest.

The other Indians ignored her, preoccupied with picking through their plunder, unrolling bundles and comparing stashes. Through their wild gesticulating and loud discourse she understood they were negotiating an exchange of prizes. By watching and listening she came to understand some words. Her great thirst drove her to speech.

"Minne," she pleaded, her voice a hoarse croak.

The Indians looked up from their bartering, as if surprised to see her there. She repeated her plea for what she understood to be water.

Pierce grimaced but stood and came to her with a cup in his hands. He sipped from it first, as if to demonstrate its cleanliness. As he proffered it, Annabelle stretched against her binds, leaning toward the water. She drew near the cup, not wishing to spill a precious drop. As Annabelle came closer, Pierce held the cup steady so she had to lean forward to reach it.

She stretched as much as she could, but the cup drew no nearer. She looked to Pierce, understanding dawning in the sight of his twisted smile as he drew the cup away. Gravity took hold and she fell face-first. While the Indians cackled like cruel children, he poured the water into the dirt beside her. If she could have moved, she would have lapped it up before it disappeared into the dust, but she lacked the strength even to crawl. The muscles and sinews in her shoulders, already sore from leading a horse all day, screamed with the strain from being bound behind her, and all she could manage was to roll to her side and allow exhaustion to overcome her.

She might have lost consciousness. A thrumming in her head drowned out the sound of the Indians' chattering. When the pale Indian returned, the others fell quiet. He spoke for a minute, maybe two, his voice softer than the others but clear in her mind because no one else spoke when he did.

He came to her, unfastening the bindings on her hands. Despite his light skin, his high, sharp nose and expressionless features bore no resemblance to a white man. Though smaller than the others, the taut muscles in his shoulders and arms rolled beneath his skin in thick bands as he worked. His black eyes avoided her, like a shy schoolboy.

Once the binds were loose, he helped her to her feet. Her ankle still throbbed, but she managed to put some weight on it. Annabelle sensed tension in her captor, and his gentleness did little to dissipate her fear. He placed a wreath of fine feathers on her head, and Annabelle was too terrified to object, wondering if the gift signified a mark of sacrifice to whatever pagan gods they worshiped — or a symbol that he was taking her as a wife, at least for the night. Her apprehension mounted as he led her to the other side of the fire where his blanket lay.

Now it's time.

Between death and rape, Annabelle hadn't been sure which she feared more. She'd heard stories of white women shunned on returning to their people, as if tainted by their use among savages. If Josey treated her that way, if he disowned his baby because of what happened to her, she would regret not saving a last bullet for herself.

She trembled as the Indian leader eased her to the ground, each kind gesture escalating her dread of what cruelty might come next. When he offered a cup, she sought his gaze in vain as if that could hold him in place while she savored the water. She drained it, holding the cup at such an angle that every rivulet reached her parched throat. He offered a piece of dried meat and watched her chew. In her hunger, she ignored the strong taste. She shrank back when he reached for her. Her hands moved to her belly.

"I am with child. I have a baby in here."

She followed his gaze to her stomach.

"So you do understand some English."

His eyes met hers for the first time, holding a moment before flickering away.

"You understand me?"

The pale Indian gave no indication of even hearing. He reached for her again and re-tied her hands. The task completed, he turned from her, settling into his blankets and leaving her to lie on the cold ground beside him.

She still had her buffalo blanket, and she sought what warmth she could in it. Despite her exhaustion, Annabelle's mind buzzed with thoughts too many and too varied to catalog. Whatever relief she felt at the man's apparent disinterest was lost in a swirl of apprehension that something might change his mind before morning. She had survived a day among the savages. She drew comfort in that, even as she pondered the possibility they might kill her on the morrow.

CHAPTER SEVENTEEN

Annabelle endured more of the same on her second day with the Indians. She rode all day in the midst of their single-file line, leading a second horse behind her.

After drinking plentifully before starting in the morning, she noticed the Indians carried little sticks in their mouths that they chewed. On mimicking them, she found this created enough saliva to prevent the terrible parching she'd suffered the first day. Another piece of dried meat did little to satisfy her hunger, but at least it settled her stomach.

Such small comforts taught her something about the will to survive. When they unfastened her bonds in the morning, the feel of blood in her fingers shocked at first, then gave her such relief she felt nearly delirious. Her ankle throbbed when she walked, but the respite that came on returning to the saddle helped her forget all the places made sore from so much riding. "Pleasure" seemed a strange word to describe the absence of torture, yet the previous day's sufferings made the lack of pain now feel like a cause for joy. Hope budded within her. If they hadn't killed her by now, there was a chance they wouldn't kill her, a chance she might escape, a chance she might find Josey.

Her optimism lasted until mid-morning, when a stumble by the horse she led down a steep bank caused her to drop the rope — and brought on an outburst of furious whipping from Pierce. She cowered from the blows, her hope revealed as a mirage. Their leader might want her alive for some reason for now, but it was clear Pierce did not agree.

His eyes followed her, alight with anger as if flames burned within him. She'd been watched by men before, and she recognized in his appraising glances that his wish to see her dead might be mixed with . . . other desires. She couldn't bear to give words to what he might do. Even after he finished whipping her, more from a lack of breath than pity, she shuddered with certainty that this man would not be content until she was dead — and if death came at his hands, it would not come quickly.

They halted late in the afternoon in a small glen. The site seemed ill suited to a camp, with no apparent water source. The Indians dismounted and unpacked their booty, their voices rising in an excited chatter that reminded her of squirrels at play. No one paid her any mind, and for a moment she hoped an opportunity to escape might present itself. But in what direction would she go? How far might she get before they ran her down? The hopelessness of her situation would have brought tears if there had been any water in her.

The Indians tore through their plunder, casting aside their robes in favor of whatever finery they discovered, the more elaborate, the better. She stifled a laugh at the sight of a grim-faced brave beneath a plumed lady's hat she had brought for Margaret Carrington. The boy with the wounded arm shaded himself beneath a tiny parasol, another intended gift.

Only Pierce and the light-skinned Indian refrained from further adornments. Pierce had taken control of the mules with the bodies of the fallen warriors. He bid farewell to the others and led the mules in a different direction. Annabelle breathed easier watching him depart.

After the others had completed their

wardrobe change, they led her from the glen into an open valley bisected with a clear running stream. On the opposite side stood a massive Indian village, the white skin tepees glowing like embers in the fading afternoon light.

The village, like a city in size, stretched so far along the stream's banks she couldn't see its end. Boys playing near the water spotted their approach. Their raucous shouts drew great crowds of villagers, who greeted the returning warriors with wild dancing and voices raised in song.

The men tried to lead their horses into the village but soon gave up the exercise as futile in the face of adoring swarms. They dismounted to warm embraces and congratulatory claps on backs and arms, everyone eager to touch the returning victors as if they'd overrun the Spotsylvania courthouse rather than simply murdered five frightened miners. The injured boy was feted with special exuberance, a circle of men admiring his wound and parasol in equal measure. Great crowds of curious Indians flocked to stare at Annabelle, the women bringing their children as if she were some exotic species in a zoological garden display.

They paraded through the settlement, still accompanied by an escort of men, women, and children. Annabelle remained on her pony, a boy claiming the reins like a trophy and leading Apple among the maze of tepees until they reached one that stood out for its modesty. While ornaments of brilliantly colored porcupine quills or fringes of matted fur distinguished most of the tents, this one held no such embellishments. She knew instinctively that it must belong to her captor.

The boy gestured for her to dismount and enter the tepee. It resembled a Sibley tent used by soldiers during the war but was made of animal skins sewed together and stretched across a number of poles that reached at least three times her height. Pulling aside one of the skins that served as a door, she leaned down and stumbled in on her bad ankle.

It took a moment for her eyes to adjust to the dim light inside. A fire burned down to ash filled the center of the room. A small hole at the top where the poles met provided egress for the smoke. Around the fire buffalo robes served as a carpeting, with more skins and robes piled along the edges of the tent for bed areas.

On one of these sat an old woman as still as a figure in a shop display. Her dark hair was mottled with gray, like a dusting of snow across a pine forest, but her age showed in an impassive face deeply lined with what Annabelle imagined to be decades of toil and sorrow.

"Hello." Annabelle felt stupid for not knowing enough of the woman's language to greet her. "I believe I'm meant to wait here."

The woman showed no sign of recognition. Annabelle drew closer but saw no awareness in the woman's empty, rheumy eyes.

"I suppose you won't mind some company."

Annabelle spoke more for her own benefit than the old woman's. She stirred the ashes and added some wood from a small pile. The stench of smoke and animal musk filled the tent, and Annabelle had to breathe through her mouth to keep from growing woozy. She nestled in among a pile of furs across from the old woman, thinking a brief rest might clear her head and ease her pain. Her hostess never moved, and Annabelle closed her eyes.

She woke with a start. Judging from the darkness in the tepee, she must have slept for hours. The fire had died out, and no light leaked through the hole at the top of the tepee. Disoriented and heavy-headed from her first good sleep in days, it took a moment for Annabelle to focus on the face before her.

Her captor showed no emotion as he gestured for her to rise and follow him. Annabelle nearly tripped when stepping through the low-slung doorway. Night had fallen, but she had no idea of the hour. A crispness in the air caused her to rub her arms to stimulate warmth. Her lithe captor had no apparent need for a robe, wearing only leggings and a deerskin shirt as he moved among the tepees.

Her pace slowed on seeing an orange glow ahead, forcing the pale Indian to take her arm and lead her forward. Her stomach tightened, and her legs trembled as they stepped into a huge clearing where every Indian in the village appeared to be gathered around a bonfire as big as a sloop.

Braves painted in full war regalia circled frantically around the flames, flourishing torches and brandishing weapons as they barked and yipped and shouted to the heavens. Annabelle stopped, transfixed by the image and rooted by fear of what it portended.

"My baby . . ." The pleading in her voice left no need for translation.

He ignored her pleas. He pulled her along,

the strength of his grip impressing on her the futility of resistance. She swallowed and tried to still the rolling drumbeat in her breast. If she must die, she would display the courage she imagined her brothers had shown at Sharpsburg.

Some of the Indians at the outskirts of the gathering noticed their approach and cleared a path through the throng to the fire. The dancing stopped when they reached the center and a silence fell over the crowd that reminded Annabelle of silent prayers at a church service.

Annabelle tensed her muscles in an effort to quell the trembling in her legs, yet she stumbled as her captor dragged her forward. The heat from the fire buffeted out in waves like a desert wind. She grew dizzy and felt her face and chest redden. Her hands shook so badly she gripped her captor's arms to still them. He misunderstood the gesture and barked a command at her. His voice softened on seeing her face, but his words meant nothing to her. He repeated himself, then shook his head in frustration. He called to a nearby warrior who stepped forward with a long lance. Annabelle blanched at the sight of the sharpened iron at the end of it.

Do they mean to impale me before they fling

me into the flames?

The warrior handed the spear to her, positioning her hands on the narrow wooden staff so that she could hoist the blade aloft. It was heavy with decorations, a fringe of small animal pelts that smelled like polecat. The two men urged her to lift her arms, raising the lance as high as she could. The gathered Indians cheered wildly and resumed their dancing around her.

The man beside her grinned, nodding like a woodpecker in his enthusiasm. She returned his smile, relief flooding over her as she realized her fate was not to be roasted in sacrifice but to serve as a human maypole to their demons' dance. The warrior gestured for her to hold the pike higher, but its weight tested her strength.

She braced its end against her hip but nearly lost her grip. It twisted in her hands, and she steadied the staff against her forehead. The stench of the rotting skins choked her, and she craned her neck back as far as she could. In the bright light of the flames she studied the animal skins. Bile surged in her throat, and if there had been anything in her stomach she would have lost it.

The lance was not decorated with animal skins. They were human scalps. And the one hanging before her eyes was not the white streak of a polecat but all that remained of the gray head of poor Old Ben.

CHAPTER EIGHTEEN

Josey found Fetterman at the bar in the boardinghouse dining hall. The room had cleared out, the only sounds coming from the kitchen, where the Wheatleys were cleaning up for the night. The scent of strong soap mingled with food smells. Fetterman's glass stood empty.

"I'd fill that for you, but I seem to be in the same predicament."

Josey turned his bottle over, watching one beaded drop of liquor slide into the neck.

"Are you feeling all right, Josey?"

"Under the circumstances . . ."

"I've heard," Fetterman said. "The whole fort has heard by now, I expect. I'm sorry for your —" He stopped himself.

He was going to say "loss."

Fetterman finished. "I'm sorry to hear what happened."

"Annabelle's not dead."

Josey set the bottle on the bar more firmly

220

than he'd intended. The clunk of the empty glass against the pine board reverberated inside his aching head.

"The Indians take women as captives. We can ransom her."

"Yes, yes, of course."

"We can *rescue* her."

Fetterman stepped from the bar and pulled over a bench from a nearby table.

"You should sit down. You don't look well."

Josey stepped back. "Don't doubt me. I do as I say."

"I don't doubt you." Fetterman spoke as if coaxing a horse.

"You won't need eighty men if I'm one of them. We'll kill every Indian until we find Annabelle."

Fetterman squinted. "I don't follow."

"What you said! 'Give me eighty men, and I'll ride through the whole Sioux nation.' "

"Did I say that?" Fetterman studied his empty glass a moment. "I suppose I said something like that. I never meant it literally, of course."

"But you said it!"

"I said that so the men would believe it could be done. You've seen how they are. After all these attacks, the Indians picking them off one by one, they act as if it's

Napoleon in all his glory at the gates instead of a bunch of primitives. They needed to be reminded: this is the army that defeated Robert E. Lee!"

Josey sank onto the bench. The captain put a hand on his shoulder.

"Carrington was right to insist we wait until the men are better trained. I see that now. In a couple of months, when the tribes break into smaller camps for the worst of winter, we'll hold the upper hand. If the Sioux have taken Annabelle, I promise we shall find her."

Josey sat in brooding silence. A whoosh of frigid air followed the noise of an opening door and a bellicose shout from the Colonel.

"Josey, I've been looking all over the fort for you." He looked drawn and worn, as tired as Josey had ever seen him. He glanced at the bottle and frowned. "You're not going to find help for Annabelle inside that bottle."

"It seems I'm not going to find it here, either." Josey cut a glance toward Fetterman. "The captain is all talk."

"It wasn't just empty boasting." Fetterman turned to the Colonel. "The men have to *believe* they can defeat Red Cloud's warriors, and that confidence won't come from numbers and weapons alone. They have to have conviction in their training — and faith in the man who leads them."

"Faith in you?"

Josey's head thrummed, and his stomach felt queasy. He tried to remember when he'd last eaten, but he shuddered at the thought of food.

"How I am perceived is just as important as how I perform." Fetterman still directed his speech to the Colonel. Josey blinked to see him better.

"I know how that sounds," Fetterman continued. "We have both, I am sure, known officers whose reputations exceeded their abilities. Don't confuse me with one of those paper-collar officers. A great officer both performs on the field *and* is perceived as such. For it's that perception, that *legend* if you will, that can inspire troops to perform beyond what their training, numbers, and munitions would dictate. How else do you explain Alexander's success at Granicus? Caesar at Alesia? Hannibal at Cannae. And, yes, even Lee at Chancellorsville."

"I believe I am going to be sick."

Josey's head spun. He thought he'd just heard Fetterman compare himself to Alexander and Caesar. He doubted he was as well as he'd felt when he'd come into the room. He stumbled to the door, waving away the Colonel's offer of assistance.

The cold air brought a momentary reprieve as he staggered in the direction of the privy. The stench put him off, and he headed toward a clump of sage growing beside the road to the fort. He felt even worse recalling the night he'd found another man out here in a similar state. *Guess I'm no better than Grummond.* The thought turned his stomach and helped him accomplish the task.

Feeling much better, he returned to the boardinghouse. The Colonel and Fetterman were deep in conversation. In his absence, Fetterman's glass had been refilled, and the Colonel had one standing untouched on the bar before him. Josey slapped a gold half eagle onto the bar and reached for the glass as he called into the kitchen.

"Wheatley, another bottle."

"I thought that was supposed to be ranch money you're throwing away on whiskey," the Colonel said.

"There's no ranch without Annabelle."

The Colonel shook him. "I won't have you talking about her like she's dead. I've talked with Fetterman. He's going to give us two scouts. With them, you, me, and Byron — we can find her. If we can't rescue her, we'll negotiate a ransom and bring her back."

The Colonel waved Wheatley off before the proprietor could bring another bottle. Josey didn't object. He thought back to the time he'd been shredded with shrapnel, how the Colonel made sure he was among the first at the field hospital. The time Josey went after four Union soldiers responsible for raping and killing a widow woman. Josey had killed them — the army would have called it murder — but the Colonel made sure he and Josey were gone before suspicion fell on him. So he didn't object when the Colonel threw back the shot and led Josey away from the bar. Still drunk, Josey said, "You've always been there to save me."

Chapter Nineteen

Annabelle's days fell into a pattern of servitude and anxiousness. After not being consumed in flames on her first night in the Indian village, she no longer feared imminent death. But the absence of any understanding of her current plight or what the future held was its own form of torture.

She was not mistreated. On the day after her arrival, a woman with some knowledge of healing had wrapped her ankle and braced it with sturdy sticks and leather thongs. The woman felt her belly and spoke some words and smiled. Understanding came from her expression and tone. Annabelle smiled. The baby was well.

Annabelle lived in the light-skinned Indian's tent with the woman Annabelle assumed to be his grandmother. The old squaw never spoke, and at times her mind seemed to have left her body. Yet she was alert enough to maintain her grandson's household, if the interior of a tepee could be called that, and through hand motions and gestures she trained Annabelle in the ways of Indian domesticity.

From what Annabelle could tell, the only difference between a squaw and a household slave was that the Indian women were also responsible for breeding the next generation of warriors. All other tasks disdained by men fell to women.

Each morning the old woman woke Annabelle before dawn to fetch water from the stream, a task she repeated each evening. Winding between the lodges, she passed big leafy trees that were cut down and dragged into the village so that the horses kept close to the tepees could graze on the upper branches. Once bare, the trees would be chopped into firewood, which was piled here and there about the camp. Fetching wood was a constant chore as the days grew cooler and the nights turned frigid. Snows were coming. Annabelle could feel it on the wind and see it on the mountains, where each week the snowy peaks stretched longer, like an old man's beard. She feared if she weren't ransomed soon, she would be doomed to remain at the Indian camp until spring — if the Indians ever intended to release her.

The rest of the day was filled with assorted tasks often performed in the company of other women. On pleasant days they sat outside on the ground, their weight balanced on one thigh with their legs and feet tucked modestly to the side, their toil-worn hands in constant motion.

Two sisters — married to the same warrior — instructed Annabelle in many chores. Like all married women, they wore their hair in long braids that hung in the front. Working so closely with them, she learned that the strong smell she associated with Indians was caused in part by oils and other materials from animals. The women treated their hair with bear grease so that it glistened. They tried to apply it to Annabelle's hair, which they seemed to find dry and unruly, but she demurred.

While they gossiped and teased among themselves, the women treated Annabelle like a simple-minded mute, patiently correcting her as they went about tasks that were as foreign to Annabelle as the language. They cut meat into strips and built low, smoky fires under high racks to jerk the meat. Another kind of meat they pounded until it had a dried, sausage-like consistency. They left the village to dig prairie turnips or gather sage and sweet smelling grasses and plants that they used inside the tepees.

Though kind in their way, the sisters delegated the worst of the chores to Annabelle. Her stomach turned at pinning stinking animal hides to the ground for scraping. They taught Annabelle to use a mixture of jellied buffalo brains to rub into the fleshy side of the skin so it penetrated into the pores. They left the stretched skins to dry in the sun for several days before washing them in the river until they were pliable. They repeated the stretching and rubbing process. After another several days, Annabelle and one of the sisters would grab either end of the hide and draw it across a tree trunk for hours. While the sisters took turns, Annabelle received no relief until the skin was soft enough to fold.

While the women worked, children played everywhere. Dogs ran underfoot, always alert for an opportunity to steal a morsel of food. Men squatted on the ground in groups around fires for hours on end, the lazy brutes doing nothing more than smoking their pipes or repairing weapons and recounting their exploits.

Her captor was an exception. He did not loaf with his friends or take his ease in his lodge. Annabelle rarely saw him about the village. The few times she spied him, he was training horses near the brush corral outside the village. He often returned late to the tepee and spent any free hours there making arrows or sharpening weapons while Annabelle and Old Grandmother labored at dyeing porcupine quills, beading moccasins, or sewing thick hides with a bone awl.

The work was hard and without end, but at least she lived. In time, Annabelle even came to feel relatively safe. She still shuddered whenever she saw Pierce. If he was out lounging with the other warriors while she worked, his dark eyes followed her. If she intended to leave the village for water or wood and saw him, she would take up another task until he was gone. He had never spoken to her or attempted to harm her since their arrival in the village, but she understood from the way he watched her it was not wise to give him an opportunity to catch her alone away from the village.

The pale Indian treated her well enough. He gave her a white cotton gown that reached below the knee and a red scarf to fasten it at the waist. When her ankle was better, she received a pair of moccasins, embroidered with beads and porcupine quills. She kept her riding clothes rolled in a bundle beside the furs where she slept, hoping she might have occasion to wear them again.

She also received her buffalo robe and a few other belongings that hadn't been plundered by the Indians, including a dress she'd planned to let out and wear on formal occasions at the fort. The dress was of little use to her without her petticoats and drawers, but she valued the possession above all others once she realized the Indians had paid scant attention to it. She laughed to think what a mystery it must have been to them, a tangle of heavy fabric with its elaborate lace collar and secret pocket sewn into the lining. She stowed it beneath the robes like a pillow, a reminder each night of home.

For a month in captivity, Annabelle gave little thought to escape. While free to leave the village for fetching water and wood, Annabelle had nowhere to go. There were no road signs or maps pointing the way to the fort. She believed the fort lay to the south. Even if she headed in the right direction, she couldn't expect to get far before the Indians ran her down. Her captor hadn't killed her. He showed no interest in marrying her. She assumed he meant to ransom her, but her patience wore thin, and her frustration in not being able to communicate with anyone threatened to drive her mad.

She found hope in a stranger who came to the village. While his skin and hair were as dark as any Indian, he wore his hair too short to braid and covered it with a felt hat. He had boots instead of moccasins, trousers instead of leggings, a cotton shirt buttoned at the wrists, and a bandana around the neck in the cowboy way.

The first time she saw him sitting with some of the warriors she stopped so abruptly, the woman walking behind her bumped into her, and both almost spilled their water buckets. She caught his eye for but a moment on that occasion. He stared at her with such palpable curiosity she must have blushed.

Annabelle watched for him after that. Though not much older than a boy, like many of the young men she had seen in this country he carried himself with an air of experience beyond his years. While he spoke easily with whomever he was with, Annabelle imagined that he must speak English to be dressed in such a manner. She feared to approach him directly, and, when she caught him glancing at her, he looked away and never left the company of the men.

Returning one evening with water, Annabelle shivered as an icy breeze snaked its way between the tepees. She breathed in the smells of the village, the odor of wood smoke, and scraped hides, fresh stew cooking within the lodges. She was later than usual, and the days were growing shorter. She had watered the pale Indian's favorite horses, which were tethered close to the lodge. She suspected he was still away at the corral outside the village where he kept the rest of his horses.

She pulled on the rawhide rope that raised the tepee door. With a graceful sideways swoop learned with much practice, she swung her way into the tent with her heavy load. Inside, she stopped, arrested by the sight of the stranger who dressed like a white man speaking with Old Grandmother.

The young man nodded in her direction but continued speaking to the old woman. She didn't respond, and in the smoky light from the fire Annabelle saw no indication that Old Grandmother took notice of her presence.

Annabelle added water to the pot for their stew, wishing she understood what the man said. It was a moment before she realized he had switched to English, the words sounding nearly as strange as Indian patois after so long without hearing it.

"I asked, who are you?" the man repeated. He continued to look at Old Grandmother, though his choice of language made clear he addressed Annabelle.

She told him her name, the words coming slowly at first in her confusion. As she began to describe the circumstances of her capture, words came in a torrent, like water through a burst dam. He turned to face her, palms held out in surrender.

"Not so loudly. It is right that I should pay my respects to Old Grandmother, but it would not do for anyone to overhear us speaking English."

Annabelle bit her lip to still her voice. She looked to the skin door, wondering when the pale Indian would return and what he might do on discovering this man with her. The stranger seemed to have read her thoughts.

"Do not be afraid. He will not be back for a while." His voice held an amused tone. "No Water is away on a hunt, so he went to visit Black Buffalo Woman."

Seeing her confusion, he laughed. "You have much to learn."

Annabelle didn't know where to begin. Taking pity on her, he didn't wait for a question.

"I am John Hutchins. I am pleased to

finally meet you, Annabelle."

He told his story quickly. His father had been a soldier at Fort Laramie, an officer who took an Indian woman as his "fort wife." He abandoned her and the child when he rotated back to the states, leaving nothing to his son but his name.

Growing up at the fort, the boy learned English as well as his mother's tongue. He was still a boy when he began working for the army as an interpreter, and he seemed pleased with himself.

"A private at the fort makes about fifteen dollars in a month," he told her, youthful pride betraying his age. "I get fifty."

"But you're not working now?" A thought occurred to her, and she whispered her next words with breathless urgency. "Are you a spy?"

The boy leaned backed, his eyes growing wide.

"No, no. It is important that I be able to move between both worlds. My mother still lives with her people, and I am able to do some trading when I am not working as an interpreter. If either side thought me a spy, my life would be worthless."

"But you must *know* things."

For days Annabelle's curiosity about her surroundings had been building with no

235

outlet, and the questions tumbled out of her. *What did they plan to do with her? Why were so many gathered in one camp? Who was the strange Indian who kept her?*

Hutchins held out his hands to forestall the barrage.

"I cannot stay long enough to answer even half of your questions."

He settled in among the skins that covered the lodge's floor, any pretense that he was there to speak to Old Grandmother forgotten. His curiosity almost matched hers.

"Who *are* you?"

"I've told you." She didn't understand why her name shouldn't be enough. "I'm just a captive."

He shook his head. "Those feathers you wear — did he give those to you?" A nod of his head to their surroundings indicated he meant her captor.

She nodded, almost too nervous to ask the question that plagued her since receiving them. "Do they mean we are to be married?"

He laughed, almost a boyish giggle. "The wreath of feathers is a token of his protection. So long as you wear those, no other Indian will bother you."

"Why would he do that?"

"That's what everyone in the village wants

236

to know. That's why I am here. If I can find out why Crazy Horse has kept you I won't have to cook another meal the whole time I am in the village."

Gossip. So that's what he wanted. He wasn't here to help her, only to enhance his currency of stories to share among the others. Annabelle tried to conceal her disappointment. There had to be a way she could use his curiosity if she could just keep her wits.

"I wish I knew." She tried to sound helpful. "Did you say his name is Crazy Horse?"

He nodded.

"Tell me about him. If I knew more, maybe his actions will make sense."

Hutchins shared what he knew, confirming that, despite his light skin, Crazy Horse was full-blooded Sioux. As Hutchins described him, Crazy Horse was something of an enigma even among his own people. They whispered about his visions, that he was immune to bullet wounds.

The greatest wound he'd ever suffered was a broken heart. The woman he loved, Black Buffalo Woman, had married a childhood rival called No Water. Crazy Horse lived alone with his grandmother long after most warriors his age had wed.

"And he went to visit her tonight?" Annabelle asked.

Hutchins arched an eyebrow in response.

Annabelle drew some comfort in learning her captor's romantic attentions lay elsewhere. She even felt a pang of pity for a man so devoted. Her hand moved over her belly, little more than a bump suggesting the life inside.

"He won't take my baby, will he?"

Hutchins looked embarrassed, his eyes seeking out the painted rawhide storage containers arranged along the walls of the tepee. He stammered his words.

"Has he shown an interest in that way?"

Annabelle understood and nearly laughed at his awkwardness.

"Not at all. He doesn't even look at me in that way. The one who does is that big, brooding man who was with him. I call him Pierce."

Hutchins laughed. "Pierce? I see why you would think that was his name. He is Climbing Bear, a Cheyenne. He probably blames you for the death of two of his people in the raid when you were captured."

"He frightens me. It seems he's always watching me."

"You should avoid him."

Annabelle turned the conversation back to Crazy Horse. She wondered if there was a chance the Indians would ransom her.

"That's what He Dog thinks." Seeing her confusion, he added, "He Dog is his closest friend. He says Crazy Horse means to ransom you, to take you to the fort himself."

Hope surged in Annabelle's breast, and she hurried to mention Josey and the availability of ransom goods or money.

Hutchins held out a cautionary palm. "Do not let your hopes run away from you. No one else believes it."

"Why not?"

"Crazy Horse never keeps anything for himself. You see how he lives." He gestured to the meager contents of the tepee. "It is part of his vision, like a priest's vow of poverty. Some say it is why Black Buffalo Woman married another man — her father would not see her married to a pauper. If Crazy Horse would not betray his vision for her, he surely will not enrich himself with you."

Hope drained from Annabelle, and with it all the strength she had left. Her body collapsed. Hutchins seemed embarrassed to witness her distress and rose to leave.

"I will try to visit again before I leave." He sounded uncertain. "If I can."

He moved to step past her, but she caught

239

his hand and brought it to her face, wet with tears.

"You must help me. Take me with you when you leave."

"I cannot do that." Hutchins tried to pry loose his hand. "If I helped you, I could never come back. They would kill me."

With a wrenching tug, he freed himself of her, but before he could stoop to escape the tepee, she called after him.

"If they kill me and the soldiers find out you did nothing to help, you won't be able to work for the army again."

And Josey will kill you. Of that she was certain.

Hutchins paused at the flap, his expression a mixture of pity and something else. It took a moment for Annabelle to recognize it. Fear. That's what it was. When he left, Annabelle was certain Hutchins wished he had never come to see her.

CHAPTER TWENTY

The clouds clustered over the mountains burned orange like the glowing embers of a campfire when Light Hair rode one of his stolen ponies back to the village. The horse had promise.

Light Hair liked to walk his horses uphill to save their strength before turning them loose for a loping stride downhill. This one, a bay with matching white socks reaching to its front fetlocks, he rode hard even on the ascent, just to test its character. He liked how the bay responded. The horse pushed harder anytime Light Hair started to ease up, as if to prove itself to the man.

"You have pride." He patted the bay's neck, wiping clear a sheen of sweat from the hard run. "Pride is a good thing in a horse, so long as you mind your master."

The other warriors had long retired for the day, leaving a couple of boys charged with watching over the herd within the brush corral. Light Hair knew the others thought him too hard on his horses. In a community that calculated wealth by the number of a man's horses, Light Hair was a spendthrift, riding his horses until they wore down, giving away many of those he stole to widows and old men who had not seen a raid in a dozen winters or more.

Light Hair never named his horses, and he prized them in his own way. When pursued after a raid, Light Hair wanted to know his horse would burst its heart before it would fail him. There was value beyond wealth in a horse with that kind of pride.

The young warriors who mocked Light Hair for what they saw as his profligate ways could learn from a horse like this. Their pride was the boastful, boyish sort. Instead of victory, they pursued feats of valor they could crow about around a fire.

He still simmered with anger over losing the Cheyenne brothers in the last raid. Impatient with bloodlust, they had taken foolish risks. If it had been a Cheyenne or Lakota woman, they would have been more careful, but they did not fear a white woman and one man. They thought Light Hair an old woman for demanding caution, and they paid for their pride. Light Hair suspected the white woman had shot one of the brothers, but he kept that to himself. It was difficult enough to stop Climbing Bear from killing her in his grief over the brothers' deaths. Light Hair had his reasons for keeping the woman alive and well.

Back at the corral, Light Hair loosed the bay to graze with the others. Most of the stolen horses and mules were broken and would take to a travois harness. For his personal use, Light Hair preferred mounts with more spirit.

High Backbone was waiting for him. Even in the faint light of dusk, Light Hair recognized his friend's broad-shouldered silhouette. They admired the bay as it danced away to mingle with the other horses in the corral.

"Good horse. Even after a hard ride it shows you it has more to give."

"It will make a good warhorse." Much of what Light Hair knew of horses he had learned from his older friend.

"Obedient, is he?"

"Obedient yet proud."

High Backbone moved off to another horse, a white-faced sorrel with shoulders even broader than his. The horse was roped to a post, its wild eyes showing its displeasure.

"What do you intend for this beast?"

"Buffalo hunter."

"Yes, that might be its only hope." A horse that could not be broken was destined for a stewpot. High Backbone moved toward the horse, but it skittered away as far as its tether would permit. "How long have you kept it tied here?"

"Four days."

The horse had not eaten in that time. All of the ground around the post had been picked clean. Starving the horse would make it more docile, at least to the one who fed it. Light Hair brought a bucket of water to the horse and tried to coax it to drink. The sorrel's huge nostrils flared, and it took a step forward. Light Hair raised the bucket to its muzzle — and the horse reared back, straining against its ropes and forcing Light Hair to back away. He threw the water on the horse.

High Backbone laughed.

"Do not pretend to be angry, Crazy Horse. This horse is much like you. A buffalo hunter should not be broken too easily."

Light Hair let his smile show. For buffalo hunts, he needed a horse with even more spirit than a warhorse, a young, fast horse with a reckless nature. A horse like that could be trained to overcome its natural fear

244

of buffalo. The sorrel might never be an obedient warhorse like the bay, but it showed promise, too.

"Another day or two, and we will see." Horses lasted longer without water in the cooler temperatures.

High Backbone turned from the horses and looked west. The fire over the mountains had burned out. Darkness settled over them.

"It is late. I have been sent to ensure you come."

Red Cloud had called all the Big Bellies together. Even Spotted Tail had left the fort at Laramie to come.

Light Hair shook his head. "I am not a chief."

"Neither am I."

"But you will be one day."

High Backbone shrugged. "Red Cloud wants the Big Bellies to hear your vision."

Light Hair turned away to replace the bucket. He had no vision, not yet, just an idea for how they might take the fort. The vision of victory, he hoped, would come later.

"I have told Red Cloud. He can tell the others."

"You know he will not. He will sit back and watch which way the wind blows the grass, and he will follow."

The *wasicu* treated Red Cloud as a great chief, the leader of all the tribes, but among the people he was seen only as a war leader. He had killed the Crow chief Little Rabbit, helping to end the war for the Powder River country, and most of his followers were young warriors eager to fight the soldiers. It was no secret that Red Cloud viewed this war as an opportunity to enhance his standing among the people.

High Backbone placed his hands on Light Hair's shoulders and waited for him to meet his eyes. "The chiefs must hear it from you. Their warriors will follow a plan of your devising, just as I do."

Light Hair sighed. "I will be at the front of the battle. I always am." He kicked at a stone with his moccasin. "It is not my place to lead the talking."

"I will be there with you." High Backbone smiled. He had taught Light Hair how to fire-cure his first bow, and Light Hair trusted him more than anyone. "You cannot shirk your duty."

Light Hair went to retrieve his saddle and bow. The herd grazed in the corral, and as he watched the horses his bay raised its head, as if awaiting new commands. Yes, the horse had promise. He turned to the sorrel, still wide-eyed and pulling against its ropes. There was promise here, too, but of a different kind.

As he followed High Backbone into the village, Light Hair thought again of the Cheyenne brothers who died on the raid. He had blamed them for their impulsiveness because it pained him too much to admit his culpability for their deaths. Now he saw. He had taken buffalo hunters into a fight that demanded obedient warhorses.

Light Hair resolved not to repeat that mistake. In the coming battle, he would need men like High Backbone, who would trust in his vision and follow his commands. He would also need warriors like Climbing Bear, whose lust for soldiers' blood would overcome the caution of a more prudent man. He needed both warhorses and buffalo hunters — and a white woman whose life the soldiers valued above their own.

CHAPTER TWENTY-ONE

The Colonel woke Josey before dawn. He'd hardly slept, his imagination torturing him with thoughts of Annabelle and the Indians. Every time he sensed sleep approaching, an image came of dark hands against her fair skin, Annabelle helpless to stop them, perhaps calling his name in a plea for help that went unanswered. At least he hadn't dreamed when he drifted off, though it seemed like mere minutes before the Colonel roused him. His head ached. His stomach turned revolutions. He groaned.

The Colonel showed little sympathy. "Is that from nightmares or whiskey?"

"Whiskey, I expect." Josey made a new vow to avoid the stuff. "Thanks for waking me. I would have overslept."

"Well, don't count on me always being around to wipe your ass." For all the Colonel's gruff talk, Josey saw concern in the old man's eyes. "Think you can ride?"

They were gone before the sun's first rays crested the horizon. Besides Josey, the Colonel, and Byron, two army scouts joined them: Jim Bridger, recently returned from Fort Smith, and a full-blooded Crow named Waters Run High, who, after generations of warfare between his people and the Sioux, hated them more than any white man.

Josey checked his impulse to ride hard. This was a journey of a couple of days, not a couple of hours. Bridger had heard the Sioux were gathered in large numbers in a camp along the Tongue River, about midway between Fort Phil Kearny and Fort Smith, which was ninety miles distant.

Bridger set a measured pace on his mule, Hercules. The old mountain man, who was sixty if he was a day, claimed he could ride all day without getting sore because of the animal's shorter, more comfortable gait. He led them on a path north that paralleled the Bozeman Trail, which he said the Indians watched.

"It's when you don't see 'em that you know they's skulking in them hills, lying low under their wolf skins watchin' you."

The path wound among the foothills that descended from the Bighorn Mountains. The mountain-fed streams were low this time of year, and they crossed in places

Bridger said wouldn't be possible with the snowmelt in spring and summer.

The rising sun proved a small blessing, hovering low and weak in the sky. It was warmer than it should have been for autumn in the mountains. Even without snow, persistent winds whipped down from the heights, twisting their way along streambeds and between hills, finding their way beneath upturned collars and between gloves and sleeves. The cold didn't bite like a winter wind, but it penetrated deep into the bones just the same and made it impossible to feel warm, even when they stopped for the night and hunched over a low fire that wouldn't be seen at a distance. They built it slowly and used dry wood to reduce the smoke.

Bridger's path took them closer to the road to Virginia City the next day. Once when cresting a hill, Josey smelled smoke and saw white puffs coming from a distant ridge, what Bridger called "signal smoke" from Indian scouts watching the route.

"We should go find those Indians," Josey said. "Maybe they know something about Annabelle. News of a captive white woman is sure to spread."

"You're right about that, but we'll never get the jump on Indian wolf lookouts," Bridger said. "Better we look for some hunters and catch 'em unawares."

They had their chance late in the afternoon. Waters Run High had been ranging ahead and came back to report he'd found a hunting shelter hidden among a copse of cottonwoods. The crude hut was built of willow poles covered with brush and horse blankets. No one was there, but someone had been there the previous night and left blankets and bedrolls beside a fire pit made of stones that were still warm. The Colonel ordered everyone into sentry positions around the shelter.

They didn't have to wait long. The Indians returned around dusk, two of them, an older brave and a younger man, not much older than a boy. An antelope carcass was strapped to drag poles behind the older man's horse. They never heard Waters Run High until he was standing before them, a pistol pointed in the young man's face.

Within minutes they had the warriors trussed up like dressed turkeys. Bridger and Waters Run High did the talking while Byron and the Colonel set a guard to make sure no other Indians came upon them. Bridger and Waters Run High communicated with the Indians through a series of hand gestures and words common to the Crow and Sioux languages. The Indians were grim-faced and refused to speak. Josey resisted an urge to intervene with the Bowie knife he carried at his waist. Eventually, Bridger got them talking. When he was done, he came to Josey.

"Well?"

Bridger had a swollen goiter in his neck, like a misplaced Adam's apple. When he swallowed, it looked like he'd choked down a whole egg. He swallowed now and scratched his bristled chin.

"They heard of a white woman in the village taken during a raid."

"Annabelle?"

"No way a knowin'. They haven't seen her. They were with a war party down our ways. They stopped on the way back to the village to chase some game. Guess they didn't count on bein' hunted themselves."

"Is that all they know?"

"They said there's a half-breed trader who does business with the tribe and speaks English. He camps near the village and might know more."

Josey wasn't sure what he'd hoped to learn. It wasn't like they could ride into the village and demand a parley with Indians who'd been stalking the wood wagons and marauding their stock. He took comfort in the news of a captive white woman.

It has to be Annabelle.

Again, he imagined her surrounded by leering savages, naked before them, helpless to stop them from . . . He unsheathed his Bowie knife, the heft of its long blade as comfortable in his hand as a claw.

"I wouldn't cut 'em loose before mornin'," Bridger said. "They could cause mischief for us yet."

"Not these two."

Waters Run High knew what was coming. The Sioux did, too. Josey saw it in their eyes. The older man's were hard, his jaw set so that Josey knew he wouldn't squirm. So he went to the younger one first. His eyes widened, a flicker of fear from one who hadn't seen as much death as the older man. The young man bore no scars that Josey could see. Maybe he imagined himself invulnerable. Many Indians did, convinced by visions and luck that spirits or magic protected them. When they died, as all men must, their friends and family blamed the death on a disobedience of the vision, a betrayal of the magic.

The young Indian knew his magic had fled as Josey pulled his long braid away from his neck and turned him to face the ground. He said something, gibberish to Josey's ears, repeated three times, the last one drowning

253

in a gurgle of blood as Josey wrenched the knife across his throat.

The older man groaned as if he, too, had felt the cut. He leaned his head back, eyes closed, murmuring a chant. A death song, Josey suspected. He admired the older man's demeanor, how he tilted his head back as if to welcome the knife.

It was over so fast Bridger hadn't had time to say a word. He swallowed, the egg-like protuberance swelling with the movement.

"I told them we wouldn't harm them if they told us what we wanted to know."

Josey wiped his knife against the younger man's buckskin leggings and stepped clear of the growing puddle of blood. His nose wrinkled at the sour, metallic smell.

"Every Sioux I kill is one less between me and Annabelle."

Waters Run High grunted something in his native tongue and kicked the bodies to the side.

"He said if you hadn't done it, he would," Bridger translated. He swallowed again as the separate puddles of blood coalesced into a single dark pool. "You could have at least let the scoundrels butcher the meat before you killed 'em. Now one of us will have to do it."

Josey took the first watch, knowing sleep would elude him so long as Annabelle was a captive. The men's hacks and coughs as they settled into bedrolls sounded like rifle shots in the cold, thin air. There were so many stars in the clear sky Josey didn't need a torch to see. He wondered if it was his imagination that there could be more stars here in the territories than he recalled back in the states. He recognized the constellations, so he knew the sky itself wasn't different. Just brighter.

The Colonel found him sitting against a large boulder near the shallow stream. He brought a mug of coffee, which Josey accepted, more for the warmth in his hands than the taste.

"How long did I sleep?" the Colonel asked.

Josey looked to the heavens, noting the Big Dipper's position in relation to the North Star.

"It's about midnight."

The Colonel stretched his legs. Tried to squat but stopped when his knees popped. As he stood, he rubbed his lower back.

"Getting old. I don't recommend it."

255

"Better than dying."

The Colonel coughed. "I suppose that's true, least for a little while. I ain't so sure about the end."

They sat in silence, enjoying the night sounds. Water trickled over stones in the streambed. A wolf called from a distant hill. The tall, straight trees groaned in the breeze.

"It's good news, what Bridger learned from those Indians," the Colonel said. "I think it must mean Annabelle is alive."

"I do, too."

"Means the Indians didn't kill her, even though they could."

"Guess the ransom is worth more to them."

"Maybe."

Another wolf answered the first. Sound carried so far on the night air the howling could have come from anywhere. The Colonel pulled out his pipe and packed the bowl.

"Those Indians you killed . . . they were our captives, same as Annabelle is somebody's captive."

"It's not the same."

"Because they're Indians?"

"A day or two ago they were stalking the wood trains, looking to get off a shot at me or one of the woodcutters. A few months back they might have been in the war party

256

that tried to kill you."

Josey doubted he'd ever forget the sight of the Colonel being struck down by a pale Indian who wielded a stone war club. The blow to the head had laid out the old man for days. Josey had thought he was dead. The sight so shocked him he froze on the battlefield. The same Indian might have killed him. Instead, all he did was touch Josey as he rode by, an act of bravery the Indians called counting coup.

The Colonel lit the pipe, drew on the stem with three quick breaths. He was quicker than Josey to forgive an enemy.

"Today they were just hunters."

"And tomorrow they could have been killers," Josey said. "They can't hurt us now."

The Colonel pursed his lips and exhaled smoke in a thin stream. Josey enjoyed the smell of the Colonel's tobacco, though he never cottoned to the taste. Sometimes he could smell the tobacco on the Colonel even when the old man wasn't smoking. He had a sudden image of his father smoking a pipe while he sat in a chair by the hearth in their home when Josey was a boy. A lamp stood on a small table beside the chair, but Josey's father preferred to read by the light of the fire. Josey had forgotten his father smoked a pipe until that moment. The memory left him feeling hollow.

"Dammit," the Colonel said. "I'm trying to tell you something. You don't make it easy."

Josey turned to face him. He'd seen this coming from the moment the Colonel handed him the coffee. Josey wasn't sure why he'd killed the Indians. They could have posed a threat if he'd let them go, but he might have figured out some way short of slaughtering them to reduce the risk. He was angry and frightened about Annabelle, most of his anger directed at himself.

The Colonel cleared his throat. "War forces us to do things we're not proud of — I know you know that. But killing like that. It will haunt you, son."

"Every one of them haunts me. I can see the face of every man I've killed. I even see the faces of men I never saw up close before they died."

Josey's voice was louder and harsher, and he'd said more than he intended. He added in a whisper, "It's the price I pay."

"The price of what?"

"The price of living."

"Those are just nightmares."

Just nightmares? They had started during the war. The only escape Josey could imagine was another death — his own. On surviving the war, he tried to distance himself from the memories with drink. That led to bar fights and more gunplay and more deaths. He headed west with the Colonel and Byron in hopes that he could leave all that behind, but killing and death followed him here, too. Annabelle had given him hope of an escape. Being with her brought him peace. She gave him something to live for, something to *want* to live for. He never felt more alive than when making love with Annabelle.

Except that's not entirely true, is it?

Josey pulled off his hat and ran a hand through his thick hair and looked up. A thin layer of clouds lit from behind by a moon he couldn't see had spread across the sky like a gauzy curtain. Beside him, the Colonel puffed away on his pipe like he was short of breath. For once, it seemed the old man had run out of things to say.

Josey said, "Every man's death diminishes me, for I am involved in mankind."

"Are you turning philosopher?"

"It's from a poem my father read me as a boy. John Donne. He said no man is an island. Every man is a part of the main."

"It comforts me that you know that." The Colonel drew on his pipe but sucked only air. He studied the pipe a moment before knocking it against his boot to empty it. "It would comfort me even more if I knew you believed it."

Their progress slowed as they drew nearer the Tongue River. Bridger got down from his mule to study broad scuffs left by travois poles and Indian ponies. He found a few marks of horses he said were stolen from whites because they were shod. Fearing they might be detected, they abandoned the trail and bushwhacked through dense forest.

At midday they came to an open field littered with long-rotted buffalo carcasses, so many Josey couldn't count them all. The bleached bones gleamed in the sun. Decayed flesh still clung to some, for there were more dead beasts than even the scavengers that roamed the plains could eat. Bridger eased his mule among the remains. Josey knew he didn't like being in the open, but the sight was too strange to go unstudied.

"What a waste," Josey said. "I thought the hunters made use of every part of a buffalo. How can they claim to be starving if they've killed so many?"

"Indians didn't do this," Bridger said. He crouched beside a pile of bones. "I've heard of such things but never seen it for myself. All they took were the skins and the tongue, the best-tasting part."

Bridger stood. "White hunters did this. Shot 'em down from over there." He pointed to a small rise to the east, an impossible distance for most guns, but not a buffalo rifle. "Large-bore Sharps, I 'spect."

"A single-shot rifle?" Josey figured there had to be at least a hundred carcasses spread across the field. "How could they kill so many?"

"Buffalo's big but not bright. They stampede when the Indians hunt 'em 'cause the Indians have to get close. From that distance, the hunters could pick 'em off one by one, like shootin' targets. Buffalo'd never know what was happenin'."

The Colonel had been quiet, squinting against the sun, his gray mustache drooped in a frown.

"Army might have better luck driving off the Indians by just killing all the buffalo," he said.

"It's almost enough to make me pity the Sioux," Bridger said. He mounted his mule and turned back for the cover of the tree line. "This many buffalo could have fed all the tribes for two winters."

As they drew closer to the Tongue River,

Waters Run High ranged ahead, seeking a way that avoided any more Indian encounters. Bridger explained that the Crow and Sioux had been sneaking up on each other's camps for so many generations, it was in their blood. Waters Run High returned and reported seeing a half-breed trader headed to the Sioux camp from the direction of Fort Smith. He recognized the trader from his white man's clothes. He rode a roan pony and led two mules loaded with goods.

"Let me go talk to him," Bridger said. He looked at Josey. "Do I need you to promise me you won't kill him?"

He seemed to take Josey's stone silence as assent, and he ambled ahead with Waters Run High.

The others waited. It wasn't long before Bridger returned with the trader, introducing him as John Hutchins. Bridger couldn't restrain a crooked smile.

"John here says Annabelle is alive and in the Indian camp."

"You've seen her?" Though he had remained hopeful, the fear that the Indians might have killed Annabelle had been twisting in Josey's gut like a Bowie knife.

"I've spoken with her."

If not for his dark skin, hair and eyes, Hutchins might have passed for a white man. He spoke better English than Bridger.

"Is she well? Have they mistreated her? The baby?"

"She is fine. No one bothers her. She wears a wreath of feathers given to her by Crazy Horse."

"Crazy Horse? I've heard of him," Bridger told the others. "The Crow believe he's touched by spirits."

"Like a medicine man?" Josey hoped a holy man might treat Annabelle with more kindness.

"No, he's a warrior, but a strange one," Bridger said. "The Crow hold him in some kind of awe. In battle he always rides in the front. Some say he can't be hurt by bullets or arrows."

"I would like to test that," Josey said. He recalled the pale warrior who'd been riding in front of the other Indians when he struck down the Colonel and could have killed Josey.

"You don't understand," Hutchins said. "Crazy Horse protects her."

"Why would he do that?"

"Some say he plans to ransom her at the fort."

Indian faces were too impassive for Josey to read, but he thought he saw a flicker of doubt in Hutchins's eyes.

"You don't look confident."

"It is hard to know the mind of a man like that. I fear war is coming."

"Then help us," the Colonel said. "Convince the Indians to give her up for a ransom. Maybe there doesn't have to be any more bloodshed."

Hutchins looked skeptical.

"My mother is Lakota, but that won't protect me if they think I'm helping you."

Josey asked, "Can you get a message to Annabelle?"

Hutchins didn't look pleased, but he nodded.

"Tell her we haven't given up. Tell her I love her."

CHAPTER TWENTY-TWO

Red Cloud's lodge was about four times the size of those that housed a single family, with as many as twenty pine poles used to raise his tent. Brilliantly colored porcupine quills adorned the sides, and the front was fringed with matching strings of dozens of scalps.

The chiefs and their seconds were gathered in a circle when Light Hair and High Backbone arrived. Respected warriors from all the tribes, eager to hear the deliberations of the Big Bellies, filled out the rest of the lodge. The room was dark and smoky, the only light coming from a large central fire that had burned down to ash and embers. Light Hair knew most of the chiefs: Old Man Afraid of His Horse, Little Wolf, and Spotted Tail, among others.

Red Cloud motioned for the newcomers to take a position at his right. He was tall with a regal mien accentuated by the full eagle-feather war bonnet he wore on formal occasions. Each white feather denoted an enemy killed, and Red Cloud's bonnet was arrayed with dozens of feathers. He had greased his long, dark hair and braided it around the wing bone of an eagle.

Even with everyone gathered, no one spoke. Red Cloud drew out his pipe, as long as his arm and as ornate as his headdress. Red Cloud murmured words of prayer, beseeching guidance as he packed the bowl with a painted wooden tamper and used a hot coal to light the tobacco. He offered the pipe first to Grandmother Earth, then to the four directions and lastly to Tunkasila, the spirit above.

He took three puffs from the bit with a kissing sound that exaggerated the leanness of his slender face. Red Cloud was some twenty winters older than Light Hair but looked even more aged from the deep creases that bracketed his eyes and mouth. He passed the pipe to his left, and each man in the circle took a turn. The pipe reached Light Hair last. He did not care to smoke, but the occasion demanded it. A pipe ceremony represented a gesture of harmony among those who partook, the tobacco a sacrifice with the smoke rising to carry the words of their council to the spirit beings.

The tobacco was bitter, and Light Hair took two puffs. Instead of handing it off to Red Cloud to complete the circle, he sent the pipe back the way it came so that each man would have a second turn. The deliberateness of the ceremony set a tone for the discussions that would follow, ensuring that whatever decisions were reached were supported by a consensus of chiefs.

Though his following was not the largest among the gathered chiefs, Red Cloud spoke first. As a young man of twenty winters he had killed a Lakota chief who feuded with his chief and adopted father, Old Smoke. The act won Red Cloud respect as a warrior but tainted his standing as a leader in times of peace. He had been first to make the call for war when the *wasicu* sought peace with a Laramie treaty. He saw duplicity in their plan to build forts along the trail and reminded the others of this.

"The Great White Father offered us presents because he wants a new road," he said. "But at the same time, he sent soldiers to steal our land before the people can say yes or no."

The other chiefs nodded in agreement, the lone exception Spotted Tail, who had signed the treaty. The others looked to Old Man Afraid of His Horse, who had the biggest following among them. He was the third chief in his line to carry the name, which implied that he caused such dread among his enemies even the sight of his horse inspired fear. His son, Young Man Afraid of His Horse, sat at his side.

"The *wasicu* ask to pass through our lands. We would not mind if they were like the wind. The wind stirs the grass. It might knock over a dead tree, but it passes and becomes nothing more than a bad memory."

The old man paused, allowing his words to sink in. Alone among them, he had been a chief when the first Laramie treaty had been signed, the one that granted the *wasicu* passage along the Platte River on what the Indians called the Holy Road.

"Now the wagons come here, and more will follow. They will drive our game from the hills. They will slaughter the buffalo for its skin, leaving our women and children to go hungry. We cannot allow what happened at the Holy Road to happen here. No man should live to see his children go hungry."

The man's words washed over Light Hair as he stared into the fire. He watched Spotted Tail from the side. His uncle had once been a warrior chief as feared as Red Cloud. But when the white soldiers began to hunt down his people, he turned himself in and went to their prison to save others. He came back a different man.

Like Red Cloud, he wore a war bonnet, his accentuated with a raccoon tail. It was whispered by younger warriors that it had been years since Spotted Tail added a white eagle feather to his bonnet, that instead of killing enemies he longed to die in his sleep and be wrapped on a scaffold where wild animals could not get at his corpse. It pained Light Hair to see his uncle cowed by white soldiers. He had lived with Spotted Tail for a time as a boy. Now he avoided him.

Spotted Tail remained a chief, and the pipe ceremony demanded that all voices be heard. He spoke in a low voice, and Light Hair closed his eyes to focus on the words lest they be lost among the sounds of the smoldering coals and the men shifting around him.

"If a hornet threatens your child, kill it where it flies. Do not pursue it to its nest and stir up a thousand more."

Some of the younger warriors made noises deriding his fear, but the Big Bellies listened. Spotted Tail had traveled far beyond Sioux lands, as far as the River of Canoes, what the *wasicu* called the Mississippi. He had seen things.

"You cannot imagine how many of them there are. I saw one village as big as all the Lakota lodges."

Some of the younger men who had not heard Spotted Tail's stories smirked. A big village so far away did not frighten them.

Spotted Tail's voice rose as he continued.

"They have *hundreds* of such villages. You may kill as many as the leaves in the forest, but their fathers will not miss them. Destroy the fort, and they will send a hundred soldiers for every one you kill. They will hunt us like dogs. Slaughter us, man, woman, and child, in the villages where we sleep. The *wasicu* do not understand war the way we do. They are killers. They measure victory only by how many they kill. We cannot defeat a people like this. We can only hope to drive them away."

His words stirred an angry reaction among some of the warriors. Light Hair bowed his head, embarrassed for his uncle's fear even as he considered his words. His uncle was no fool and not a man to exaggerate.

Little Wolf, the last great chief to speak, cut through the din.

"That is why we must fight. We must show the *wasicu* that we are strong, too. Sharpen your knives, and string your bows. Load your rifles, and whet your tomahawks. We will teach them what it means to fear us."

Some of the younger warriors rose from their seats, yipping and shouting. They quieted when Red Cloud raised a hand. High Backbone nudged Light Hair. *The direction of the wind is clear now.*

"Friends and sons, listen to my words," Red Cloud began. He spoke with a measured tone intended to add the gravity to his words that seemed to come naturally to the other chiefs. "You are a great and powerful people. The *wasicu* have proven themselves inferior. We extended a hand of friendship to them, and they demonstrated how false and cruel they are. You will find no truth in their words, only deceit."

Red Cloud's voice rose, the rhythm of his words filling the room like a drum beat, a powerful man speaking powerful words, his strength all the greater because he no longer made the effort to sound dignified, the words alone giving him the authority he sought.

"They have earned our hatred, and the people cry for vengeance. The wretches who would steal our fathers' land will die by our hands, and our feats of valor will never be forgotten. Our songs of victory will be sung at scalp dances by our children and our children's children."

The words struck the inside of the lodge like a gun-that-shoots-twice, first in his booming rhetoric, then in the explosion it set off among the young warriors who sat outside the circle. They stood as one, shouting war cries and boasts of courage. The chiefs were more restrained, nodding approval. Their impassive features did not reveal whether they approved of Red Cloud's call to war or merely the effectiveness of his words. Stoicism, Light Hair realized, is part of being a chief.

Only Spotted Tail seemed immune to the enthusiasm. Even before the room quieted, he leaned in toward Red Cloud and said, "The *wasicu* live in forts from which they can shoot their big guns. No tribe has ever defeated the white soldiers in their fort."

Red Cloud's lean features stretched into a smile. He had been waiting for this. He lifted his hand, stilling the noise in the lodge, and gestured to his right.

Light Hair felt the eyes of every man in the room turn to him, like a sudden hot wind on his face. He held his gaze on the fire, imagining himself smoldering among the embers. The commands of his vision demanded a modesty that for Light Hair extended even to the meeting lodge, so it was left to High Backbone to speak for him.

"Many of you know Crazy Horse has captured a white woman. I have heard some claim he means to keep her as a wife. You should know better. My friend keeps for himself only what he needs to kill more *wasicu,* the white woman included."

The words touched on a source of camp gossip that fired the curiosity of everyone in the tent. Most men of Light Hair's age had at least one wife, but after losing his bid to marry Black Buffalo Woman, Light Hair had shown no inclination to take a wife. His continued interest in Black Buffalo Woman created concern among some of the chiefs, who feared a confrontation with No Water, her husband. By speaking of wives for Crazy Horse, High Backbone seized everyone's attention.

"The woman is wife to a great white warrior. She carries his child. We will send an emissary under the flag of peace to seek ransom for the woman's return. We will demand ammunition for the buffalo hunt. The soldiers will refuse. They will offer food and blankets, and we will agree."

One of the warriors in the circle began to interrupt, but Red Cloud stayed him with a gesture. He knew High Backbone was not finished.

"Crazy Horse will lead the party that

returns the woman. Once they are inside the fort, they will break for the walls, killing the soldiers who fire the guns-that-shoot-twice and those who open and close the gate."

High Backbone paused to look at Light Hair, knowing his friend's fate in such a plan, then turned his gaze to the chiefs around the circle. "You will be in hiding with your warriors in the trees near the fort. Crazy Horse will hold the gate until your army can sweep in and kill all the soldiers inside."

The plan was met with silence. Light Hair's cheeks burned. Red Cloud had roused the room with his words. Light Hair's plan had silenced them. Did they see dishonor in his stratagem?

Spotted Tail spoke, directing his words to Light Hair in a way that forced the younger man to look from the fire. "Your plan may succeed in giving us the fort, but it will end in death for you and every man who joins you."

Light Hair met his uncle's gaze. As a boy, Light Hair viewed this man as a hero. The *wasicu* had stolen that from him, leaving the husk of the warrior he had been. Now Light Hair spoke.

"Better to die young on the battlefield

than to live to be an old man wrapped up
on a scaffold."

CHAPTER TWENTY-THREE

The Indians broke camp with an alacrity Annabelle found startling. One moment she was bringing back an armful of wood from the forest, enjoying the quiet of the village in the morning. In the next moment a swirl of activity overtook the tepees, like a sudden wave roiling among shoreline rocks.

Squaws hurried back and forth. Children screamed and laughed. Dogs yipped and snapped. Horses stomped and snorted. Annabelle wondered if they were under attack, if the army had come for her. But there was no sign of panic among the women, who set about their tasks with a precision that would have impressed even General Robert E. Lee.

The sisters from the nearby tepee who often instructed Annabelle in the methods of women's chores approached. They'd already dismantled their tepee with a speed that bewildered Annabelle. Their words of instruction meant little to her, so the larger sister pantomimed what Annabelle should do. She lowered herself on all fours beside the tepee as if to crawl. The more slender of the sisters climbed on her back, straining to reach the wooden pins that held in place the skins of the tepee. Once the pins were removed, she and Annabelle peeled away the cover from the long wooden poles, winding it into a tight bundle that reminded Annabelle of helping her mother fold a bed sheet.

While they were occupied with that, the other sister dismantled the poles and fastened the longest to Annabelle's pony and a couple of other horses Annabelle recognized from Crazy Horse's stock. The long ends of the poles dragged on the ground behind the horses, and the sisters showed Annabelle how to attach crossbeams to the poles where they could pile most of the household goods. The rest they wrapped into tight bundles and loaded onto the dogs, which dragged little travois of their own.

Within a matter of minutes evidence of Annabelle's home of more than a month had been swept from the grassy field along the river, ready to be moved to wherever the Indians chose.

Annabelle helped Old Grandmother pack

the last of their belongings onto their travois, and they headed out. Men and older boys mounted the best Indian ponies and rode ahead, leaving the women and children with the drudgery of the move.

Leading her horse by the bridle, Annabelle carried a bundle on her back with all the things she couldn't fit among the rest of the loads. The cavalcade of women, children, horses, and dogs kicked up a dusty cloud that appeared to stretch for miles.

Old Grandmother led another horse, walking with the steady stride of a much younger woman. It always surprised Annabelle how capable the old woman was once set to a task. It was when idle that her eyes glazed and her mind turned inward to a place only of her knowing.

The day was warm for the season, with blue skies and puffs of white clouds overhead that chugged like locomotives from the Bighorn Mountains in the west. The summer sun had browned the grass since the first time she crossed the Powder River country. If she closed her eyes, she could almost imagine herself among a train of wagons, with Josey out there, somewhere, riding ahead and keeping them safe.

The morning's activity so preoccupied Annabelle she had no time to consider the move's meaning. She held no illusion it portended her release. There would be no need to move the entire camp if they intended to take her to the fort. She assumed they moved for more practical reasons. Annabelle and the other women needed to walk farther from camp every day to find wood for the cook fires. The grass the horses grazed on had been eaten away. And when the winds shifted, she could smell the stench of the privies dug outside camp.

As much sense as the move made, it left a pit in Annabelle's stomach. She'd been with the Indians too long to harbor hopes for a quick rescue, yet she couldn't escape the sense that the move would complicate whatever efforts were being made. At times she feared the worst for Byron, convinced that if he'd succeeded in reaching the fort Josey would have already come for her. Yet her faith in the man was such she didn't doubt him. Of course Byron lived. Of course he made it to the fort. Of course Josey was doing everything he could to find her. The Indians couldn't go far enough away to keep Josey from finding her. To believe anything else would be giving in to despair.

Annabelle's mood brightened at the sight of John Hutchins. She hadn't seen the half-breed trader since the day she'd begged him to help her, and she'd convinced herself he was avoiding her.

Hutchins was on foot, leading his horse by the reins. A trio of tethered pack mules loaded with trade goods trailed behind. As he had on their first meeting, he came first to Old Grandmother, speaking in soothing tones and lending an arm for her support as they crossed some uneven terrain. When he switched to English, Annabelle knew he addressed her.

"It is a fine day for a move. The old ones warn we will pay for such a warm autumn with a bitterly cold winter, but I am not so sure. Sometimes I think it is the duty of the old to frighten the young with their superstitions."

Annabelle removed the bandanna she wore across her mouth and nose to shield her from the dust and smell of the animals. "It must be the duty of the young to doubt their elders — until they have the years to earn such wisdom."

Hutchins smiled, and Annabelle felt a wave of relief to think he harbored no ill feelings after his abrupt departure from their first meeting. She spoke to him of the move, realizing she was blabbering but continuing anyway, just to keep him talking and hear the sound of English a little longer.

As they spoke a hawk circled overhead, gliding in lazy circles on unseen currents of air. She tried to imagine the view from such a height — snow-capped mountains bristling with pine forests, hills that rolled to the opposite horizon like folds in an unkempt blanket, clear streams gleaming like silver in the sun as they sliced across the scrub-filled plains.

"This is beautiful land."

"You see why the Lakota fight for it."

Hutchins told her about learning to hunt with his uncles and cousins, enumerating the game that lived in the region like checking off a list for Noah's ark. Black and white-tailed deer. Antelope. Wolves. Rabbit. Sage hen. Prairie chicken. Beaver. Otters. Brants, geese, and ducks. Grizzly and black bears. And buffalo. Buffalo in numberless herds. Enough buffalo to sustain a population of hunters and their families.

"Before the whites came, Lakota and Crow fought for generations here. The Lakota did not take this land from the Crow to give it to the whites."

"The whites don't want to take it from them. They just want to pass through."

"My uncles told me stories about when the whites first started following the path

281

along the Platte River. The whites said they needed only land wide enough for their wagons to take them to Oregon and the Great Salt Lake. They offered food and tools to the Indians so that they could pass in peace. The Indians knew if they did not agree, they would have to fight the soldiers."

They walked in silence for a moment. Annabelle did not need to ask how the exchange worked out for the Indians. Her wagon train had followed that path, past tribes decimated by disease, across lands once teeming with buffalo and other game, now littered with broken wagon parts and abandoned goods. She'd never seen a buffalo until she reached the Powder River country.

"The Indians will not give away this land in a treaty," Hutchins said.

"Even if it means war?"

"They would rather die fighting than watch their families starve."

Annabelle protested. She didn't want to see the Indians lose their land. She didn't want to see Old Grandmother go hungry. She didn't even want to see Crazy Horse shot down by an army cannon. The tenderness she'd seen in his treatment of his grandmother and people softened her impression of him.

"It doesn't have to be those two options," she said. "Indians could learn to farm. Their children could learn to read."

"They could become white Indians like me." With a sad smile and a sweep of his arm, Hutchins gestured to his clothes. "You would make them a people who do not belong anywhere."

Annabelle coughed from the dust kicked up by the animals, unsure of what to say.

Hutchins continued. "The Lakota have a saying: 'It is better to die young on the battlefield, than to die old, rotting on a scaffold.' "

"That's horrible," Annabelle said, wrinkling her nose.

"It sounds better in Lakota."

"They don't bury their dead?"

"We bury many where we can. But the most revered dead are wrapped in robes and placed on a scaffold to encourage the spirit's journey into the sky." Seeing her skepticism, he added, "It also keeps animals from disturbing the body."

They walked in silence for a few minutes, long enough for Annabelle to fear Hutchins might leave, and she would be swallowed again in her homesickness. Beside her, a squaw she did not recognize led a heavily laden horse. A small child was bundled

283

within a makeshift saddlebag of buffalo skin draped over the back of the pony. Annabelle wasn't good at judging children's ages and wondered how long before her baby reached a similar size. The thought made her frown. *I don't want to raise my baby in an Indian village.*

Hutchins was studying her face and must have misread her expression as something he'd caused.

"I apologize," he said. "I did not come here to sadden you with talk of death."

She forced a smile. "You have no need to apologize. I'm glad you're here. I thought you were angry with me for asking your help. I asked too much of you."

"I cannot blame you."

Annabelle continued watching the child as they walked. The horse's gait jostled the boy in such a way that he gurgled as if being bounced on his grandfather's knee. *Indians love their babies as much as we do.* Annabelle didn't know why she might think differently. She'd just never considered the matter before.

Hutchins brought her out of her reverie. "Do you understand what this move means?"

"I think there is to be a final big buffalo hunt, to gather enough meat for the winter."

284

"That is right. You are learning some of the language."

The real significance of the move, he explained, was that the village traveled as one entity. Tribes often come together in summer. In winter, when the hunting is not as good and the need for wood is greater, they break into smaller groups that are better able to sustain themselves.

"So this village is too large for a winter camp."

He nodded. "And it is not breaking up into smaller groups. That can mean only one thing."

"War?"

"A kind of war I have never seen."

"What do you mean?"

"The fighting I spoke of with the Crow is not something your soldiers would call a war. Indians do not fight battles the way the whites know them. They go on raids. If people die, it is cause for great mourning in the village."

Annabelle thought of the battle where her brothers died. Tens of thousands had been killed in a matter of days, more people than were in this village.

"Look at the mothers around you," Hutchins continued. "Most of them have one or two children at most. We are a nomadic people, not like the white people who settle in one place and have so many children they can lose half in a war and call it a noble sacrifice."

The comment hewed too close to her family's mourning. Annabelle didn't appreciate having her own observation turned back on her.

"I can assure you white mothers love their children as much as Indians."

Her hand moved to her belly, and he apologized.

"I would not know," he said. "What I know about white fathers is not encouraging."

Now it was Annabelle's turn to feel bad. Was there any hope her people and Indians could ever understand each other? She asked Hutchins, "What would war mean for you?"

He seemed surprised by her concern. "I do not know. Nothing good, I fear."

In an all-out war, he would not be free to move between the two peoples, he said. His family is Indian, but his livelihood depends on the whites.

"You don't want to see war any more than I do," she said.

"Not like this."

She listened as he explained the potential

for disaster both sides risked. The Indians might be strong enough to destroy the fort, but the army would retaliate. They would send even more soldiers, and they would hunt down the responsible tribes and exterminate them. Everyone he knew would be killed.

"What can you do to stop it?"

He smiled at her. "I happen to be walking beside the key to their plans."

"Me?"

He nodded.

"I don't understand."

"You do not have to. All you need to understand is that I have a powerful reason for seeing you escape. Do you trust me?"

Annabelle's mind whirled. *Escape?* She'd almost dismissed all hope. She looked over her shoulder at the women and children around them, now worried about their being seen together. No one seemed to be taking notice of them, but she had an irrational fear that someone might overhear and understand. She lowered her voice to a whisper.

"You said they plan to ransom me. Maybe I should wait. If they catch me trying to escape, they might kill me."

Hutchins shook his head, almost violent in its movement. "Do not trust in the ransom. A war is coming, one neither side can afford."

As much as she wanted to flee, Annabelle still harbored doubts. The risk should she be recaptured seemed too great. Hutchins must have seen her hesitation. He grabbed her hand to draw her close, a fierce whisper in her ear giving her courage.

"Your men are looking for you. I can take you to them."

CHAPTER TWENTY-FOUR

A bugle call split the icy morning air.

"The wood train is under attack!" a private called from the sentry tower.

Josey hurried to the stables. Thirty cavalrymen and a score of infantry scrambled about, some pulling on boots over extra layers of woolen socks, others fumbling with cartridge and cap boxes and Springfield rifles that were too long to be used effectively on horseback.

Horses whinnied and blew, their iron-shod hooves pounding an impatient drumbeat against the frozen earth. After weeks of unseasonably warm temperatures, a late autumn freeze had struck as if to make up for lost time. Josey's Gray stood saddled, along with every other horse capable of carrying a man. Today, if everything went as Carrington intended, they would make the Indians pay for their harassing attacks on the wood wagons.

As he readied for battle, Josey thought through Carrington's plans. It had taken all the persuasive powers the Colonel and Jim Bridger could muster to convince him to return to the fort and give John Hutchins a chance to secure Annabelle's ransom. Josey agreed only once he realized the others wouldn't return without him. Any attempt at a rescue in such a big Indian camp would have risked the lives of his friends as well as his own.

On returning to the fort, Josey and the Colonel met with the commander in the post headquarters. A skeptical Carrington listened to their report, including what they relayed of the half-breed trader's estimate of the size of the Indian camp.

Carrington asked, "Did you see so many warriors?"

When told they hadn't gotten close enough, Carrington acted like that proved his point. "We've never seen more than maybe a hundred Indians attack the herds or wood trains. If they have so many warriors, why haven't we seen them?"

"Maybe they're still gathering their strength." The uncertainty in the Colonel's voice undercut his argument.

"Or maybe the camp is filled with women and children," Carrington said. "We've killed a fair number of Indians, gentlemen. Perhaps we've dealt them a blow that limits the fighting force they can put in the field."

The commander sounded like he needed to convince himself. In their absence, Carrington had received direct orders from General Cooke to mount an offensive.

"His directive says we must respond to their 'murderous and insulting attacks.' Sitting in Omaha more than seven hundred miles away and he's insulted!"

Carrington stalked about the map table in the center of the room, his face red and his breath coming in quick gasps. He was not a robust man, and Josey worried he tried too hard to command the men's respect. His success in planning and overseeing the fort's rapid construction should have made any officer proud. But with no experience leading men into battle, Carrington resorted to a pedantic focus on rules and discipline. He'd issued one set of orders since Josey's arrival chastising officers for the use of profanity in reprimanding the men. That provoked more whispered comparisons to fearful "Ichabod" while he dallied over plans to take the offensive.

"I apologize, gentlemen. I speak out of turn." Carrington pulled on his tunic, smoothing out the folds on his blue uniform, and swept his dark hair back from his eyes, where it fell when he became agitated. He turned his attention to the maps, tracing his finger along the route between the fort and the wood camp. His finger stopped at the wood road.

"The next time the Indians attack the wood wagons, I'll send Fetterman with the cavalry from the fort. The Indians won't stand against an armed and trained squad. They always retreat to the north, here, around the far side of Lodge Trail Ridge and into the Peno Creek valley."

The Colonel nodded. "They know our riders can't keep up with them."

"Exactly." Carrington continued. "My plan is to lead a second column along the Bozeman Trail to the east of Lodge Trail Ridge. We'll swing around here and be waiting for them at Peno Creek."

He pounded a fist into the palm of his hand. "Fetterman will chase them right to us, and then we'll have them."

Josey slipped his loaded Henry rifle into the scabbard latched to his saddle and led Gray out of the stables. The plan was sound, just the sort of thing a West Point instructor would have approved, but Josey worried how the untested recruits at Fort Phil

Kearny would respond when faced with targets that returned fire.

At least the prospect of battle gave the troops a sense of purpose. Josey heard it in their excited chatter. There were no grumblings about Carrington this morning. Nervous tension invigorated the soldiers in a fashion Josey hoped would keep them vigilant.

"What the Indians need, I tell you, is one solid whippin' to send 'em skulking back to those hills for good," a pudgy corporal with apple-red cheeks explained to a pair of privates as he tightened the front cinch on his saddle. "If they had the courage to stand and face us in the field, we'd crush 'em, I tell you, just like we did those rebel bastards. Red Cloud's no Robert E. Lee, of that you can be sure. Once we hang 'im, that lot will give us no more trouble."

Josey kept silent. He felt their eyes on him, heard the whispers when he passed. Enough of the men he'd fought with in the summer during the ambush at Crazy Woman Creek were around to tell the tale. The Colonel had nearly been killed in that fight. Josey took comfort knowing the old man would not be riding out today — though the Colonel had protested at being left out. He'd offered to ride alongside Carrington, but the commander demurred.

The Colonel waited at the gate when Josey rode up. Carrington and Grummond were already there. The smell was not so bad that morning, the cold having frozen over the latrines.

"Fetterman just left with Lieutenant Bingham and the cavalry to relieve the wood wagons," the Colonel said. "You'll have to hurry to get into position before the Indians retreat to Peno Creek."

The Colonel looked ready for war, armed and wearing his thick coat. His brown-spotted Appaloosa stood tethered to the guard stand beside the gate.

"Carrington won't change his mind?" Josey said.

The Colonel said something foul under his breath. "Says he needs me here so that if something goes wrong Captain Ten Eyck will have the benefit of my 'wise counsel.' 'Wizened' is what he means. He thinks I'm too old! I've led more attacks than he's even read about in his damn books."

Josey held a stern expression, not wanting his friend to see the relief he felt. "It's his plan. It won't help him if the men think you're riding out as his nursemaid."

That seemed to mollify the old man. "I don't like the timing," he said. "Some of these poor boys had never even ridden a horse before they were posted here and declared 'mounted infantry.' They're no match for Sioux."

He'd like the plan more if he were riding with us. Josey held back his reaction. "We won't have to chase them if we get there first."

"Then you better hurry."

Josey eased his horse outside the gate to where Carrington was saying some parting words to his wife. Grummond was off to the side and seemed to think no one was looking when he pulled a quick draft from a flask stored in his coat pocket. He shrugged when he noticed Josey and proffered the bottle.

"A nip to ward off the cold, perhaps?"

Josey shook his head and sidled Gray beside Carrington, who took the hint and spurred his horse forward. He called the men to follow. His big, thick-chested bay, the best horse at the fort, sprang ahead as if shot from a cannon. Josey made to follow, but Margaret Carrington took hold of his stirrup. Her thin lips were set in a grim expression. "Look out for him," she said. "See that no harm comes to him."

Josey nodded, but he feared she asked too much of him.

CHAPTER TWENTY-FIVE

Josey loped after the squad, which had bunched up at Big Piney Creek. He arrived in time to see Carrington, on his ass, sputtering in the water.

"His horse slipped on the ice," Grummond said, making no effort to conceal his mirth.

The commander was soaked from head to boot. His wet hair hung limply over his eyes until he swept it back. A private retrieved the hat and brought it to him. Carrington's big bay stood on the opposite side of the creek, shaking itself dry, tossing off beads of water that glinted like ice crystals in the bleak sunlight.

Josey led the others across and waited for Carrington, who sat by the stream pouring water from his boots.

"You have to go back," Josey said. "You'll catch your death out here."

"I can't go back." Carrington spoke in a

fierce whisper, mindful of the troops just out of earshot. "The men already think I'm weak. They'll think I'm a coward if I turn back now."

He pressed his hands against his pants, wringing what water he could from the thick wool. He remounted the big bay. "Better they tell the story of how I pressed on and led them to victory than that I retired after wetting myself."

He tried to smile at his joke, but the creases that bracketed his mouth were rigid with cold. His deep-set eyes looked sadder than usual, as if he'd come to realize that drawing up battle plans isn't anything like designs for a fort.

A sergeant interrupted with a shouted call at seeing three Indians on horseback on the hills ahead. Grummond, who'd ambled ahead with three soldiers, took off in pursuit.

Carrington called after him, but it was no use.

"You should get him," he told Josey. "We can't risk dividing our forces."

"I'm not leaving you," Josey said, mindful of Margaret Carrington's request. "Grummond will return after he fails to catch those scouts."

They pushed on, north to Lodge Trail

Ridge. On the ascent, Carrington warned the soldiers against scattering. Some were such bad riders they strung out at the top of the serrated ridge. Josey circled back to try to keep them on pace, offering words of advice for controlling their mounts as they descended into the valley.

He turned at the sound of gunfire as they drew within sight of the bare cottonwoods along Peno Creek. He eased up alongside Carrington. The commander had out his binoculars. His body shivered so much he couldn't focus. He handed the glasses to Josey.

"I think the sound is coming from near that bend in the creek, but the echo carries so far among these hills I can't be sure."

Josey looked, but the trees and the slope of the ridge obscured his view. Shadowed gullies among the hills made ideal ambush spots, and their steep confines stirred echoes that scattered sounds across the valley.

Carrington said, "It must be Fetterman and the cavalry, right?"

"Could be Grummond." They hadn't seen the lieutenant or the three troopers who'd gone off with him. Josey had expected to find them on the ridge. "If it is Fetterman, we need to get into position."

"Right." Carrington seemed distracted. His features were pinched, his jaw clenched. Probably to stop his teeth from chattering. They'd come too far to turn back. Once the rest of the riders caught up, they pushed on. Josey held back his surefooted mustang to allow the others to match his pace.

The hour was approaching midday, but the morning chill lingered in the shadows of the hills. The cold grew worse as they descended. Josey kept an eye on Carrington, who'd gone quiet, one hand on his reins, the other pinching together the ends of his sodden overcoat at his heart. As they neared the valley, Josey no longer heard gunfire. Was the fight over? Or was it a trick of the echoes?

The valley was a narrow stretch of flat grassland that wound between the hills that overlooked Peno Creek. The brown grass crunched beneath the hooves of their mounts. Bare cottonwoods and dogwoods grew thick along the water's edge. Too thick for Josey's comfort. While Carrington and the others turned west, looking for Fetterman or the Indians who'd attacked the wood wagons, Josey studied the tree line. Brambles and chokecherry shrubs formed an almost impenetrable thicket beneath the trees everywhere but —

There.

Before Josey could shout a warning, dozens of mounted warriors burst from a gap in the thicket, their war whoops and whistles sending a chill through the troops that bit deeper than the mountain winds.

In their panic, a few of the men shot their rifles to no effect. Horses reared at the noise, and three men were thrown. Two horsemen spun their mounts to flee.

Josey leaped down and grabbed their bridles. "If you run, you'll be slaughtered. Get down and fight."

Behind him, Carrington muttered, "They shouldn't be here." His plan in disarray, confusion furrowed his brow and glazed his eyes. Josey helped him dismount.

"Pull yourself together," he said.

Carrington nodded. His training took over, and he ordered the men to form into two outward-facing firing lines. The troopers took what little time they had to reload and aim their muskets.

"Hold your fire," Josey called. "Wait until they're closer."

Josey pulled extra cartridge boxes from his saddlebags and took a position on one knee beside the commander. Carrington remained standing so his orders would be heard. He organized the lines to stagger their shots so that half the troops could reload while the others aimed. The cracking of rifle fire reverberated in Josey's head and deafened him.

The Indians broke off their charge when they realized the soldiers were prepared, veering off into a wide orbit at the last moment. The Indians outnumbered them, so the soldiers were forced into a defensive position. Few of the Sioux carried guns, and while they were more accurate with bows, the steady fire from the soldiers compelled them to maintain a distance at which bow shots posed little threat. They rode with such speed that the soldiers' rifles weren't much of a danger either, though they kept firing anyway. The result was an oddly bloodless melee, more like a sport than the battles Josey had known in the war.

"They're waiting for us to run out of ammunition," he called to Carrington, unsure whether he could be heard above the din.

The commander shuffled among the troops shouting orders. His mouth moved, but Josey couldn't make out the words. Powder smoke hung over them like a pungent mist. The sharp smell enlivened Josey, like breathing smelling salts.

The encircling parade of horsemen moved like the spinning figures on a carousel. The

Indian ponies were painted with colorful stripes and patterns. The warriors, too, had painted their faces. Despite the cold, some were stripped to the waist and bore markings across their chest and arms. They were waiting for an opening, a moment when they could charge to within range and launch a volley of arrows into the soldiers' ranks.

Josey no longer felt cold. The air seemed warmed by the motion of their action. The rifle ready in his hands felt like a part of his arms. He no longer heard the percussive beat of the rifle shots around him. He felt them as a part of his being, a pounding of his heart that sustained him so long as it continued. Josey held his fire. His breath came measured and slow, as if he were reading a book and lingering over every word as the drama intensified.

Carrington placed a hand on his shoulder, and he sensed more shouted commands, but Josey's focus remained on the moving figures. A rider on a pinto turned in from the circle. The wide brown splotch across the horse's chest resembled a shield as the horse leaped forward on a dare ride. The speed of the charge tested Josey's aim. He tasted the powder on the air as he inhaled. The warrior crouched low over the horse's back, slipping to the side of his mount as he drew within range, preparing to fire an arrow. Josey exhaled. Tracked the warrior's pace over the rifle's front sight. Leading him just enough. Waiting for the moment when he showed himself from underneath the pinto's neck. Josey's lungs emptied, his body still.

Now.

With the first shot the warrior slipped from the pinto's back. Josey levered in a second shot. The cartridge casing spun from the rifle in a graceful arc. He fired again before the momentum of the tumbling body stopped.

The warrior's death incited the others. They broke into a sudden charge toward the soldiers. They rode in swerving paths to throw off the soldiers' aim. One warrior with crimson streaks painted on sunken cheeks swung from either side of his horse's neck as he hurtled toward the line. Josey aimed for a spot between the horse's eyes, firing in time with its bobbing head.

The horse collapsed into a heaving pile, hooves akimbo. The rider flew over its head as if launched from a cannon, crashing into the hard ground with a lifeless thud. Josey had already levered in another cartridge, his hand sliding down the edge of the Henry's steel barrel. Heady on the scent of burned powder, he looked for another target.

They were everywhere, all at once. A melee of panicked horses, flying arrows, yipping warriors, and shouting soldiers burning with fear and rage. Carrington held the men in their lines. A well-timed fusillade turned a charge from the warriors. Josey chased off three others who persisted in the advance. Aim. Fire. Lever. Repeat. On spending his last cartridge, he twisted open the Henry's loading sleeve and dropped in new cartridges from the box on his belt. The blue steel warmed his ungloved right hand. Sweat, icy against his skin, ran down his back beneath his woolen shirt.

Josey looked up. Carrington had been watching him. He looked like he was about to say something when sudden movement from the right diverted the attention of both men. Josey raised his rifle, but it was too late. The Indian whose horse he'd shot had recovered, red-painted streaks like blood smears across a face contorted into an unearthly death cry. He raised his stone war club and leaped at Carrington. The startled commander fell back a step. Years of training on parade grounds had forged an instinct that steeled him. He fired his revolver. Once. Twice. Again. The first shot halted the warrior. The second dropped him to his knees, a glazed look passing over his eyes before the third shot knocked him onto his back, dead in the dirt.

Carrington watched the corkscrew of smoke waft from the barrel of his revolver, the crease between his eyebrows deepening as he pondered what he'd just seen. The gunshot echoed in Josey's ears, so he had to read the man's lips.

"I shot him."

A range of emotions competed for expression on Carrington's face. Surprise. Horror. Pride. Josey saw it all in the furrows in the man's forehead and the lines that bracketed his mouth. He stood beside Carrington, a hand on his shoulder as he leaned in and shouted to be sure he was heard.

"Reload."

The Indians withdrew into their containing circle, tempting the soldiers to exhaust their ammunition. The fighting continued for what seemed like hours in the way that only time in battle can telescope. Later, in looking over his spent shells, Josey figured no more than twenty or thirty minutes had passed.

The arrival of Fetterman and the rest of the cavalry drove off the Indians. The captain explained that they had been caught in a similar melee but suffered no casualties. While the new arrivals continued their report to Carrington, Josey took a mental roll call of the troops, their faces and hands smeared with powder stains. One man suffered an arrow wound in the shoulder. His comrades had already cut out its barbed end and were stanching the flow of blood with a field dressing. Another man had his arm in a sling after injuring it in a fall from his horse. Several mounts had been killed or stolen. Josey was about to congratulate Carrington on emerging largely unscathed from what could have been a calamity when he finished his count.

Grummond.

Carrington had already figured it out. Grummond and the three soldiers who'd followed after him were missing.

"Lieutenant Bingham, too," Fetterman said. "His horse bolted when we came under fire. We lost sight of him when the Indians circled us."

They gathered their horses and remounted, some of the infantry who'd lost their mounts having to double up. Fetterman led the way, ascending Lodge Trail Ridge for a better vantage. They heard shots in the direction of the Montana road.

Carrington scanned the horizon with his binoculars, and they heard a shout.

"For God's sake, come down here quick."

Looking to the road, Josey saw a small Indian raiding party pursuing Grummond and two soldiers. They pushed their horses as hard as they could, Grummond jabbing the blunt end of his saber into his horse's flanks to urge it to greater effort. Fetterman formed a firing line on the hillside, and a single fusillade ended the pursuit.

The riders reached the safety of the ridge, and the next minutes were a confusion of shouted questions until Carrington could bring some order. Grummond reported that he and his group had linked up with Bingham in pursuit of the fleeing Indians. Grummond and Bingham pulled ahead of the others but found themselves surrounded by a much larger war party. With ammunition exhausted, the officers used their sabers to cut a path through the Indians while the enlisted men lay a covering fire.

The soldiers tried to make a stand on the hill as the other groups had done, but their numbers were too few. The Indians closed in. Two men and a horse were wounded before Grummond ordered the soldiers to remount and attempt another break through the Indian lines. Bingham and Sergeant

Bowers didn't make it. Grummond saw them pulled from their horses by the Indians who'd surrounded them. Fetterman led a column of cavalry in search of the bodies. They found Bingham and Bowers a little east of the Montana road, their bodies riddled with dozens of arrows.

It was a quiet ride back to the fort, at least at the front of the column. Carrington appeared preoccupied, whether with questions of how his plan disintegrated or reflections on the man he'd killed, Josey couldn't tell. He left him to it, falling back to the rear, where Grummond retold the tale to every trooper within earshot.

"Old Ichabod is either a fool or a coward to allow his men to be cut to pieces without offering help," he concluded.

Josey maneuvered his horse to block Grummond's path. The men around him stopped to watch.

"You broke ranks," Josey said, pointing his index finger toward the larger man's face. "Those men are dead because of you."

A stunned silence fell upon the troopers as Grummond collected himself. When he did, his voice came as a roar.

"How dare you speak to me like that? You're not even commissioned."

"I don't need to be an officer to know you

308

led those men into an ambush. The only question is whether it's because you're a fool or a drunk."

The other horsemen fell away as Grummond's free hand dropped to his waist where his Colt was holstered. Josey was ready, his fingers already tapping a beat on the grip of his revolver.

"Do it," he said. "The way I figure it, one more corpse today will save lives tomorrow."

Josey waited. Grummond's hooded lids gave the man a sleepy look most times, but his eyes were wide open now, darting about the crowd who had stopped to watch. He swallowed with some difficulty. The corner of his lips twisted into a semblance of a grin. He lifted his arm, his fingers splayed to display an empty palm.

"I fear we will have to reschedule our performance," he said to the gathered men. "I spent my last bullet on the Indians."

He made it sound like a jape, but the murderous look in his eyes convinced Josey he'd better not ride with his back to the man next time his gun was loaded.

CHAPTER TWENTY-SIX

Annabelle woke early the morning of the season's last buffalo hunt, excitement flittering in her breast like a hummingbird and making sleep impossible. Crazy Horse was already awake. She lay still, feigning sleep, fearing her face would betray her intentions.

She listened as he stirred the fire so the inside of the tepee would be warm when Old Grandmother awoke. After a month, she knew his sounds well enough to picture his actions with her eyes closed. She felt a pang on realizing she knew his morning noises better than she knew Josey's.

Not much longer now. When she was with Josey again, she vowed to savor even mundane moments such as these.

Crazy Horse shuffled around the narrow confines of the tent. He leaned over the old woman to kiss her lined forehead before leaving. A puff of cold air stole into the room after he raised the flap and stepped into the pre-dawn darkness.

Annabelle sprang from her bed furs, more from anxiousness than hurry. She couldn't leave until the men departed on this final opportunity to store meat for the winter. All warriors were going, and even many of the women, who were responsible for butchering the fresh kills. Annabelle would slip away from the village as if fetching firewood, and no one would suspect a thing until nightfall.

Then it would be up to John Hutchins. He had departed the Indian camp two days earlier so he wouldn't be implicated in her escape. He planned to camp downstream from the village where he would be easy to find. Then he would lead Annabelle past Indian scouts to the fort.

Worry gnawed at her, despite the simplicity of the plan. What if she couldn't find Hutchins? What if he betrayed her? The escape had been his idea, yet it left her uneasy to put her trust in a young man she hardly knew.

She took what precautions she could. Sorting through the things she kept in a roll beneath her furs, she found a knife they used for carving meat. It wouldn't be much good in a fight, but it was better than nothing. She set it aside with her buffalo robe and the riding clothes she would change into after she cleared the village.

She took out the formal dress she had packed from Virginia City and turned it inside out before rolling it tight. Through the exposed lining of the dress, her hand clasped the hard object within the pocket, still surprised it had escaped the warriors' attentions. *I might yet have need for this.*

Hearing the camp stir, she left the tepee to fetch water. She couldn't abandon Old Grandmother without fresh water. She shivered, glad for the chill, the sound of the hunters outside the village at the horse corral carrying clear on the cold air. Closing her eyes, she willed them to be gone already. She had to control her own pace so as not to draw attention.

As she trudged back from the stream, the sounds of so many horses leaving in unison rolled over the camp like thunder between the hills. She smiled. The bucket no longer felt heavy, and there was a lightness in her step she hadn't known since before injuring her ankle.

She pictured Josey's face on her return. Even his impassive countenance would crack with the joy of their reunion. She imagined herself tight in his embrace. Her body was different now, and she wondered if he would notice. He would notice her breasts, which were growing so large she expected they would spill out of any of her old dresses. Her belly wasn't showing much, but she was confident it would soon. It would be good to be checked by the fort surgeon.

Thoughts of homecoming and a healthy baby so preoccupied her, Annabelle almost didn't notice the man sitting alone beside a fire outside a tepee. She wouldn't have seen him at all but for the wisps of smoke that rose from the low-burning fire. She couldn't see his face in the dim light, but she knew him from the way his eyes, glowing red in the reflected embers, followed her as she walked.

Pierce.

She looked away and increased her pace, water sloshing from the bucket in her haste. *Why hadn't he left with the other hunters?* The answer that came to mind chilled her more than the morning air.

Annabelle pushed the thought from her head as she ducked into her tepee, wishing Indians lived in houses with doors that could be locked. Pierce — it was hard for her to think of him as Climbing Bear — hadn't bothered her since her arrival in the camp. A full moon had passed since then.

313

Why now? Again, the answer was obvious.

She swallowed back her fear. Old Grandmother had woken. Annabelle spoke with her in soothing tones, finding comfort in the routine of speech even as her mind whirled. The old woman stared into the fire, giving no sign that she heard a word Annabelle said, much less understood any of it.

Annabelle dared not go to the tepee's opening and look for Pierce. She knew he would be watching. Seeing her might encourage him. She couldn't wait him out, either. Every hour she delayed left less time to get far enough away with John Hutchins that no one could catch them.

She went to her bedroll and took up the carving knife. If she cut a slit in the backside of the tepee, she might slip away before Pierce knew what she was doing. She needed to act soon. If he came and discovered her gone, he would search for her, maybe raise an alarm. Hutchins had promised to have a horse for her, but she had to flee the camp on foot. It would be easy for Pierce to run her down.

On her knees, knife in hand, she hesitated as she faced the backside of the tepee. There would be no turning back once she made the cut. She closed her eyes and took a deep breath when a burst of cold air enveloped

314

her. She opened her eyes with a start, saw a flash of light in the room, as if someone had lit a candle, and then it was gone. The cold air settled around her, stealing her breath. She willed her heart to be still, and she listened.

For a moment she heard nothing, a silence as heavy as a deep snowfall. Then she heard his breath, deep and ragged behind her. She gripped the knife in her palm as she turned to face him.

"You shouldn't be here." She fought to control the tremor in her voice, feeling stupid for speaking to a man whose only knowledge of English were vulgarities.

He was bare-chested, having removed his robe, and wore only deerskin leggings. He spoke to her as he approached. *He's telling me there's no one to hear my screams.* She didn't need to understand the language to realize he had planned for this morning as carefully as she had.

She started to rise, but he held her in place with one powerful hand on her shoulder. He spoke again, his voice low and menacing so that she understood: how much pain he inflicted would be her decision as well as his. Annabelle's eyes found Old Grandmother, but she stared into the fire as if unaware of the man's presence.

There was no one to help her.

Pierce jerked her hair, braided Indian style, pulling her head back as if to expose her throat to his knife. She had no doubt he intended to murder her, but it would not come so quickly or painlessly. He had waited too long for this.

She brought up her knife, seeking to plunge it somewhere, anywhere. He laughed at the futile gesture, catching her hand and twisting her wrist until she dropped the knife with a yelp of pain.

Jerking her hair again, he pulled her down and clambered on top of her, his weight pinning her to the ground. He gripped the collar of her cotton gown and tore it open, pausing a moment and smiling at her nakedness. It was not lust that drove him, she realized, but the pain and fear he inflicted. He took her knife, showing it to her before he cut away the rest of her gown, leaving her open to him.

She slapped at him, tried to scratch at his eyes. He caught her hands, pinned them over her head, her fingers splayed against the slick fabric of the gown she'd packed earlier. She leaned forward, tried to bite any part of him she could reach. He pounded his forehead against hers, knocking her back, dazed. Holding her legs together, she resisted him as the lower half of his body ground against her, but she was no match for his strength.

He thrust against her again and again, the stench of his sweat choking her breath. He gripped her wrists with one hand, so that he could use the other to loosen his leggings and free himself. As he tugged at his pants, she twisted against him, hoping, somehow, to get out from under him, to get away, to wake from this nightmare.

His grip on her hands loosened. Her fingers felt the bundle of things she had rolled earlier, the riding clothes, and the dress that had so baffled the Indians who first seized it, with its rolls of heavy fabric, lace collar and secret pocket.

With a final grunt, Pierce kicked free his leggings. He wrenched her legs apart and slid forward.

The look of triumph on his face fell away as Annabelle used the moment to break his grip on her hands just long enough to bring her right hand up and press it to his throat — the snub nose of her derringer pistol digging against the soft skin.

"I suppose you've never seen a gun so small." Her voice trembled, and her body shook, but the gun remained in place. "Believe me, it's big enough at this range."

She held the gun in place with all her strength, but she was no match for the warrior. She felt his hand sliding beneath her, reaching for his knife. She twisted the barrel deeper into his throat and pulled back the hammer.

Hearing the click, he stopped. His eyes grew wide, not with fear but with a hatred that burned with the intensity of the sun. Annabelle returned the look in equal measure.

"What is it you Indians say? Better to die in battle than as an old man in bed?" His body was so tense she could see his heart pulse beneath the skin of his neck. She positioned the gun there. "I wonder what they will say about you."

Annabelle pulled the trigger.

CHAPTER TWENTY-SEVEN

Still angry over the white woman's escape, Light Hair rode alone into the hills. He had returned late to his lodge from the buffalo hunt. He went first among the other tepees, sharing his spoils with those who had no warrior to ride in the hunt. Light Hair had been pleased with his new buffalo-hunt horse, and it left him feeling more generous than usual. His plan to attack the fort left him little need to stock meat for winter.

Everything changed on his discovery of Climbing Bear's corpse. Old Grandmother had built up the fire and started a soup, but she had ignored the body. Light Hair needed little imagination to figure what had happened, and he was so angry to see his plans thwarted he did not mourn the Cheyenne warrior's death.

It was too late to mount a search that night. He picked up the woman's trail the next day but lost it in the stream. She had been gone too long. For a day, he clung to the hope that she might intend to return, that she had gone into hiding after killing Climbing Bear. For two more days, he scouted the trails to the fort, but he found no sign of her. He Dog convinced him she had gotten lost in the woods, that a hunting party would one day find her body after she had starved or been killed by wolves.

The ride into the hills cleared Light Hair's mind. He rode toward the mountains. Green and dark at their base, the peaks gleamed white in the sun. Light Hair had hoped a long ride might inspire a new vision for defeating the soldiers, but instead his thoughts turned to Spotted Tail. The old chief had sought him out the day after the meeting in Red Cloud's lodge before heading back to Laramie, where his band of followers lived off handouts at the fort. Though no older than Red Cloud, Spotted Tail resembled a man diminished by age in Light Hair's eyes.

Spotted Tail placed his hands on Light Hair's shoulders, forcing the younger man to face him. "You have become the man I always knew you would be. You bring honor to your father's name."

Light Hair thanked his uncle. He tried to look away, but there was nowhere to turn his gaze.

"I, too, killed many *wasicu* when I was your age, but it was like swatting locusts to halt a swarm. When I went to their prison, it was not because I feared death. I feared watching my children killed. Hearing your words last night, I wonder if I was wrong."

Spotted Tail lowered his hands and began to walk. Light Hair fell into step beside him.

"Fear has no place in a young man's heart. The *wasicu* made me an old man before my time. I see that. It is only now that my children are grown that my vision is clear enough to see the true nature of the *wasicu* threat."

Light Hair felt his anger toward the old man melt away. He tried to imagine his life if he had married Black Buffalo Woman and had children. Would he choose living with the *wasicu* over watching the soldiers murder his children? "Tell me, uncle."

"The *wasicu* hate our people. They think us no better than animals. Their deepest desire is to make us like them."

"I do not understand. If they hate us —"

"They wish to be gods." An urgency overtook Spotted Tail's voice, and when he turned, Light Hair saw a wildness in his eyes that hinted at madness. "They believe their god created them in his image. They would shape us in their image to satisfy a desire to be like their god."

Light Hair shook his head. He had thought his uncle weak, but that had been better than mad.

"Listen to me." Spotted Tail took Light Hair's arms in hands that had once drawn the biggest bow Light Hair had ever seen. "You will fight the white soldiers. You may even win. But they will come back in ever greater numbers, and you will have to fight them again. And again. Every time you win, you lose, because the only way to defeat them is to become like them. If the people become like the white man, it will be like we never existed. That is what the *wasicu* want. I swear it."

Light Hair shook himself free. He should have tried harder to avoid the old man. He invented an excuse for leaving, still scoffing at the frightened chief's words. What danger was there that he would become like a white man? Would he live in a fort? Would he dig in the dirt for his food? Light Hair would never become like the *wasicu,* and he would not watch that happen to his people, either.

"The white woman is gone, so now you come to me?"

Black Buffalo woman stepped into a small

clearing in the woods. It was the middle of the afternoon, and they were far enough from the village to expect not to be disturbed. Light Hair had seen her at the lodge where women went during the time of their moon blood. One glance was all it took. It was all she had ever needed.

She made him wait. She always made him wait. He challenged her about it once. She could have said it was hard for her to steal away from a husband and three children or from the other women who seemed to gather at the lodge at the same time of the moon. She could have said she was being careful. He might have believed her.

Instead, she said the waiting whetted his appetite for her. He told her his appetite was sharp enough. Their time together was so rare and fleeting, he could never be sated. She said that was why he still waited, ten years since he fell in love with her.

The sun shone, but it was low in the sky and cast long shadows among the trees. Black Buffalo Woman moved between dark and light, and he could not read her expression to know if she was teasing him about the white woman's escape. She wore a fringed deerskin dress that hung below her knees. Her dresses were taut through the hips and across the chest, more so than when she was a girl. The tanned hide pulled against her body as she moved in a way that reminded him why he had come.

"I came to you even while she was still here," he reminded her.

She stopped where the light fell across her plaited hair so that it glistened. "She was not enough for you?"

"I never had her. You know this."

The twist in her smile betrayed her knowledge. She liked hearing him say it.

She came to him, seeming to glide across the forest floor without stirring the dried pine needles and leaves so that he was unaware of her steps. All he saw were her eyes, dark as caves, looming large enough to envelop him. She stopped, tilting her head toward him, and waited.

He never made her wait long. His mouth covered hers with a hunger he would have denied until that glance by the lodge. His hands were everywhere at once over the familiar angles of her lithe body. She was another man's wife, but in Light Hair's grasp she was still the girl of fifteen winters he had first tasted in a wooded clearing away from the village just like this one.

He would have swallowed her whole. He would have crushed her body to his until they were a single being. Breathing her in dizzied him, and his knees trembled. Her knowing fingers traced the slope of his hips and reached beneath his breechclout. He broke their kiss with a gasp.

It had been like this from their first time when, still a boy, he had been uncertain of what to do once he grasped her. She had known. She always knew. He suspected that was what she liked.

There was no mystery to his lust. For her, it was another matter, he suspected. In her hands, the fierce warrior Crazy Horse trembled. The noble Shirt Wearer, so dedicated, so disciplined, became her plaything. Hers alone. The greater his standing among the people grew, the more she enjoyed her control of him. It was no secret in the village. They were discreet enough to spare her husband's pride, but the women in the lodge knew she did not disappear so long merely to wash away her moon blood in the river.

Women gave themselves to their husbands. They were slaves in a man's lodge — and among his bed robes when he desired it. Black Buffalo Woman was a good mother, a good wife in every other way, but in her hands the great Crazy Horse bowed to her whims. Her power over him, Light Hair understood, was as intoxicating as his desire for her.

With a few frenzied movements, she brought him to a precipice. He threw his head back, groaning with pain and delight. She could have felled him with a finger. He lay back, catching his breath, the moment abating, extending his desire.

He was naked below the waist and peeled off his shirt. He gestured for her to do the same, but she demurred. She lifted her skirts and straddled him, and he thought no more of what she wore.

Light Hair had expected to marry Black Buffalo Woman. He had courted her at her father's lodge like many other young men. He would have known himself to be her favorite even if not for their trysts in the woods. Though he did not come from a distinguished family and was not wealthy, he was a young man with a growing reputation as a warrior.

When Red Cloud, Black Buffalo Woman's uncle, announced plans to lead a raid against the Crow, Light Hair determined to capture enough horses to press his suit with Black Buffalo Woman's father. All the young warriors joined the raid, but No Water turned back, complaining of a toothache. When Light Hair returned to the village, he found that No Water had married Black Buffalo Woman in his absence. Light Hair left to live with another tribe, thinking never to return.

But he did return.

Their bodies moved together like a ritual dance. Light Hair watched Black Buffalo Woman's face as she took her pleasure. It was as if her mind left her body to play among the spirits. Black Buffalo Woman was the only person to still call him by his boyhood name. Light Hair liked it best when she used it in these moments. He smiled with satisfaction — and anticipation, knowing she would not neglect his pleasure. His mind shut off every thought as he gave his body over to her.

Afterwards, she lay beside him, her head on his chest and her legs twined with his. The warmth of her body stayed the chill of the shadows that swallowed them. He smelled rain on the air and suspected a freeze would follow.

Is this our last languid day in the sun?

Her fingers traced the outline of the muscles in his chest. "I am glad the white woman is gone."

He studied her. She never confessed to jealousy.

"I did not intend to keep her."

Her brows knitted the way they did whenever he said something foolish or asked her to leave her husband. "They would have killed you when you took her back."

"Perhaps. But Red Cloud and the other chiefs would have destroyed the fort."

"And then what?"

He did not understand the question.

"The *wasicu* would build another," she said. "They would bring a bigger army."

"You sound like Spotted Tail."

He did not like the sharp tone in his voice. He had so little time with Black Buffalo Woman, he did not want to squander it arguing. His hand moved to a place she liked, but she pushed it away.

"What will you do now?"

"Find another way."

"Another way to get yourself killed?"

"It is better —"

She stilled him with a hand over his lips. "I have heard these words. Who is made better by a young warrior's death? Is it better for his children to be without a father? Is it better for his wife to be a widow, left to go hungry and poorly dressed?"

"A widow remarries."

"Yes, she will be the second or third wife to another man, a slave to his first wife. Is she better for her husband's death?"

Black Buffalo Woman would leave soon, and he did not wish for hard words to linger between them. He kissed her fingers. Calloused and hard, they were the hands of a woman who knew hard work.

"The *wasicu* leave us no choice. We must fight to keep our lands."

"You will never force them to leave, sweet Light Hair." Black Buffalo Woman softened her words with kisses that followed the line of his jaw to his ear. She nuzzled against him. "You must make them *want* to leave."

An idea clicked in Light Hair's mind, but before he could consider it he became aware of Black Buffalo Woman's hand. The fingers had grown rough with years, but they moved with a practiced surety that left him no room for any other thought.

The light had risen from the ground and was climbing into the trees when Black Buffalo Woman rose with the same girlish grace he remembered from their first time. She rearranged her skirts with fastidious detail.

From her expression, he saw she was already gone from him, her mind on a list of tasks she must accomplish before the day was gone. Light Hair wondered where he fell among those tasks. If No Water was her traveling horse, was he her warhorse, fierce, yet obedient? Light Hair swallowed back the bitterness he felt every time she left him.

Contented with her appearance, Black Buffalo Woman planted a kiss on his forehead and played her fingers through the curls on his head. It looked like she might say something for a moment, but she forced a smile to her lips and turned away without a word.

Light Hair watched her slip away into the trees. He lay back under the crushing weight of his shame. It was always the same after she left. He tried to placate his mind with memories of their bodies together, but the images no longer aroused him. He thought more clearly in her absence. He saw their actions for the betrayal they were. To No Water, her husband, and to the people who had made him a Shirt Wearer. They held him to be a man of virtue and strength, but here was only selfishness and weakness.

He had sought to free himself of her in his battle plan, to redeem himself with a penance that would cleanse his conscience. The white woman's escape had robbed him of that. His friends mocked Light Hair for having no sense of humor, yet he recognized the amusement others would take in his predicament. The great Crazy Horse, a warrior no man could stand against, turned powerless by a pair of women.

The thought reminded him of the things Black Buffalo Woman and Spotted Tail said. The *wasicu* were dismissive of the people, thinking them no better than beasts. Light Hair knew they were wrong, but in his anger he neglected to see what truths the statement revealed. The people could not write their words. They did not live in stone houses. They could not make things the *wasicu* valued. Of course, the *wasicu* perceived them as little better than animals.

Light Hair had been planning for battle with the pride of a warrior when he might have used the guile of a prairie dog. He did not have to destroy the fort to kill the white soldiers. He merely had to draw them away from their burrow. *Let them think of us as mindless beasts.* Like a bird that feigns a broken wing to lead a predator from its nest, there was advantage in perceived weakness. Light Hair needed the vision to see how to make that work.

CHAPTER TWENTY-EIGHT

Henry Carrington sat at the desk in the commander's headquarters and pinched the bridge of his nose as if warding off a headache. The skin beneath his eyes, dark as bruises, sagged in deep crescents. He looked thinner than usual to Josey. A plate of food delivered by his wife for his midday dinner sat untouched on the corner of his desk.

Alone with Carrington for the first time since the ill-fated attack, Josey didn't know why he'd been summoned. Carrington had shut down the wood trains while they buried their dead, and there had been no sight of Indians in two days since.

Josey hoped the summons meant there was some news of Annabelle. He had no idea how long it should take the half-breed trader to arrange a ransom, only that it seemed too long. Had Hutchins misled them? Had Crazy Horse changed his mind about a ransom? Had some harm befallen

Annabelle? The nagging doubts plagued Josey's mind, making him wish he'd stayed near the village so that he could be there whenever Annabelle was released. Anything seemed preferable to this uncertainty.

Carrington seemed to have other things on his mind.

"I've ordered a doubling of the guards for the wood trains when they resume tomorrow," he said, staring at his clasped hands. "I've also issued orders to keep the serviceable horses we have left saddled and ready to sally from dawn to dark. If there's another attack on the wood train, we'll be ready, but I won't order any more attacks until we see the promised reinforcements, horses, and supplies from Fort Laramie."

Josey wasn't sure why the commander shared his plans with him. "That seems prudent, sir."

"You don't think we're capable of defeating the Sioux in the field." The commander's gaze alternated from the papers on his desk to the wall behind Josey.

"It's not my place to say."

Carrington's thin-boned hands washed each other, the dry skin of his palms making a scratching sound. "I'd heard you were too plain-spoken to last as an officer in this army. It seems you've honed your diplomatic skills since then. But what I require from you now is candor."

Josey stared at Carrington until the commander met his eyes. "Grummond is a threat to you and every man under his command."

"Grummond?"

"He disobeyed your orders and rode into an Indian ambush that cost the lives of Lieutenant Bingham and Sergeant Bowers. He's done it before. He will do it again. You must know this."

"I'm familiar with his record," Carrington said.

Josey only knew stories he'd heard during the war, and he'd seen enough here to convince him the camp gossip had been true. They said Grummond had been drunk in battle when he ordered a suicidal charge. That the men under his command were saved because one was clever enough to fire a few shots near Grummond, convincing him they were already under attack.

"Grummond was court martialed and punished for his actions," Carrington continued. "When he re-enlisted after the war, he lost his brevet rank of lieutenant colonel, and the army sent him here. With so few officers at my command, I need to put every one of them to use. I spoke with him. He knows his mistake. If some of the officers are overeager to make their mark, it is because there is no other way to climb through the ranks except by proving themselves in combat. I think the men appreciate his valor."

"It's not valor Grummond finds at the bottom of those bottles. He is a bully and a coward. Battle terrifies him."

Carrington looked up from his papers at that. "How do you explain his charging after the Indians?"

"The liquor helps," Josey said. "Plus, the only thing that terrifies a bully more than a fight is the notion that he'll be found out as a coward."

Carrington stepped away from his desk to look out the window of his office at the parade ground where Fetterman led the men in a training exercise. With his back to Josey he said, "You think that's why Grummond despises you so?"

"I think he's uneasy seeing anyone familiar with his past."

"Your reputation can be intimidating to anyone plagued with doubts as to their own abilities." Carrington turned to look back at Josey.

"Are we still speaking of Grummond?"

A twist at the corner of Carrington's

mouth suggested a smile, but it was a rueful expression. "You know my experience in the field is limited."

Josey kept his face blank.

"I thought I was prepared for it. I thought it would be exhilarating." Carrington forced a sound that would have been called a chuckle under other circumstances. "It was not what I expected."

Josey recalled his first taste of battle. He'd been so frightened, so overwhelmed by every sensation that he forgot to fire his weapon. He said nothing, doubting that Carrington would have heard him anyway. The commander returned his gaze to the parade grounds and the men marching in formation.

"That Indian would have killed me. I know that. I'm glad I shot him. I'm glad the Indians suffered worse losses than we did, to punish them for what happened to Bingham and Bowers. That's what I told myself as I wrote letters to their families. But when sleep eludes me, I can't help but wonder about the man I killed. A savage, I know, but curiosity plagues me. Did he have a family? A squaw, perhaps? Children? Who told them of his death?"

Listening to Carrington, Josey recalled the two Indians he killed in the woods while searching for Annabelle. *Murdered.* That was the word for what he'd done. Those deaths were different than any he'd caused during the war, and yet through his haze of anger he'd failed to recognize the difference in the moment.

Carrington turned back from the window. "Not every man is as suited to combat as others. That doesn't mean he isn't a good soldier."

The commander's words hadn't been formed like a question, but Carrington looked at him as if he expected some confirmation. Josey formulated a response as he thought back to a time when he'd been as troubled as Carrington by the men he had killed.

The first time Josey shot at a man he'd been so terrified there was no time for remorse. Later, he justified the deaths as a consequence of war. If men were going to shoot at him, they accepted the risks when Josey fired back, no different than a man who sits down to a game of poker and risks everything he has. And in this game, it *was* everything. By the end of the war, meting out death was a matter of survival. Kill to live. Dead men couldn't come back the next day and kill you.

In the light of day he could justify those

deaths as the rotten fruits of war. Even in his troubled dreams, he imagined another man responsible, like watching an actor on a stage. In the nights since he'd killed those trussed-up Indians, Josey found no escape from his culpability. His hands were red with their blood, and he stood alone on the stage. He had feared the Indians, if freed, might expose the group's intention to rescue Annabelle. And so he had killed them. Without a second thought. Without a moment to ponder other options. Without consulting the others. He had dispensed death as if he alone possessed the power to do so.

During the war, Josey had felt he was God's instrument. He carried out His will. And he cursed the god he'd worshiped as a child for His bloodlust. But what if it hadn't been God's bloodlust? *What if it had been mine all along?*

The thought left Josey quaking when he awoke from his nightmares. He had wanted to believe his guilt checked his worst impulses, yet when the time came it was no match for his anger. What did that make him? What kind of father would he be if he held life in so little regard?

He felt like a man come to a fork in a path. One choice led into the mountains, where sunlight sparkled off a quartz rock face. The other descended into a shaded wood. Josey felt like he'd taken the second path, and now night had come, and with it darkness. As much as Josey wished he'd taken the sunny path, he didn't know how to get back to it.

Before Josey could respond, they were interrupted by a courier. Josey recognized the round-faced cavalryman, though he didn't know the private's name. He saluted Carrington but turned to Josey as he delivered a message that riders had arrived at the fort. Josey's thoughts went to the half-breed trader.

"Do they bring news of a ransom offer?"

The private couldn't restrain a smile.

"Better."

Josey was out the door without hearing another word.

He found Annabelle at the post commander's quarters. Margaret Carrington greeted him at the door but wouldn't let him in, explaining that Annabelle was with Doctor Hines.

"Is she all right?"

"She is unharmed." Margaret Carrington spoke as if measuring her words before pouring them out. "The doctor believes her body will recover."

"The baby?"

A smile compressed her thin lips. "He's still examining her, but, yes, he believes the baby is well."

"I need to see her, to let her know I am here."

"She knows you're here, Josef. Give her time. Her captivity couldn't have been easy. The journey from the camp was difficult, too. An Indian trader brought her. They had to avoid being seen by scouts and raiding parties."

John Hutchins. Something must have changed his plans to seek her ransom. Josey wondered about it, but it was unimportant next to his concern for Annabelle.

"Please, Mrs. Carrington. If I could see her for a moment —"

Margaret Carrington placed a fine-boned hand on his arm.

"Give her time, Josef. She needs rest and opportunity to set her mind right. Something must have happened during her escape. She won't talk about it. She was so afraid the Indians might catch them for so long, I think she still fears they might sweep down from Lodge Trail Ridge any moment to retake her. Come back tonight. She may be ready for visitors then."

Josey resisted the impulse to push past the woman and burst in to see Annabelle. *Visitors?* Was that all he was? Seeing him was what Annabelle needed to feel safe again. If Annabelle knew he was here, she would want to see him.

Wouldn't she?

That flicker of doubt sent him away from Margaret Carrington's door. *Is it possible Annabelle doesn't want to see me?* Josey trudged along the mowed path from the commander's quarters to the flagpole at the center of the parade grounds. The sun hung low in the sky, throwing deep shadows across the fort. Despite plummeting temperatures, he wanted to stay near in case Annabelle called for him.

The soldiers were gathering for evening dress parade. A bandstand stood at the foot of the flagpole. Josey sat there with a view of the commander's quarters. The Colonel and Lord Byron found him, long after Carrington had completed the evening inspection while the band played. It was dark, and another freeze was coming, yet Josey remained at his vigil.

"Mrs. Carrington sent us," the Colonel said. "Annabelle is ready."

CHAPTER TWENTY-NINE

Annabelle wore a simple cotton dress with a high collar that reached nearly to her chin. She had pulled back and parted her dark hair instead of letting it fall loose the way Josey liked it. Her cheeks were thin, but there was a rosy glow to them that spoke to good health. Her eyes cast about the parlor in the Carringtons' home as if seeking something. Margaret Carrington sat in a chair beside the hearth, leaving Annabelle to face her male visitors.

She went first to Byron and embraced him, having to stretch onto her toes to put her arms around the big man's neck. Byron was so taken by surprise he looked alarmed.

"I would not be here today without you," Annabelle said before placing a kiss on his cheek. When she stepped back, Josey would have sworn Byron blushed.

Annabelle turned next to the Colonel.

"Dear Marlowe, I feared I might never see

you again." She hugged and kissed him as well, forestalling any objections from the old man regarding the use of his given name.

Finally, she came to Josey. She said nothing as he folded her to his breast and held her as if he feared her being wrested from him. He shook with joy to hold her again, and he didn't trust his voice. He just wanted to breathe her in, a heady scent of soap and lavender and something else he'd never known except when close to Annabelle.

"Let the girl breathe, Josef," Margaret Carrington said, setting off an explosion of laughter.

He released Annabelle enough to look into her eyes, but she looked away. His hands moved from her waist to cover her stomach. There was a fullness to her belly, but no sign that he could see that any being could be in there.

"The baby . . . is fine?"

She nodded. "It's still just a wee thing. The doctor says I have another six months."

"June." He forced a smile, wishing she'd return the expression. "It's a good month."

She spoke so only he could hear. "You told me once you didn't want children."

Anxious to prompt a reaction from her, Josey recalled Annabelle's love of poetry.

343

" 'When I said I should die a bachelor, I did not think I should live till I were married.' "

"Shakespeare." Annabelle's lips stretched into a smile, but the expression did not reach her eyes. " 'The world must be populated.' "

The Carringtons lived in a comfortable home that would not have been out of place back in the states. There were wood floors instead of the oilcloth and sewn burlap sacks Josey had seen in other houses at the fort. The chairs were cushioned. A brightly colored quilt hung on one wall, and a large Franklin stove added a pleasant scent of burning pine.

Margaret Carrington served coffee and gingersnaps, yet despite the convivial circumstances, Josey felt an underlying tension, like the pull of an unseen river current. He attributed it to his impatience to be alone with Annabelle, to hold her with no eyes upon them and talk to her where no ears could overhear.

Annabelle told the story of her escape, how she used the distraction of the last buffalo hunt to slip away from the village. She spoke in a monotone, the way a student might recite lines of a memorized poem she didn't understand. Her eyes stared, unfocused, at a spot on the far wall where no face could distract her. To Josey, the account sounded incomplete, and he wondered at what she left out in her retelling. He knew better than to ask.

She finished by explaining how John Hutchins had led her to the fort, taking a circuitous route to avoid Sioux scouts. Afterwards, a silence settled over the room, like cold air after a fire has gone out.

Josey spoke first. "Where is Hutchins? I want to thank him."

"He stayed only long enough to get provisions for the journey to Fort Laramie," Margaret Carrington said. "Henry offered to reward him for his service with a position here, but he declined."

"He's convinced the Sioux intend to assault the fort," Annabelle said, still staring at the far wall.

"But without the ruse of your ransom, there's no way the Indians could breach the walls," the Colonel said. "Now that you're gone, they must know we'll be prepared for them."

Josey pictured the village Annabelle had described.

"With so many lodges, Red Cloud might have as many as two, three thousand warriors. That would be enough to overwhelm any defenses."

"Don't frighten the women, Josey." The Colonel smiled awkwardly in Margaret Carrington's direction. "We've never seen more than a couple hundred of the savages."

"They're not savages." From Annabelle's vacant stare, Josey had thought she wasn't listening. "They have reasons for what they do. I can't pretend to understand them, but they are not wicked by nature. No more wicked than any other people."

The only sound in the room was the hiss and popping of burning wood in the fireplace. Annabelle clasped her hands in her lap while she rocked in the sort of chair mothers use to soothe newborns. It warmed Josey to imagine Annabelle nursing a child in such a chair, but her face revealed nothing of that promised joy. He'd been so intent on her safety, he'd put from his mind the coolness that hung between them on their parting.

"I wish we could pack up and leave this fort," Annabelle said, so softly it wasn't clear she meant the words for anyone else. "We don't need to be here. There are other routes to Montana. Soon there will even be a railroad. We should leave this land to the Indians the way it's always been."

"Darlin', even if we could leave now, you know the army won't agree to that," the Colonel said.

Annabelle fell quiet. The moisture in the wood popped and sizzled. Margaret Carrington cleared her throat and stood.

"I had better go fetch my boys. They're probably driving their father to distraction."

The Colonel and Byron made excuses to leave as well. Annabelle remained seated while Josey watched her.

Josey followed Annabelle into a rear bedroom in the Carrington home. From the two small beds and the toys on a table by the window, he figured Margaret Carrington's two young sons slept there.

Annabelle sat on the edge of one of the beds beside a pile of clothes and necessities the other women at the fort had gathered for her. The tension he'd noticed in her earlier was even stronger now. She turned to face him with an expression he didn't recognize.

"You left me."

Josey blinked as if smacked. "I didn't leave you."

Her voice cut as cold as the wind off the Bighorns. "You were gone. I remained. What do you call it?"

"I came to get the Colonel."

She spoke as if she didn't hear him. "Were you going to come back?"

"Of course."

"When?"

"In the spring." He picked at a splinter on the bedpost. "After the snows passed and the wagon trains came. It would be safer then."

"You weren't so concerned about safety when you left me."

"I didn't leave —" *What was the point?* He had left her. The Colonel had given him a good excuse, but it wasn't the reason he left. Not the only reason.

Maybe Margaret Carrington was right when she said every man had doubts at the prospect of marriage. Every woman, too, she had said. Josey had never doubted his love for Annabelle, though he wondered sometimes how she could love in equal measure. He felt in the pit of his stomach that one day she would look at him with fresh eyes and see him for what he was. How fast would she run away then? If Margaret Carrington was right, he left Annabelle despite the pain it caused him so that he could avoid the hurt of watching her leave him forever. *How mad is that?*

"You're safer without me." He must have

mumbled the words.

"What?"

"I'm a lodestone for trouble, Annabelle. People die wherever I go."

"So you left me to keep me safe?"

This isn't going well. Annabelle seemed to be getting angrier the more Josey talked.

She said, "You expect me to believe that?"

"I couldn't live with myself if anything happened to you."

"How well did that work?"

"If you had stayed in Virginia City —"

Josey had thought she was angry before, but her heated interruption showed her temper at a level he'd never seen.

"What am I? Some kind of doll you can leave on a shelf when you don't feel like playing? Use me for your pleasure and cast me aside when you're done?"

"No. No. That's not true." He reached for her, wanting to wrap her in his arms and show her how much she meant to him, but she slapped his arms away.

"Just go." Her eyes were rimmed red and her voice trembled.

He reached to her again.

"Leave me." Her voice was hard as slate. "I don't want you to see me cry. Go."

Josey stepped past her. He imagined he felt the heat of her anger, and he shivered

349

as he opened the door and stepped out.

Josey stalked away from the commander's quarters and across the parade grounds. He walked fast at first, an anger to match Annabelle's driving his steps. It was full dark now, and the night had turned bitterly cold. His anger seeped away like heat from an unchinked cabin. His steps slowed as he passed through the stockade gate with a nod to the shivering sentries.

He found Byron seated on the steps of the boardinghouse porch. Even in the dark the big man's gap-tooth smile lit up his face.

"I didn't expect to see you until morning. And late in the morning at that."

His tone changed once he got a good look at Josey. "What's wrong?"

"Annabelle's angry." Josey's breath emerged in silvery puffs in the glow of the half moon.

"She must be some kind of angry to send you out in cold like this."

"Angrier than I've ever seen her."

"Come morning, she may cool off," Byron said. He didn't sound confident.

Josey sat beside him, sharing his blanket so it covered their shoulders. "I've always felt a fool when it comes to women. I suppose it's hopeless to try to figure them out."

"It ain't as hard as you make it."

Josey wished he could believe his friend. Someone else's problems always looked simpler. He listened to the wolves howling and scratching at the fort's walls. The butchers had been slaughtering cattle to salt meat for winter and the smell of the offal drew the packs near. Byron's low-throated rumble drowned out the sound.

"The day I was sold started like any other. I thought we's going to the fields, so I never said goodbye to my Rae or my boy or baby girl. I used to wonder what they thought when I didn't come home. Did they know I'd been sold? Did they think I's dead? How long was it before they knew? Not a night passed I didn't think of them. I would lie awake, thinking of all the things I wanted to say when I saw them again."

Josey knew how the story ended. The white slave owners fled when Sherman's army came through. Byron — people called him "Ol' Hoss" then — went looking for his family only to learn all three had died of fever the previous winter.

Byron's eyes glistened in the soft light, and his voice thickened as he continued. "If I could go back to being a slave, I would —" He cleared his throat and swallowed. "I surely would, if it meant I could see them again."

The wolves yipped and growled as they fought over what scraps they could find. Shadows cast by clouds passing over the moon slid over the cottonwoods that grew along Big Piney Creek.

Byron stood. His knees popped as he stretched. He drew a deep breath and cleared his throat. Before going inside he said, "Your woman is back. What's keeping you from being with her?"

CHAPTER THIRTY

Light Hair gathered with his closest friends in a small sweat lodge he had built away from the camp. He usually went there alone to purify his spirit and encourage visions, but it was time now to share what he had seen.

The low, dome-shaped lodge was built of red willow frames and covered with hides to hold in the heat. A fire built in the center of the floor was ringed with stones that sizzled and steamed when Little Hawk poured a cup of water over them. High Backbone fed sprigs of sage into the fire and waved the aromatic smoke over himself. He Dog, Lone Bear, and American Horse, a young leader from another band of Lakota, sat back with Light Hair, their bare shoulders touching within the confines of the lodge.

The encampment had swelled to a size none of the men had ever seen. Nearly every band of Lakota was represented, along with

353

Cheyenne and Arapaho. Rumors swirled of an attack on the fort when the moon was next full. That was a few days away, and though the Big Bellies met every night in Red Cloud's lodge, they had not settled on a plan.

"You should be with them," Little Hawk said to Light Hair. "It is not your fault the white woman escaped. That was a good plan."

"I suspect Crazy Horse has a new plan" — High Backbone looked at Light Hair — "or we would not be gathered here."

Light Hair was not yet ready to speak his mind and was glad when Little Hawk missed the implication in High Backbone's words.

"You should not be here either," Little Hawk said to High Backbone. "The Big Bellies would welcome you at their meeting. At least then we would know what they are saying."

"I can tell you. They are arguing. Everyone wants the glory of victory, but no tribe can afford to lose a hundred warriors in a reckless attack."

"We will have to fight soon." The agitation in Little Hawk's voice made his impatience clear. "The people have never gathered so many warriors. The camp is too big for us to remain together long. We must attack while we are strong."

"We are many, but the soldiers have more bullets," High Backbone said.

American Horse had been silent while listening. Like High Backbone, he was the son of a chief, and his reputation as a war leader was well established. Light Hair had been watching him to measure his temperament. When he cleared his throat, the others fell silent.

"The people are impatient for vengeance, but it is not enough to win this battle if it costs us the lives of many warriors. We have greater needs than one day of glory."

He leaned forward and added sprigs of sage to the fire and watched the pale smoke circle over their heads.

"We must win back our land from the *wasicu*. The whites have trod upon our hearts. Now we will seize their horses and mules and add them to our herds. We will take their women to be our slaves as so many of our women have been enslaved to them. We will slaughter their soldiers and spit upon their scalped corpses."

American Horse sat back and folded his arms. The burning sticks in the firepit crackled.

High Backbone said, "American Horse

speaks what all of us hold in our hearts."

Lone Bear poked High Backbone with the end of a kindling stick. "American Horse speaks like a man whose woman sleeps with her legs crossed."

All the men laughed, even American Horse, who tried to appear stern but could not hold his grave countenance. He told Lone Bear, "That is why I take my pleasure with *your* woman."

They spent the rest of the night smoking and talking of past battles, the memories gilded by the glow of nostalgia. They teased unlucky Lone Bear, challenging him to recall a raid when he had not been hurt. When American Horse sounded too proud, they insisted he retell the story of how he interrupted an attack on the Shoshones to kill a black-tail deer and eat its raw liver before springing upon the enemy raiding party. The others doubted the tale and reveled in the inconsistencies their sharp questioning exposed.

As the hour grew late, they stopped feeding the fire and the rocks no longer steamed. The heat within the lodge smothered them, and they lingered longer than they might have because no one wanted to be first to step into the freezing night. When it was time to leave, Light Hair held back High

Backbone and American Horse, the chiefs' sons, for a final word.

"You have had a new vision?" High Backbone prompted.

Light Hair nodded. American Horse said, "Why have you not told Red Cloud?"

"Red Cloud blames me for the escape of the white woman. His ears are closed to me."

"It was that fool, Climbing Bear," High Backbone said. "He could not check his anger."

Light Hair shrugged. "It is the same with the young warriors. They cannot curb their impulse to attack."

"Young warriors will seek to win a name for themselves in battle. It is the only way they know," American Horse said. "We were the same when we were their age."

"But we were not fighting white soldiers," Light Hair said. "The people must fight with more discipline now. It is the way to defeat the *wasicu.*"

"Perhaps you ask too much," High Backbone said.

Recalling the differences between his warhorse and buffalo-hunting horse, Light Hair said, "No. I have asked the wrong people."

High Backbone tilted his head and studied

Light Hair. "What do you mean?"

"We cannot rely on large numbers to set an ambush. It must be a small raiding party, no more than ten warriors specially chosen so that every man can be relied upon to do exactly as he is told — at exactly the time he is told to do it."

"You speak of us."

"There is no one I trust more."

American Horse said, "You would take ten men against all the white soldiers?"

"No," Light Hair said, permitting himself a smile. "I do not think we shall be so lucky as to face all the white soldiers. I would be content with a hundred."

High Backbone narrowed his eyes. "You saw victory in your vision?"

In response, Light Hair rubbed his palms together, a gesture of grinding stones. To the Lakota it signaled the destruction of a thing, a rubbing out of the enemy. He shared the rest of his plan with both men and urged them to go to their fathers and beseech Red Cloud.

When Light Hair was done, American Horse smiled and shook his head. "You are well named, Crazy Horse."

CHAPTER THIRTY-ONE

Two days after Annabelle's return to the fort, Josey rejoined Byron on their work detail guarding the wood wagons. Carrington was eager to bring in enough firewood to last through winter before heavy snows set in.

When Josey returned that afternoon, the Colonel told him to expect a visit from Annabelle. He had just enough time to bathe and change into his cleanest shirt before she arrived at the boardinghouse. She took one look at the crowded dining room and declined the offer of a meal. It was just as well. His stomach felt tied in knots, and he had no appetite. She surprised him by suggesting they go to his room for privacy.

"I don't care what anyone thinks," she said. "We need to talk."

Josey didn't have much experience in such matters, but anytime he'd heard a woman say that, it didn't portend good things. He swallowed hard and followed her outside to the stairs that led to the second floor.

His room was small and plain. A pineboard bed with rawhide strips stretched across the frame supported a tick stuffed with dried prairie grass. A small cast-iron stove fought against the encroaching cold. A window high on the wall permitted a sliver of light to enter the room. His nose wrinkled at the room's musty smell. He stoked the coals in the stove and added wood.

"I know it's not much —"

"I don't care about the room, Josey."

Of course, she doesn't. He had been rehearsing what he wanted to say for a day, but it all fell away when he saw her. She'd always had that effect on him, clouding his thinking for some things even as other thoughts became clearer than they'd ever been.

She wore a borrowed dress of linsey-woolsey that pulled tight across her midsection and hung short on her lithe frame. It barely covered her calves and revealed a generous stretch of dark stockings beneath a petticoat that had been quilted for warmth. He didn't know why the glimpse of stockings should fascinate him, yet his eyes kept returning to them.

With a dull ache he recalled the first time he'd seen her undressed. He'd been bathing in a stream near Laramie when she joined him. *Not entirely by her choice.* He smiled at the memory of her falling in and inhaled deeply at recalling what happened next.

Being with her that first time proved better than the dream of it. He knew he would do whatever it took, say whatever had to be said, to have her again. Nothing else mattered. He'd feared he would never see her again. Now, all the reasons he'd invented for not being with her fell away at the sight of her. He could no more deny her than he could stop breathing. Eventually, his body would betray him and gasp for more.

She turned to face him. Her dark eyes seemed to expand to the size of silver dollars in the dim light. Her hair was done up, fastened with pins or something that pulled tight and piled high the mounds of dark curls. He longed to take her hair in his hands and hold it to his face, breathing in the scent of her until he grew dizzy with it.

There was a price to pay first. He lit the kerosene lamp, and it appeared they were four, the two of them and their outsized shadows, moving like a dance of dark giants against the wall. He picked up a sheet of paper that rested on the table beside the lamp.

"I started a letter to my parents."

She smiled. He felt off to a good start.

"I told them I was well and apologized for not writing sooner. I wanted to tell them about the baby, but I didn't know what more to say."

"What do you want to tell them?"

She stood at least two arm's lengths away, but when he shifted his body their shadows merged on the wall. "I want to tell them we are to be wed."

"Is that a proposal?" A half smile. She turned her gaze to the floor. The movement divided their shadows. He felt his momentum slipping away.

"Do you wish it to be?"

The question sounded weak even to his ears. He shifted his weight to one leg, thinking to close the gap between their shadows, but the distance increased.

"I'd like nothing more," she said. "But . . ."

"But?"

"You take these risks. You're so quick to place yourself in danger. It frightens me."

"It's not so dangerous. The way most men shoot?" He tried to make it sound like a jest, to win another smile, anything to narrow the gap between them.

"I don't think it's funny, Josey. It's almost like you wish to be killed."

"I don't want to be killed."

The words were true, but they didn't sound convincing. There was a time he hadn't cared if he lived or died. Everyone he knew expected to die. The worst he'd ever been hurt, he'd been cowering in a hole while artillery poured down like a heavy rain. After that he knew when it was his time, it wouldn't matter if he hid behind the lines or charged ahead at the front. Fate could find a man anywhere.

He thought to tell her but doubted she could understand. *How could she?* It all sounded as superstitious as the boys who talked before every battle about how they were sure the next would be their last. Later, if they lived, no one spoke of their prophecy. Only if they died would others recall their words. It was a comfort to survivors to think that when death came, they would see its approach. Josey knew the lie of this. Death didn't come for men like him; it was always there, stalking his steps like the shadow that loomed against the wall.

"I know you don't want to be killed," Annabelle said. "But I don't think death frightens you the way the thought of your death scares me. I thought I could live with it, but not now."

Her hands moved to her belly. Josey wondered if she could feel the baby within.

She looked at him, moist eyes burning with reflected light. "Josey, I need to know you'll be here for me." She looked down, eyes resting where the baby grew. "I don't know if I can do this alone."

He closed the distance between them. He moved to kiss her, but she took his hand and placed it over her stomach. He felt nothing but the warmth of her body. He said nothing, uncertain if he was supposed to feel something, a kick or flutter of life. He smiled because he thought that's what she expected.

Should I feel more? Josey wondered what his father had felt when his mother had been heavy with him. His father was a good man, kind and wise. If a man could feel his unborn baby inside the mother, Josey's father would have felt it. Maybe that's the way it was supposed to be . . . if a man could feel anything.

There's the rub. It hadn't been enough to avoid being shot or falling ill. To survive the war, a man had to curl himself up, like toes squeezed in boots that were too small. Walk around like that long enough, a man stops feeling anything. Which was good. That way, when the soldier riding next to him falls with a bullet in his brain, a man can sleep and do what he has to do to survive the next day. Day in. Day out.

It wasn't until he tried stepping out of those boots that a man came to know he wasn't feeling anything. His toes uncurled, spasming with pinpricks, so painful he'd rather keep wearing the boots than feel what it's like without them. *Better to be numb than in pain.*

The only time he didn't feel that way was in a fight.

And once he explained that, he would lose her forever.

The thought of being with Josey again had sustained Annabelle during her weeks of captivity, like a lamp in a window, guiding her home through the darkness. Then Pierce had come for her, and she'd killed him. She still smelled his blood in her hair, no matter how many times she washed, an oddly metallic scent like a house key or the buttons on a man's coat.

She barely spoke over the days it took her and John Hutchins to ride to the fort. While she never wavered in her feelings for Josey, by the time she saw him again she felt herself a different woman than the one he'd left behind in Virginia City. Maybe it was the baby. Perhaps it was what she'd had to endure. When she saw Josey again, she no longer needed a light in the window. She knew her way home.

She'd been glad to see Josey leave for the day. After the harsh words they'd exchanged on their reunion, they didn't speak the following day. In Josey's absence, the Colonel came to see her. She wondered if Josey had put him up to it, but she didn't ask. She was glad of the company. Even Margaret Carrington had been timid around her, afraid to ask if the Indians had ravished her, though Annabelle knew the matter was top of mind for every gossip at the fort. Let the devil take their curiosity. She was too proud and had overcome too much to accept anyone's pity.

She expected the Colonel to talk about the weather or news around the fort, but he got right to it. "After all you've been through, it's natural you should need some time alone," he said.

"I'm not the one who needed time alone." Her voice was harsher than she'd intended, making it sound as if she'd been bothered by Josey's retreat from her — which she had determined she wasn't. She softened her tone. "I won't trap Josey into marriage. I would do anything for Josey — even sending him away if he doesn't want to be with me."

"Josey loves you as much as you love him. Anyone can see that. Josey's problem is he doesn't feel worthy of that kind of love."

"But Josey —"

The Colonel held up a hand to still her. "Josey hasn't forgiven himself for what he's done in this life. Feeling unworthy of your love, he'd put it in his head that you're better off without him."

"He's a fool then —"

"All men are fools in love."

No arguing with that. She ran her hands across her belly, a compact swelling that stretched against the fabric of the dress she'd borrowed from Margaret Carrington. Soon, she would need clothes from a more full-figured woman. Annabelle longed to feel the baby's movement. Until then, despite the assurances of the doctors, the idea of a child within her seemed beyond belief. If it didn't seem real to her, how could Josey come to terms with it?

The Colonel's words had their intended effect. Now that she was alone with Josey, he stepped away from her, rubbing the hand that had touched her as if it was numb. He stared at a place on the wall behind her, and Annabelle wondered what he saw.

She held out her arms. "Josey, come back."

"No. I have to tell you something, Belle. When you hear it, I'm not sure you'll want to be in the same room with me."

"Josey, I can't help loving you. Nothing you say can change that." She stepped toward him, but he held up a hand.

"The reason I never could write to my mother is because I knew she would want to see me. If that happened, she would see what I've become."

"A father? A husband?"

"A killer."

"Josey, it was —"

"The war. I know. But it didn't stop with the war. It still hasn't stopped."

He looked in such anguish, she wanted to go to him, to wrap him in her arms and soothe him with kisses the way a mother would with a sick child. Something in his voice held her back. She measured her words.

"You killed to protect yourself and the wagon train. You killed to rescue me."

"I keep killing."

He told her about the two Indian hunters he'd come across when he went out with the others searching for her. She tasted bile in her throat.

"They were tied up, Belle. They couldn't hurt me, and I killed them anyway."

"Josey —" She didn't know what to say.

He could tell. She'd never seen him look sadder.

"I suppose I had a lot of reasons for leaving you. I was confused. I was scared. I was worried about the Colonel . . . The thing I never told you is that I missed it."

"Missed . . . what?"

Her stomach roiled, and she felt dizzy. She wanted to sit down, but she was afraid if she moved, the spell that had overtaken him would break. He would stop talking, and she would be left with this image of him slaughtering two bound Indians. In her mind, the young hunter he'd described was just a boy. She thought of the Indian mothers she'd met in the village and how they adored their sons, no less than her mother had loved Annabelle's brothers. She couldn't blame Josey. He'd meant to save her. But she wished her child could be born into a world where war and death were not so pervasive.

She waited out his silence.

"Have you ever played blind man's buff?"

"Of course. Every child has. What does

that —" She bit back her question.

"The way we played as children, we tied a scarf around our heads. It covered our eyes and our ears. When the game was over and you took off the scarf, the light was so bright it hurt your eyes. Everything looked and sounded so clear. Can you imagine that feeling?"

She nodded, not wanting to interrupt him.

"That's how it feels when I'm out there."

She wasn't sure she understood. "Out where?"

He held up his arm, making a sweeping arc, his meaning no clearer to her. "I know how mad it sounds."

Understanding began to dawn. *That can't be right.* "Do you mean out there . . . when you're being shot at?" She already knew the answer. "Josey, you could be killed."

"I know. It's mad, I told you. But when I'm not out there, life feels like blind man's buff. Everything is muffled."

"Even a life with me?"

CHAPTER THIRTY-TWO

Annabelle remained in the room. That had to mean something. As many times as Josey had imagined talking through a reconciliation, he had never expected the conversation to turn in this direction. He'd been reluctant to admit it even to himself. *What kind of man takes joy in killing?*

Joy wasn't the right word. And it wasn't the killing that enlivened him. Maybe it was the danger, the thrill that came from being so alert to everything around him he felt a part of the world instead of apart from it. Josey had come to terms with what he considered his God-given skills, assuming the death he caused on a battlefield to be his life's purpose, the way a fire burns away the underbrush in a forest so that new life can take root. Fires burn themselves out once the brush is gone — or they risk turning into a conflagration, uncontrolled, a threat to all life. Josey feared that's what he had become.

Everyone had been quick to excuse his actions. Annabelle, her family, the Colonel — they forgave Josey. The deaths he caused came in defense of others, they said. Yet there was something in the moment when he meted out death that he'd never shared with anyone, a sublime harmony — with nature, the universe, with God, even. Josey never felt so alive as in the moments he dealt death like God's sword. In moments when other men panicked or froze with fear, Josey *thrummed.* The way a tuned violin string resonated and filled a room with sound. The way a match struck in a darkened room cast a perfect light, all its hues visible in a brilliant flare.

Yet Annabelle had hit upon something. The thrill of battle was not the only time he felt so alive. Earlier, when his hand rested on her belly, he imagined it sliding down, reaching between her legs, probing with his fingers. His face flushed, and he tried to push the thought from his mind. She wouldn't understand his thinking of that now. *He* didn't understand it.

"You're right, Belle," he said. "That's the only other time I feel so alive. When we . . ." He blushed again.

"That's a good thing, Josey."

"I feel connected to you —" He paused, realizing how his words might be taken. "Not just *that* way. Connected to the world."

"Like a return to God's Eden?"

He smiled at her reference, recalling their time in his cabin in Virginia City. The attachment he felt to Annabelle was more than sexual, yet those feelings were impossible to separate from the rest. Just being near her affected him. She liked to sit close, to *feel* his presence beside her. He preferred to sit where he could look at her or, even better, touch her. He liked to lose himself in the geography of her, exploring her coves and fissures. In the dark, when no words passed between them, their bodies locked into the puzzle of a single being. Pure transcendence. He never felt shame for what they did in the dark, though they were not yet married, and he knew other people might find it sinful. It was in those moments, too, that he felt closest to God.

Before he could begin to arrange these thoughts into words, she came to him. Their shadows on the wall merged into a single void of light, like the mouth of a tunnel. She lifted a hand to his face, warm against his skin. He placed his hand on her belly, hoping he might feel something now.

"If you can feel connected to the world

through me, imagine how connected he will make you feel."

"He?" *Does a mother know these things?*

"Or she." Annabelle smiled.

He felt like a hummingbird had taken flight in his chest.

"I don't know what's in here," she said. "I only know it's yours, and we need you."

Josey stroked Annabelle's thigh with a finger, watching the skin dimple beneath his touch in the cool air. He wasn't certain how much time had passed. The oil was low in the lamp. The light from the window had shifted across the room, transforming from gold to silver.

"I've walked halfway across the country and survived capture by Indians, yet you touch me like I'm made out of china or something precious and fragile."

"You are precious to me."

"Stop." She rolled her eyes, an expression that told him: don't stop.

"I mean it." He used all the fingers on one hand now, tracing the ridge of muscle that extended from her knee. "How many times have you touched your leg? A thousand?"

"In my lifetime? I don't know."

"If you had a thousand emeralds, no single one would be precious to you. If you had just one, you would cherish it."

"I don't think it's the same thing."

"Close enough." He closed his hand over her thigh, feeling the skin alive beneath his stroke. "I haven't touched your leg a thousand times. Every time I do feels like the first."

"My leg is no different than any other."

"It's unique to me by the fact that I may touch it."

"You've never touched another leg?" Her voice held a playful quality, but he tacked away from that shoal.

"Every time I caress you, I notice things I hadn't before. Like how soft the skin is at first touch. How taut the muscle is beneath the skin when I grab hold." He held her thigh with a soft grip that turned into another stroke.

"I had no idea legs fascinated you so."

"It's not just legs." His hand moved in demonstration. The sound she made reminded him of a purr.

"I knew *that* fascinated you."

"It's precious to me, too." He continued his demonstration. Her breathing stopped until he paused.

"You only get one of those," she said as she caught her breath, "so it had better be precious to you." She stopped talking.

■ ■ ■ ■

Afterwards, they talked for hours. Annabelle didn't know Josey could talk so much. She should have been tired, given the hour, but she felt energized at hearing the words animate him, like a soldier unshouldering a heavy pack. Some of the things he said frightened her as he spoke of God and death. He said at times he felt bereft of emotion, but his regret was a palpable thing, and she told him remorse was a feeling, too.

His need to unburden himself was obvious, and she allowed him to continue long after she'd forgiven him. She kissed his fingers one by one, the metallic scent of the oil he used to clean his guns filling her with an odd comfort. He spoke of death as if he were the only person who'd ever killed another, and she grew quiet. She felt a need for confession, too, but she pushed it from her mind and steered their conversation to lighter matters. She told him of a lunch she'd had with Margaret Carrington and Frances Grummond and the gossip at the fort.

"Fannie's a sweet girl, but I don't know how her husband can be so big eating what she cooks. She may be even worse in the kitchen than I am." It was a joke between them that Annabelle had little experience cooking aside from over a campfire. "She brought this pie to dinner that she had baked. I was afraid to ask what kind it was supposed to be. Neither Margaret nor I could tell."

"At least there were no casualties." Josey laughed as he shared the story of Frances Grummond's ill-fated attempt to make biscuits. "You'd think being married so long she would at least be capable enough not to pose a threat to herself."

"What do you mean?"

He looked at her, confusion clouding his eyes. "The way she cut herself slicing biscuits, of course. I told you about that."

"No, not that. I didn't realize a year of marriage should seem such a long time. Is that an insight into the mind of a bachelor?"

"A year?"

"Yes. They were married in September, after the war." She could tell Josey's mind had turned elsewhere. "What is it?"

He shook his head. "Nothing, I'm sure. You know my memory plays tricks on me sometimes."

Annabelle wasn't sure she believed him. Josey had fallen silent as the first gray light of day appeared in the window. He'd been so open with her, but she'd held back what troubled her, and she suspected he could sense it.

He had spoken again about the helpless Indians he'd killed. When she pictured the older hunter, she saw the face of the Indian she'd known as Pierce. For a moment, she was back in Crazy Horse's tepee. She remembered being covered in Pierce's blood and crawling out from under the body, like being buried alive and digging herself out. She shook with a start.

"Are you falling asleep on me?" he said. "I've kept you up too long."

"No. We needed this."

"On that, we are agreed."

A movement of his hand informed her they were speaking of different needs. She caught his hand in hers. He deserved to know.

"I haven't told you everything about how I escaped."

His hand tensed in hers. He gripped her hand so tightly as she told the story, her fingers lost feeling. He didn't relax even after she told him she hadn't been ravished. Josey, more than most men, knew the suffering a survivor of violence bore. By the time she had finished, she had to pry his fingers loose, like pulling splinters from her hand.

"Are you angry with me for not telling you sooner?"

"At you?" His voice was so loud she shushed him, certain they risked waking other boarders. "I wish the savage still drew breath so that I —"

"No." She put a finger to his lips. "Your anger doesn't help me."

"I'm not angry at you." The anguish in his voice was heart-rending. "If I'd stayed, I could have sent the others back. If I'd come for you —"

"You'd be dead. And my escape may have been made impossible." She rubbed her hand, returning feeling to her fingers. "You are not responsible for me, Josey. I have to make my way in this world just as you do. But we can choose whether we walk our path alone" — she took his hand in hers — "or with another."

He swallowed and nodded. His downcast eyes studied their interlocked fingers. "My father used to tell me: a fist is stronger than five fingers."

She lifted their hands, shaking them like a victory salute. "And two fists are stronger than one."

He didn't share in her smile. "What if I

379

can't change, Belle? I feel remorse for what I've done, and minutes later I can feel so angry I want to" — he stopped himself — "to *hurt* someone."

"Don't you see, Josey? We have to choose between life and death. Both paths lead to God, and He grants us the choice of which we will take."

"Because you can't live with both."

"Not for long." She looked in his eyes and inhaled. "Can you make a choice?"

Chapter Thirty-Three

Having seen to his horses, Light Hair returned to camp. With the day's light slipping away, the tepees were wrapped tight against the cold. The warriors would ride south to the fort at dawn, so most had retreated to their lodges for a final evening with their families.

Light Hair considered seeking out the decoys he had selected, to review with them again the plans to initiate the battle, but he knew they would mock him as a nervous old woman for going over the same thing so many times. Yet he would do so again on the ride south and again on the morning of battle. He knew the repetition would impress upon them the importance of patience. Success depended on it.

A swirling wind darted among the lodges, snatching smoke as it poured through the opening at the top of the tepees and filling the air with the smell of burning wood. A few men gathered outside at large fires. While they fletched arrows and sharpened blades they swapped stories of battles they had seen. Light Hair might have joined them, but he did not want to talk of the past. Too many memories pained him.

A line of children raced around a lodge, mimicking the war cries of their elders and nearly toppling a drying rack. A pack of camp dogs chased after them. Light Hair quick-stepped out of their way. Their barks cut through the brisk air, sharp as an arrowhead.

Some older boys in thick-skinned moccasins passed him carrying the painted stones and long, peeled willow rods used to play snow snakes. Their faces glistened from the bear fat their mothers rubbed on to protect their skin from the cold. Part of the river had frozen over at a bend where the water eddied into a pool, and Light Hair was tempted to follow the boys there and test his skill at sliding the rods across the ice to see which could come closest to the stone. *I should find He Dog and Lone Bear, and we will teach these boys a thing or two.* Instead, he headed to his lodge to check on Old Grandmother, maybe eat something and pray he could manage sleep.

His mind turned to other distractions

once he saw Black Buffalo Woman. She stood near his lodge awaiting his return. She was usually more discreet, and he thought something must be wrong. Then he saw her eyes, dark as coals. He felt himself stir from the intensity of her gaze. She turned from him and walked away the moment she was certain he had seen her. The furs she wore from her neck to her toes concealed the figure beneath, but Light Hair pictured her in his mind as if she stood naked before him.

He took a different route into the woods. The snow rose higher among the trees, and he made slow progress. He walked to his sweat lodge, tucked in among the trees and brush. A man might walk right past if he did not know its location, but Light Hair was confident Black Buffalo Woman would find it. She knew all his secrets.

On arriving at the lodge, he stood outside, stamping his feet to ward off the cold. She always made him wait, so he was surprised to hear someone already within. He half expected to see someone else when he pulled back the furs and crouched through the door into the dark room. She was bent over the center pit so that the furs no longer concealed her figure. She had carried burning coals in a small bowl and used them now to light some dried sage among the stones.

It was not Black Buffalo Woman's time for the moon blood, and Light Hair had no idea what excuse she had invented for slipping away. He did not care. He watched her blow at the embers, coaxing a flicker of flame that cast her cheeks in an orange glow and set her coal eyes afire. He caught her gaze for a moment before she returned to her task, adding sticks to the pile and blowing again. Light Hair rubbed his hands together to warm them before sidling up behind her. Her skin beneath the heavy pelts was almost hot to the touch. She tried to wriggle away from him while she completed her task, but her movements incited him further.

He shed free of his robes, pulled loose his leggings with one hand while the other continued its explorations. His peremptory movements violated the rules of their game. He had always been *her* plaything, but Black Buffalo Woman had never come to him on the eve of battle. Old men joked with leering, toothless grins that they knew the best place for a warrior to seek peace from battle-bred anxieties. Light Hair meant to discover the truth of their words for himself.

Black Buffalo Woman got the fire going and swatted at his hand. He put both hands on her, so that she would feel his urgency. Light Hair had not known how much he needed this until her dark eyes had locked on his. He gave himself over to the rush of longing, so much like battle lust, his body moving on instinct alone, his mind disengaged as if in flight.

His need was so great he almost spent himself in the first minute. He willed himself back, like a raptor gliding on the wind to extend its flight. He felt his heartbeat throb within her. Her body clenched him tight, releasing and clenching again, a new rhythm that pleased her so that when she called his name the need in her voice set him off, too.

Afterwards, they lay together, bodies slick with sweat. Her moist hair fell in thick clumps across his chest. He had held her close while their breathing evened, until the air in the lodge grew stifling from the fire. They watched its orange flames cast strange shadows against the willow-rod walls when they moved. Light Hair amused himself by imagining the display that had played out a few minutes earlier.

Black Buffalo Woman did not speak, which was odd, and Light Hair filled the silence, which was odder still. He told her how the chiefs had sent a seer to ride among the hills that surrounded the fort. The seer rode in a zigzag pattern to inspire a vision. The first time he returned, he told the chiefs he envisioned a handful of soldiers delivered into their trap. The chiefs sent the seer back out twice more. On the third try, the seer returned and told the chiefs he saw more soldiers than he could hold in both hands. Some of the warriors were already calling the battle to come "A Hundred in the Hands."

"We will kill all the white soldiers," Light Hair vowed. "This will be a battle worth recording in the winter count."

While he talked, Black Buffalo Woman rebraided his hair. He had done it himself because Old Grandmother's fingers could not pull the strands tight enough, and he was too proud to ask anyone else. Black Buffalo Woman pulled with a savage intensity. Her braids held tight. Her continued silence was unnerving. Had he been too brusque with her? Was she troubled to be away from her lodge for so long? When she spoke, her words were the last Light Hair expected.

"Take me away, Light Hair. Leave with me tonight."

He turned to face her, not understanding

her joke. Her eyes sparkled like quartz, but her face betrayed no sign of humor.

"I would be your woman, Light Hair. I would give you children if you want them."

She was not joking, yet Light Hair still did not understand. For ten years he had wanted to marry Black Buffalo Woman. Even after she wed No Water, once he had nursed his heartache, he continued to wish for it. By turning out her husband's possessions from their lodge, a Lakota woman was free to marry another. It did not happen often, and in many cases the new husband provided payment in horses or other goods. Light Hair had been too proud to ask this of Black Buffalo Woman, and he had given up hope that she would ever offer.

"We could be together, just us, forever. We could go north and live with the tribes far from the *wasicu.*"

"Do you think I fear the *wasicu*?"

"No. You fear no one." Her eyes cast down.

He could see that she knew what his answer must be.

"Do you think we will lose this fight?"

She shook her head. "You never lose."

Light Hair grabbed her by the shoulders to compel her to look at him, but her eyes, brimming with tears, avoided his. By offering to run away with him instead of leaving her husband, she was acknowledging his status as a Shirt Wearer and the shame that would come upon him for stealing another man's woman. Even being with her like this violated the trust the people had placed in him, and she knew how it troubled his conscience. Yet he chose to be with her anyway. She was the only thing he had ever wanted that he could not win for himself. She had expected his love for her would overcome his pride, his devotion to the people . . . everything he was.

"Why now? This battle — Lakota warriors will speak of it for generations. You did not like my last plan. *You* told me to think of another way, and I did."

She still could not look at him. "This battle will destroy you."

"The *wasicu* will not kill me." Light Hair laughed to hear such a childish fear. His vision had shown him what he believed was his death, and the *wasicu* played no part in it.

"They will destroy who you are. They will destroy who *we* are." She looked at him, her voice strong and sure. "You may kill every one of them, but they will return in greater numbers. They will never stop coming until our bones are buried in the sands

388

and we are forgotten like the giant sky horses."

Her words reminded Light Hair of what Spotted Tail had said, but he pushed them from his mind. Doubt could be as lethal to a warrior as an enemy's rifle. Black Buffalo Woman should know this. She had come to him on the eve of battle, he thought, to give him the comfort a warrior needs. Instead she filled his mind with reservations.

"It is you who would destroy me," he said. "You are a trickster spirit."

His words struck as a blow, and she fell away from him. She was as inconstant as the wind. Even if he went with her, how long before the season changed and the wind blew from a new direction? How long before she returned to her children, her husband, her people? She would rob him of everything that defined him as a man and leave him with nothing but shame and a blackened name.

He stood and turned from her.

"Do not go, Light Hair."

He looked down on her. Tears streaked her cheek. She was the only one who still called him by his childhood name, the name he had when he first loved her. The people had honored him with his father's name after his first battle, and he had devoted the years since to earning it. In the battle to come he would add to the name's greatness.

"Do not call me that anymore," he told her. "My ears will be shut to you. From now on you will call me Crazy Horse."

CHAPTER THIRTY-FOUR

The cavalry stables were empty when Josey arrived. Thirty-seven army horses remained strong enough to ride, and every one of them had been saddled and tied off by the wagon park so they would be ready to relieve the woodcutters if they were attacked.

The stable boys had shoveled the stalls clean and brought in fresh hay. Josey liked the earthy smells of the stables, but it was strange not to hear the restless shuffling and snorting of the horses. It felt like walking through a cemetery. He pulled his coat a little tighter where it was fastened at his throat.

Only Gray remained. The mustang gelding must have smelled Josey coming because he saw its nose peeking out from the stall as he neared. Holding his palm flat, he proffered a hand dusted in sugar, and the horse's raspy tongue wiped it clean. With his free hand, he stroked the horse's neck.

"Got to get you a new home so you won't be so lonely," he cooed. Gray perked its ears at his voice and turned its muzzle to his other hand, hoping to find it covered in sugar, too. "Sorry, boy. That's all I could get."

After his nightlong talk with Annabelle, Josey had resigned his post guarding the wood wagons. The commander hadn't ordered him to remove his horse, but Josey felt he should move Gray into the civilian stables. Carrington hadn't been happy when Josey quit, not until he revealed his motivation for leaving. A wedding.

That's where a night of talking had led them. The gray light coming through the window in his room had brightened into golden rays that crawled across the floor toward their bed.

"How long will it take to build the ranch house?" Annabelle asked with a yawn. It was the first time they'd spoken of where they would live once they left the fort. Josey had been afraid to raise the topic.

"What about Virginia City, your family's store?"

"I won't have time to work in the store once I'm a mama."

He pulled her tight and smiled, feeling

confident enough to broach a subject that had nagged him for weeks. "What about leaving for San Francisco? London?" He thought, too, of the newspaperman always sniffing around her but swallowed back his jealousy.

She tilted her head, squinted toward him in the window's glare. "I wanted to visit those places, Josey. I never thought we would live there."

Annabelle nestled in tight against him. "My mother always told me: home is where you feel loved. My home is Angel Falls."

He looked at her, not sure what she meant.

"The name of the ranch you're going to build," she said.

"I'm not sure I like that name." He'd never much cared for being called angel, especially the suggestion of being a fallen one. "It sounds like a place where someone gets hurt. Or fails." One was pretty much the same as the other to Josey.

"Or it's just a beautiful waterfall. A place where people fall in love."

He kissed her hard on the mouth, drunk with joy — or lack of sleep; it didn't matter in the moment. They might have stayed in bed all day, but they were famished, and the smell of bacon from the kitchen lured them downstairs. Josey had it all figured out before Annabelle finished her first cup of coffee. The post reverend could perform the ceremony. The Colonel would give Annabelle away, with Margaret Carrington as her maid of honor and Byron standing beside him.

Annabelle agreed. Whatever concerns she had about not having her family present were outweighed by a desire to be wed before returning home obviously with child. The only thing left was to pick a date.

"Christmas is coming," Josey said. "Wouldn't that make for a grand celebration?"

Annabelle laughed. "We can't be wed on Christmas, Josey. It's Christ's day." Seeing his frown, she sought to mollify him. "What about New Year's Day? That's also a cause for celebration. I'll need the extra time to get ready, anyway."

"You would make me wait until a whole new year?"

She laughed, and she never looked more beautiful to Josey. Her cheeks flushed with joy, and her eyes sparkled like icy snow in the sun. He kissed her pert nose for no reason, and she laughed more to see him so giddy. Josey couldn't remember when he'd been so happy. Maybe as a boy, when the world seemed full of magic and possibilities, all work felt like a game, and the only evil he knew came in books with happy endings.

After he finished brushing down Gray, Josey saw to his saddle. He wiped it clean and rubbed saddle soap into the leather. The flank billets were more worn than he liked, the leather cracked from so much hard riding in the cold. He headed across the stable yard to the saddle shop to see about a replacement.

The wide sky was flat and gray, and Josey sensed another turn in the weather. A fortnight without a freeze had melted most of the snow and ice they'd seen at the start of December. With Christmas five days away, it was just a matter of time before more snow forced everyone to batten down for winter.

That was part of the reason Josey didn't feel too bad for leaving his position. He wouldn't have been needed much longer anyway. There'd been an Indian attack the previous day, the first in a couple of weeks, but the soldiers had driven off the Indians without a fight. Carrington had sent out a large patrol with strict orders to relieve the woodcutters and return to the fort. The patrol returned without casualties.

Annabelle had asked him if he would miss

the activity.

Josey shook his head. "I've made up my mind. If I'm to be a father, I can't go taking needless risks."

She smiled as if she believed him, and Josey hoped it was true. When he walked out that morning, he left his guns in his room. If a bugle call alerted the fort to an attack on the wood train, Josey wouldn't have time to retrieve his guns and join the relief force even if he wanted. He wouldn't have to kill again if he kept himself free of dangerous predicaments.

Without the twin Colts, cartridge box, and powder flask he usually carried, Josey felt light, as if he could have leaped onto Gray's back without stepping in the stirrups. He hop-skipped the final few yards to the saddle shop. Josey grinned to think the movement might have been described as a dance step if anyone had been around to see him.

The saddle shop was just as empty as the stables. The smell of leather and cut wood filled the small shack. A wood stove stood at the back of the room against the wall, but no heat came from it. A collection of different-sized leather sewing awls, hole punches, hoof nippers, and burr setters lined the plank walls, and horseshoes hung from nails in the roof beams. Rivets, pieces of leather, an iron fire poker, and more tools were scattered across a workbench. Josey hefted a maul, a three-pounder he judged, feeling its head-heavy weight in his hand as he looked about the room.

Spare flank billets dangled from a peg on the opposite wall. Josey inspected the collection until he found one the length he wanted. He could do the work himself and settle with the saddle maker later.

A stirring from behind startled him. The saddle maker must be in after all. The sound came from a small room he hadn't noticed off to the side of the entrance. Through the open door he saw the end of a cot. Its wooden legs groaned, and hinges creaked as a great weight lifted.

Light from a window in the bedroom left the man in silhouette and obscured his face, but Josey recognized Grummond's powerful figure. He closed the door behind him, throwing the shop in shadow. On unsteady legs, he moved to stand between Josey and the stable yard. Little flakes of spittle had gathered at the corners of his mouth, and his eyes were rimmed red. He wore his revolver on his hip. The unbuttoned flap had been turned out so that the Colt's butt stood free. He yawned and stretched, his hands balled into fists, his arms reaching so far it seemed he could touch both walls at the same time.

He smacked his lips, a tightness in the lines around his mouth suggesting a bad taste. When he looked to Josey, his hooded eyes and great height lent him a haughty demeanor, like a man accustomed to looking down on the world.

"Were you planning on just taking that?" Grummond nodded toward the flank billets. "I wouldn't have pegged such a man of honor for a thief."

"I would have settled with the saddle maker later," Josey said. "Where is he?"

Grummond made a gesture like brushing away a fly. He stepped toward the workbench, narrowing the distance between them. "I ran him off. Too much noise with all that pounding and grunting. I needed someplace quiet."

"To sleep off your drunk?"

"Don't tell me you're a damned teetotaler," Grummond growled. "Carrington's bad enough. A little nip now and then never hurt anyone."

"To take the edge off?"

"Naw, edge is good." He picked up a pair of hoof nippers and studied how the clips came together. The tool looked like a child's toy in his large hands. "You never know where danger could lie."

Grummond smiled beneath his mustache as he snapped the clips together a couple of times. "I'm glad we have this chance to talk. Sort of clear the air between us."

"What's to clear?" Josey kept his eyes on Grummond's hands and the butt of that Colt. He felt naked without his guns.

Grummond's hands traced the outlines of the workbench. "I had asked you to leave my wife alone."

"I never bothered your wife."

"You talk to her."

"Talk never hurt anyone."

Grummond smiled, but the expression was colder than the wrought-iron stove at Josey's back. He picked up an awl, tapping his fingers against its pointy end one by one. "Tell me what you talk about."

"We talk about Tennessee. The gallant Union officer she met while treating the wounded at the hospital."

Grummond's hooded eyes narrowed. "You don't talk about Michigan?"

"Frances has never been to Michigan."

He stood erect, his mustache flattening into a smile. "That's right." Grummond nodded, as if conceding a good play in a card game. "But you recall that I am from

Michigan."

"You and your other wife."

Annabelle's revelation that Grummond had wed Frances after the war had clicked something into place in Josey's brain. He remembered all that he'd forgotten about Grummond, including a letter from his wife at home that he'd read aloud at a campfire where men were gathered during the march through Georgia. The recollection explained why Grummond had been so uneasy about seeing Josey with his wife.

"Does Frances know you were already married?"

Grummond's gaze fell to the ground between them. "Fannie never would have married me if she'd known. The divorce is final now." He returned the awl to the workbench and leaned his weight against it. "I fear she would leave me if she knew. I'd lose everything."

At its highest ranks, the army was an insular culture. Even a whiff of scandal would scar a man's record. Given Grummond's past and the court martial, there would be no chance to redeem himself. Frances carried his child. The child would need a father. Yet when Josey thought of the young mother, her bright manner and laughing eyes, he wondered if she wouldn't be better off without him.

"She has a right to know."

Grummond's shoulders sagged. "So that's how it is." His face twisted into a snarl. "Josey Angel, the noble warrior. So brave in battle. So composed under fire. An example to all the men. I was sick of hearing about you before we even met. Then I saw what a little man you are. You're nothing special. You're nothing at all without your guns and that rifle of yours."

Josey kept his eyes on Grummond's Colt. The man had made no move toward it. He picked at the rivets scattered across the workbench, lining them in rows like an infantry firing line. Though angry, Grummond didn't seem drunk enough to shoot Josey and risk being brought up on murder charges.

"There's no need to bring guns into this," Josey said.

Grummond turned away from his line of rivets. "I suppose you have no need of your guns now that you've turned coward, hiding behind the skirts of a woman." His hands remained on the workbench, too far to make a grab for the Colt. "You can act all high-minded with me, but at least I didn't make my woman into a whore."

Josey's jaw clenched. "Only a bigamist."

401

The movement came so fast Josey almost failed to register it. He'd been so focused on Grummond's revolver he hadn't noticed the man had taken hold of the fire poker. Grummond's long frame unwound like a spring as he lashed out.

Josey turned from the blow so that the long iron rod didn't break his arm. His shoulder exploded in pain. The next swing came at his head. Josey stumbled forward, saving his skull, but the blow across his back knocked him to the ground.

"I won't be lectured on manners by a craven little man."

Josey heard Grummond, but the words sounded far away. He rolled over, thinking of escape until the lieutenant's cavalry boot caught him under the chin, rocking his head. He saw black for a moment.

Relying more on instinct than strategy, Josey curled into a ball, covering his head as best he could as Grummond kicked him again and again.

The blows stopped once Grummond was spent, heaving for air as if he'd just run up Pilot Hill. Josey felt smothered in pain. More pain than the time he'd been shredded with shrapnel. More pain than he'd ever known. *Grummond means to kill me.* The thought arrived as a curiosity to be studied more than a fear. He hurt too much to be afraid. He tried losing himself in the pain, like burrowing under thick blankets on a cold morning, the pain shutting out whatever Grummond said, the pain engulfing him, shielding him from thoughts of those who would mourn him, the Colonel, Byron, Annabelle.

"— maybe I'll pay her a visit next. That's a sweet quim."

Annabelle.

"I expect she has a taste for red men now. Maybe being with a real man will restore her affections to her own race."

"Fight me" — Josey managed the words through pain-strangled breath — "like a man."

"Fight you? You still have fight in you?" Grummond mocked him. "Can you even stand?"

Josey rolled to his knees. He felt nothing in his left arm. He breathed in short gasps to avoid a stabbing sensation through his chest. His back felt afire. Pinpricks of light orbited his head, like twinkling stars. His vision blurred so that he faced three Grummonds. He saw them raise the rod for another blow. On his knees and unable to move, Josey knew he could not protect himself.

Grummond lowered his arm. "I suppose that wouldn't be very sporting." He cast the poker aside and rolled up his sleeves, assuming a pugilist's stance. "Well, come on now."

Josey pictured himself standing, but his body wouldn't budge.

"Do I have to do everything for you?" Grummond strode forward. His long arms extended under Josey's armpits, raising him like a stuffed doll. Josey's face fell against his chest.

"Lower your legs," Grummond commanded. "I can't do that for you."

Josey's feet touched the ground. Grummond released the pressure under his arms as Josey tested the strength in his legs, hoping they would hold him upright.

"Do you think you can stand?"

Josey tried to nod.

"Good. Now —"

As Grummond leaned away, Josey pushed off with all the strength left in him. Even with every ounce of effort, the movement was more of a fall than the graceful spring he imagined. Gravity worked in his favor, lending momentum that gave a power to his movements his body didn't possess. As his left hand dropped to Grummond's waist, his fingers twined around the butt of the

Colt before he fell back to the ground.

The pain of the impact helped clear his head. Josey saw Grummond's surprise in a single focused image. He switched the gun to his good hand and pulled back the hammer.

"I expect" — he still couldn't manage his breath — "this is loaded."

Grummond backed away without answering.

Josey kept the sight leveled at his chest.

"You better leave" — Grummond kept backing away — "before I test the truth of that."

Chapter Thirty-Five

The day dawned cold, the coldest day they'd seen yet, with heavy clouds that threatened snow. Annabelle hurried from the boardinghouse to the fort's main gate, her arms wrapped about herself for warmth, her toes already numb in the thin shoes Margaret Carrington had loaned her. She should have anticipated the cold. She'd overheard someone remark in the dining room that it was the winter solstice, the shortest day of the year. Annabelle hoped to catch Margaret at home. She had much to discuss with the commander's wife.

Annabelle hadn't slept. After the saddle maker found Josey, the Colonel and Lord Byron brought him to the boardinghouse. Josey refused to talk. From the way his jaw was swollen, they weren't sure if he could. His left arm hung at his side, and he breathed with a wheeze that pained her to hear.

The Colonel was spitting mad. "Grummond did this. I'm sure of it."

The Colt they found in Josey's hand mystified them once they accounted for all his revolvers. "Do you think Josey shot Grummond?" Annabelle said.

"I hope so. The rascal deserves whatever's coming to him. I'm going to find him as soon as we know Josey's all right." From his stolid expression, it was clear Byron agreed with this course of action.

Annabelle summoned Doctor Hines and sent the men away in hopes that Josey might talk once they were alone. The Colonel took Josey's rifle and gun belts. "If he kills Grummond now, he could face a murder charge," he said.

"I don't think he'll be going anywhere for a while," Annabelle said.

She felt a little better after Doctor Hines examined Josey. He diagnosed broken ribs as the worst of his obvious injuries, though he worried that his head was concussed. He spent a long time looking into Josey's eyes. He refused to prescribe anything for the pain until they were certain of Josey's head wound. He offered to stay that night, but Annabelle took the duty. James Wheatley, the boardinghouse owner, brought up a rocking chair, and she dozed between periodic checks of Josey.

Josey never spoke. When she asked him questions, he closed his eyes and turned from her. He seemed content when she sat with him. With her hand resting in his, he squeezed weakly and stroked her finger with his thumb. Along with the hurt, she saw the love in his eyes.

Doc Hines returned in the morning. He was a fine-boned man with limbs that seemed more delicate than Annabelle's. A wispy mustache and tousled hair lent him the distracted air of a man with more important things on his mind than the whereabouts of his comb. Annabelle was encouraged to see that focus applied to Josey, and the doctor seemed pleased with his patient's condition. Josey communicated his reaction to the doctor's proddings with nods, grunts, and, once when the doctor tried to get him to sit up, a gasp of pain. Doc Hines sent Annabelle to the kitchen to get porridge.

The doctor provided a dose of laudanum to help him sleep and stayed with Josey so that Annabelle could go to Margaret Carrington's house and retrieve the rest of her things.

The fort's main gate bustled with activity. Repeated bugle calls tore through the frigid air, while dozens of soldiers in heavy over-coats scurried about. A score of men struggled to control horses agitated by the excitement, and officers shouted to be heard above the din. Annabelle threaded through the crowd to avoid being knocked down.

On the parade ground nearest the guard-house, Captain Fetterman brought some semblance of order, calling together infantrymen for inspection. Annabelle overheard soldiers tell of flag signals from the pickets on Pilot Hill alerting the fort that Indians had attacked the wood train.

The cavalry assembled behind the infantry. Grummond sat astride a thick-chested roan stallion, a full head taller than any of the men he inspected. Was it just her imagination or did he smirk at her? She clenched her fists until her nails dug into the palms of her hand.

"Annabelle, you best keep to the side or you'll be trampled." She stepped back as the Colonel drew up his Appaloosa. Beside him, James Wheatley rode an old mare that looked better suited for pulling wagons. Both men were dressed for the cold with heavy boots and coats.

"You're not going out there, are you?"

"Byron's with the wood wagon. With Josey laid up, somebody needs to look out for him. How is the boy? I take it as a good sign you felt he was well enough to leave his side."

She summarized the doctor's assessment. As she spoke, she noticed the Colonel had Josey's rifle scabbard fastened to his saddle. Wheatley carried his own Henry rifle. He noticed Annabelle's gaze.

"I've been meaning to test this out since we got to the fort," he said. "Captain Fetterman said we could ride with him."

Annabelle looked to the Colonel. Even with the overcast sky she had to squint. "Are you sure that's wise?"

He responded with a throaty chuckle. "Are you saying I'm too old? I've been leading men into battle longer than most of these greenhorns have drawn breath."

Annabelle's cocked eyebrow drew a scowl once he realized the contradiction in his statement. "Don't say a word."

She couldn't help but smile at the old rogue. "Just be careful."

"You watch out for Josey." He nodded in the direction of Grummond and the cavalry. "We'll deal with what happened when I get back."

They were interrupted by shouted orders, and Fetterman, riding a bay stallion, led the infantry out the gate, marching double time to meet the besieged wood wagons. The Colonel tipped his hat and spun around his Appaloosa to follow, Wheatley trying to keep up.

Annabelle shivered against the cold. She spied Margaret Carrington near her husband and the rest of the officers outside the post headquarters. Frances Grummond stood with her, swaddled in so many furs Annabelle couldn't tell she was six months into her term, about twice as far along as Annabelle.

Most of the time when Annabelle looked on Frances, it was with a sympathetic pang, as if looking into a crystal that foretold her future. She felt no sympathy this morning as she strode over to the women. Margaret smiled and squeezed her hand in greeting, but Frances didn't even acknowledge her.

Margaret sensed her unease. "Don't mind Fannie. She's afraid for her husband. He hasn't been out on a sortie since the time he was surrounded by Indians."

She'd spoken in a whisper, but Frances must have overheard.

"I begged him to ask for an administrative assignment, but he was in such a state last night we quarreled about it. I don't know what got into him. He was so angry he stormed from the house. I think he slept in the cavalry barracks."

Perhaps he just wanted to avoid any place where someone might seek him. Annabelle kept her thoughts to herself.

Her face pinched with worry, Frances pulled on Margaret's arm. "I have a bad feeling about this. Can't Henry hold him back today? He could send Captain Powell instead."

"You know your husband won't appreciate such coddling, Fannie. We must be strong for our men. They have enough on their minds. Let him do his job."

Frances nodded, yet her agitation increased as her husband gathered the cavalry and trotted toward the gate. She paced along the path in front of the post headquarters. From atop the sentry platform, Henry Carrington called for the cavalry to halt. Frances stopped her pacing and turned with the other women to watch.

"Report to Captain Fetterman, and stay by his side," the commander called. It was difficult to hear over the sound of the horses stomping and snorting and the flag snapping in the biting wind. "Return to the fort after you relieve the wood train. Do not pursue the attackers across Lodge Trail Ridge."

The wind drowned out Grummond's

412

response, along with whatever Carrington said in reply. With a final salute, Grummond ordered the cavalry to advance. He turned and tipped his hat to his wife. Despite the cold, Annabelle felt her face burn with indignation when he winked as his eyes passed over her. She held her tongue in front of his wife, who fought back tears.

Frances resumed her pacing. Margaret placed a hand on her shoulder to still her. "You heard Henry. They'll drive off the Indians and return. George will be back before supper."

"I've had bad dreams since the last time he went out." Frances's voice quaked, and she spoke in breathless gasps. "I picture him in my mind, surrounded by those savages, fighting his way through. I —"

"Maybe you should lie down. Rest could do the baby good," Margaret offered.

Frances nodded with a vacant stare directed toward the gate and the brown rolling hills that extended to the horizon.

"I'll come check on you after I speak with Henry," Margaret said.

After Frances left, Margaret looped her arm in Annabelle's, and they walked together toward the headquarters. "I commend your restraint," she said. "Is Josey doing better? Henry told me about his injuries."

Annabelle repeated what the doctor had said. "Josey still hasn't told anyone what happened . . ."

"You have your suspicions. I understand." Margaret patted Annabelle's arm with a gloved hand. "If Lieutenant Grummond is responsible for what happened to Josey, rest assured that Henry will find out and will mete out the proper punishment. Please don't let Josey take matters into his own hands. If he does, I'm not sure Henry can protect him."

"Josey's in no condition to do much," Annabelle said. "He's fortunate to be alive."

Margaret made her apologies. "I should see after Frances. You heard her. I'm sure she has no idea of what happened."

"I know." Annabelle set aside the bitterness. "You go. I'll stay and bring you news if anything happens."

Near the gate, the sentries were abuzz about a new signal from the flagman on Pilot Hill. She overheard a sergeant explain that the Indians had broken off the attack on the wood wagons. A thin cloud of dust, like a brown smear on the gray horizon, marked where the cavalry had galloped off in pursuit of Fetterman and the infantry.

"Does that mean they're coming back?"

she asked the sergeant, but he moved off without answering.

Annabelle hurried over to the guard tower, pushing past a red-faced private who blocked the ladder. Ignoring his protests, she climbed the steps, the wind whipping at her long coat and skirts as she climbed. Henry Carrington was there, scanning the area outside the fort with a pair of binoculars while receiving a report from a courier.

The fields around the fort were a mottled brown, the hills stripped bare of all but some scrub by the persistent winds. Even without field glasses she saw the signalman on Pilot Hill, his tower and flags standing out like a sail on an ocean horizon. On the stockade wall beyond the main gate a dozen or more crows roosted like sentries, their black heads turning at every sound, hoarse caws cutting through the din of the soldiers' movements.

Carrington set down the glasses. The courier read figures from a notebook, his ungloved hand shaking in the cold.

"The captain left with forty-nine infantry from companies A, C, E and H." The courier spoke through gritted teeth to keep them from chattering and needed one hand to hold his cap in place from the wind. "The lieutenant mustered twenty-seven cavalry."

"Plus two civilians," Carrington said, referring to the Colonel and Wheatley.

"Yes, sir. And Captain Brown rode out after them."

Carrington's goatee twisted into a smile. "So Fetterman finally got his eighty men," he said before turning to Annabelle. "Is Doctor Hines still at the boardinghouse with Josey?"

Annabelle nodded.

"I'm going to have to order him to see to the wood trains in case there were injuries." Pulling off a glove, Carrington scribbled a note for the courier to take.

While he wrote, Annabelle snatched up the binoculars and peered in the direction she'd seen Carrington looking. What she saw made little sense. Instead of pursuing after the infantry in the direction of the wood road to the west, the cavalry moved east, the infantry following them, circling around Sullivant Hill toward Big Piney Creek and Lodge Trail Ridge.

If the soldiers were no longer needed at the wood train, why didn't they return to the fort? "Didn't the signalman send word that the Indians have fled?" she asked after Carrington dismissed the courier.

Carrington pointed toward the base of Lodge Trail Ridge. "I suspect Fetterman is hoping to catch the Indians in retreat. You can see a few Indian scouts there on the ridge. If he can get to the Peno Creek valley first, he may catch them unawares."

Annabelle noted a hint of pride in the commander's voice.

"He's adapting the plan I drew up for the attack three weeks ago."

"I thought that didn't go so well." She spoke softly to avoid giving offense.

"A matter of unfortunate timing." Carrington patted her on the shoulder as he took back the binoculars. "Don't worry. This is the biggest single force we've ever sent from the fort. We learned our lesson after the last time."

Annabelle looked out over the stockade wall. The crows took flight. Their glossy black wings beat a steady rhythm that carried them toward Lodge Trail Ridge. A sudden gale from the west blew loose the tie that held her hair and obscured her vision. Without the glasses, she couldn't see the soldiers or the Indians Carrington had pointed out. She squinted as she brushed her dark hair from her eyes. It looked as if one of the Indians on the ridge had dismounted from his horse.

CHAPTER THIRTY-SIX

His eyes gummy with sleep, Josey blinked hard to bring into focus the figure in the chair beside the bed. Gray light streamed through the window in the boardinghouse room. His nose wrinkled at the sour smell of the chamber pot in the corner.

He blinked again and looked about. Turning his head stirred a wave of pain. Swallowing brought more. He raised his hand toward his jaw — and stopped with a sharp intake of breath and a gasp.

The pain focused his vision. Instead of Annabelle's familiar figure, the crazy-haired doctor slumped in the chair. He stirred. With a yawn and cat-like stretch, Doc Hines opened his eyes and fumbled for a pair of glasses at the bedside table.

"How do you feel?"

"Hurts." Josey's voice sounded like a frog's croak.

"At least you're speaking." The doctor

rose and brought a cup of water to Josey's mouth. Raising his head to meet the cup, Josey wasn't sure what hurt more, his mouth or his ribs. By the third swallow, he was certain: the ribs.

"Where's Annabelle?" He felt he should know the answer, but his brain seemed sluggish, like cotton stuffed his head.

"She went to the fort to retrieve some things. She was with you all night." The doctor pulled a bottle from his leather satchel and measured out a small draught of dark liquid into a shot glass and brought it to Josey. "This will help you sleep."

"I've slept enough."

"Then it will help with the pain."

Pain helped him think through his cotton head. Gritting his teeth, Josey blocked the proffered glass with a hand. "Don't trust that stuff."

"There's no harm if it's used sparingly." Hines set the glass on the table. "I'll leave it in case you reconsider — which I expect you will by the time I've completed my examination."

Josey accepted the words as a challenge, biting his lip when the doctor felt along his swollen jaw. Josey imagined he looked like a greedy chipmunk. Hines tried to be gentle, but almost every touch landed like a hammer blow.

"I don't believe anything's broken, just bruised. When the swelling subsides, you'll feel up to eating solids again."

The pain lit a path through Josey's mind, and he recalled everything. The saddle shop. Grummond. The fire poker.

"Where's my rifle?"

Doc Hines lit a candle and asked Josey to follow its light with his eyes. "Your friends took your guns. They were afraid you'd do something foolish."

Josey started to nod until the pain forced him to reconsider. He'd had Grummond's Colt. He could have shot the bastard dead, and people would have called it self-defense. Lying on the ground with the weapon pointed at Grummond's chest, Josey recalled his promise to Annabelle not to kill again unless he had to. He'd been thinking of those Indian hunters when he made the promise, and Annabelle wouldn't have blamed him if he'd killed Grummond. She'd have done it for him, if she'd been there.

The thought of Annabelle killing Grummond was what stopped him. She'd killed three men since she'd met Josey. While she didn't talk about it, Josey could see the toll those deaths took on her. He knew the punishing meanderings of a mind bedeviled by guilt better than anyone.

So when she'd asked him to choose a path of life, it wasn't just his salvation that concerned her. Josey had read it in her eyes as she watched him. If Josey couldn't change paths, what hope did she have?

He'd let Grummond walk away. And if Grummond stood before him now, Josey would have to do the same. The choice wasn't about Grummond. *Let the devil take him.* The choice was about Josey. It was about Annabelle. It was about their child.

"This is going to hurt." Hines pulled back the bed covers and placed a hand over various points on Josey's bare chest. Next, he pulled from his velvet-lined field case a tubular device, split on one end so that he could place matching buds in his ears. The other end he placed against Josey's chest and asked him to breathe. He repeated the command several times, moving the device as he listened. When finished, Hines withdrew from his satchel a thick roll of gauze and motioned for Josey to lean forward.

"Your ribs are cracked and should heal on their own in about six weeks." He circled Josey's chest with the wrap. "By immobilizing the area with these bandages, you may be able to move more freely."

By holding his breath, Josey found he could manage the pain better. He couldn't hold his breath long enough for the doctor to finish the task.

"I wish you'd reconsider the laudanum. Adequate pain relief will help you to breathe normally, so you don't develop pneumonia."

"I'll think about it."

Doc Hines completed the wrapping. As he repacked his satchel, a knock came at the door. He opened it to a courier. Josey couldn't see the new arrival. He heard him explain about the attack on the wood wagons and orders for the doctor to report.

"I was finished here anyway." Hines looked back at Josey. "I'll see if I can have the Colonel come and stay with you."

From the hallway, Josey heard the courier. "He rode out with Captain Fetterman. He and the man who owns this place."

Hines stepped into the hallway, and Josey couldn't hear the rest of the exchange. By the time the doctor returned for his bag, Josey had on his pants.

"What are you doing?"

It was a fair question. The answer would have been obvious except Josey couldn't bend over far enough to pick up his boots. He used his feet to grasp one boot at a time and raise it to where his hands could grab hold.

"My friends are out there."

The courier leaned past the doorway to watch, his thickly bearded face failing to conceal his curiosity. Josey said to him, "I'll give you five dollars to fetch my horse and tack. He's a gray gelding. Do you know the one?"

The man nodded. "The mustang."

"That's right." Josey shooed him. "Hurry, now."

He managed to step into his boots, stomping his heel against the floor to get his foot all the way in. The doctor shook his head. "You can't ride a horse."

"It won't kill me, will it?"

The doctor shrugged. "No. I —"

"Then I have to try."

Hines nodded. Josey wanted to think the look on the doctor's face was one of admiration rather than derision, but he wasn't about to ask. He handed the doctor his shirt. "You'll have to help me with this."

With a heavy sigh, the doctor dropped his bag and took up the shirt. He helped with Josey's buffalo-skin coat as well. Josey maintained his breathing through all the movement, which he took as a good sign.

Hines disagreed. "You have no business

423

going out there."

"You're going out there."

"I have orders."

Josey picked up his thick fur hat and wondered at the best way to get it on his head. "Let me ask you this, doc: If there's trouble, would you rather have me here in my bed" — he held his breath and raised his arms over his head to place the hat — "or out there with you?"

Josey flashed a self-satisfied grin at the doctor once the task was completed. "Now where did you say my guns were?"

CHAPTER THIRTY-SEVEN

Crazy Horse woke before dawn. A full moon hung over the Shining Mountains to the west, casting enough silver light to allow swarms of warriors to move about their camp. They numbered at least two thousand. No one knew for sure. Even the old men had never seen so many warriors gathered in one place, and no one could say what two thousand gathered warriors looked like.

Each greeted the dawn of battle in his own way, some alone, others with companions or in small groups. Some sang war songs. One battle-scarred Cheyenne lifted his face and bellowed, venting his anger and fear to the spirits. A young warrior swung a rifle about his head, then lifted his hands and face in prayer until a tear trickled down his face, an old Lakota tradition known as crying for scalps. A few young warriors disappeared into the trees to heave up the contents of their stomachs in private so that the others would not witness their shame.

Lone Bear greeted him while he saddled his warhorse. Like most of the Lakota, Lone Bear dressed in his finest clothes for battle. He wore leggings of blue woolen trade cloth that his wife had beaded with blue triangles on a white background that ran the length of each leg. The beads matched those on his winter moccasins. An eagle feather war bonnet covered his braided hair.

His warhorse was a blue roan stallion as big as an American horse. The horse's breaths emerged in the cold as giant puffs of cloud, as if the beast breathed fire. Lone Bear had tied golden eagle feathers in its mane and tail and painted lightning streaks from the mount's ears to its fetlocks in the front and from hip to hoof in the rear. He had painted his face with a similar design. Standing tall, he preened like a meadowlark while he watched Crazy Horse tighten the cinch on his saddle.

"You look beautiful," Crazy Horse assured him.

Lone Bear nodded, ignoring his mocking tone. "I would offer you something suitable to wear, but you would make a mess of it."

Crazy Horse's vision forbade ostentatious display. He wore a plain buffalo-hair shirt and pants beneath a heavy robe that he would set aside when it was time to ride. He did not tie anything in his sorrel's tail. He did not paint his face, and he did not wear a war bonnet. The finest clothing he owned were the winter moccasins Yellow Woman had sewn and beaded for him before she was killed at Sand Creek. He wore those to honor her memory.

"Even if my vision allowed such finery, I do not see the sense of wearing it into battle where it could be torn or bloodied."

Finished with the saddle, Crazy Horse rubbed a pinch of dirt from a prairie dog mound between the ears of his horse. Prairie dog magic would help protect the sorrel from bullets. He rubbed more dirt onto the gelding's chestnut flanks and threw a light dusting of what remained across its back.

"That is the point, my brother," Lone Bear said. "If I fall in battle, I do not want others to pass and sneer, 'Here was a poor man. See how shabby he dressed.' " His appraising look implied Crazy Horse risked a different fate.

"That is where we are different," Crazy Horse said. "Many will die today, but I know that I shall not be one of them."

By dawn Crazy Horse stood on the ridge looking south over the fort. The morning horn bellowed like an angry swan, calling the soldiers from their lodges. They gathered and watched two men pull a rope to raise the giant flag that drooped in the still air.

Crazy Horse turned and walked his horse to the other end of the ridge where High Backbone waited. A narrow valley stretched before them. The white man's road ran along a small rise through the middle of the valley. A creek flowed across the far end, but its forks flanked the road on either side. Thick brush, dogwoods, and cottonwoods grew in the marshy land there, obscuring his view of the water. As cold as the morning was, the temperate weather of the past few days favored them. High Backbone understood this, too.

"It is good most of the snow has melted," he said. "The soldiers will not see the tracks of our warriors hidden among the brush."

They watched while the warriors from every tribe took positions in the gullies where the creek forked. The Cheyenne had been given first choice of where to hide. Their chiefs selected the end of the western gully nearest the ridge so that their warriors would have the best chance of avenging Sand Creek. The Arapaho took a position alongside their longstanding allies. Most of the Lakota massed at the northern end of the valley. A smaller band hid behind the eastern gully. They would circle behind and close the trap once the soldiers entered the valley.

Still angry over the white woman's escape, Red Cloud had been slow to accede to Crazy Horse's plan. They had tried a similar attack two days earlier, but the decoys had failed to lure the soldiers into the valley. After that failure High Backbone and American Horse convinced the chiefs to follow Crazy Horse's vision. His plan relied on ten decoys. He believed any more might intimidate the soldiers after the near disaster of their fight earlier that moon.

Crazy Horse surrounded himself with his friends and trusted allies from the other tribes. It had been important to involve the other tribes, American Horse had told him, and he recruited Big Nose, a Cheyenne warrior he admired. Big Nose brought another Cheyenne and two Arapaho warriors so that all the tribes would share in the success if the plan worked.

They just had to make sure the soldiers

followed them into the valley.

At midmorning the wagons with the wood-cutters left the fort. Crazy Horse had moved the decoys off the ridge and into a position among the trees nearest the fort where they could see the wagon road. What they could not see were forty warriors who had been chosen to feign an attack on the wood wagons. They were hidden farther down the road.

The decoys dismounted when the wagons approached. They caressed the snouts of their horses to keep them calm and quiet while the wagons passed. More soldiers than usual marched with the wood wagons. The *wasicu* were nervous. Crazy Horse worried for a moment they might prove too careful. Perhaps he should have planned an attack on the wood wagons. But no. They wanted to kill blue coats. They would wait. Once the hidden band of warriors attacked the wagons, more soldiers would come. He was sure of it.

They did not have to wait long. The crack and pop of gunfire carried far in the frigid air. Most of the Indians carried bows, reinforced with parts of buffalo horn tied to each end to give them more range and velocity. The gunfire meant the wagons had pulled into a circle to fend off the warriors and their bows. Another trumpet call from the fort signaled the soldiers' response.

The air had grown colder in the early morning hours. Even once the sun rose, it hovered low in the sky and did little to warm the air. Crusted snow clung to the shadows, piled deep in wind-blown drifts in the defiles that stretched out from the hills. The decoys waited, stiff and cold beneath thick buffalo robes. Minutes dragged like hours. When Crazy Horse had been part of the attack, it never seemed to take so long for the soldiers to respond.

The fort's gates opened, and foot soldiers marched out. Their rhythmic steps appeared unnatural, even laughable, moving together like a giant caterpillar inching along the road. Crazy Horse counted about fifty men. Maybe more. They passed with an almost musical noise, the beat of their footsteps accompanied by the jangling of metal equipment and shouted commands from a man on horseback.

The Indians had learned to distinguish the leaders among the soldiers from the markings on their coats. This one wore two golden bars. His gaze shifted as he rode. For one breathless moment he seemed to look at Crazy Horse and the rest of the decoys, but they were hidden too well, and the soldiers passed without stopping. They were in a hurry to save the wagons.

Crazy Horse was disappointed to see just three horsemen, and two of those did not even wear the blue coats of soldiers. Men on foot would be harder to lead into a trap so far from the fort. When a large party of horse soldiers emerged from the fort's gate, he let out a breath of relief. He used the farseeing glass to study the horse soldiers. One stood out. A big man with a hairy face. From the bar on this one's shoulder, Crazy Horse knew him to be their chief. He recognized him as the fool who chased their decoys in the attack earlier that moon. Crazy Horse smiled. *The spirits favor me.*

It would not be long now. The sound of gunfire from the wagons was already petering out. The soldiers might return to the fort once they knew the wagons were safe — unless they had a reason to stay.

Crazy Horse led the decoys from their place of cover among the dogwoods. They charged their warhorses toward the horse soldiers, who did not notice the advancing Indians. Crazy Horse carried a rifle and a revolver. He would not use a bow against white men, preferring to kill them with their own weapons or the stone-headed war club he carried for close combat. He normally dismounted to fire his rifle so as not to waste a shot, but he did not care where the bullet went now. If they killed a white soldier too soon, the others might lose heart. Better to play to their confidence.

His single shot had its intended effect. The decoys had the attention of the horse soldiers now. Crazy Horse imagined the foot soldiers heard the shot, too. The soldiers' surprise gave the decoys time to draw close enough for the others to loose a volley of arrows. They veered off without even taking notice of where the arrows landed, charging toward the ridge that overlooked the valley. Wild shots sounded behind them as the soldiers returned fire. Crazy Horse looked back to see that the others were with him. Little Hawk grinned like a boy taking his first gallop, and Crazy Horse matched his expression, forgetting the cold, the danger, and everything else in the exhilaration of the moment.

They took to the ridge at full speed, their nimble ponies finding purchase among the stones and brush almost as if they were on flat ground. Crazy Horse halted at the crest and waited for the others. He reloaded his rifle, holding steady until the whine of bullets drew near. One of the Arapaho warriors, the youngest among them, stood on his saddle, flipped up his breechcloth, pulled down his leggings and waggled his backside to the pursuing soldiers.

The big horses the soldiers rode struggled to make the ascent. "It is good they are so slow," High Backbone said. "It will give time to the foot soldiers."

For the ambush to work, they needed the soldiers together when they entered the valley. The foot soldiers reached the bottom of the ridge as the horse soldiers struggled up. Through the farseeing glass Crazy Horse saw their faces glistened with effort, their expressions tight with hatred.

Was that hatred enough to draw them on? He rode to the far side of the ridge where he could see into the valley beyond. The white man's road cut through the center along a slight rise that split the valley like a backbone. The trees that grew along the creek banks marked the borders of the valleys like the fences the *wasicu* liked so much. Two thousand warriors were hidden among those trees, but Crazy Horse saw no sign of them unless he used the farseeing glass. If the soldiers saw them and turned back, all his planning would be for nothing.

"When the soldiers come, their hatred needs to be so great they do not stop to look at what waits for them in the valley," he said to High Backbone.

Crazy Horse dismounted and gathered handfuls of dried grass and a few sage and greasewood sprigs. Sitting beside his horse, he started a small fire, wanting the soldiers to see him like that when they crested the summit. He warmed his hands over the fire, waving the scent of burning sage over him. He rose once he heard the cracks of rifle shots and the whine of bullets and saw tufts of grass near him explode from approaching shots. He smiled as he leaped onto his sorrel. High Backbone had been watching from the downward slope.

"The spirits protect you, but don't ask too much of them," he said.

"The spirits want this as much as we do. We are their instruments."

As the soldiers gathered on the ridge, the Indians started down the other side to the sound of a few wild shots. Soldiers did not have to concern themselves with how many bullets they wasted.

The horse soldiers were faster coming down the ridge. The decoys had no choice but to ride hard to keep ahead. Crazy Horse kicked his heels into the sorrel's flanks to pull ahead far enough that he could pause and look back with his glass. The hairy-faced chief led the charge, the other horse soldiers riding hard to keep up. They came so fast they had separated themselves from the foot soldiers.

"The fool will blow out those heavy American horses before he even gets halfway across the valley," Crazy Horse said.

High Backbone pulled at Crazy Horse's sleeve to urge him on. The soldiers fired at him whenever he paused.

"Do not fear, my brother. Their arms quake with fear and weariness from the ride. They will not strike me."

High Backbone grinned. "I am not worried for you. I am worried they will hit me while aiming at you."

Laughter helped ease the tension that had gripped Crazy Horse all morning. "Then I will see you at the creek. Do not wait for me."

Without another word, Crazy Horse kicked the sorrel's flanks and turned its muzzle toward the onrushing soldiers. He rode straight at them, using his revolver to fire into their ranks, scattering them like stampeding buffalo. The unexpected movement stunned the soldiers. Some stopped to aim at Crazy Horse. Others fled from his charge. He was past them before they recovered, and their confusion bought him more time as he drove his horse back toward the ridge.

Separated from the other decoys, he was in danger of being caught between the horse and foot soldiers in just the sort of trap he had planned for them. The foot soldiers had made it to the top of the ridge, where they milled about in confusion. He squinted until he saw the chief with two bars on his shoulders. He was peering into the valley with long glasses, saying something to the horsemen beside him who did not wear blue coats. The two horsemen kicked their mounts and rode down the slope after the horse soldiers, but the foot soldiers remained on the ridge.

Crazy Horse dismounted and pulled out his rifle. Using his mount to steady his aim, he focused on Two Bars. The soldiers had seen him. They were pointing and shouting. He could hear the crack of their rifles, but he had been true to his vision and knew his magic would protect him at least a little longer. Behind him, the sound of hooves pounding on the hard, frozen ground grew nearer. A cold, damp wind had risen, wending its way between the folds of his clothing to chill his neck and back. He emptied his mind of distractions and adjusted his aim to account for the breeze.

The shot was perfect. He knocked the wide-brimmed hat from Two Bars. The man whirled around in response and pointed to Crazy Horse. Shots drew nearer as the soldiers adjusted their aim to account for the downward slope. Crazy Horse leaped onto the back of his warhorse, waved his rifle overhead, and yipped a war cry that He Dog and Little Hawk answered. They had turned back to harass the horse soldiers who had come after Crazy Horse.

Together they rode back through the valley. The other decoys were far ahead, and the horse soldiers were spread across the land that sloped down from the ridge. Crazy Horse looked back over his shoulder just long enough to see that the foot soldiers had started down the slope. *Not long now.*

They pushed forward. Crazy Horse felt his sorrel shudder beneath him. The horse had been well trained and would die before it stopped to rest, but it could not last much longer. He leaned forward over its neck and stroked it. *Just a little farther.*

High Backbone and the others had slowed to allow Crazy Horse to catch up along with He Dog and Little Hawk. Together they raced along the rise where the road ran, down to where the land flattened and the creek turned to cut across the valley. With the horse soldiers chasing them, the two parties of decoys crossed paths just before they reached the creek. It was the signal to spring the trap.

On reaching the tree line, Crazy Horse had just enough time to dismount and look back. For a moment, the scene seemed frozen in Crazy Horse's mind, like a drawing on a wall. Two thousand warriors emerged from the dogwoods and cottonwoods in the gullies along the creeks. The horse soldiers rode on, unaware of their presence. Crazy Horse could not see the foot soldiers on the rise at the far end of the valley, but he knew they were there. They had followed the decoys into the trap. A hundred in the hands.

The collective war cries of the assembled warriors echoed like thunder, and when they loosed their first volley of arrows they numbered so many they blotted out the sky. Crazy Horse felt like his heart soared — and plummeted — with them.

"Come, brother." Little Hawk pulled on his sleeve. "We have not yet bloodied our war clubs."

Crazy Horse inhaled, his chest shuddering as cold air filled his lungs. "My horse will not survive another charge."

"Then find another. Come and share in

the glory you have won for us."

Crazy Horse shook his head and waved his brother forward with the others. Everything had gone just as he planned it, yet he shivered as if a shadow had passed over him while he reflected on the words of a frightened old man and a woman who professed to love him.

CHAPTER THIRTY-EIGHT

From the top of the ridge, the bodies looked like fish left to rot on a riverbank.

Cold burned at Josey's cheeks and nose. His eyes were so dry he blinked to be sure of what he saw. Corpses were scattered across a rocky outcrop at the head of the valley below. Dozens of them. Stripped of their uniforms, the carcasses were so white Josey thought at first they were clumps of snow. The wagons bringing up the rear of the relief column halted. No one spoke. Even the horses were still. The soldiers' greatcoats whipped in the wind. Great blackbirds cawed. Josey heard them before he saw them. Their cries rent the air, and the crows chased away a pair of larger buzzards from their fresh meal.

A quick count gave him hope. Fetterman had nearly a company of men with him. Josey saw half that many. *Maybe some escaped. Maybe the Colonel's alive.*

Mindful of the doctor's warnings against shallow breathing, Josey tested a deep breath. The cold cut at his throat, but he breathed without pain so long as he remained still. Holding his breath, he urged his horse forward, terrified of what he might find among those rocks.

After retrieving his pistols from the Colonel's bedroom at the boardinghouse — he'd been unable to find his rifle — Josey accompanied Doctor Hines to the fort. On arriving at the ambulance wagon they learned the wood wagons were safe. *At least Byron is all right.* By that time gunshots echoed over the hills from the opposite side of Lodge Trail Ridge.

Henry Carrington had assembled every available soldier at the fort. Fewer than forty men remained until the guards who had ridden out with the wood train returned. The soldiers marched on the double quick along the route taken by Fetterman. The ambulance and a couple of wagons carrying extra ammunition trailed behind.

The soldiers removed boots and socks before wading across Piney Creek. The sound of a few scattered shots from the far side of the ridge carried across the thin air. The rate of fire had been greater when they'd left the fort, a fusillade of regular volleys that echoed like thunder. Now the sporadic shots sounded like individual handclaps in an empty theater. The soldiers in the relief column couldn't move fast enough. They scaled the ridge, struggling to keep their footing while carrying their long Springfields.

Despite the pain it caused him, Josey urged Gray forward. He'd reached Carrington and the front of the column by the time the soldiers straggled to the summit. From the crest, he could see for miles. The road to Virginia City stretched out along the ridge before descending into Peno Creek valley. Mounted warriors filled the valley, as many as two, perhaps three thousand. More Indians than Josey had ever seen at one time. The church-going Carrington gasped and blasphemed at the sight. His face lost all color.

The warriors took note of their arrival. Hand mirrors flashed signals, and those on horseback raced back and forth, trying to taunt the soldiers into entering the valley. The nearest warriors, a group of about a hundred, were gathered around some boulders a half mile away.

"We should have brought cannons," Josey said. "They fear the big guns more than anything else."

A dazed Carrington looked like he didn't believe what he saw. "I told them not to cross the ridge," he said, so softly Josey doubted anyone else was meant to hear.

The commander called for a courier and sent orders for a howitzer to be brought up. Once the ambulance and supply wagons crested the ridge, the Indians began moving north through the valley toward Peno Creek.

"They think we've already got cannons in the wagons," Josey said.

Like a receding tide, the Indians' retreat exposed what was left in their wake. Josey saw what he'd taken for rotting fish near the boulders where the Indians had been clustered. For the second time that day he heard Carrington blaspheme.

"This can't be happening," he added.

Josey couldn't blame the commander for doubting what he saw. Indians had been sparring with the soldiers and workers at the fort for five months. Men had died on both sides. The fort's cemetery had filled with victims of violence, but they'd been buried in increments of one or two at a time. Carrington had sent his largest force yet out this morning. The idea that none might return seemed as fantastic as stories of ghosts and monsters. Nothing like it had ever happened to the American army. The generals would blame Carrington for this. Josey had no doubt. They would need a scapegoat, and no one would have the stomach to point the finger at the men martyred on this field.

"I see about fifty," Josey said.

He meant bodies but choked on the word. The Colonel was down there somewhere, but until he saw the old man's corpse he would hold out hope.

The statement woke Carrington from his trance. Josey wondered if his mind had already turned to how he might shift blame for the massacre and salvage his career. Carrington ordered the column forward, sending armed sentries wide on their flanks to watch for a return from the Indians. As the soldiers moved toward the road, the last of the Indians disappeared from the north end of the valley.

On reaching the boulders, Josey dismounted. Doc Hines had come up on foot from the ambulance wagon, the little man hopping about like a circus monkey in his agitation, issuing orders for the men to examine their fallen comrades for signs of life.

It was obvious to Josey they would find none living here. He crouched beside one of the naked corpses. The body was almost unrecognizable as a man. He had been scalped. The eyes were gouged out, displayed on a nearby rock as if to watch over the scene. Ears, genitals and fingers had been sliced off. As many as a hundred arrows protruded from the torso so that it looked more like a pincushion than anything human.

Hines cursed the Indians. He'd been recording in his notebook the condition of the bodies. "Couldn't they see they were already dead?"

"Each of the fletchings is unique," Josey said. "Every warrior wanted to leave his mark, to count coup for the death."

"I thought they counted coup by touching an enemy."

"Different kind of coup."

Josey thought of the pale Indian who'd touched him rather than taken his life in the battle at Crazy Woman Creek that summer. Annabelle said he was called Crazy Horse, that he was the Indian who'd taken her, though Josey still found that hard to believe. If the rest of the tale was true, the young warrior had wanted to use Annabelle to get inside the fort so his band could kill soldiers. *Looks like he didn't need Annabelle after all.*

They found Fetterman, at least the body

they believed to be Fetterman, near the center of the ring of boulders, surrounded by other corpses. His throat had been slit almost to the point of the head being severed from the torso.

The hardiest of the soldiers began loading the bodies into the wagons. They had a few hours until dusk, and Josey figured it would take all that time just to load the bodies they could see. They totaled forty-nine. Thirty-two remained. Somewhere.

The weapons along with the uniforms had been taken as trophies, at least those weapons that still functioned. Josey found some rifles broken on the ground, probably used as clubs in the last desperate moments when ammunition had run out or there had been no time to reload. Among the broken Springfields he found a Spencer. The carbines had been issued to the cavalry. Because there were no dead horses among the corpses, Josey had assumed all the dead were infantry.

He looked out across the valley, but the road dipped below a small rise a few hundred feet away, and he couldn't see past that point. Buzzards circling overhead provided a clue.

"Fetterman didn't advance here," he said. "This is where he retreated." The higher ground and the boulders provided at least some cover for a final stand.

"What's that?" Hines said.

"I need to push on."

"I'll go with you."

"I'm not sure it's safe."

The doctor looked at the scattered bodies. Those that were whole, soldiers loaded like cordwood onto the wagons. For others, they tried to match severed limbs with bodies. A few men could be heard retching alongside the wagons.

"I'm of no use here," Hines said. "Maybe we'll find survivors ahead."

Carrington didn't like the plan.

"If anyone lived, they did so by making it back to the fort." He gestured to the north across the valley. "We won't find any living here."

The commander might have been right, but Josey couldn't rest knowing the Colonel might be out there.

CHAPTER THIRTY-NINE

The doctor wasn't a horseman, so they walked into the valley, Josey leading Gray by the reins. Walking was easier on his ribs. He managed to breathe better without the jostling of riding a horse.

They discovered more bodies strewn along the road to Virginia City. They weren't hard to find. Thousands of arrows covered the road like a carpet. At the points where the arrows were concentrated in greater numbers, Josey and the doctor found bodies. All were in the same condition as those they'd found among the boulders.

From the road, Josey couldn't see the creeks that flowed alongside their path, but he heard the water rushing over rocks in the creek bed. The dogwoods that grew along the creek's course had long lost their leaves, but plenty of bushes and thick clumps of grass remained.

"The Indians meant to lead them here."

Josey pointed to the thick brush. "They waited in ambush in those gullies."

They made slow progress because they stopped to examine each body. The doctor checked for vital signs and recorded details in his notebook. Josey watched for a familiar face. When there wasn't much left to recognize, he checked the bodies. An old man would stand out. Along with the men they found a few dead horses. One still lived, and Josey used his revolver to end its misery.

"These men were cavalry. They were trying to get back to Fetterman."

"How did they get so far ahead?"

"Grummond." *It had to be Grummond.* Josey could picture it as clear as if he'd been riding with the bastard. Just as he had in the attack three weeks earlier, Grummond must have given chase to the Indians he saw. Decoys, most likely. "He must have led the cavalry all the way into the valley before they sprang the trap."

"Fetterman had to know it was a trap," Hines said. "Couldn't he have turned the infantry back?"

Josey looked back across the valley. If Fetterman had started his descent from the ridge after Grummond, he would have only heard the shots when the ambush started. He wouldn't have seen what was waiting for him and his men.

"If he had marched back to the fort, he might have saved every infantryman in his column," Josey said. "But he would have doomed every member of the cavalry."

An officer with such self-regard and ambition that he compared himself to Alexander, Caesar, and Lee would never abandon his troops. If Fetterman had saved Grummond and the cavalry, he would have been hailed on a level with his heroes. If he abandoned his men, he would have been called a coward. He'd have no future in the army. Fetterman led his men down from Lodge Trail Ridge knowing his legend would be made, either as hero or martyr.

"Roland waiting until his dying breath to call Charlemagne."

"What was that?" Hines asked.

Josey shook his head. "Fetterman didn't have a choice but to come to the cavalry's aid. He probably figured there were no more than a hundred, maybe two hundred warriors. By the time he realized his mistake, his best option was to retreat to those boulders."

"I guess the cavalry tried to turn back, make a run to Fetterman and the infantry."

"They were fools then."

"Why fools?"

"Retreating from Indians on horseback? They never had a chance."

Josey studied the ground ahead. *They weren't all fools.* He knew at least one who would have kept his head. "Once they realized they were surrounded, the smart thing would have been to make a stand from a defensible point."

About a quarter-mile off, at a point just before Peno Creek crossed the trail, another cluster of boulders stood on a small rise. A crow perched on the biggest rock, its wings glistening in the fading light.

"It's getting dark," he told Hines. "You should head back. I need to check something out."

Josey rode up the rise to the rocks, which rested among thick brush of thistle and sage. He looked south across the valley. The rolling landscape stretched under a gray sky. His view of Carrington and the wagons was blocked, but he saw movement in the middle distance. *Doc better hurry back.*

He dismounted when he came across the first of the bodies. The carcass looked more like a butchered side of beef than human. He counted about ten more bodies among the boulders. Along with the twenty he passed since leaving the wagons, he figured this had to be the last of them. None of the bodies looked old enough to be the Colonel.

Closer to the boulders he found a mound of spent Henry cartridge casings. *Must have been a hell of a fight.* The nearest body, he guessed, must be Wheatley. He was naked, like the others, unrecognizable without his eyes and scalp. The new rifle he'd been so eager to test was nowhere to be found.

It wasn't pain that made it difficult for Josey to draw breath. The pit in his stomach felt big enough to choke him. He stepped past Wheatley.

Two of the boulders lay together, like blocks set one against another. They formed a small crevice where they joined among the thick sage. Josey wouldn't have seen the opening if he hadn't been following the trail of spent shells.

The body looked like it had been pinned beneath the rocks, concealed beneath a thick buffalo-skin coat. Josey fell to his knees, feeling the old man's bony shoulders and head beneath the folds of the coat. He got his hands under the Colonel's arms and pulled him free from the rocks. He tugged aside the coat. The head of an arrow was buried in his chest. The Colonel must have snapped off the end before crawling under the rocks. The old man's face was as serene as if he'd been sleeping. Josey tried to breathe, but the air came in sputtering gasps as he fought back tears.

When the Colonel's eyes fluttered open, Josey thought he'd imagined the sight through blurred vision.

"About time you showed up."

Josey laughed, not even minding the pain through his chest. He wiped his eyes. "Looks like you gave them hell, old man. Did you run out of ammo?"

"Ran out of Indians." The Colonel tried to laugh but choked on blood that bubbled up from his mouth, staining the white whiskers on his chin.

"Just be quiet." Josey stood to look back across the valley. He saw no movement. The wagons would never get this far today. He sat down and cradled the Colonel's head in his lap, realizing he wouldn't be leaving this place with his friend. "Help is coming."

"You were always a terrible liar."

Josey pulled a handkerchief from his shirt pocket and wiped the blood from around the Colonel's mouth.

"Why did you follow Grummond?" He regretted the question as soon as he'd asked it. This was no time for blaming the dead. He tried to shush the Colonel, asked him to save his breath, but the stubborn coot refused.

"He ran off with the cavalry after some Indian scouts. I told Fetterman I'd bring him back. We were too late. Never saw so many Indians." The Colonel coughed, spraying blood over his chest and arms.

"Hush. I need you strong. Who's going to see that Byron and I build that ranch house proper? We'll build a veranda that wraps around all four sides, and you can nap in the shade no matter what time of day it is."

"That sounds good. I'm so tired —"

"Of course you're tired, you foolish old man. What were you thinking coming out here?"

"— tired of wiping your ass."

Josey laughed but it came out a sob. Tears dropped across the Colonel's face.

"It's too damn cold for rain."

"Be quiet. Save your strength."

"Ain't got none left."

"The wagon's coming —"

"I won't be getting on the wagon, not breathing at least. It's time for you to move on."

The Colonel closed his eyes. His body shook with a spasm. Josey brushed at the wisps of hair that crossed his age-speckled head. The body felt frozen in his lap. *The cold probably kept him alive this long.* About the time Josey figured the Colonel had spoken his last, he drew a faltering breath.

"Forget the war. Forget me. Don't turn me into another ghost who haunts the rest of your days. Take that woman and —"

His eyes closed, and Josey kissed his forehead, the first time he'd kissed a man other than his father. He listened to the old man's ragged breathing, determined not to leave until it was done.

The Colonel's eyes fluttered open, surprising Josey.

"Promise me."

"What? Anything."

"Don't name that baby Marlowe."

The Colonel's droopy mustache flattened out one last time in a smile, and he was gone, as quick as turning a page in a book and finding the next one blank.

You always had to have the last word. Josey closed the Colonel's eyes and pulled his body close. He forgot to breathe, and when his straining lungs forced him to inhale, Josey felt the pain of it, grateful that he could feel anything.

CHAPTER FORTY

Once more soldiers arrived, pulling wagons with their guns that shoot twice, the warriors melted away like snow beneath a heavy rain. Crazy Horse and his friend High Backbone watched the retreat from the gully where they had launched the ambush.

The seer the chiefs had sent out before the battle had been right about a great number of soldiers. No one counted the dead, but it may have been a hundred as the seer predicted, and the warriors had killed every one. The last to die was a dog, discovered among the bodies.

"Do not let even a dog get away," a young man called out. He and his friends shot arrows until one found its mark.

Many of the retreating warriors sported blue uniform coats they had stripped from the dead. They flaunted captured rifles and revolvers, even if they lacked the ammunition to fire them. They had cut off ears,

457

fingers, and other parts from the corpses for trophies. The mutilations assured the dead would be cursed in whatever spirit world soldiers went to.

Crazy Horse believed they called it hell.

"The scalp dance when we return to the village will be remembered for generations," High Backbone said. "Red Cloud will claim a great victory for the people, but you brought us to this, my brother."

The words of Spotted Tail and Black Buffalo Woman still echoed in Crazy Horse's mind, numbing him to the thrill he normally felt after battle. "We will have warriors to mourn."

"A dozen? Maybe a score? They will be celebrated as martyrs. The greatest honors will fall to them."

Will such honors feed their children through winter? "More will die of their wounds once they return to camp."

"And still it will be little compared with the soldiers' losses." High Backbone turned his mount to face Crazy Horse. "No warrior has ever known a greater victory than what you gave us today."

Crazy Horse urged his horse forward from the gully for a better view. The cold had hardened the marshy ground along the banks of the creek. Scanning the mile-long valley, the land appeared flat until Crazy Horse sought something as small as a single body. Then he noted the undulations, small depressions and rises, thick with sage and greasewood and scattered boulders.

"Have you seen Lone Bear?" Crazy Horse asked.

"He is not with the others?"

Crazy Horse shook his head. He had found his friend He Dog and his brother Little Hawk after the fighting. At the time he had thought Lone Bear rode with High Backbone.

"He must have gone ahead," High Backbone said. The warriors had a temporary camp a half-day's ride north of the fort.

"Without any of us?" Crazy Horse scanned the valley again. Lakota never left their dead on the field. "What if he is wounded?"

The white man's road cut across the center of the valley between two creeks. High Backbone nodded toward the tree line that marked the far creek. "I will ride there. You follow this side. If I find anything, I will come back to you. Otherwise, we will meet at the base of the ridge."

They set off. The light of the day was fading beneath heavy gray clouds, and Crazy Horse lost sight of High Backbone. He kept to a point about midway between the road and the creek, scanning for signs of life in either direction. He found only death. Crows big as puppies alighted on the exposed bodies, picking at flesh exposed by the sharp blades of trophy hunters. They flew off in angry flurries when Crazy Horse drew near. The sky grew darker. He smelled rain on the air, but it was far too cold for rain.

He reached the ridge without finding what he dreaded, yet he felt no relief. High Backbone watched the soldiers on the ridge from the cover of a small embankment. With a hand gesture, Crazy Horse signaled him to retrace his path. Lone Bear was known to be unlucky in battle, yet he had always returned.

Back at the north end of the valley, where the forks of the creek converged with the road, he found Lone Bear. His friend must have been struck down soon after emerging from the hiding spot within the gully. Thousands of warriors had charged out at once, loosing a rain of arrows that blotted out the sky. Some found their mark, but many more flew too far and wide. Crazy Horse had seen many warriors wounded by the arrows of their fellow warriors.

Lone Bear's luck had never been so bad

as this. Two arrows pierced his chest. His ruddy skin looked almost as pale as Crazy Horse's own. Crazy Horse abandoned his horse and robes the moment he saw his friend among a tangle of brush near the ravine.

"I knew you would come for me." Lone Bear's voice was soft and ragged, his eyes unfocused. "We have won a great victory."

"Hush, my friend. It is too steep a price if you do not return home with me."

Crazy Horse did not recognize the fletching on the arrows and assumed they belonged to another tribe. He cut away Lone Bear's buckskin jerkin, stiff with frozen blood, to see the wounds. The blood seams along the long shaft of the arrows had done their work. Even though the skin had closed around the shaft, blood had flowed through the three grooves cut along the length of the arrow. The cold had kept Lone Bear from bleeding out. Removing the barbed heads now would hasten his death.

Lone Bear knew. Crazy Horse saw it in his oldest friend's eyes.

He smiled. "The white men will leave this place. They will never return."

Crazy Horse wiped his eyes. Blood from his hands smeared his face, tasting bitter on his tongue. "Even if we burn the fort to the ground, they will return, as locusts in their time."

"Then we will kill them all again." Lone Bear closed his eyes. "I have seen it."

Lifting his head, Crazy Horse removed Lone Bear's war bonnet, careful not to displace the feathers from the leather skull-cap. He could read the story of Lone Bear's life in his bonnet and glistening hair. The tiny red bow twined in the braid signified his first coup. The white, black-tipped eagle feathers in the bonnet marked all the enemies Lone Bear had slain. Red-painted feathers told of how he had been wounded in the encounters. Lone Bear had more red feathers than anyone Crazy Horse knew. If Crazy Horse thought hard, he could recount the occasion of every feather Lone Bear had won. Now there would be no more feathers added to Lone Bear's headdress.

Crazy Horse cradled his head in his lap. "Tell me what you see."

Lone Bear's eyes remained closed. "I see you on a field of grass, so much grass the water near the fields is greasy with it. The sun is on your face. It is warm. The Moon When the Berries Are Good."

Crazy Horse smiled. "Warm would be good."

"Dead soldiers cover the hills around you.

So many that men will forget the 'Hundred in the Hands.' "

"I will not forget. Rest now, brother."

Crazy Horse looked across the valley. *More dead than this?* He could not imagine such a thing, though he had heard stories of the white man's war where so many dead covered the fields their blood soaked the ground like a heavy rain. Only the *wasicu* could kill so many and have the stomach to kill more.

The white men went to war to destroy their enemy. To the Lakota, war was a way of life. War turned young braves into men. Men made their fortunes in war, stealing horses, sometimes slaves. And if a man grew too fat and happy with his spoils, someone else would go to war with him and take what he had.

Warriors died in war. The weak. The foolish. The proud who defied the spirits and the demands of their visions. But a Lakota never thought to destroy. If a man destroyed an enemy village, where would he go to steal horses the next summer? Where would young men go to prove their valor?

"We have already lost, brother." Crazy Horse wondered if his words were heard. "We have lost, and I have brought us to it."

For as long as he could remember, Crazy

Horse feared watching the people become like the *wasicu*. That is what white men *wanted*. They wanted the people to pray to their dead god, to scrape the ground with iron and grow crops, to live in stone or wooden houses. They gave the people whiskey and colored beads and flour and coffee and told them they could have more until the people grew lazy and hungry and turned beggar. All his life Crazy Horse had fought against this. As a Shirt Wearer, he swore he would protect the people from becoming like the white man — even if he had to kill every white man.

"Now I see the truth."

Spotted Tail had warned him of this. Even Black Buffalo Woman saw it. But Crazy Horse's ears had been closed to them, dismissing the old chief's warnings as the rants of a man turned coward, his lover's words as the pleas of a frightened woman. For so long he had vowed to kill the *wasicu* that he did not see how much like them he had become.

Crazy Horse thought of the dead soldiers scattered like leaves across the valley. The way their white bodies gleamed against the brown grass and gray rocks brought to mind the buffalo carcasses white hunters left to rot in the sun. The hunters stripped the beasts of their skins and abandoned the rest to the buzzards and wolves.

"Where is the honor in this?"

The ambush had succeeded because the warriors had remained disciplined. They forsook individual honor so that they might kill every white man. They had emulated the *wasicu* in order to kill them.

"We have become them."

Crazy Horse looked down at Lone Bear, glad his friend could no longer hear. A lone tear dropped from his face. Crazy Horse could not remember the last time he cried. Had it been at Little Thunder's village all those years ago when he found everyone dead but Yellow Woman? Was that the fate today's victory had won for the people? A winter of waiting for the soldiers to return in even greater numbers, to destroy their village and kill everyone in it?

Lone Bear was right. Crazy Horse would kill more *wasicu,* but he could no longer fool himself about his motives. He did not kill the *wasicu* to stop himself from becoming like them. It was too late for that. He killed white men to punish them because he had become like them.

A heavy snow began to fall, and Crazy Horse shivered from the cold. He had left his buffalo robe with his horse. The warriors slathered themselves with bear grease to ward off the wind's bite, but it was no match for this kind of cold.

Giant flakes floated on the still air around him, like seeds from the cattails that grew in marshes by the village. He remembered as a boy with Lone Bear cracking open their long husks and blowing the seeds into the air to watch them dance on the wind. It was so long ago, it seemed the memory belonged to another man's life. Though he knew this to be snow that dusted the ground around him, he turned his gaze toward the water looking for cattails.

A shape emerged from the ravine. Through tear-blurred eyes Crazy Horse was slow to recognize the figure as a man. It could not be High Backbone, for he was on horseback and on the other side of the valley. The figure moved with the shambling gait of a spirit but wore the clothes of a white man.

How had he survived? Perhaps the man had hidden in the brush along the gully in the confusion of the attack. The prairie dog magic must be strong in this white man. Perhaps he was one of the soldiers who came after the battle to retrieve their dead. Yet this one looked more dead than alive. His face was as dark as one of the people, dark like death.

The man's eyes were wild, like a panicked horse, but they found their focus on Crazy Horse. His empty expression filled with something else, more than hatred, more than vengeance. Crazy Horse was not surprised that he could not put a word to it, for he was certain white men could hate more than the people. The people had no word for such hatred.

The man raised his revolver. Crazy Horse felt no fear. *Perhaps it would be better to die here.* He had been robbed of this victory in realizing what it cost his people. All that was left to him was to see them fall further under the white man's control. Yet Crazy Horse knew that was his fate. No white man would kill him. He had seen it. He would kill more white men. Lone Bear had seen that.

Crazy Horse heard the man pull back the hammer on the gun. He said something in his white man tongue. Crazy Horse was not afraid.

CHAPTER FORTY-ONE

Josey stood, his legs stiff from the cold and bearing the Colonel's weight in his lap. The lowering sun gilded the overcast sky with a falsely warm glow, the shortest day of the year setting too late for the soldiers of Fort Phil Kearny, too soon for the men who would retrieve their corpses. The wagons weren't coming for the Colonel. Not today. Josey wasn't strong enough to lift his friend onto his horse. Not with his busted ribs. He covered the old man with his buffalo coat and vowed to return in the morning.

Mounting his gray pony, he started back through the valley. It hurt to ride, but Josey needed to hurry. Carrington would have to leave with the wagons soon, and Josey's absence would slow them down.

The bodies he'd passed earlier gleamed in the dusk. Josey avoided them, circling wide of the road to the marshy land near the creek. The pain in his ribs punished him with every step. Snow began to fall. Flakes big as primrose petals dusted the valley. They swirled about on air stilled by the cold. Flakes alighted on Josey's cheeks and eyelashes, his body too cold to melt them. Within minutes they covered the landscape. It was not the burial the fallen deserved, but Josey hoped it was enough to keep the wolves and carrion birds away.

The falling snow muffled the steady plod of Gray's hoof falls and created a gauzy haze that played tricks with Josey's vision. He squinted at what he expected were more boulders on the road ahead. Shrouded in snow, their outline looked almost like horsemen. He drew his coat tight to his throat and trusted Gray to find his way.

Some sound or movement through the gloom drew Josey's eyes to his right. A copse of dogwoods stood by the creek. Their bare limbs reached out from the gully like skeletal fingers in search of a handhold. Josey peeled off his glove and pulled his Colt free, but what he saw stilled his hand.

A plainly dressed Indian sat alone on the ground. He wore unadorned buckskin leggings and was bare chested but for a woolen sash that crossed his torso from one shoulder, where he'd slung a rifle. With his back to Josey, the Indian hadn't noticed his approach. Josey slipped from his horse and stepped closer. The man seemed frozen in place. Josey might have thought him a vision if Annabelle hadn't described him so well.

Crazy Horse, she'd called him. She believed the Indian who'd taken her captive was the same warrior who had nearly killed the Colonel with a blow to the head that summer yet merely touched Josey when he might have struck him down. Josey had dismissed the idea as an unlikely coincidence, but he reconsidered as he studied this man. He was pale enough that he might have been a half-breed, with brown hair that he plaited into two braids.

The Indian wasn't alone. He held a man's head in his lap. Josey watched the man a moment, struck by how similar he must have looked not much earlier. The pale Indian spoke to the man he held. Josey couldn't make out the words, just the familiar sounds of mourning and regret. He watched until the Indian stopped talking and embraced his comrade a final time, just as Josey had done for the Colonel. Josey holstered his weapon.

He turned back to his horse but stopped on sensing more movement. From the tree line along the creek a large figure in army blues shambled out from the brush. Arrows protruded from his back. A hand clasped another stuck in his midsection. It looked like the figure had broken off the shaft but was unable to remove the barbed head. Through the snowy haze, Josey might have thought him an apparition as he moved toward the Indian until the man raised his arm, a revolver in his extended hand.

Grummond.

How is he still alive? Josey started toward him, setting aside the anger he'd felt for the man when he'd been whole. Grummond would not survive such wounds, but if Josey brought him back to the fort now he might grant Frances Grummond some tender parting with her husband.

Grummond pointed his gun at the pale Indian. His face was dark, as if smeared with blood, and his focus on his target so complete he didn't notice Josey. He cocked back the hammer of his revolver.

"Don't," Josey said.

The look of bewilderment that crossed Grummond's face suggested he didn't believe his eyes anymore than Josey had.

"How — ?" Grummond shook his head. "It doesn't matter." He turned the gun from the Indian and pointed it at Josey. "I have enough bullets for both of you."

471

Josey had been looking past Grummond, toward the impassive Indian who'd been watching his approach. The floating snowflakes in the last light of day created an impression of movement in the distance, shimmering shapes that grew more distinct one moment and were lost to the glare in the next.

"Let it go," Josey said. "Come back with me to the fort, while there's still time."

"A false show of concern isn't going to save you, Josey Angel." Grummond gestured with his gun to the revolvers at Josey's waist. "I know why you're scared. You don't think you're fast enough to kill me."

"I'm not scared, and I won't kill you. You're already dead."

Raising the hand that had been pressed to his gut around the arrow shaft, Grummond looked at it, stained dark with blood.

"At least I will die knowing you went first."

He raised the gun again. The snow fell even heavier than before, cutting short what remained of the day and making it night. All movement on the horizon stopped behind the curtain of white, but the figures Josey had imagined were clear in his mind.

Josey shook his head.

"I told you: you're already dead."

The gunshot split the air with an echoing crack. Grummond fell to his knees, registering a moment of dumbfounded surprise, as if he believed somehow Josey had fired the shot.

"Faster than I thought —"

Blood poured from his mouth, choking off the rest of his words before he fell face first into the snow.

Josey checked the body to be sure. The bullet had blown away a portion of the back of Grummond's head. He peered through the snow and waited for the shapes he'd seen earlier to materialize.

"You waited long enough to take the shot."

Even through the thick snowfall, Byron's gap-toothed grin gleamed like a crescent moon. "I thought you meant to talk him to death."

He was leading his horse by the reins. A smaller figure trailed behind. They were covered in so much fur Josey thought of a bear sow and cub.

"What are you doing out here?" Josey asked.

"Making sure he didn't miss." Annabelle peeled away the thick scarf that covered her face. "I might ask the same of you. You're supposed to be in your room."

Worry, relief, and something more powerful than both competed to control her expression. Josey felt the same wash over him.

"I love you."

"I know you do," she said. "I've always known."

Her face turned somber as she took in the surroundings. He could tell she had a question but feared the answer too much to ask. She left it to Byron.

"The Colonel?" he asked.

Josey shook his head. He stepped toward his friend and put a hand on his arm. "He went the way he wanted to go, at least."

No one spoke until Annabelle broke the silence. "It is better to die young on the battlefield, than to die old in bed."

"What's that?" She'd spoken so softly Josey wasn't sure he'd heard right.

"It's something the Indians say."

Josey tried to picture the Colonel napping in the shade of the house Josey intended to build for Annabelle. It had always been his fantasy, never the old man's. "I think he would have agreed."

Byron nodded. "We best get him. Bring him home."

Josey pointed through the swirling snow toward the rocks where he'd left the body. "I'll be along in a minute."

Byron mounted his horse and rode off, leaving Josey alone with Annabelle — and the pale Indian.

Crazy Horse.

They went to him. Crazy Horse had remained seated, the head of his dead friend still in his lap. Josey walked to him, blowing on his bare hand to keep it from going numb. Crazy Horse watched everything without a word. He remained still. His eyes followed Josey's footsteps as he approached.

"Is this the man?" he asked Annabelle.

She had replaced the scarf over her face, and all he saw was a nod of her fur-covered head. Josey looked down on Crazy Horse. The Indian had meant to kill the Colonel that summer. He'd intended to use Annabelle to gain entry into the fort so that the Sioux might massacre everyone inside. No doubt he bore responsibility for much of the day's slaughter.

None of it mattered now.

Josey reached out with his hand and touched Crazy Horse on his bare shoulder. The skin was slick and cold as ice. The muscles in the man's shoulder tensed, then relaxed. Josey rested his hand there a moment. Then he turned and took Annabelle's gloved hand in his. Together they went to the horses to follow Byron.

ABOUT THE AUTHOR

Derek Catron, author of the critically acclaimed *Trail Angel,* has hiked and camped throughout the West to research his novels. A career journalist who's won numerous awards for investigative reporting and feature writing, Catron is the managing editor at the *Daytona Beach News-Journal.* He lives in Florida with his wife and daughter. Read more about the author and *Angel Falls* at derekcatron.com or on Facebook at Derek Catron-Author.

The employees of Thorndike Press hope you have enjoyed this Large Print book. All our Thorndike, Wheeler, and Kennebec Large Print titles are designed for easy reading, and all our books are made to last. Other Thorndike Press Large Print books are available at your library, through selected bookstores, or directly from us.

For information about titles, please call:
(800) 223-1244

or visit our Web site at:
http://gale.com/thorndike

To share your comments, please write:
Publisher
Thorndike Press
10 Water St., Suite 310
Waterville, ME 04901